By Claudia Gray

STAR WARS
Lost Stars
Bloodline

FIREBIRD
A Thousand Pieces of You
Ten Thousand Skies Above You
A Million Worlds with You

SPELLCASTER
Steadfast
Spellcaster
Sorceress

EVERNIGHT
Evernight
Stargazer
Hourglass
Afterlife
Balthazar

BLOODLINE

STAR WARS

BLOODLINE

CLAUDIA GRAY

DEL REY
NEW YORK

Copyright © 2016 by Lucasfilm Ltd. & ® or ™ where indicated. All rights reserved.
Excerpt from *Star Wars: Aftermath: Life Debt* by Chuck Wendig copyright © 2016 by
Lucasfilm Ltd. & ® and ™ where indicated. All rights reserved.

Published in the United States by Del Rey,
an imprint of Random House, a division of
Penguin Random House LLC, New York.

DEL REY and the HOUSE colophon are registered
trademarks of Penguin Random House LLC.

This book contains an excerpt from the forthcoming book *Star Wars; Aftermath:
Life Debt* by Chuck Wendig. This excerpt has been set for this edition only and
may not reflect the final content of the forthcoming edition.

ISBN 978-0-425-28678-4
ebook ISBN 978-1-101-88525-3

Printed in the United States of America on acid-free paper

randomhousebooks.com

2 4 6 8 9 7 5 3 1

Special Barnes & Noble Edition

Book design by Elizabeth A. D. Eno

THE DEL REY

TIMELINE

I — THE PHANTOM MENACE

II — ATTACK OF THE CLONES
- THE CLONE WARS (TV SERIES)
- DARK DISCIPLE

III — REVENGE OF THE SITH
- LORDS OF THE SITH
- TARKIN
- A NEW DAWN
- REBELS (TV SERIES)

IV — A NEW HOPE
- HEIR TO THE JEDI
- BATTLEFRONT: TWILIGHT COMPANY

V — THE EMPIRE STRIKES BACK

VI — RETURN OF THE JEDI
- AFTERMATH
- AFTERMATH: LIFE DEBT
- AFTERMATH: EMPIRE'S END
- BLOODLINE
- THE PERFECT WEAPON (EBOOK ORIGINAL)

VII — THE FORCE AWAKENS

A long time ago in a galaxy far, far away. . . .

BLOODLINE

An entire generation has prospered during an era of peace. The New Republic, governed by the Galactic Senate, has held power for more than two decades. The wars that divided the galaxy are fading into legend.

Yet conflict has begun to take shape within the Senate. In the absence of MON MOTHMA, former leader of the Rebellion and first chancellor of the New Republic, two unofficial but powerful factions have formed—the POPULISTS, who believe individual planets should retain almost all authority, and the CENTRISTS, who favor a stronger galactic government and a more powerful military.

Only the greatest heroes of the war are still honored by all. A ceremony honoring the memory of BAIL ORGANA has drawn the Senate together in rare harmony. It is a day of celebration, but even now, the divisions among the worlds of the galaxy are growing wider. . . .

CHAPTER
ONE

"When we look back upon the war against the Empire—upon the billions of lives lost—sometimes it seems as though nothing could ever have been worth the terrible price we paid. But when we think of those people who perished in the conflict, let us remember that they died for justice. For liberty. For the extraordinary peace we now enjoy." Senator Tai-Lin Garr held out his arms, taking in the entire celebration on Hosnian Prime: the brilliant sunshine, the aquamarine sky, the countless citizens of a thousand different species gathered together beneath the colorful flags of their worlds. The beauty and promise of the New Republic seemed to be laid before them all. "*This* is what we fought for."

Everyone applauded. Many cheered.

Senator Leia Organa clapped along with the rest and thought, *Too bad it's falling apart.*

To the majority of the observers, most of them among the enormous number of citizens who had traveled to Hosnian Prime for the dedication ceremony and concert, the many senators clustered in the stands would appear to be a sign of solidarity and strength. Planets from the Core Worlds to the Outer Rim were represented; humans wore the cloaks, robes, and ceremonial gear of countless different cultures as they watched the ceremony alongside species from the Aqualish to the Ithorian, from the large-eyed Mon Calamari to the small, woolly Ashaftan, in what looked like perfect unity. Leia's sharper eyes traced the invisible line between the two halves of the gathering: Centrist senators on one side, Populist senators like herself on the other. The physical gap couldn't have been measured, but the philosophical one widened every day. Soon that gap would broaden into a crevasse, one deep enough to reveal how fragile the peace really was.

Stop it. Leia forced herself to think positively. Rationally. *Galactic politics has always had its parties, factions, divisions. It always will. Not every ideological conflict leads to a complete governmental breakdown.*

But the unease that stirred just beneath the glossy surface of this ceremony reminded her of the final days of the Imperial Senate. Polite words cloaking implied threats, a near-complete lack of trust among worlds: The mood felt all too familiar.

Then again, the Imperial Senate actually made decisions once in a while. See? History isn't repeating itself after all, she thought sourly.

Leia took pleasure in exactly one aspect of this gathering: the new statue they had come together to dedicate. The seventy-meter-high statue had been carved of Jelucani fogstone, which sparkled transparent as diamond in bright light, then turned a pale, opaque gray-green in darkness. As Tai-Lin finished his speech to applause, a cloud passed in front of the sun. The fogstone's glittering dimmed to reveal the fine detail on the statue of Bail Organa, portrayed in his robes of the office of viceroy of Alderaan and with a hand outstretched toward all peoples, in classic hagiographic form. Yet his face had been as accurately and lovingly carved as the most intimate portrait. Maybe the different senators and planets could agree on little any longer, but at least her father's legacy endured.

Tai-Lin nodded to Leia as his pod hovered back into place; for

ceremonial functions, such pods were allowed, though their us_
the Senate was now considered "overly hierarchical." His nod served
as both an acknowledgment that her turn had come and genuine encouragement. She gave him a quick smile before she pressed the controls that would bring her pod forward from the stands and focus the
amplifier droids on her voice. A warm breeze fluttered the dark-blue
folds of her cape and gown as Leia stood before the gathering.

"I stand before you not only as a senator, but also as Bail Organa's
daughter." Leia's voice rang out, clear and strong, revealing none of
the doubts that had haunted her day. "And yet everything I have done
in my career as a senator has been rooted in the valuable lessons he
taught me about courage. About strength. About leadership."

Leadership was something the Senate badly needed at present.
Mon Mothma had remained hugely influential even after her term as
chancellor . . . more so than Leia had realized before Mon Mothma's
illness. Without someone able to bridge philosophical gaps and create consensus, the political process they'd forged for the New Republic was showing its weaknesses.

She continued speaking smoothly as the flags flapped in the strong
breeze. "He stood as viceroy of Alderaan at the beginning of a dark
time for our entire galaxy." A hush fell over the crowd at the mention
of her dead planet's name. Leia pretended not to notice. Her pod hovered so high above the ground that the hundred thousand people
from a thousand species and worlds, vibrant in their individual skins,
scales, and furs, were indistinct to her now—a mass of color and
noise, hard to connect with. But Leia tried. "He helped Mon Mothma
create the Rebel Alliance, even while still fighting valiantly to preserve what little integrity and authority the Imperial Senate had left.
I have no doubt that he would have continued the battle alongside
our rebel soldiers if he had not so cruelly been taken from us in the
destruction of my homeworld."

She continued, "It was my privilege to know him as both a leader
and a father. As proud as I am to think of his courageous stand against
Palpatine's tyranny, I also smile every time I remember how he used
to get down on the floor to play blocks with his little girl." Fond
laughter rippled through the audience.

Good. She'd woken the crowd, won them over. Time for Leia to say the words her listeners *wouldn't* want to hear.

"He taught me so much about politics, leadership, and war, but above all he taught me that no price is too great to pay for our ideals. Bail Organa was willing to die if that meant the Empire would fall. He believed in the New Republic we have been able to create, and in the promise of fair, equal government for everyone under the law." Applause welled up, and Leia paused to let it subside before continuing, "He believed in unity, and he knew that unity came at the cost of compromise. Mon Mothma, one of his earliest and most enduring allies, shared those convictions and let them guide her leadership of the Senate. She wanted the worlds of the New Republic to find balance, and to always seek the middle ground where we can work together for a better tomorrow."

This won more applause, but the sound was muted, now. Populists and Centrists agreed on only one point these days: Compromise was for the weak.

Leia looked at the statue and imagined herself speaking directly to Bail Organa as she concluded. "My father gave us one legacy more precious than any other—a galactic peace. All of us here today have inherited the responsibility to preserve that peace from this day forward. Only by doing so can we truly honor and remember him."

Applause and cheers welled up, deafeningly loud, in a display of enthusiasm greater than any Leia had seen in a long time. Had people actually heard her message? Did they understand how fragile peace had become? Would they now urge their senators to overcome their endless petty bickering and finally give the galaxy the leadership it deserved?

Then she heard the high, silvery sound of X-wing fighters overhead. The military air show had begun. *That* was why the crowds were cheering. They hadn't heard her last words at all.

That was . . . a disappointment. But not a surprise.

As the X-wings split into a dramatic new formation, Leia sighed and hit the control that would levitate her pod back into the senatorial stands. If nobody was listening, she might as well enjoy the show.

"You're such a pessimist, Leia," Senator Varish Vicly insisted after the ceremony, as various leaders milled around the base of the glittering statue of Bail Organa. Like all Lonerans, Varish had long, silky fur the color of gold and a quartet of thin, extended limbs that allowed her to walk on two feet or all fours with equal ease. Now she ambled along on only two, the better to keep waving and shaking hands. "Of course people cheered for the air show! X-wing maneuvers are more exciting than the best speech ever made."

Leia tucked a stray lock of hair back into her one long braid. "I just wish we could get people to listen."

"Look at it this way." Varish's golden fur fluttered in the breeze, and her long, narrow face split in a wide smile for someone waving in the distance. "People love the X-wing pilots because they think of them as the great fighters of the Rebellion. See? People haven't forgotten the war. It's just that it was all so very long ago."

"I suppose it was." Leia remembered sitting in the Senate as a fourteen-year-old junior legislator and feeling sure she was the youngest person among all those thousands; these days, she sometimes felt like the oldest. The war had taken a toll on her generation, culling so many who would otherwise have gone on to lead. Among the crowds and the Senate itself were many who hadn't even been born when the Battle of Endor was fought.

Leia ought to have felt that her obsolescence stood as a badge of honor. The populace couldn't have become so complacent without decades of relative peace, which had been given to them by the New Republic. But she couldn't relax. Couldn't stop worrying. That was what happened when someone grew up on the run, under siege, always expecting capture or death at any moment. Paranoia became the only way of seeing the world, unable to ever be fully set aside.

"Come, now. If you don't cheer up before dinner, I'll seat you next to Count Jogurner, see if I won't . . . oh, Feleen, over here!" Varish squeezed Leia's arm once before darting into the crowd to greet yet another of her political friends.

Leia shook her head in fond resignation. Behind her seemingly frivolous interests, Varish Vicly was a person of integrity, as staunch a Populist as Leia herself, and one of the very few senators it was actually fun to spend time with. (Unlike, for instance, Count Jogurner, who meant well but could not converse at length on any subject other than Cheedoan whiskeys.) But she wasn't a good audience for Leia's darker fears.

Nobody wants to hear about the war any longer, Leia told herself. *No one wants to be afraid of more chaos and turmoil. Isn't this what I fought for—so they wouldn't have to be afraid?*

She scanned the crowd, picking out friend and enemy alike. Tai-Lin Garr, conspicuous in his trademark scarlet cloak, listened gravely to a group of spectators who had apparently come all the way from Tai-Lin's home planet of Gatalenta. His thick black hair was pulled back into a topknot; his dark eyes were thoughtful, even solemn, in a way that did not conflict with the gentle smile on his face. Nearby stood a cluster of Centrist senators fawning over one of their movement's rising stars, a young politician from Riosa named Ransolm Casterfo. Certainly Casterfo cut a dashing figure. He was tall, handsome, charismatic, and only thirty-two years old—an age that had once sounded mature to Leia, and now seemed impossibly young. Too young to have fought in the war, or to have any substance whatsoever, but apparently the Centrists chose their new figureheads by asking themselves who would look best in their propaganda. Leia's mood brightened when, in the far distance, she spied Admiral Ackbar. He'd made the voyage all the way to Hosnian Prime for the ceremony, though he was now in his eighties—but of course he wouldn't have let anything keep him from honoring Bail Organa. Leia began pushing through the throng toward him, hoping for a chance to catch up with someone else who remembered the old days.

"Princess Leia?" The melodious voice calling Leia's name would have sounded alluring to most people. Only Leia's diplomatic training allowed her to keep from cringing. "Princess Leia, if I could have a word?"

Leia managed to put on a convincing smile before she turned. "Lady Carise. What can I do for you?"

Lady Carise Sindian, senator from the Centrist world Arkanis, was of the same generation as Ransolm Casterfo but came across as even younger. Perhaps that impression of immaturity came from Lady Carise's priorities, rather than her lovely face. Her long silvery robes were embroidered with jewels, displaying her world's wealth and power, in a contrast with Leia's simpler and more elegant blue. Lady Carise began, "We must discuss the governorship of Birren. As you know, Lord Mellowyn has passed away—"

"Of course. I was sorry to hear of it." Lord Mellowyn had been a distant kinsman to Bail Organa. Over the years, Leia had made a few trips to visit him, since Mellowyn had been one of the few people who still remembered her father and had called him friend.

(When she thought of her father, she thought only of Bail Organa. He had been her father in spirit, and surely that was more important than anything else.)

"Well, the governorship passes down through the elder bloodlines—" Lady Carise began, her dark-brown eyes alight at the thought of royal titles. Virtually no one took the concept of hereditary nobility seriously any longer, not even the other members of the Elder Houses. However, Lady Carise seemed unable to imagine any greater honor. "But as Lord Mellowyn had no children, the title has now passed to you."

Leia covered her mouth as if in surprise. Really she hoped to conceal her dismay. One of the few things she remembered about Birren was that their rituals invariably lasted for several weeks. Birren was a small, sleepy Inner Rim world that might provide an excellent vacation spot . . . but a frustrating exile for a senator with important work to do. "The title is purely ceremonial now, isn't it? I can't imagine that the people of Birren are in any hurry to replace a figurehead governor."

"But the *title*!" Lady Carise's eyes widened. Maybe unconsciously, she shook her head—*tsk, tsk*. "How can we deny the people the certainty, the reassurance, of knowing that this ancient tradition is being upheld?"

"I'll task my staff with looking into this immediately." This was Leia's stock escape for official conversations she wanted to end; it sounded official but promised nothing. Lady Carise smiled and nodded as she turned away, satisfied for now.

The X-wings streaked overhead again. Although the air show had ended, the pilots were still showing off, enjoying themselves. For now they required no greater purpose, no sacred duty, only the sheer exhilaration of flight.

How long has it been since I was that carefree? Leia thought. *Was I ever?*

Probably not.

The brief window between the ceremony and Varish's dinner for the Populist senators gave Leia no chance to relax. Instead, she needed to meet with her staff. Fortunately, there she could at least count on rational conversation.

Mostly.

"What a marvelous celebration!" C-3PO shuffled through the broad oval of Leia's state office. Afternoon sunlight streamed through the windows, gilding the white-on-white furnishings; the droid's golden metal plating shone as though he were new. "Such an illustrious gathering. I daresay everyone in attendance will share the memory with their grandchildren someday."

"Never imagined this," Han had murmured, sitting up in their bed late at night, Ben's tiny head resting in the crook of his father's arm. *"Having a kid. Even wanting a kid. But now he's here, and—"*

"And you're a dad." Leia had leaned closer, unable to resist the chance to tease her husband. *"Just think, hotshot. Someday you might even be a granddad."*

Han's chuckle had warmed her. "Speak for yourself, sweetheart. Me, I ain't ever getting that old."

"Princess Leia?"

Leia snapped out of her reverie, back into the here and now. "I apologize, Greer. It's been a long day. You were saying?"

Greer Sonnel, Leia's assistant, continued as smoothly as if her boss had not just spent several seconds lost in thought. "You've been invited to the reception for Senator Bevicard on Coruscant, which I said you would consider. Shall I refuse immediately or tomorrow?"

"Give it until tomorrow." It didn't do to become too predictable.

Greer nodded, her fingers dexterously working on her datapad. Her thick, blue-black hair had been tucked into a simple bun, and the coarsely woven shawl she wore over her bodysuit came from her rugged homeworld of Pamarthe. Greer preferred the plain and practical, always; Leia knew she was finding her transition to work in the Senate difficult, probably because there was so much formality and even more nonsense. However, Greer had always risen to a challenge, and she had sharpened her diplomatic skills in the past several months. "Shall I refuse with ordinary politeness or extra courtesy?"

"Extra, I think. Honesty deserves courtesy. Bevicard's a snake, but he doesn't lie about what he is." Leia shook her head ruefully. "That's about as much as you can expect from a Centrist these days."

"But—" Korr Sella—Sondiv's daughter and the office intern, only sixteen years old—caught herself and shrank back. "Excuse me, Princess Leia. I spoke out of turn."

"You'll find I'm not a stickler for protocol, Korrie." From the corner of her eye, Leia saw C-3PO swiveling his torso toward her, no doubt appalled to think of anyone, anywhere, ignoring protocol. "What is it you were going to say?"

At first the girl looked so stricken that Leia feared she'd put her in an awkward position. Before she could withdraw her question, however, Korrie found her courage. "I was going to say, shouldn't you accept the invitation? To help build friendships and consensus between Centrists and Populists?"

"In an ideal galaxy, yes. Unfortunately, that's not the galaxy we live in." Leia sounded so jaded she even disgusted herself. More gently, she said, "The invitation was symbolic, not genuine. If I actually accepted, Bevicard would be mortified."

Korrie nodded, but her expression remained uneasy. "Are the two parties really that far apart?"

Leia leaned back in her chair, rubbing her sore neck. If only Varish weren't hosting a banquet tonight, so she could let down her hair. "I'm afraid they really are."

"Oh." Korrie bowed her head, but not before Leia caught a glimpse of the girl's confusion and dismay.

I was that young, once. I believed so strongly in the power of government to accomplish anything. Leia had joined the Imperial Senate at fourteen; she hadn't completely given up on the rule of law in the Empire until the moment she saw Alderaan die in front of her eyes. *How I miss that feeling—the sense that justice would always win in the end.*

"I've prepared a statement on the dedication for us to send to the planetary news services. You can take a look and let me know what edits you'd like, if any." Greer tapped her datapad, sending the document to Leia. There was no need. Leia knew exactly what it would say, just as she knew the precise, subtle shades of spin the Centrist senators would put on their own statements. "That more or less wraps up our business for this afternoon, Princess Leia. You have another hour before Senator Vicly's banquet. What would you like to do next?"

Leia realized the answer only moments before it came out of her mouth. "I want to quit."

Korrie frowned. Greer paused before she said, "I beg your pardon, ma'am? You want to quit—having this meeting, or—"

"I want to leave the Senate. To leave government completely." An exhilarating, unfamiliar sensation blossomed within Leia. Maybe this was what freedom felt like. "*I want to quit.*"

CHAPTER
TWO

———————————

Han said, "Now, this I gotta hear."

The uplink between Hosnian Prime and the Theron system was clear tonight: no static, no delays. Leia could see her husband's face clearly, and behind him the broad window of his temporary quarters on Theron. His gray jacket lay across a nearby chair, and the amber liquid in a slender glass on the table was most likely Corellian brandy. Small, darting lights in the night sky behind Han were no doubt podracers getting some practice weaving in and out of the planet's famous spiral stone formations.

None of that mattered compared with the sight of Han's smile. Despite the skeptical tone of his voice, Leia recognized the light in his eyes.

"The Senate is turning into a political quagmire." She folded her legs beneath her on the sofa and began unbraiding her hair, a lengthy process she had always found calming. "And it's our own fault. After

Palpatine, nobody wanted to hand over that much power again, so we don't have an executive, only a chancellor with no real authority. Mon Mothma got things done through sheer charisma, but almost every chancellor since her has been . . ."

Han finished the sentence for her: "Useless."

"Pretty much." At the time, Leia had been grateful for Mon Mothma's leadership, but now she realized that one individual's ability had disguised the fundamental flaws in the New Republic's system. If Mon Mothma had stepped aside earlier, might they have realized their errors? Amended the constitution in time? At this late date, it was impossible to know. "The conflict between the parties gets worse every day. Most Centrists and Populists are still polite to each other, but barely. Every debate on the Senate floor turns into an endless argument over 'tone' or 'form' and never about issues of substance—"

Han kept nodding, but his eyes were starting to glaze over. By this point in their marriage, Leia could predict down to the nanosecond when Han's patience for all things political would run out.

Now, finally, she was just as sick of it as he was.

"So why shouldn't I quit?" Leia loosed the final strands of her long hair, allowing it to tumble free to her waist. "Nothing keeps me from resigning in the middle of my term. I could announce that I'm stepping down sometime in the next few weeks, which would give me time to tie up loose ends before an interim election has been called. Greer already agreed to draft an announcement—well, she kept calling it a 'hypothetical' announcement. She doesn't think I'll actually follow through."

"Neither do I," said Han, not unkindly. "Listen, Leia, I never understood exactly what you got out of politics, but you must get *something* out of it, because it's been your whole life."

"Since I was fourteen." As a girl she had been so proud to represent Alderaan. So impatient for her chance to do something meaningful. Why hadn't she taken a little more time to simply be a kid? Even princesses could have fun sometimes—her mother had tried to tell her that, from time to time, but Leia had never listened—

Han continued, "You've been fed up with the Senate before. I've heard you gripe about factions and deadlock a thousand times. But it's not like you to give up."

"This isn't giving up. It's just . . . facing facts." Leia sighed as she took up her hairbrush and began working out the few tangles at the ends. By now a few strands of steely gray shone in her brown hair. "I can't do this forever, Han. Eventually my time in the Senate has to come to an end. Why not now?"

Han's face filled more of the screen as he leaned forward, perhaps to study her expression. Although he still looked skeptical, she could tell he had begun to play with the idea in his mind. "Don't take this the wrong way, but—what would you do with yourself?"

It was a fair question. Leia had given so much of her life to the Rebellion and then the New Republic that even she had sometimes wondered whether she had anything left.

But she did, of course.

"I've been thinking." She pretended to mull the question over. "What if I decided to go flying around the galaxy with some scoundrel?"

Han raised his eyebrows and pointed toward his own chest.

Leia laughed. "Unless you had another scoundrel in mind."

"Hey, hey. I'm the only scoundrel up for the job." He shook his head in—surprise? Disbelief? Leia wasn't sure. What mattered most was the warmth in his smile. Even if Han wasn't convinced she intended to do this, he liked the idea.

Down deep, buried where she could almost ignore the fear, Leia hadn't been sure he would.

They'd been apart too often in their marriage. Too long. Han's restlessness had been a large part of that, but he couldn't take all of the blame. Leia had remained stuck here, mired in the political muck. Now she could finally do her part to change things for them.

"You really think you'd enjoy the life of a racer?" Han asked. "Bouncing around from one system to the next, working on ships, never knowing where you're headed next?"

"Doesn't sound that different from being a member of the Rebel Alliance."

"Maybe not," Han conceded with a tilt of his head. "Still, it's a pretty wild ride. You sure you're ready?"

This was something of an exaggeration. Han often raced for charity, and he was as likely to sponsor a match as he was to compete in one. He'd traveled to Theron to oversee the prestigious piloting championships known as the Five Sabers, which tested skills on everything from starfighter atmospheric runs to hyperspace orienteering. In other words: Han Solo was in charge of *enforcing the rules.* Although he ran his shipping company on the go, he was a far more vigilant, responsible owner than he liked to let on. The life he led these days took him all around the galaxy, but it was a far cry from the dangerous existence of a smuggler.

Compared with stagnating in the Senate? Han's world sounded like *paradise.*

"Freedom and adventure." She sighed. "Yeah. I'm ready."

Han studied her for a few moments, then began to grin. "You realize—after three months on the same ship, we're gonna kill each other."

Leia leaned closer to the terminal so he would see the wickedness in her smile. "But won't those three months be fun?"

She was thinking of a sublight run they'd undertaken together early in their marriage, which had begun with a great deal of bickering. However, all that time alone, with no one to interrupt them, had eventually led to much more enjoyable pursuits. Given the timing, she was fairly sure those pursuits had directly led, some months later, to Ben's birth.

"Oh, we'll have fun." Han brushed his fingers near the holocam, as if he could touch her face. "You better believe it."

The next day, in the Senate, Leia found herself remembering the way Han had said that, turning it over and over in her mind like a young girl daydreaming. Of course she was being ridiculous, and she was rarely so easily distracted while the Senate was in session.

Then again, the Senate gave her very little worth concentrating on, these days.

Clapping from the Centrist benches drew her back into the here and now. Via the console at her position in the broad, flat, and utterly maddening Senate chamber, she could see screen images and holos of Ransolm Casterfo as he bowed to the cheers of his colleagues, ignoring the stoic silence of the Populists. Leia mentally replayed the last few words he'd spoken . . . yes, he'd been complaining about the number of Populist speakers at the statue-dedication ceremony. In other words, he'd said the exact same thing every other Centrist senator had said so far today, albeit more eloquently. For all their applause, the Centrists were no more interested or engaged than the Populists; they responded by rote. As she scanned the vast chamber and all its representatives from its multiplicity of worlds, Leia thought they looked like a theater audience struggling to endure the last act of a dull play.

"How many Centrist speakers have there been now?" she murmured under her breath to C-3PO, who occasionally accompanied her to record the proceedings—not that there was much worth recording.

"Seventeen, all of whom addressed irregular protocol during the dedication ceremony," C-3PO said with his usual cheer at being able to supply an exact answer. Then he turned his golden head toward her and added, in a lower tone, "I must say, their attention to these points of etiquette seems . . . excessive."

Leia nearly groaned. *C-3PO* thought they were overdoing protocol? That was a very bad sign.

She touched the small screen in her pod that would show her the order of business for the day, then straightened. For once, the senators would be expected to stop talking and listen.

The speaker droids intoned at once, "Acknowledged on the floor, Yendor of Ryloth, emissary to the Senate."

Leia sat up straighter as Yendor walked in. Tall for a Twi'lek, he made an imposing figure with his long blue lekku hanging from his head down the back of his deep-brown cloak. Although the Senate floor was more than a hundred meters in front of her, she could see him well thanks to the various screens and holos displaying his image on her console—some in different wavelengths, for those species whose eyes differed greatly from those of humans. She had known Yendor slightly during the war, when he had served as an X-wing pilot. Although Leia doubted they had spoken more than two dozen times, right now the mere sight of someone from the days of battle cheered her.

"To the esteemed representatives of the Galactic Senate, greetings." Yendor stood tall and straight, despite his advancing years and the long staff he used to steady himself. "The history of my planet and my people is well known. For centuries, we suffered under the oppression of the Hutts and their criminal enterprises. The Empire's domination doubled our difficulties. Only in the past few decades, in the era of the New Republic, have we been able to assert our own independence and our own rule. Though we stand apart from you, we salute you, and appreciate the peace the New Republic has given to the galaxy."

Leia applauded, as did many others—both Populists and Centrists. Ryloth was an independent world, apart from the New Republic, and so one that could not be said to belong to either party. Besides, the Hutts had earned bipartisan loathing.

Yendor bowed his head briefly, acknowledging the response, before he continued. "Now, however, our independence is again endangered. The Hutts have lost much of their old power, which means others are rushing in to fill the gap. Of these, the most dangerous are those cartels run by the Niktos."

"The Niktos served the Hutts for centuries," C-3PO said to her. Leia understood this perfectly well, but she didn't waste time interrupting him to say so. She knew the droid well enough to be sure he'd keep talking anyway. "They've never had a truly independent government of their own. Hardly even a world of their own, really."

Then Emissary Yendor's tone took on a sharper edge. "Among the many promises the New Republic made after Palpatine's fall was that organized crime would never again become as powerful a force as it had been during the age of the Empire. Financial regulations and comprehensive patrols of the shipping lanes were meant to protect Ryloth and every other world in the galaxy from large-scale criminal corruption. But those regulations are enforced only sporadically, and the patrols have yet to materialize, even though more than twenty years have passed. In that time, the cartels have begun to assert their power again." Leia felt ashamed for her part in this and hoped others in the Senate did as well. By bickering over the minutiae—who would enforce what, and when, and how—the Senate had once again failed to take the bigger picture into account. Now the price of their inaction had come due, and it would be smaller, poorer worlds like Ryloth that had to pay most dearly. "One cartel in particular has become a risk to the commercial shipping lanes in our sector," Yendor continued. "Although our information is incomplete, we believe this criminal organization already rivals that of any of the most powerful Hutts at the zenith of their influence. We know only that our pilots are being raided, that our merchants have been pressured for protection money, and that the cartel is led by a Kajain'sa'Nikto known as Rinnrivin Di, operating at least in part from the planet Bastatha."

Low murmurs went through certain sections of the Senate chamber, from both parties. *More of us should have heard of this guy,* Leia realized, sitting up straighter. *We should've been alerted to a cartel of such size long ago.* But of course nobody had been paying attention to anything that really mattered. Frustration made her clench her jaw.

Yendor held up his hand, both calling for their renewed attention and signaling the end of his address. "Today Rinnrivin's cartel presents a danger to Ryloth's future, and to free trade in our part of the galaxy. Tomorrow, however, it could threaten the rule of law in the New Republic itself, as the Hutts did in both the Old Republic and the Empire. Therefore, I ask for the Senate to investigate the reach and influence of Rinnrivin Di's cartel and to take the actions necessary to restore order, on behalf of the Twi'leks of Ryloth—but for the benefit of us all."

The silence that followed lasted for only a few seconds . . . and then the Senate dissolved into an immense amount of talking, and very little listening. Senators jabbed commands into their terminals, and the sorter droids programmed to display viewpoints equally weighted from both parties flashed different ones onto the main screens.

An Ottegan speaking through a vocoder that translated his words into humanlike speech: "How can we be sure the emissary's information is accurate?"

Senator Giller, an elderly, mustachioed Centrist who still wore his war medals every day: "There have been rumors of Twi'lek criminal enterprises as well! Maybe this is merely an attempt by the Twi'leks to force us to eliminate their rivals!"

Lady Carise Sindian, with a jeweled hairband atop her head: "Senators are not lowly planetary constables to be sent out on every possible minor law enforcement errand. We must think of the dignity of our office. Are we to be reduced to mere investigators?"

Varish Vicly, brushing back her golden fur: "This is an intrasystem matter. Even if the worlds involved belonged to the New Republic, as Ryloth and Bastatha do not, the Senate would be overreaching its authority by interfering."

Leia found herself remembering the stench of Jabba's palace, where every breath had smelled of grease and smoke from half a dozen illegal substances. In her mind flickered the anguishing memory of Han frozen in carbonite, his grimace of pain as hard as stone—the raucous sound of laughter from those watching Luke fight for his life in the rancor's den—and the heaviness of a metal collar tight around her neck.

Ultimately she had hated Jabba the Hutt nearly as much as she'd hated Emperor Palpatine. But her loathing for Jabba had come to a far more satisfying conclusion.

Leia saw Yendor of Ryloth leaning on his staff and realized, with a jolt, that he was wearier than he'd let on. He'd made this journey across the galaxy to speak to a governing body most Twi'leks still distrusted, all in the hope of changing something for his people. And the best response the Senate could give him was yet more bickering?

Leia felt a galvanizing sense of purpose rush through her as the idea took shape in her mind. Maybe she could do one last bit of good before she resigned and left the government forever.

She rose to her feet, a signal to the moderator droids that a senator urgently wished to take the floor. Senators were not allowed to overuse this privilege, but Leia had not bothered to avail herself of it in months. Almost instantly, the hovering holodroids rushed toward her. From the corner of her eye she could see herself in her long white dress, graying hair roped in its braid down her back. How august and official she looked. How dignified. Nobody would have any reason to expect her to say anything that deviated from the party line.

So it was with great satisfaction that Leia proclaimed, "Honored members of the Senate, it is my opinion that the emissary from Ryloth has brought an important matter to our attention, one that demands further inquiry. Therefore I volunteer to lead the investigation myself . . . and as such, will leave Hosnian Prime for Bastatha immediately."

Silence followed—out of what Leia expected was sheer astonishment. How long had it been since somebody in the Senate had stood up and actually offered to do something useful?

Too long, she thought. *But damn, it feels good.*

CHAPTER
THREE

———————————

Leia knew her proposal to lead the mission to Bastatha was sensible, useful, and direct.

Obviously, the Senate didn't know what to do with it.

"We could hardly be certain of assuring your safety, Princess Leia," said Lady Carise Sindian, the only senator who called Leia by her royal title, rather than her elected one, while on the Senate floor. "We couldn't put you at risk."

"Have you no faith in the soldiers of the New Republic, Senator Sindian?" This objection actually came from another Centrist, Senator Arbo, one of the war hawks of Coruscant. "Senator Organa will travel with an entire squadron of guards to protect her at all times. Do not doubt their ability or their valor!"

Tai-Lin Garr shook his head. "We could hardly expect Senator Organa's investigation to run smoothly if such a large military presence accompanied her. The people of Bastatha would consider it an intrusion, perhaps even an invasion."

This was the first useful thing someone had said since Leia had volunteered for the mission. Given that the tone of the overall conversation was turning toward safeguarding her trip to Bastatha, rather than objecting to it, she was beginning to feel encouraged despite herself.

And if she'd realized what a charge she would get out of the mere idea of being out in the field—the chance to work with ordinary people instead of politicians, to evaluate a situation for herself without any committees in the way—she would've come up with another potential mission a long time ago. The journey to Bastatha would be the perfect way to end her career in the Senate: doing something interesting and meaningful again, at last. Then she could walk out with a sense of satisfaction that at least she'd been able to accomplish some real, tangible good before she left.

Who knows? she thought. *Taking on one of the spice cartels— I might even wind up with some stories to rival a few of Han's.* Already she couldn't wait to tell him about this.

However, Lady Carise wasn't done speaking. "The question of this mission's worthiness remains. As others have stated, we have only the testimony of the emissary of Ryloth to go upon. What has been characterized as criminal activity may be no more than the Niktos attempting to rebuild their economy after escaping the influence of the Hutts. Furthermore—and forgive me, but it must be said—such an investigation could not be left to a Populist senator alone. Although Princess Leia is no mere conspiracy theorist, some of those on the Populist benches are determined to see the worst in any larger organization, whether governmental, military, or economic."

"I can be objective," Leia began, but her voice was almost immediately drowned out. Protests bubbled up from the Populist senators, and it was all Leia could do not to groan. Now her own party would keep her from being heard.

C-3PO's gold head swiveled from side to side as he attempted to record the entire debate. "I should have thought the Senate would welcome your generous offer," he said. "Oh, dear."

" 'Oh, dear' is right." Leia kept her chin high, determined to wait this out. Now that she'd tasted even the hope of going into action again, she wasn't going to give it up easily.

One of the moderator droids intoned, "The floor is granted to Senator Casterfo of Riosa."

Even as his name was announced, Ransolm Casterfo had already risen to his feet, all the better to look impressive for the holodroids. The dark-green velvet cloak he wore testified to his wealth and privilege. Leia wondered sourly whether he'd chosen the clothing to make it seem that he was from a more powerful, prestigious world than Riosa, or because the colors suited his complexion. There was a touch of the celebrity about him . . . as there was with too many of the younger senators, for whom government was more about fame and influence than duty.

"My fellow senators," Casterfo proclaimed. His narrow, aristocratic face looked out from the screens and holos; he'd already mastered the politician's trick of seeming to make eye contact with everybody at once. "Senator Sindian has raised a valuable point. This should be a bipartisan mission. In fact, I am ashamed on behalf of my own party that one of our own did not volunteer first—because as Centrists, we value law and order, do we not?" Murmurs of agreement rose from various Centrist senators. Casterfo went on, "Not only is there a need for both Populist and Centrist perspectives on the question of the Nikto cartels, but we should also be more generous than to repay the courage of the esteemed Senator Organa by requiring her to make such a potentially hazardous journey alone."

Smooth, Leia thought with grudging admiration.

Casterfo continued, "I therefore volunteer to accompany Senator Organa on her mission to Bastatha. We will work together to present a comprehensive, objective set of findings to the Senate upon our return."

The sensation in Leia's chest then felt a bit like riding on a sailboat in full furl only to be jerked to a stop by an anchor. Her great last adventure had just turned into a . . . babysitting job.

"I knew it was too good to be true," she muttered.

"I beg your pardon, Princess Leia?" C-3PO gestured toward Casterfo's image on the holos. "I failed to record your last comment. If you would like it to be part of the record—"

"It doesn't matter, Threepio. Forget it." Leia heard other voices rise up to debate further points of protocol, but she knew how the Senate worked well enough to know how this would all end: She'd go to Bastatha, but with Ransolm Casterfo by her side.

"You could've let us know you were planning on doing this," Greer said in Leia's offices afterward.

"I would've let you know I was going to volunteer if I'd had any idea myself."

"So, you'll be taking the *Mirrorbright*?" Greer's tone was casual as she worked with her datapad, but she couldn't disguise the small smile on her full lips.

"I'll give you the answer to the question you're really asking, which is, yes, Greer, you'll get to pilot the ship." Leia paused. The Bastatha mission had a small but genuine element of danger. This might not be a mere pleasure cruise. "If you're sure . . ."

"I'm sure." Greer beamed. As good as she was at her office duties, she hadn't entirely lost her love of piloting. *A pity Greer had to give up racing*, Leia thought, not for the first time.

Next Leia would have to verify as accurate every datapad containing visual, sound, and sensory records of the day's Senate session, just one more layer of New Republic bureaucracy she had to sort through every day. "Let's get through this as soon as possible. I want to head to Casterfo's office right away."

"But—" Korrie looked from Leia to Greer and back again, a stack of datapads in her arms. "Shouldn't he come to you?"

"Indeed he should!" C-3PO sounded delighted to have something meaningful to contribute. "Proper senatorial protocol demands that the junior senator should always be the one to call upon the senior senator. No doubt Senator Casterfo will be here first thing in the morning."

"No doubt," Leia agreed. "Which is why I'm going to his office instead, before he has a chance to leave for the night. I want him to understand that we're not standing on 'protocol' on our mission to Bastatha, and I want to catch him off his guard."

Greer caught on immediately; she usually did. "He'll be surprised. Flattered. You'll get a chance to see what he says and how he acts when he doesn't have a Centrist script to go by."

"Exactly." Leia began verifying the datapads one after the other—a thumbprint here, a retinal scan there. Korrie overcame her surprise to keep the datapads circulating speedily. "Besides, this way we can start making concrete travel arrangements right away. The sooner I get off Hosnian Prime, the better."

She pretended not to notice the glances Greer and Korrie shared.

Before long, Leia was able to leave her offices for Casterfo's. Over C-3PO's objections, she went alone. If Leia had no staffers with her, she could reasonably ask Casterfo to excuse his own. Taking the measure of a man would be far more easily done if he had to answer every question himself, and if he was divided from his usual sources of support.

The senatorial complex on Hosnian Prime was a vast structure, mostly housed in a single long, flat building only one story tall. This had been done to avoid any sense of offices on higher towers being "more prestigious" than others—which had seemed to make sense at the time—but it meant Leia would need to travel nearly a kilometer and a half to reach Casterfo's office. She stepped onto one of the automated sidewalks, drawing her white hood over her head. It wasn't as though this would prevent anyone from identifying her, but it might delay recognition long enough for her to avoid getting pulled into any inconsequential conversations that would only waste time.

Broad transparent panels revealed wide slices of the twilight sky overhead. Leia glanced up at the statue of Bail Organa—cool white in the encroaching dark—as she passed it by. Her father seemed to be watching her go. The numerous citizens of various worlds milled around, both on the mobile sidewalks and around them: a group of Bothans growling to one another in front of one office's door, a Gungan having an animated conversation via the comlink in his hand,

and two Wookiees far ahead of her on the sidewalk, being propelled forward past the throngs of politicians, workers, lobbyists, and visiting constituents that perpetually filled the complex. Only the sight of the Wookiees made Leia smile.

I wonder how Chewbacca's doing. Her husband's old Wookiee partner had settled back into a peaceful domestic life on Kashyyyk. As difficult as it was for Leia to imagine Chewie being content at home, he'd remained there long enough that she had to conclude he was enjoying himself. *Han never passes along Chewie's holos; I need to make some time to catch up, and soon.*

The planet Riosa was a faded center of manufacturing in the Inner Rim, one still struggling to rebuild itself. Accordingly, it had been assigned senatorial offices at the far edge of one of the building's wings. So much for the supposed "equality" of the office arrangements; status could be carved out of any substance people desired—and in Leia's experience, they always did desire. This meant almost nobody witnessed her walking into Casterfo's offices. When she entered, for a moment his staffers simply stood there, agog.

"I take it Senator Casterfo is still here?" Leia asked pleasantly, clasping her hands in front of her within the wide white sleeves of her robe. "Can you ask him if he has time to meet with Senator Organa?"

To Casterfo's credit, he hurried out of his private office almost instantly. "Senator Organa?" He smiled as he finished shrugging his green cloak back on; apparently he'd already begun unwinding from his day. "I had expected to visit you in the morning."

"When there's work to be done, why delay?" Leia returned his smile as politely as she could manage.

"My opinion exactly." Casterfo had the same sort of aristocratic accent Grand Moff Tarkin had spoken in, the one so many senior Imperial officers affected, the one she'd mocked when she and Tarkin last stood face-to-face. She tried not to let that put her on edge. "Please, do come in and sit down. Can I offer you tea? Water? Anything?"

Leia waved off refreshments as she followed Casterfo into his personal office—and then stopped in place, as though frozen.

On the walls of Casterfo's office hung artifacts from the Empire.

A stormtrooper's helmet. The black control box of a TIE pilot's atmospheric suit. Flags and banners of the Empire, the individual stormtrooper legions, and one—faded, slightly torn, but still searing to Leia's eyes—dedicated to Palpatine himself.

It was one thing to see such items in a museum . . . not that Leia would have ever gone to such an exhibit, but she would have understood its historical purpose. This adulation, however, was grotesque.

"Senator Organa?" Casterfo stared at Leia, somehow completely oblivious to the source of her discomfort. "Are you well? You look pale. Perhaps you should sit down."

"In here?" Leia held out her hands, gesturing to the array of artifacts surrounding them. "In the middle of your shrine to the glories of the Empire?"

Casterfo *smiled*. How could he dare smile? "Now, now, Senator. Don't overreact. These are historical relics, no more."

As though the war against the Empire had taken place millennia before, rather than the space of one generation. Leia wondered if Casterfo thought of her as a historical relic, too.

"You consider yourself a collector, then." Her tone remained cool, but she took a seat in one of the chairs. As she'd anticipated, Casterfo didn't go sit behind his desk—which would have been an assertion of his authority. He didn't want to insult her in that way, but he wasn't sure what else to do, and so was left standing in front of her, slightly at a loss.

But he remained eager to talk about his hobby. "Yes, exactly. I was only a small boy when the war ended. The adventures you all must have had! When I look around at these things, I imagine the battles so vividly I feel as if I had been there."

If Casterfo had *really* been able to imagine himself in the great battles of the war, he wouldn't have enjoyed the experience. Leia had dealt with enough shell-shocked former Rebellion troops to know that much. However, his guileless enthusiasm soothed her somewhat. *All right, he's not a warmonger. Just an overgrown kid who thinks he missed out on all the "excitement."*

She had never been so close to Casterfo before, and saw now that his polished appearance was not entirely perfect. His sandy hair had perhaps been grown longer in order to hide his ears, which protruded somewhat sharply from his narrow face. But he'd practically lacquered his hair in order to make it look sleek, no doubt because it otherwise would have curled tightly. Even the flowing cloak was probably meant to disguise how reed-thin he was. Before, Leia had seen Casterfo's obvious concern for his appearance as vanity; now she realized it was at least partly vulnerability, evidence that Casterfo wanted to look older than his years, more prosperous than his planet. He wanted to stand in the Senate and look as if he belonged.

Her judgment of him gentled . . . for the remaining second it took him to add, "Besides, even if we cannot respect these soldiers' methods, we can at least honor their dream."

"Dream?"

"The dream of empire, of course." Casterfo smiled like a man remembering the best days of his childhood. "If the galaxy truly could have been united under a wise, authoritative leader, such an empire might have stood for a thousand years, to rival the Old Republic itself."

Leia realized she was gaping at him, mouth open. "You wish the Empire were still standing?"

"Not the Empire we had, led by a man so corrupt as Palpatine. But if the Empire could have been *reformed,* perhaps, turned over to better and more responsible leadership—"

"You mean, if the Rebellion could've been defeated," Leia snapped. Her temper had heated beyond the point of restraint. "I regret that we so disappointed you, Senator Casterfo, by fighting and dying to set the galaxy free."

His face flushed. "Oh, don't misunderstand me, please. I would never have wished for the Rebellion to lose the war. I only wish that the war had not been necessary."

"You think Palpatine was the only problem with the Empire? Think again. That kind of power structure bred corruption from the highest levels on Coruscant down to the smallest outposts on border worlds. When the people with authority don't have to answer to citizens of the galaxy, the result is tyranny."

Casterfo's boyish dismay had faded and was now replaced by anger as poorly concealed as Leia's own. "So the answer is to give power to no one? In order to ensure that no evil can be done by those in authority, we make sure no good can be accomplished by them, either?"

"What 'good' do you think the Empire had to offer?"

"Very little, it seems. But if the Old Republic had not been flawed in its own right, Palpatine could not have come into power in the first place."

This made a certain degree of sense, as Leia was uncomfortably aware. She had heard her father's stories about the final days of the Old Republic too many times not to have absorbed his warnings about how liberty came to die. But Casterfo had never learned these lessons; he only wanted to excuse the rise of the Empire. "A republic can be changed as needed, because it remains answerable to its people."

"A wise and just Emperor would listen to his people as well," Casterfo insisted. "The only problem was that we had the wrong emperor."

The only problem? There was a limit to the amount of stupidity Leia could tolerate in one day, and she'd just hit it. She got to her feet. "I don't have time for a conversation about galactic politics with someone so profoundly ignorant of their greater implications."

Casterfo drew himself up to his considerable full height. "Nor do I have time to discuss these matters with someone so intolerant of other points of view."

By that point Leia's temples were throbbing, hinting at the headache her anger was carving within her skull. "I'll have my protocol droid come by tomorrow to exchange details about our travel." She wouldn't dream of forcing Greer or Korrie to deal with the man one moment longer than necessary. Besides, C-3PO would be thrilled to have something to do. Never had Leia been more grateful for a protocol droid. "My assistant can handle all other details of the trip. There's no need for us to see each other again until it's time to depart—if, of course, that's all right with you."

Casterfo folded his arms. "Believe me, I would find that arrangement a great relief."

"The feeling's mutual." Leia strode out of his office, through the thicket of staffers pretending not to eavesdrop at the door, and back out into the corridors.

As she stepped back onto the moving sidewalk, she covered her face with one hand. Her temper had gotten the better of her often enough in her life, but not many people had incensed her as quickly as Ransolm Casterfo and his collection of "historical items," which insulted everything she had fought for. Soon she'd be stuck with him for days, or even weeks—however long it took to get to the bottom of the situation with the Nikto cartels on Bastatha.

So much for an exciting last mission. It looked like her final days as a New Republic senator were going to be a royal pain in the ass.

CHAPTER
FOUR

Joph Seastriker had been born and raised on the planet Gatalenta, a world as warm as it was tranquil, famed for its tea, its meditative retreats, and lengthy, erudite poetry. People slept to the sound of wind chimes and woke to thank their suns for rising each day. Gatalenta offered serenity, silence, and calm.

Joph hadn't been able to get off Gatalenta fast enough, because he was bored as hell.

For as long as he could remember, Joph had longed for excitement. For adventure. In his class he was always the loudest, the most restless, and the least content. So his mothers placidly accepted Joph's desire to join the New Republic military. Maybe it wasn't like the old days, when you got to be a hero, but at least he could fly the best starfighters and travel around the galaxy. Although he'd left Gatalenta for the Academy only four years ago, Joph felt sometimes as if he'd lived on his home planet in a completely different lifetime. He'd never once looked back.

(Well, sometimes he missed the wind chimes. But that was it.)

Upon graduation a few weeks before, he'd been assigned to the precision air team; less than a week ago, he'd been doing starbursts high above the statue dedication ceremony, grinning in triumph as he swooped high into the clouds. At the time it had seemed about as good as duty got.

But now he'd been assigned as a military escort to a senatorial mission—to one headed into the criminal underworld, no less. *That* was the kind of excitement he'd been craving all along.

Joph brought his X-wing fighter into the Senate hangar, spinning it around sharply to land next to the ship even now being loaded with supplies. Sure enough, the info grid on his console told him this was the *Mirrorbright,* personal spacecraft of Senator Leia Organa herself. He took some satisfaction in determining that he was in fact the only X-wing pilot around; during the past few days, his orders had fluctuated several times, from being part of an entire squadron to accompany the senators on their mission to being told that there would be no military escort at all. Apparently there had been some bickering higher up about this. Joph neither knew nor cared about the details.

The air in the hangar smelled of rubber, grease, and solder. In the distance, he saw low-level maintenance droids shuffling from craft to craft and sparks flying from repair torches. The *Mirrorbright* stood out from the others the way the moon outshone the stars, its surface a glossy white and its edges curved, broadcasting its status as a civilian craft.

Joph hopped out of the cockpit with a grin on his face. As his boots thudded on the tarmac, he caught a glimpse of the person he assumed was the *Mirrorbright*'s pilot, sitting on a storage crate with her back to Joph as she checked in the material being loaded aboard. Her gray jumpsuit was civilian issue, as was the heavy woolen shawl draped across her shoulders. Her thick black hair hung loose down her back, another hint that she'd never been military.

Still, she's your copilot for this entire mission. So play it cool, make a good first impression, and for once in your life don't try too hard, Joph thought.

As he stepped closer, she heard his approach and turned.

She was the kind of pretty that wasn't merely *seen*—instead it hit you like a tidal wave. Lustrous black hair, full lips, deep coppery skin . . .

But no sooner had the rush of infatuation spilled over him than it subsided. This woman was so far out of Joph's league that even a crush was impossible. It would've been like getting lovesick over a sunset.

He relaxed and walked forward with a grin. "I'm Lieutenant Joph Seastriker, and I'm your escort for the mission."

She frowned. "You're Seastriker?"

Joph had run into disbelief before; he kept promising himself not to get defensive about it, but it was hard to resist. "You can check my ID and everything. If you think I'm too short, well, I'm one and a half millimeters above minimum regulation height."

"One and a half," she repeated, and he could've winced. Joph could never quite keep himself from adding the half. But he *hated* it when people thought he was a mechanic instead. Still, her smile was warm rather than mocking, and she held out her hand. "I'm Greer Sonnel, the senator's assistant and pilot of the *Mirrorbright*. Glad to have you along."

A political staffer and a pilot? That seemed like a strange combination. Before Joph could inquire, though, Greer continued, "If you ask me, we ought to bring a couple of extra starfighters. Bastatha's no place for law-abiding people."

"Have you been there?"

"No, but I've worked with pilots who have. All underworld space-ports are potentially dangerous. Bastatha isn't one of the worst, but we'll have to watch ourselves." Greer patted the nose of the *Mirrorbright*. "At least we've made a few custom modifications that should allow her to hold her own if we run into any trouble."

Joph realized the *Mirrorbright*'s unconventional W-shape allowed for weapons stations to be tucked into the corners, unobtrusive and almost invisible. While the average transport would have no weap-onry save perhaps defensive shielding, this ship could probably hold its own in a firefight. "So the senator believes in peaceful negotia-tions, huh?"

Greer's full lips quirked in a smile. "Let's just say she believes in being prepared. Her husband and I installed these guns a few years ago, when I first started working for him."

". . . her husband?" *Stay calm. Do not freak out. Don't say the name Han Solo unless you're totally sure your voice won't squeak.* "You, uh, know Captain Solo?"

"I won the Junior Sabers competition a few years back." Greer shifted from foot to foot. "Ancient history."

Anyone good enough to win a Sabers race, even at the junior level, knew what she was doing. Joph wanted to be impressed, but instead he felt intensely jealous. While he'd been taking exams at the Academy, she'd been out winning races, flying with *the* Han Solo, and having all the exciting times he'd been denied. Not that excitement was a finite resource some people used up before others could get their share—but still.

I'll get my chance, he reminded himself. From the sound of things, Bastatha might provide plenty of opportunities for action.

"Good morning." Across the hangar walked Senator Organa, although it took Joph a moment to recognize her; instead of formal senatorial robes, she wore a simple cream-colored tunic and leggings, and her hair was gathered into a braid down her back. "How's she looking, Greer?"

"She's ready to fly when you give the word," Greer promised. "And our X-wing escort just showed up. Senator, this is Lieutenant Joph Seastriker. Joph, this is Senator Leia Organa."

"Pleased to meet you, ma'am." Wait. Was that right? "I mean, Senator. Or, uh, Princess—no, Your Highness!"

A golden protocol droid shuffling up behind them said, "Either Senator or Your Highness at first reference. Ma'am or Princess Leia is acceptable thereafter."

"That's See-Threepio," Princess Leia said with a skyward glance and a shake of her head. For a legendary war hero, she turned out to be pretty grounded. "Don't worry. He'll tell you more about etiquette than you ever wanted to know; Threepio worries about it so I don't have to. And this is our staff intern, Korr Sella."

Korr couldn't have been more than sixteen, which meant Joph

wasn't the youngest person on the mission. Compared with her, he was experienced. Worldly, even. He felt more confident already, and the mission was looking up—until a male voice called, "Are we ready for departure?"

Everyone tensed. Joph turned to see a tall, pale, skinny guy walking toward them in a blue velvet cloak that would've been appropriate on the floor of the Senate or at a wedding but was absurdly posh for a hangar bay.

"Very nearly, Senator Casterfo!" C-3PO said cheerfully. "You're right on time, sir."

Casterfo stopped short, apparently taken aback to see everyone else in standard space jockey attire. Although Princess Leia smiled at Casterfo, it was the kind of smile that hit harder than a punch. Korr bit her lower lip, and Greer's sigh clearly meant something like, *Oh, brother, here we go.* Joph could almost have felt sorry for the guy, if Casterfo weren't so obviously in love with himself.

"Well." Senator Casterfo didn't seem to know what else to say to the shabbier people around him. "I'll have the droids load my trunks aboard."

"Please do." With that, Princess Leia headed onto the *Mirrorbright* herself, either to check things over pre-launch or to avoid Casterfo as long as possible. Probably both.

Once all the higher-ups had walked away, Joph muttered, "Is it my imagination, or did the temperature in here just drop almost to freezing?"

Greer gave him a sideways glance. "Let's put it this way. You're going to have a way more comfortable ride in that X-wing than we will on the *Mirrorbright*. Because it's only getting colder from here."

Leia remained in her cabin for as long as possible during the voyage to Bastatha, using the hours to snatch a quick nap, and then send another communiqué to Luke and Ben. (The Force alone knew when they would hear it. Luke's last message to her had been a while ago, and badly corrupted by radiation interference; wherever they were in

the galaxy, they were cut off from communication for the time being.)
Only at the end of the trip did she prepare herself for the diplomatic
visit. Her deep-maroon gown had been richly embroidered in blue
and silver at the edges, and she had ornamented her long braid with
dull pewter pins inset with small, glittering stones. More flashy than
valuable, but in a place like Bastatha, where style was forced to stand
in for substance, a little theater went a long way.

When she could procrastinate no longer, Leia emerged from her
cabin, determined to face Casterfo as calmly as possible, but he was
nowhere to be seen. From the cockpit, Greer called, "He just gave up
a few minutes ago."

"Oh, yeah?" Leia went into the cockpit herself. Greer sat at the
main controls, but there was a chair for a copilot or auxiliary gunner—
currently empty. When Leia sank down into it, she saw the strange,
warped blue waves of hyperspace in front of them, beckoning and
forbidding all at once. "What did he say?"

Greer shrugged. "He tried to make conversation with Korrie until
she came up with some excuse about reviewing her work. Then he
talked with me for a little bit about racing, where he actually knows
his stuff, so, give him some points there."

Leia couldn't help chuckling. "You'd forgive anyone if he had a fast
enough cruiser, wouldn't you, Greer?"

"Or if he backs the right teams." Greer's smile made her seem even
younger than her years, like the scrap of a girl she'd been when Leia
first met her. Han had taken countless young pilots under his wing
during the past several years, many of whom remained close to them
both even now.

His willingness to take on the role of mentor was one of the first
things she'd noticed about Han Solo, years ago—well, one of the first
things she'd *liked* about him. For all his griping about "farmboys,"
Han had dedicated himself to Luke in the days after the first Death
Star's destruction. Leia had watched as Luke slowly overcame his
grief for Obi-Wan Kenobi and his aunt and uncle, while learning
about gunnery, ship repair, and countless other things from Han. The
sarcasm and wit Han used disguised his concern from Luke, and

even Leia took a while to realize that Han was looking out for her, too.

Han was just as committed to his current crop of young pilots. Leia wished she could believe he mentored them out of the same impulse that had led him to befriend Luke; probably, on some level, he did. But Han was also teaching these kids the same lessons he'd wanted to teach their son.

Footsteps from behind made Leia turn around just in time to see Casterfo stepping back into the main living area. His velvet cloak had crumpled somewhat during their journey in hyperspace, but he drew himself upright with as much dignity as he could muster. "I take it we're nearing the Bastatha system?"

"Not quite." Greer didn't glance away from her controls. "But it's only going to be a few more minutes."

Leia got to her feet and strolled past Casterfo, the better to help herself to some Gatalentan tea from the *Mirrorbright*'s stores. As she busied herself with its preparation, she said, "I take it your accommodations are comfortable, Senator Casterfo?"

She expected him to reply in kind: formal, stiff, and barely within the boundaries of courtesy. Instead, Casterfo stepped to her side, where it was impossible not to look at him. "Senator Organa, I realize our initial conference went poorly, in large part due to my own tactlessness. My conversation was more theoretical in nature—philosophical—"

What philosophy is it that leads you to worship the Empire? Leia thought but did not say. The man was trying to be polite, and she could at least respect the effort. They had a job to do on Bastatha, a potentially important one; there was no point in letting Casterfo's distasteful politics get in the way.

"—and in my enthusiasm for the concept of monarchy, I failed to take your personal experiences into account," he continued. "We both said things that were ill advised, but your reason for speaking so heatedly was far more excusable than my own. I can only hope you will forgive me."

Leia had been a diplomat too long not to recognize a good apology when she heard one. "I understand, Senator Casterfo. Please don't worry about it any longer. The past is the past, and we have work to do."

"My thoughts precisely." Casterfo straightened the collar of his cloak as he pulled himself back up to his full height. Whatever sense of humility he'd mustered had already dissolved. "On to Bastatha."

CHAPTER
FIVE

The planetary surface on Bastatha was superheated by its red giant of a sun, uninhabitable by all but the most ineradicable bacteria and the sturdiest mining droids. As the *Mirrorbright* sliced through the hazy golden sky, it drew trails in the clouds of sulfur and methane that boiled in the valleys.

On Bastatha, the underground was *literally* underground.

Leia watched as the *Mirrorbright* dived straight toward the surface of the planet, nimbly turning sideways just in time to slip into a narrow crack that turned into a cavern. Joph Seastriker's X-wing followed behind, keeping close despite the numerous stalagmites and stalactites now breaking up the narrow spaces they had to traverse. The thin rays of the sunlight above soon faded into nothingness, and the air cleared into something humans could breathe. Greer cut their speed as they began to navigate by sensors and running lights alone.

Finally they reached the platform where the "municipal authorities" were waiting for them—an oasis of light amid the stony gloom. As Greer lowered the *Mirrorbright* for its landing, Leia smoothed her hair. "Let me do the talking."

Casterfo didn't like this any better than she'd expected him to. "The local authorities will no doubt wish to hear from us both."

"The local authorities are merely puppets. They do whatever the cartel leaders want. Our job is to reveal little and promise nothing." Leia raised an eyebrow. "Understand?"

"Perfectly." Casterfo sniffed. "If at any point we run into anything in the galaxy you don't already know, please alert me. I shall wish to record the event for posterity."

Did he just say—

Before Leia could lose her cool, C-3PO chimed in. "Oh, sir, you need not trouble yourself! I am programmed to record all essential conversations, and as you know I am fluent in nearly seven million forms of communication—"

"Yes, we know." Leia gestured to silence the droid, then forced herself back into diplomatic mode. Casterfo didn't like her any more than she liked him: fair enough. If he just had the sense to shut up and let her handle this, they'd be fine.

The magistrates—both of them Niktos—practically fell all over themselves to welcome the New Republic envoys. "What an honor," said Magistrate Tosta, one clawed hand to his chest. "To meet the famous Princess Leia Organa in person!"

"But of course we are just as pleased to meet Senator Casterfo," hissed Magistrate Xun. "So new to the Senate, and yet already so well respected."

Their flattery applied to everyone, and they even insisted upon inviting her staffers and pilots along to dinner as well. Everyone accepted, save Greer, who insisted so convincingly upon remaining with the ships that anyone would think it was her personal preference, not Leia's cautious orders. They set out—Leia and Casterfo in the lead, with Korrie and Joph just behind—to a chorus of praise from Tosta and Xun for the New Republic, for Leia's war record, for everyone's clothing, and so on. Even C-3PO was plied with flattery.

Such an unusually sophisticated droid. Had he truly been with her so long? *Extraordinary.*

Luckily, C-3PO was the only member of the team whose head could be turned by such stuff. The rest of them stayed on track as they were led deeper into the caverns of Bastatha. All business and personal life was conducted within these enormous tunnels of stone, most of them carved until they seemed to sweep up into majestic arches and vaults. The natural colors of the rock had been polished until they shone in mottled clouds of black, red, and every shade of gray. Air traveled through the tunnels in erratic gusts and gales, sometimes catching the edges of Leia's long robes but mostly blowing overhead.

Where it steals the sound, she thought. Otherwise every word spoken here would echo. Were Bastatha's strange air currents truly ungovernable by modern climate technology? She doubted it. No, this place was designed to keep its secrets close.

"We have prepared a table for you all at our grandest establishment," fawned Tosta, whose gaudy, gilt-edged robe put even Casterfo's finery to shame. "Amid the splendors of the nightlife Bastatha is coming to be known for."

Meaning Rinnrivin Di didn't want to hear about any of you getting a chance to speak with the senatorial delegation in private, Leia thought. "Yes, you're positioning this world as a resort, aren't you?"

"The market for gambling in this region has too long been monopolized by the uncivilized," Xun interjected. "We can offer a far more sophisticated experience here."

Indeed they could. Leia's party was ushered through gigantic doors that sectioned the tunnel—an arbitrary, but effective, split between what was considered "outside" and "in." Glinting metal tiles spiraled upward along the richly carved columns that appeared to hold the ceiling fifty meters overhead. Perhaps a thousand visitors lounged at the long oval tables, some of them merely eating or drinking, but most of them gaming. The dealer droids had been uniformly plated in shining copper so that they looked more like ornaments than tools as they dealt cards, spun wheels, and called out the winners and losers.

"And here we are." Tosta held out his scaly hands to present their table, which was placed nearly in the middle of the gaming hall. "We even have Riosan mead, to honor Senator Casterfo."

Leia accepted her glass without acknowledgment. She liked mead, but she couldn't enjoy the sweet taste while Casterfo preened before the Niktos' flattery. "Are we only here to eat," she said, "or will we be able to enjoy Bastatha at its best?"

The Niktos went still, their confusion obvious. Xun began, "Senator Organa—I beg your pardon, but if the arrangements are not to your liking—"

"Your arrangements are splendid." She smiled warmly before gesturing at the games of chance nearby. "But after our meal, will we not be allowed to play?"

Immediately both Niktos brightened. Tosta said, "But of course! What game would be the noble senator's pleasure?"

"Sabacc, if you don't mind."

Their smiles sharpened, the telltale sign of those who expected to make some money in short order. Sabacc was notoriously tricky, and the odds were always in the house's favor.

But few sabacc players had learned the game from Han Solo and Lando Calrissian.

"Honestly," Casterfo whispered as he leaned closer to Leia. "Is this the kind of example we should be setting as representatives of the Senate?"

"These people don't respect decorum. They respect cunning." Leia gave him a sidelong look. "Besides, if you're so worried about setting a good example, maybe you shouldn't spend so much time staring at the upper gallery." Above them, on a wide balcony, strolled scantily clad people of a dozen species and at least four genders Leia had spotted thus far.

"I wasn't—I didn't intend—" Casterfo's pale skin flushed. "The guests there seem determined to catch our eyes."

"Of course. That's because they're not guests. I would guess the casino refers to them as independent contractors." Leia took pleasure in watching Casterfo's face as he realized he'd been ogling the paid escorts—and with no intention of buying, which was rude on any planet. He sank back into his seat, obviously caught between embarrassment and ill-concealed umbrage.

The banquet itself was pleasant enough, with food that was popular on several worlds, all of it prepared well. Leia made polite chitchat about "economic development" with her Nikto hosts, paying more attention to what they didn't say than what they did. For instance, Tosta and Xun spoke often of "investors" without ever identifying who any of those investors might be, or what their main financial interests were. They praised the New Republic in terms that might have been thought flattering for a Populist—"*respect for independent worlds,*" "*a less controlling approach,*" and so forth—but were borderline insulting to Casterfo, who clearly wasn't sure how a good Centrist ought to respond. Of course, the Niktos weren't actually declaring their allegiance to a party; they just didn't want anyone interfering in their business.

Leia's eyes took in even more information than her ears. Some of this was merely amusing—for instance, the sight of towheaded Joph Seastriker trying hard to come across as grown-up and experienced, when really he looked as young and bright as a meadow flower. Meanwhile, Korrie adeptly talked her way through the usual courtesies while working hard to recall every word. If Greer had been here, her quick mind would've been able to replay the conversations nearly as accurately as C-3PO. But Greer had been teaching Korrie all her best tricks, and it appeared Korrie was learning fast. Casterfo made a point of complimenting the food, the arrangements, all of it—and Leia noticed that he drew people's eyes even without openly trying to. This wasn't the same kind of fascination she knew she commanded, the sort that caused whispers: *Princess Leia the Rebellion the senator the princess* and so on. Ransolm Casterfo wasn't that famous, at least not yet. But his good looks and youth, combined with his evident power and prosperity, gave him a luster few could deny. Most of the attention focused on him was open curiosity, though with many the interest clearly involved attraction as well.

Leia smiled as she imagined Casterfo as a shiny bauble she could dangle before the crowd . . . a perfect distraction.

She particularly noticed a nearby table of humans. None of them were playing cards; although they held drinks, they appeared to be nursing them rather slowly. This wasn't a group of hard-core gamblers or even people out looking for a good time. They were quiet. Watchful. Curious. Leia focused hardest on an older woman, perhaps ten to fifteen years her senior, whose long, dark, curly hair was boldly streaked with silver. Her face showed the impact of small scars she hadn't bothered to have healed—maybe she'd been in the war. Although she said little, body language alone proclaimed that this woman was in charge. Her dark eyes scanned the room constantly, back and forth and back again, as inexorably as any security sensor.

Never once did her gaze linger on Leia or on Casterfo. They might as well have been inanimate objects. But it was this very inattention—or the appearance of it—that tipped Leia off. Anyone else would at least notice the sudden arrival of a senatorial mission in the center of the room. This woman's impassivity was a clue that she did not want to be noticed in return.

Who was she? And why was it so important to her to remain unseen?

So, after the meal, when the dealer droid offered to start a game of sabacc for her table, Leia shook her head. "Not enough at stake for a truly exciting game. If you could direct me to one of the larger tables—"

"Senator Organa." Casterfo leaned closer to her, appalled. "What can you be thinking?"

"I'm thinking I'd like to play some cards."

"These are professionals. Do you realize that if you were to lose to them, they could try to hold your debts over you for favors or political bribes?"

Leia patted Casterfo's arm. "Relax."

He didn't relax, even though—two hours later—his complaints had totally changed direction. Casterfo leaned over her shoulder at the gaming table, crushed in closer to her by the throngs who had come to watch. "They think you're cheating."

"I doubt it." Leia tossed a card into the interference field, an opalescent octagonal column of energy in the center of the gaming board. Around her were clustered the only remaining players: a human man with dark skin and a frown, a Loneran who kept pushing his fur back from his eyes as if improving his view of his cards might also improve his hand, and a dark-blue, long-snouted Toydarian woman who hovered fitfully at the end of the table. In front of Leia was piled a good portion of her winnings to date. But she'd already pushed a lot of those winnings into the pot for this hand, and she was tempted to push forward the rest. "Why would they think I was cheating, Casterfo? You said so yourself: These are professionals. They know I'm on the up-and-up."

"Your streak of good fortune would seem to go beyond chance," Casterfo said primly.

"It's not about luck. It's about probabilities."

Han and Lando had both taught her the likelihood of each card coming up. The trick was to play those odds and never, ever deviate in the heat of emotion. For all the excitement surrounding her—the Nikto officials pleased the senator was enjoying herself, Joph and Korrie laughing with delight—Leia kept her cool.

The randomizer flickered, changing the cards in their hands again. Her eyes widened as she recognized the final card she needed, and she hit the control. "I call."

Immediately all the hands went on display. The Loneran's hand, with a mere sixteen points, was barely worth considering. Both the Toydarian and the other human had nineteen points, however. Leia's hand showed the Ace of coins and the Ace of sabers—thirty points and well over maximum—but there, glittering in the interference field, was the Star, value negative ten.

"Twenty points!" Joph started to applaud, and others followed suit. "You won again!"

The dealer pushed yet more chips over to Leia as the crowd murmured and clapped. Instead of claiming them, Leia called out, "These aren't for me. They're for everyone. I'd like to buy a drink for every single being in the house!" Wild cheering followed, and immediately droids began to roll out, their trays filled with tall glasses of something green that wafted wisps of smoke.

"I ought to have expected it." Casterfo crossed his arms in front of his chest. "A cheap trick to win over the crowd."

"Not that cheap." Leia watched as her pile of winnings began to diminish; the drinks on Bastatha were of the highest quality and therefore the highest prices. But this was exactly what she'd won the money for.

"Very well played, ma'am," Korrie said, her glass of green stuff already in hand. "Would you like a tally of your wins and losses? Not that there are that many losses to mark down . . ."

"That's all right, Korrie. Enjoy yourself, but be careful. That's a lot stronger than Riosan mead." Leia turned her attention to one of the server droids, one that appeared sophisticated enough to answer questions. "Is everybody enjoying their drinks?"

"Free intoxicants are among those gifts most welcomed by sentient biological life-forms," the droid replied.

Leia casually said, "What about them, over there? The people who just got their drinks, directly in front of us?"

The table in front of her was that of the dark-eyed woman she'd seen earlier. Although she did not acknowledge Leia's win, this woman and her companions accepted their drinks quickly and quietly—attempting to avoid the very attention they had just earned.

"The party from Daxam Four have lodged no complaints during this visit to Bastatha, ma'am."

Daxam IV. Leia mentally cataloged that name for later. Maybe her curiosity had only seized upon a random group of people, frequent gamblers who would naturally visit a world like this often, calmer than most. Her suspicion of them was only a hunch, but her hunches often proved to be right.

Luke said those strong instincts of hers served as proof of the Force, evidence that it was working through her all the time. Maybe he was right. But Leia believed just as much in her experience and her common sense. All of them were telling her the same thing: The woman from Daxam IV meant trouble.

Just how much trouble—only time would tell.

CHAPTER
SIX

Leia had every intention of discussing the group from Daxam IV with Ransolm Casterfo as they all walked back to the *Mirrorbright*. While she didn't like Casterfo very much, he wasn't the type to have connections to the underworld. No doubt he had shoved his way into this mission in an attempt to raise his profile; vain as this desire might be, it meant he genuinely wanted to find something worthy of reporting to the Senate. Besides, strong as her doubts were, she knew they were based mostly on her—call it intuition. Bouncing ideas off someone else would be valuable, even if it was Casterfo.

But she never got the words out of her mouth. Casterfo never gave her the chance.

"I suppose you're pleased with yourself," he said as they left the casino complex to return to the windy tunnels that led back to their ship. The caverns arched high overhead, dark and foreboding. "You made a spectacle completely unbecoming to the dignity of the Senate—"

"Do you hear yourself?" Leia shot back. "How is playing cards in a casino a 'spectacle'?"

"It is when you insist upon buying intoxicants for hundreds of people."

"Would you rather I walked off with my new fortune? They would have hated that. Buying drinks for people makes them like us. When people like us, they're more likely to cooperate and tell us the things we need to know. Working with people to get them to cooperate is what we call politics."

Casterfo gave her a withering look. "Your brand of politics, perhaps. I prefer appealing to my constituents' reason."

Was this guy born already eighty years old? Leia managed to resist saying as much out loud. "I guess you like to keep yourself tidy. You don't understand what it means to get your hands dirty doing what needs to be done. We learned that in the Rebellion."

"Did you spend the entire Rebellion in the company of smugglers and lowlifes?"

He probably meant this to be a cutting remark. Instead Leia found herself thinking of the first time she'd really seen Han's face—in a garbage compactor aboard the Death Star, moments before he fired his blaster at the magnetically sealed walls and nearly killed them all. Leia couldn't help smiling. "Almost, Senator Casterfo. In fact, I wound up married to one."

Out of the corner of her eye, she saw Joph Seastriker and Korr Sella exchange glances. *This* was the display unworthy of the Senate—she and Casterfo bickering in front of her intern and military escort. But Casterfo's priggishness chafed at her, and for all Leia's diplomatic experience, all her years and wisdom, she'd never been good at curbing her temper.

Casterfo obviously wasn't entirely sure what to do with her reference to Han. Would he insult her husband, a war hero and a racing legend? Or would he back down?

Neither, as it turned out. Instead, he went straight for insulting the Rebellion itself. " 'Getting your hands dirty.' An interesting euphemism. I appreciate your candor, Senator Organa. Very few former rebels are willing to admit that their movement wasn't as high-minded and noble as people now like to claim." He ostentatiously straightened the collar of his billowing velvet robe, thin lips set in a smile that clearly said he thought he'd scored a point.

Leia felt her temples throb, as if her fury at Casterfo had driven a spike straight into her skull. "Excuse me?"

He shrugged, his gait never slowing—and by this late at night, this far in the walk, Leia was all too aware that his long young legs were making this trip more easily than hers. Casterfo continued, "Don't misunderstand me. Obviously the Rebellion was right to oppose Palpatine. Something had to be done. But if you ask me, that hardly condones the terrorist tactics of the Rebel Alliance."

"*Terrorist* tactics?"

Casterfo stopped mid-pace; the two of them now stood in the heart of one of the long, dark tunnels, the wind rippling their robes and chilling Leia to the bone. He said, "Destroying the Death Stars, for a death toll of nearly one and a half million people, the vast majority of whom were low-level Imperial officers or even civilian workers? The slaughter on Noult after the rebels had left, and the planet was discovered to have housed a secret base? Or what about the rebel assault on Vivonah? Or the campaigns of Saw Gerrera's Partisans? Can you condone that?"

"We did what had to be done." Leia's voice shook. "We went up against a power so much greater than ours, whose tactics were so much bloodier. Can you imagine what would have happened if the Death Stars had remained operational? What act of terror could be more horrible than what happened to Alderaan? Have you forgotten that? I was there. I saw it happen, stood there watching while they destroyed my world, my home, everyone I had ever loved—"

By now Casterfo's face had paled; he'd gone too far and he knew it.

But Leia could take no pleasure in seeing Casterfo's dismay. The death of Alderaan had never left her, but it had been so long since she'd spoken of it. So very long. A few words, and suddenly she was back there—the sick ozone smell of the Death Star's recirculated air thick in her nostrils, Tarkin's chilly smile as thin as a knife's blade, and clamped around one of her shoulders the armored hand of Darth Vader—

—her *father*—

"You understand nothing." Leia had to force the words out. "Less than nothing."

"I had not intended to—the destruction of Alderaan was of course terrible—I meant—" Casterfo held out a hand as if to soothe her. If he actually touched her, Leia would not be held responsible for her actions.

He didn't, so she lashed back with words instead. "You get to daydream about a glorious Empire because you grew up in the freedom and safety we bought for you. The price wasn't cheap, Casterfo. It was paid in lives and years and suffering and terror, none of which a spoiled brat could possibly comprehend, because you've never had to fight for what you really believe in."

Casterfo held out his arms, incredulous in his anger. "Was I just called a spoiled brat by a *princess*?"

"A princess who lost everything when she was no older than they are now." Leia gestured toward Korrie and Joph, who both looked horrified; undoubtedly they'd been hoping nobody remembered they remained standing there. In the background, even C-3PO had been rendered speechless. Leia finished, "If you'll excuse me, I'd like to head back to the ship on my own before you follow."

Nobody dared argue. Leia walked back toward the *Mirrorbright*. Although it was visible in the distance, it seemed too far away. She remained focused on it, despite the tightness in her throat and churning in her belly.

As she finally walked up the gangway, Greer appeared, one hand at the holster she wore. Her fierce expression faded as she saw Leia's face. Leia couldn't guess what she looked like now, but it couldn't be good. "Princess Leia—" Greer began, but her words halted when Leia held up her hand.

"Not now, Greer." The words came out more smoothly than Leia had expected. Good. Greer didn't deserve to bear the brunt of anger Ransolm Casterfo had earned. "The others will be along shortly."

Greer nodded and leaned back against one of the struts, staring out the opening into the dark tunnels beyond. By pretending to look for the rest of the delegation, she gave Leia a chance to protect her pride by going into her quarters unobserved. Leia felt a moment of deep, fierce affection for the girl, but the feeling drowned quickly. It was lost in the tide of memories of Alderaan.

The Cloudshape Falls with their great billowing spray that seemed like a cloud come to nest on the river. Bail Organa's ringing laugh. The white-winged birds that flew in an X-formation, always westward, circling the planet once a year so that different regions marked their seasons by the birds' appearance. A bedroom high in a castle tower, surprisingly simple for a royal residence, where Leia had dreamed and dozed and kept her most beloved possessions in a keepsake chest, in the belief that she could then have them with her forever and ever.

As the door to her quarters slid shut behind her, Leia leaned heavily against the wall. She closed her eyes and kept back the tears. It had been a very long time since she'd allowed herself to cry for Alderaan or the people she had lost there. She'd told herself she would never cry about it again; this promise had seen her through many years. But it never got any easier to keep.

Greer Sonnel did not miss racing.

She didn't. Really. Her diplomatic work challenged her intellect and fulfilled her desire to do something meaningful in the world. Princess Leia was the best boss Greer had ever had—hot-tempered sometimes, but straightforward and principled, with a sly sense of humor to boot. As frustrating as the Galactic Senate could be, working there did offer the unique satisfaction of knowing you were at the political center of the known universe.

It wasn't as though she could've raced forever in any case. She didn't have the wealth to outfit a team of her own, so where else might she have ended up? If she'd saved for her own ship and traveled around the galaxy looking for work, she wouldn't have been able to choose her employers. Bad bosses plus uncertain pay? No, thanks. She couldn't see signing up for a standard transport company, either. The same half a dozen runs, over and over? Even if you did believe in what you were doing, the routine would soon sap all the joy out of flying. And once you took no more joy in flying, you might as well crawl into the peat bog and die, to let the soil make something else out of you.

But she'd still had so many years in front of her, so many good years taken away . . .

No. She wasn't going to dwell on that. Princess Leia's offer of employment a few years ago had come just when Greer needed it most. She'd adapted to the Senate—become damn good at her job, in fact—and yet she still got to fly from time to time. Even diplomatic runs on the *Mirrorbright* could offer some variety.

And this mission was shaping up to be much more interesting than most.

"She actually spoke the words *spoiled brat*?" Greer took a gulp of her caf as she double-checked the engines first thing the next day.

Joph nodded, his thick, floppy blond hair sliding into his eyes from the motion. "And he threw them right back at her."

Greer pretended to shiver. "So the deep freeze continues."

In Bastatha's deep caverns, morning was more a concept than a reality. She and Joph were working in the same darkness that had enclosed them overnight, each of them doing routine maintenance on their engines—though, in a place as lawless as Bastatha, checking for sabotage was also a good idea.

The *Mirrorbright* checked out. But Greer lingered, mostly for the chance to check out Joph's X-wing. Back when she'd had a starfighter of her own, she'd babied it until it shone, even down in the deepest recesses of its engines . . .

Her comlink buzzed. "Greer?"

"Princess Leia. Can we help you?" Greer glanced at Joph, who was leaning closer already.

"Briefing in five."

"Yes, ma'am," Greer said with a smile. Oh, this was no routine run.

Some time later, as Greer sat in one of the chairs in the *Mirrorbright*'s main area, the briefing seemed about to wrap up until Ransolm Casterfo walked in. Unsurprisingly, he already wore his fine cloak, though by now it had begun to look rather crumpled. *Does he sleep in it?* Greer wondered idly.

Casterfo looked from person to person. "Is this . . . a meeting?"

"Why, Senator Casterfo, we are currently discussing an invitation just received by the princess." C-3PO, always glad to be of service, shuffled closer to Casterfo. "Several business leaders on Bastatha have invited her to a private conference."

"I was invited as well," Casterfo interjected, alarm clear on his face. "But I had no thought of accepting. Surely, Senator Organa—"

"I've said yes." Princess Leia poured herself more caf with studied nonchalance. Greer thought that anyone who didn't know the princess very well would actually think she didn't care. "Don't worry. You needn't accompany me."

"How can you even consider it?" Casterfo stepped into the middle of the small gathering. Maybe he was compensating for being excluded by now making it impossible for them to ignore him. "Such an invitation is highly irregular. 'Business leaders'? Need I remind you the nature of the 'business' conducted on Bastatha? Most of it is distasteful at best, criminal at worst. They even asked for us to bring only one escort. Suspicious, don't you think? If there is any truth to Emissary Yendor's allegations, and this Rinnrivin Di figure has a cartel based on this planet, then there's even potential for violence."

"I don't think they'll attack a senatorial delegation." Princess Leia didn't meet Casterfo's eyes. He might as well have been a piece of furniture in the room. *Ouch*, Greer thought. She didn't like the guy much better than the princess did, but she couldn't help pitying anyone who'd basically just been buried neck-deep in ice.

"You don't *think*. And on this basis, you'll march out into mortal danger." Casterfo gestured skyward, then sighed. "I take it nothing I say will make any difference. Why should you start listening to me now?"

The princess shrugged. "As I said, you can stay here, safe and sound."

Casterfo pulled himself back together with a sniff. "I shall take no responsibility for your safety."

"That's fine. Anything else?" Princess Leia took another sip. By now the tension in the room had risen so sharply that Greer's own caf seemed to churn in her belly. Korr stared at her feet, and C-3PO's upper body rotated from senator to senator in apparent confusion.

"Good luck," Casterfo said. "You'll need it." With that he stalked back toward his quarters.

The silence that followed endured until Korrie finally ventured, "It's not as though he's wrong."

Greer and Joph exchanged a look. Would Princess Leia blow up at that? Would she acknowledge that Korrie—like Casterfo—actually had a point?

She did neither. The princess continued staring at the corridor down which Casterfo had vanished as she said, "He's the type they liked to recruit. The Empire, I mean. Casterfo is just the sort of person they promoted in their ranks. Privileged and proper and self-important."

Nobody spoke. Greer figured the others, like her, had no idea what to say.

"I can just see him in an Imperial uniform," Princess Leia continued. "And I think that's how he likes to see himself."

"Surely not!" C-3PO sounded as indefatigably cheerful as ever. "Why, who would ever want to imagine being a part of the Empire?"

Leia's dark eyes continued to stare past the rest of them, toward a horizon only she could see. "Many people would. Far too many."

When the "businessmen" arrived—yellow-green Niktos with lowered heads and beady eyes, flanking Magistrate Tosta on either side—Leia strode from the *Mirrorbright* to meet them, a heavy silver necklace around her neck only a small part of the finery she'd donned for the occasion. The pale silvery gown she wore, with its high collar and deeply belled sleeves, was formal enough for the Senate chamber, and she was even now tugging on her finest cloak; it was a touch they would take note of, and satisfaction in.

"Is the honored senator our only guest today?" One of the Niktos gestured toward the ship. "We received Senator Casterfo's regrets, but your guard will join us, surely."

"No security." Leia smiled with all the warmth she could muster. "This is a diplomatic mission, one of the greatest importance to us both. If I didn't trust the people of Bastatha, I wouldn't have come here in the first place."

The Niktos' wide smiles told her how much they liked her answer. "Join us, Senator Organa. We have so much to show you."

They escorted her to a sort of speeder, one with a wide, variably powered base that allowed it to hover far above uneven surfaces. The transparent semi-enclosure at the top gave Leia a fine view of the caverns, particularly as they headed deeper within the world, farther away from the gauzy casino complexes. Here, she saw small outcroppings that had been turned into residence buildings, perhaps to house the Niktos and their employees. Unlike the elegant structures above, these residences seemed almost as if they were hidden— tucked away in darkness, closed in tight.

Anyone who worked here would feel that the rest of the galaxy was far away. Whoever held power on Bastatha would appear to be the only source of authority in the world.

Leia shivered as she brought her hands together, so they would be covered and warmed by her wide sleeves. Although she strongly agreed with most aspects of Populist philosophy, she couldn't deny that her party's approach had its own flaws. One of them was that planets similar to Bastatha, without much independent power or a strong economy, tended to get left behind. *We alone manage our own affairs,* Populist worlds said; the corollary to this was *We manage only our own affairs.* When each planet was focused only on its own best interests, problems on other worlds were ignored.

Failing to help those in need was bad enough for a government that claimed to represent and protect everyone. But even those too shortsighted to understand that ought to realize that one world's difficulties often spread offplanet and magnified exponentially. One world's epidemic could become a system-wide pandemic. One world's dissident faction could turn into interplanetary terrorism— *the real kind,* she thought sourly, barely able to restrain her scorn at the thought of Ransolm Casterfo's ignorance.

And one world's criminal mastermind could turn into a cartel boss capable of warping economic and political power among dozens of systems, just as the Hutts had not so long ago.

Leia startled at a flash of movement in the corner of her eye. She turned to see a hoversled weaving up toward them, piloted by a single Nikto—one who'd aimed his blaster directly at her driver.

Magistrate Tosta whispered something in his own language, sibilant and low. Leia turned toward him to see another two hoversleds pulling up alongside. One of the pilots gestured to someone behind them, no doubt covering them from behind. The firepower these Nitko had in their hands and holsters was enough to blow them all away ten times over.

"I apologize, Princess Leia," said Tosta, doing his best to sound genuinely sorry. There was no need; they both knew he'd set her up. "We appear to be surrounded."

CHAPTER
SEVEN

———————————

As her captors boarded the hovercraft, Leia remained where she sat, her posture regal. "Are you kidnapping me for ransom, or is this an assassination?"

"Neither, Senator Organa." The Nikto attacker with the largest blaster smiled toothily at her. "We are bringing you to an important meeting. There is no need to resist."

Meaning, they'll hurt me if I do. Leia had never planned on resisting. She simply folded her arms across her chest. "Then it looks like I'm going to a meeting."

Her supposed hosts—Magistrate Tosta and the "businessmen" who had led her into danger—were lowered to one of the nearest crags and told to walk to safety. This surprised Leia only because she couldn't believe they were still going through this sham, pretending that she hadn't been set up from the beginning.

Then again, could she blame them? She was pretending, too, as though she were afraid or at least unsure. Leia had suspected something like this was in the offing from the first moment she'd read the "business leaders' invitation."

In fact, she'd been *counting* on it.

The speeder dived far deeper into the Bastatha caverns, so much so that the *Mirrorbright* now had to be a couple of kilometers overhead. Broader tunnels gave way to narrow passageways barely large enough for their ship to slip through. Although Leia didn't tend to be claustrophobic, she found herself keenly aware of the heaviness of the stone overhead. Soon they were nearly concealed in darkness, except for the faint glow of lights from the windows of a small domed structure atop a plateau in the depths of the cavern. As the hovercraft sidled to the edge of the plateau, Leia put one hand to her throat as if in dismay—and pressed her fingers down hard on the central pendant of her necklace.

That pendant, broad and jeweled, perfectly concealed the miniature sensor beacon Greer had wired in place first thing that morning. Now signals were being sent to the *Mirrorbright*, broadcasting not only her exact position but also the scans of those closest to her, namely her captors. Leia's staff would immediately contact the local authorities. Although the Nikto magistrates wouldn't want to arrest criminal overlords as powerful as these, once a senator had been kidnapped . . . well, they couldn't talk their way around that one.

All Leia had to do was hold on, and stay alive.

For one moment the craft simply hung there in darkness, the deep well of the crevasse seemingly infinite beneath them. Overhead Leia heard squeaks and flapping wings—mynocks, perhaps. The only sign of civilization or light was the domed structure atop this plateau. When the door opened, a shaft of brightness cut into the gloom, and she saw the silhouette of her captor.

He walked toward them, his individual features taking shape as Leia's eyes adjusted. He was shorter than most of the others, his leathery skin redder. The white trousers and jacket he wore seemed to shine in the darkness, so elegantly cut that Ransolm Casterfo might have been proud to own them. He carried himself with as much dignity as any member of the Elder Houses, though there was something in his posture that made Leia feel Rinnrivin was mimicking humans—for what effect, she couldn't guess. As he reached the edge of the plateau, Leia lifted her head high. "Rinnrivin Di, I presume?"

"Princess Leia Organa." Rinnrivin spoke warmly, as if welcoming an old friend. He held out his hand to help her from the hovercraft. "I apologize for your unorthodox journey here. However, I thought you unlikely to accept a straightforward invitation."

"I would've appreciated the opportunity to say yes or no." Leia took Rinnrivin's hand and stepped easily onto the plateau, her cloak billowing in the breeze. If he could pretend this was any other formal visit, so could she.

He ushered her toward the dome with as much dignity and courtesy as any court minister. "Let me see if I can't make it up to you. We have so much to discuss, you and I, including matters I believe will be of great interest and benefit to us both."

"Then, by all means, let's talk."

Leia's purpose in accepting the shady "invitation" that had led her here was twofold. First, she intended to learn more about Rinnrivin Di, to determine for herself how he operated. If she was to understand the full extent of the risks he presented, she needed to better understand the man. She knew how to learn the true measure of an individual: Watch what he does to someone he believes is at his mercy.

Second, she intended to put Rinnrivin in jail. Attempted kidnapping of a senator was only the latest and slightest of his crimes, but it would do for now. Even a brief period of incarceration would give the New Republic time to go after his cartel. So Leia needed to speak with her captor at length, both to discover his true nature and to stall long enough for the Bastatha security forces to arrive.

The interior of Rinnrivin's headquarters put the Bastatha casinos to shame. The table tiled in a subtle mosaic of white and gold, the opalescent shell inlays within the domed ceiling, the beautiful holographic seascape rolling gently in its frame—this wasn't gaudy mimicry of elegance, but the real thing. Leia settled herself onto an ornately carved, amply cushioned chair across the table from the place she instinctively understood would be Rinnrivin's; it was the one spot from which nobody would be able to approach him from behind.

"Let me offer you a drink." Rinnrivin gestured for a droid to roll forward with a bottle of wine, apparently chilled. Leia was about to refuse when Rinnrivin continued, "Toniray, an excellent vintage. A wonderful year. Sadly, one of the last."

Toniray had been an Alderaanian wine. Leia's eyes widened as she took in the teal color, the characteristic shape of the bottle. It couldn't be real, could it? All the offworld bottles had to have been consumed long ago.

But when the droid poured it into the correct slim flute, Leia recognized the scent. Suddenly she was back at a royal banquet, seated at her father's right hand, taking care to slowly nurse the one glass she had been given. Ignoring Rinnrivin's avid interest in her reaction, she took a sip. Yes. It was Toniray, true Toniray. The first moment the cool wine touched her tongue, she closed her eyes to better savor the sensation.

Leia could imagine the valley where the fruit would have been grown, see the deep-green leaves of the vines—for one instant, she could taste the very soil of Alderaan again.

Home.

The intense wave of emotion she felt never altered her expression. Leia let it happen, then let it go.

When she opened her eyes again, she saw Rinnrivin studying her, though he didn't seem to be fishing for a sign of weakness. Instead he looked like any other host hopeful to have pleased his guest.

"Thank you." Leia could say this much to Rinnrivin with total sincerity. "It's been a long time since anyone gave me such a gift."

"Took a while to find the vintage. Collectors prize the few remaining casks, as I'm sure you can imagine. But when I heard you would be visiting Bastatha, I realized I had to find an appropriate way to welcome you. I so wanted to get our relationship off to a good start." Rinnrivin sat back in his luxurious chair; he seemed more at home in his finely appointed hideout than he would have in the usual rough

haunts of the Niktos. "In fact, let me put you more at ease right away."
With that he spoke to the guards massed at the door. "We have no
further need of you. Senator Organa and I are having a civilized conversation. Go on about your business; we require only a driver to take
her back to her ship when we're done."

The Nikto guards clearly hadn't anticipated this. Some shuffling
and muttered debate followed before all but one of them took off on
the hoversleds. The only guard left went and sat in the hovercraft,
arms crossed sullenly across his chest. When Rinnrivin Di turned
back to Leia, she bowed her head and smiled. "Your courtesy is much
appreciated, Rinnrivin." *And you obviously don't think a lone woman
in her late forties could represent much of a threat.*

"I meant what I said." Rinnrivin settled back into his chair. He
took none of the Toniray himself, leaving it all for her. "My unorthodox introduction may have caused some confusion, but I genuinely
would like for us to have a mutually beneficial relationship. You see,
I've been an admirer of yours for some time. Nor am I the only one.
Many among the Niktos revere you, and not for the reasons the rest
of the galaxy does. Oh, of course, your work during the Rebellion was
important, Senator, as your political efforts are now, but I personally
find some of your other accomplishments far more impressive."

Leia took another sip of the precious Toniray. "I'm not sure I follow."

"I'm about to give you another gift. One far more valuable to me
than the wine. In fact, this has been one of my prize possessions for
many years, one I've always kept with me. But when you see it, and
know what it has meant to me and to so many of the Niktos, at last
you will understand." Rinnrivin pulled a small holocube from his
pocket; its sides shone dully in the limited light. "My people have
their reasons for hating the Hutts. Jabba the Hutt we hated most of
all. So when the Hutts went through the wreckage of Jabba's sail barge
on Tatooine, looking for evidence regarding the exact nature of his
death—to settle one of their endless debates over the will, you know
how they are—well. What emerged was a bit of footage traded in
only the most exclusive circles."

The holocube flickered, and projected around it was the image of

Jabba reclining on his platform, Leia herself in dancing-girl costume shackled to his side. They were on the sail barge, and these were the last moments of Jabba the Hutt's life. Leia remembered the heat, the stench, the grit of sand against her skin, and the terrible, nauseating fear she'd felt for both Han and Luke. The risks they'd taken . . . Had they lost their minds? No. They'd only been young and courageous. Sure of their own invincibility.

It had been a long time since Leia felt that untouchable.

Jabba ordered Luke thrown into the Great Pit of Carkoon. Moments later, chaos broke out. With a kind of awe, Leia watched herself sling the heavy chains around Jabba's neck. The sheer strength it took to compress a Hutt's neck to the point of asphyxiation—she had summoned that from somewhere deep inside, remembered doing so, but found it almost unbelievable to witness. Pure hatred had fueled her. Her arms seemed to ache with remembered strain.

Of course she had been unable to see Jabba's face as he died. Leia watched him now, taking in each detail: the bulging of his heavy-lidded eyes, the protrusion of his slimy tongue. She felt neither revulsion nor triumph, only the echo of her own desperation. His death had been fulfilling to her back then, but now it was irrelevant. Only an ugly thing that had had to be done. When Jabba grunted his last, the hologram flickered out.

"Huttslayer," Rinnrivin breathed in genuine reverence. "This is what we call you among ourselves, and it is a far greater title than either *senator* or *princess* could ever be. The Niktos know you for the warrior you are, Huttslayer, and you will always have friends among us."

Leia took the holocube, slipping it into the pocket of her cloak. Footage of her committing a murder . . . well, it was either the strangest diplomatic gift she'd ever been given or very close. "There are other records of this around?"

"Only a handful. The Hutts hunted down most of the copies and vendors. They didn't want proof of their own vulnerability to circulate. As you can see, however, I have ways of getting what I want."

"No doubt," Leia said drily. Yet Rinnrivin was not the usual criminal boss, interested in the fastest, most brutish power. This was an individual who considered himself cultivated. Intellectual. He didn't only want riches; he wanted *respectability*.

If Rinnrivin had been born human in the age of the Empire, he could have turned into a figure a great deal like Grand Moff Tarkin. And had Tarkin been born a Nikto, he would have been *exactly* like Rinnrivin.

He's no thug, Leia decided. *He's much more dangerous than that. And his goals will be broader than any mere spice cartel.*

Rinnrivin leaned forward, his elbows on the table, hands clasped together as though he were beseeching her. "We honor you, Huttslayer. We will always honor you for ridding the galaxy of Jabba the Hutt. I ask only that you honor us in return."

Finally, he was getting to it. "What form do you expect this 'honor' to take?"

"We only want the same opportunities other peoples enjoy, to trade freely and grow toward greater prosperity and influence throughout the galaxy."

Leia raised an eyebrow. *Throughout the galaxy.* Either Rinnrivin Di's ambition was great . . . or his cartel was already even larger than they'd feared. "The New Republic doesn't allow the free trade of most forms of spice," she said. The weak stuff that could be mined or grown on numerous planets—nobody worried about that. And, of course, there wasn't that much money in it. Cartels went for the stronger varieties. "And coercing debtors through violence, demanding protection money . . . that's not allowed no matter what you're selling."

She expected Rinnrivin Di to deny these allegations, but he surprised her. "Rules set on Hosnian Prime often fail to reach the other worlds of the New Republic. Besides, Huttslayer—as you obviously know, sometimes violence is necessary. You didn't call Mos Eisley security to deal with Jabba, did you? No." He grinned with evident relish. "You trusted your own two hands. As do I."

"I once fought lawlessness with lawlessness, it's true," she said. "But I believe in the rule of law and have spent most of my life trying to restore it to the galaxy. In other words, Rinnrivin, I've made it this far without taking bribes. I don't intend to start now."

Rinnrivin shook his head and chuckled, like she'd told a good joke.

"A fine speech for the Senate floor. But you can't be as rigid as you claim. Otherwise, you could never have married a smuggler. Spice-running, collaboration with the Hutts, high-stakes gambling? Han Solo's record rivals mine."

"That was a long time ago," Leia said, caught off guard. No one had ever thrown Han's past in her face so bluntly before. "Before he joined the Rebellion."

"Do you believe being a part of the Rebel Alliance washed away all sins?" Rinnrivin shook his head, rueful and amused. "Trust me on this, Huttslayer. Once a pirate, always a pirate."

There had been a time when Leia would have agreed with Rinnrivin—and this, more than anything, sparked her temper. "You don't know what you're talking about."

"Don't I?"

Whatever else Rinnrivin would've said was cut off by the sound of a blaster bolt.

Leia wheeled around, alarmed. Surely Bastatha security wouldn't blindly start firing into a hostage situation. Behind her, she heard Rinnrivin hiss a Nikto curse as they both saw what was happening just outside . . .

. . . which was Ransolm Casterfo facing off with the guard.

Leia gasped as the guard swung one of his many-pointed blades at Casterfo; they grappled too close for blasters. Swift and agile, Casterfo dodged the blow, then spun around to bring the heel of his hand up under the Nikto's chin. The guard's head snapped back, and as he stumbled to the side in a daze, Casterfo kneed him hard in the gut, shoving the stunned Nikto guard backward into the hovercraft.

Then Casterfo rushed toward the door, and Leia barely had time to scramble out of the way before he dashed in.

"Princess Leia!" he shouted, leveling his blaster at Rinnrivin. "Come with me, now!"

What is he doing, WHAT IS HE DOING—but Leia couldn't argue, not without giving away the sting she'd planned in the first place. She could only stand there in equal parts astonishment and anger as Casterfo grabbed her hand.

Rinnrivin looked completely bemused. He had planned a meeting on his own mannerly terms, and perhaps had some backup that could be quickly summoned in case of a full-fledged assault, but didn't know what to do with one wild-eyed, armed senator. He never rose from his elegant, high-backed chair, and he said only, "Until we speak again, Huttslayer."

Casterfo didn't give Leia a chance to reply. He simply dragged her out of the dome and toward a hoversled. As they ran toward it, Leia yelled, "How did you get here?"

"I put a tracker on your cloak, just in case you deviated from the scheduled flight path!" Casterfo sounded triumphant as he leapt onto the two-meter-long hoversled and grasped the handlebars on the tall steering console. "When you went off course, I knew what had happened. I told you there would be trouble."

"I *knew* there would be trouble! I had my own tracker on me the whole time. Bastatha security would've been here within minutes!" Leia jumped onto the hoversled, too; her plan was ruined, so she might as well escape with Casterfo. "Did you honestly think I was stupid enough to walk into an obvious setup without guards or a plan?"

"A plan? This was part of a *plan*?" Casterfo's smug smile faded into bewilderment. "Why didn't you tell me there was a plan?"

"Because I don't trust you!"

"I just risked my life to save you from a dangerous situation that turns out to be nothing but a lie, one you set up, and *you* don't trust *me*?"

That was . . . not a bad point. Leia swore under her breath. "We can discuss this back at the ship. For now we've got to get out of here." Already she could hear the Nikto guard stirring in the hovercraft.

Casterfo put his hands on the controls, thumb sliding along the bar that brought the engine glowing back to full power. As he did so, though, Leia heard the hum of other engines, almost lost in the gale winds of the Bastatha caverns but growing louder by the moment.

"We're about to have company," she said, just as a dozen or more of Rinnrivin's men flew out of the shadows and swooped in like carrion birds ready to pounce. "*Go.*"

CHAPTER
EIGHT

When Ransolm Casterfo had realized Leia Organa was in danger, he had not hesitated before rushing to her rescue. Yes, she had insulted him, been difficult at every turn, proved touchy and defensive—but she was his partner in the delegation and a member of the Senate. She required help. That was all there was to it.

He'd been studying some of the new construction via hoversled when his monitor had informed him that the signal he was tracking had deviated sharply from the supposed itinerary for the "businessmen." Casterfo had paused only long enough to send word back to the *Mirrorbright* that things had gone horribly wrong. He hadn't asked for backup, because the caverns down here were far too narrow for either of their ships to safely navigate. He had only meant to leave word of the danger they were in so the authorities could be informed, and people would know what had become of him and Princess Leia if they did not survive. Then he steered the hoversled downward, straight into danger.

Ransolm felt he'd been brave. Decisive. Possibly even heroic.

His reward? Finding out he'd just ruined a sting operation nobody had bothered to tell him about. Wonderful.

As the mobster's thugs swooped in, Ransolm gunned the engines of the sled and took off. The sudden rush of speed made Princess Leia gasp, and he shouted, "Hold on to me!"

One of her arms went around his waist. With the other, she grabbed the blaster from his belt. As she clung to him, she shouted over the roar of wind, "Here they come!"

Ransolm couldn't afford to look too closely at the approaching attackers. He needed to lose them. Losing them meant flying fast through caverns the others wouldn't want to enter. That meant he needed to keep his eyes straight ahead.

Green blaster bolts sliced through the air directly in front of them, and Ransolm braced himself for a direct hit on the sled—but Princess Leia fired upward, and the caverns lit up with the brilliant flash of an explosion. When she fired again, another of the pursuing sleds slammed into a wall; Ransolm saw the blaze from the corner of his eye.

I'll give her this, he thought, *she doesn't lose her nerve.*

Opportunity presented itself in the form of a narrow passageway studded with stalactites. Ransolm pointed the sled straight at it and accelerated to maximum speed. He half expected the princess to cry out in alarm. Instead, she merely tightened her grip around his waist and started firing behind them.

The stalactites carved the space of the cavern into a maze he had to weave through, one where a single mistake meant death. Dull red jagged rock had swallowed them like jaws of stone. Ransolm forgot about the risks—let them go, completely. If he considered anything farther away than the controls of this sled, he'd crash within instants.

Bank left, rise, bank left again, hard right, up then down, hard! He only thought about the very next move, the very next second. Piloting a sled meant tilting your body along with the machine, feeling as if you were one with it. The stalactites zoomed into his field of vision moments before collision, over and over, and each time he bent and swerved just in time. Ransolm felt a rush of pure exhilaration that took him beyond any fear.

"They're getting too close!" Leia shouted. She fired behind them, a series of short, staccato blasts—and the stone rumbled. Had she caused a cave-in? Ransolm's momentary fear changed to satisfaction as he realized Leia had targeted some of the stalactites, ensuring they'd topple in front of their pursuers. Explosions behind them lit up the crags ahead, and the dark maw that promised an end to this cavern.

"We're heading up." He gripped the controls even tighter. "Brace yourself!"

They emerged from the crevasse into a larger pit, and Ransolm turned the sled sharply vertical. Their momentum allowed them to keep their footing—barely.

"We've still got two on our tail." Leia swore again. "See any other places we could lose them?"

"Not yet." Would they be shot down despite everything?

Ransolm heard the engines before he saw the blasterfire from above covering them. He gaped as he realized what was flying in overhead—an X-wing fighter darting through caverns hardly wider than the ship itself. It lanced through a narrow opening in the rock and spiraled over them, energy bolts streaking down toward their Nikto pursuers. At the last moment before the X-wing would've collided with stone, it looped up again, swiftly tilting sideways and pulling in its foils to slip between stalactites.

"What in the worlds is Seastriker doing here?" Leia asked.

"I've no idea. How did he even fly down this far without crashing?"

"Not a clue. But it looks like he's saved our skins."

So he had. The last of their pursuers were no more than glowing rubble amid the stones below. Seastriker dipped his wings at the hoversled, no doubt signaling for Ransolm and Leia to head back to the *Mirrorbright* while he provided cover.

Ransolm pulled the sled out of its sharp ascent, steadying them both. Leia's arm slipped away from his waist as he cut speed to a more manageable level. His breathing slowed as he realized the chase was truly over. His rescue mission had been successful.

Unnecessary, but successful.

Then Leia said, "You know . . . you're not a bad pilot."

He turned toward her. To his surprise, she was smiling.

Ransolm began to smile as well. "And you're not a bad shot."

Magistrate Xun apologized profusely to Leia about the abduction, and the failure of the Bastatha authorities to capture Rinnrivin Di. She accepted these apologies while idly wondering whether they'd even pretended to pursue him. Somehow she managed to sound regretful as she explained that Bastatha was now under conditional probational advisory of the New Republic; this was a fairly minor punishment as such things went, as much as they could impose upon a non-member world, but it would give the New Republic the right to observe and track activity around Bastatha for a while. She and Casterfo might not have the head of the cartel in their grasp, but they would have a chance to trace the cartel itself.

That was, if the cartel didn't lay low on Bastatha for a while, which they surely would . . .

"Preparing for takeoff," Greer called from the cockpit as Leia snapped off her communications with the Bastatha authorities. "Ready?"

"Just one thing." Leia walked into the cockpit and hit the comlink. "Lieutenant Seastriker, you're aware that you were operating outside standard safety protocols today." His orders had told him to summon help—not to fly an X-wing into spaces that would've led most pilots to a swift demise.

"Yes, ma'am." Joph's voice crackled slightly in the speaker. "Am I on report?"

"You are not. But watch it next time. The regulations are there to protect you, and I knew the risks I was taking. All right?"

"Absolutely, ma'am." Seastriker sounded unrepentant, but Leia shook her head and let it go.

Greer hesitated before saying, "Did Joph really dive into that cavern?"

"He did." Leia recognized the look on Greer's face now; it reminded her of Han's expression anytime he saw a brand-new racing ship: pure longing. More softly she said, "Do you miss it? Flying like that?"

Greer's smile faded as she put her hands on the controls for takeoff. "Just wish I could've seen him. That's all."

Leia didn't push any farther, simply patted Greer's shoulder as she walked back into the main lounge area of the ship. Korrie had already gone to her cabin, busily preparing the reports Leia would file upon her return, which meant Ransolm Casterfo sat in there alone, drinking his Gatalentan tea. By now his fine blue cloak had been stained and torn into a parody of itself, but to judge by the smile on his face, he didn't care. His expression reminded her a little bit of Ben's when he was little, running in after an afternoon of roughhousing with his friends, hair mussed, absolutely filthy, and proud of himself.

She gestured to her own tunic and pants. "You see now why I always come prepared."

"Very prudent," Casterfo said with a nod. "Next time I'll know how to pack."

She sat on the bench next to his. "You showed real courage today. You were also reckless—but I like that in people."

"I underestimated you," he admitted. "That's a mistake I won't make again."

She raised an eyebrow. "Do you mean you underestimated my intelligence, or my deviousness?"

Casterfo's grin widened. "You underestimate *my* intelligence if you expect me to answer that."

Leia had to laugh. This guy was going to do just fine in politics.

Encouraged, he said, "If Rinnrivin wasn't threatening you, what was he trying to accomplish?"

"He hoped I'd accept bribes to cover up his cartel's operations."

Casterfo drew himself upright, as if he'd been the one insulted. "He couldn't possibly have expected you to go along with such a thing. With your history of service to the New Republic—"

"My history's a little more complicated than you might think." When Casterfo frowned in confusion, Leia pulled her cloak from the bench where she'd tossed it and drew the holocube from her pocket. "The Niktos hate the Hutts, and . . . let's say I had a run-in with one of the Hutts a few decades ago. It didn't end well for him."

She put the cube on the low table between them; Casterfo picked it up. "Do you want me to watch this?"

"Not particularly. It's not pretty."

"You think I can't handle it?"

Leia realized that, as late as this morning, she would have believed exactly that. But Ransolm Casterfo was far more than the empty suit she'd assumed him to be. "It's up to you."

He hit the control, then stared as he saw the small flickering image of Leia and Jabba. Casterfo said not one word as the murder unfolded again. Leia studied his expression carefully, waiting to see signs of disgust or, far worse, glee. Instead Casterfo's face revealed that he understood every bit of the danger she had taken on—and also understood exactly why Jabba the Hutt had to die.

When the holo ended, Casterfo took a deep breath. "I wouldn't have believed anyone could escape a Hutt's chains with her life, much less take the Hutt's life instead."

"I wouldn't have, either, until we did it."

"This was you and your brother, yes? The famous Luke Skywalker?" Casterfo now looked as eager as a child who wanted to hear his favorite story again. "How did you come up with your attack plan?"

Leia had never actually told the tale in any detail, but she found herself warming to it: Luke's "gift" of the droids, Chewbacca's willingness to feign his own capture, her disguise as a bounty hunter. Casterfo listened raptly to it all.

She'd never been one of those former soldiers who reveled in recounting her old war stories. But finally Leia understood the appeal.

"Spectacular," he said when she was done. "As daring as any rebel mission I ever heard of."

"So you admit the rebels were daring? Not only terrorists?"

"No. Not only."

This was far from a complete retraction, but Leia figured she could cut the guy some slack. "You're not all bad, Casterfo."

He gave her an arch look. "Such high praise."

"I mean it. You're brave, and you're smart, and you fly so well I'm going to have to keep my husband from recruiting you for one of his racing teams. You've got a lot going for you, for a Centrist."

He prickled slightly. "Do you think we're all so terrible?"

"Apparently not," she admitted, "but the way you think about the Empire—admiring it, honoring it—that, I can't understand."

"It is not the Empire itself I honor. Palpatine's rule bred corruption and inhumanity, as I well remember." Casterfo's blue eyes met hers for only a moment. "I'd only just turned six at the time of the Battle of Endor, but I assure you, Princess, I was already old enough to have experienced the Empire's evil for myself."

It sounded like there was more there, but Leia knew this wasn't the time to pry deeper into the man's personal life. She leaned back on her bench, studying every small movement and shadow of his face. "So how can you proudly display stormtrooper helmets in your office? And how can you embrace a political philosophy so much like the Emperor's?"

"Oh, the artifacts, they're just a matter of history, aren't they?" Casterfo waved his hand absently, as if dismissing a banquet server droid who had come for his plate too soon. Leia's irritation lasted only the instant before Casterfo continued, "As for political philosophy, all we Centrists want is to take a fair look at what aspects of the Empire actually worked. Centralizing power, creating maximum efficiency, binding the worlds of the galaxy closer together: Can you honestly say it did no good whatsoever?"

"Whatever good came of the Empire came at too high a price."

"I agree completely. But what if we could achieve some of those same benefits without repeating Palpatine's mistakes?" Casterfo leaned forward. "Surely you won't deny the New Republic is committing mistakes of its own."

"Not the evils of tyranny and control."

"No. The evils of absence and neglect."

Leia didn't argue. She couldn't. Casterfo's words defined her own doubts about the direction the New Republic was headed in—namely, down.

Casterfo seemed encouraged by her silence. "The Populist approach is less ideal than idealistic. It requires a leader who exercises power through charisma and consensus rather than actual legal authority. With Mon Mothma, we had that. But she's gone, possibly forever, and the galaxy cannot afford the disorganization that has followed. We must find another path."

He'd seen the exact same critical flaws in their government that Leia had been discussing with Han for years. What struck her most strongly about Casterfo's speech was not how much they agreed, however. It was how passionately he spoke. She had all but given up on the thought of making a difference through her work in the Senate. Casterfo still believed.

Should she pity his naïveté or honor his conviction? Leia found she could do both. "I think you Centrists want to move too far in the other direction . . . but you're not wrong about the weakness of our constitution," she said, drawing the tiny tracker from her cloak; he'd slipped it into the metal clasp at the neck. Clever. "We see the same problem, but different solutions."

At least, she and Casterfo did. Leia had her doubts about most of the Centrist bench.

Casterfo sipped his tea, his expression thoughtful. "A pity you never stood for chancellor. You're a powerful leader, someone with lasting moral authority. More than that, you know when to stop debating and take action. If more Populists were like you, the Senate and the New Republic would be better off."

"I'm not eligible to cast a ballot on Riosa, you know. No need to flatter me for my vote." Leia couldn't resist smiling as she said it.

He smiled back, taking her joke in the spirit in which it had been intended. "I mean every word."

Even after decades in politics that had taught her to trust almost no one, Leia realized she believed him. If any hope remained for the Populists to come to honest terms with the Centrists and find a middle path, it would be through politicians like Casterfo. Maybe she could introduce him to Tai-Lin Garr and Varish Vicly before she resigned, build some bridges between them, and put the beginnings of that process in motion.

Before she could think of the future, though, she still had to deal with the present. "You realize this mission isn't over, don't you?"

Frowning, Casterfo said, "We haven't captured Rinnrivin Di, but surely that will be only a matter of time."

"The galaxy's a whole lot bigger and darker than you're giving it credit for. Rinnrivin's money will buy silence, and his reputation will create fear. He won't crawl out of his rock for a while yet." She sighed. "But that's not what I'm talking about. We still don't fully understand Rinnrivin's operations."

"Standard racketeering—"

"But on too broad a scale. Ryloth's not that close to Bastatha, and its economy is struggling. Hardly worth looting on its own. The only reason for Rinnrivin's cartel to target Ryloth is to try to get through them to the holdings of the few Hutts still in power. And anybody going after the Hutt fortunes is hunting big game."

Casterfo's gaze had turned inward, processing this information. "You said he hated the Hutts. Could this be as much about revenge as it is about profit?"

"Possibly. Or other factors could be at work."

"Other factors?"

"We were able to download some information from the droids Rinnrivin left behind when he fled," Leia said. The droids hadn't all been servitors dispensing drinks; some held significant financial data. "Korrie ran a preliminary data analysis. While this can't be the entirety of Rinnrivin's operations, this alone suggests a network beyond anything I've ever seen—even from the Hutts."

She punched her security code into the nearest terminal; holograms popped up, displaying the charts of their findings. Faint greenish light played along Casterfo's face as he took it in. "Rinnrivin's not even *keeping* most of the money," he said in disbelief. "It's being funneled into shadow corporations on various Outer Rim worlds. But of course, he must control those, too."

"That was my first thought, too. And we'll have to do a lot more digging before we can be sure. But it looks like Rinnrivin's simply . . . giving that money away. We're talking about fortunes. My guess is he's not donating it to charity."

Casterfo jerked upright, like a blaster bolt had hit him instead of a new idea. "Rinnrivin's cartel is new. Too new to have built this kind of reach from the ground up, unless he had help getting started. A sponsor."

He caught on fast. Good. "Someone else set Rinnrivin up," she said, "and in return, Rinnrivin does their dirty work and skims off more than enough profit to keep him and his underlings happy."

"But who would do this on such a scale?" Casterfo shook his head. "Criminal bosses normally don't trust other criminal bosses to handle their operations. Whoever these people are, they must have extraordinary reasons for wanting to remain out of sight."

Leia hesitated. She had no proof, only suspicions. Her observations had told her something, but not enough to act upon. Yet she felt that if she told Casterfo what she'd seen, no more, he would at least listen.

"I observed a group of humans at the casino last night." How could she describe them? Nothing had particularly stood out except their leader. "One woman specifically—older, tan-skinned, silver-streaked hair, a slightly scarred face. She made a point of *not* watching us. Like she wanted others to believe she didn't care. But it was too marked. Too obvious. That woman was acutely aware of our presence and did not want to be noticed."

"I remember her," Casterfo replied, surprising Leia. "I didn't pick up on that evasion you observed, but I didn't watch her long. She had an air of authority about her. I wondered whether she'd served in the military. The people with her acted as if she might have been their commanding officer, once."

"Have you heard of the planet Daxam Four?"

"No. Wait. A sort of desert planet, isn't it? One of the colder ones, on the Outer Rim." Understanding dawned. "The sort of place these shadow corporations might set up shop."

"Not a planet lots of people are in a hurry to visit, either. In other words, an ideal place to hide out." Leia consulted her memory of the woman's face, willing herself to remember each detail. "I found out those people we noticed were visiting from Daxam Four. They even seemed to intimidate the Niktos who ran the club."

"Are they tied to the cartel, do you think? Could they be the power behind Rinnrivin's operations?" Casterfo brightened. Once again Leia saw his youth, his eagerness, but it no longer made her look on him with contempt. Instead she saw someone overdue for a task equal to his ambitions.

Maybe she could provide that.

"I don't know if they're connected in the slightest," Leia said. "Daxam Four doesn't show up in the first set of planets we've traced the funds to, but that may simply be the first layer of false cover. Maybe this is nothing more than a hunch, but it's a hunch we share. Willing to follow that hunch?"

Casterfo's grin widened. "Wherever it leads."

As if this were an adventure instead of a very dangerous undertaking—

—but Leia had finally tasted adventure again for herself. She had something meaningful to do. She'd regained a sense of purpose, and after far too long.

A little danger was a small price to pay.

CHAPTER
NINE

———————————

"One mission is not enough."

Ransolm's voice rang out in the Senate as he stood at his console. For this speech, he was not alone. Princess Leia stood as well, with the holos and cams synced to show them standing together, even though they were separated by nearly the entire breadth of the enormous Senate chamber. They faced in opposite directions, so at least one of them would appear to be directly addressing half of the room. His elegant black shirt and cape contrasted with her ice-blue robes, as if they were both mirrors and opposites of each other.

"We have proved that Rinnrivin Di is a dangerous man," he continued. "We've seen that his cartel reaches as far as any of the Hutts' ever did. The allegations of Emissary Yendor have been proved legitimate, but our investigation must continue."

He had addressed the entire Senate only a handful of times so far. Ransolm still found the experience dizzying—thousands of faces and species staring at him, listening to his every word, assessing his arguments through rationales he could neither predict nor control. He felt as if he'd never get used to it.

This made it all the more impressive to hear Princess Leia's calm, confident voice. "During the reign of the Empire, corruption allowed organized crime to expand its influence far beyond anything the galaxy had ever seen before. Many worlds' cooperation allowed us to turn that tide and reestablish the rule of law. But we cannot afford to become complacent. It is my belief, and that of Senator Casterfo, that Rinnrivin Di's organization may represent a resurgence of organized crime, one we must put a stop to *now*."

Ransolm had argued that he and Princess Leia should present the Senate with the possibility of a shadowy power behind Rinnrivin's rise. They'd debated that point from the *Mirrorbright*'s journey home straight through to this morning, when they'd met to go over their joint address one last time. Surely, if Rinnrivin was in league with someone even more powerful and better hidden, the Senate should know of the greater danger. But Princess Leia had remained adamant. *We have to stick as closely as we can to the most concrete information we have. If we start speculating, we'll lose the Centrists immediately,* she'd said. A smile had tugged at her lips. *And if you present a conspiracy theory to the Senate, they'll think I turned you Populist.*

Ransolm knew hers was the more prudent course of action, but standing in front of the Senate and holding back information that might be crucially important felt dishonest. He had sworn not to turn into one of the backstabbing sycophants of politics, to remain true to his convictions. Now here he was, lying . . .

Merely being cautious, he reminded himself. His goal was to spur the Senate to a more in-depth investigation. After that, he could present not mere suspicions but hard facts.

He and Princess Leia weren't hiding the truth; they were fighting to reveal it.

She had begun their address and given him the chance to conclude it. He clasped his hands behind his back and lifted his chin. "Honorable members of the Senate, we hereby put forth a joint proposition: An extensive investigation into Rinnrivin Di's cartel should begin immediately and be supported by the Senate's full resources. Senator Organa and I are willing to lead this investigation, working together. We urge you to act without delay."

There. He'd been courteous but forceful, clear and concise. Although he'd felt nervous a time or two, Ransolm thought his voice hadn't betrayed it.

He felt good about his speech until the moment the moderator droid said, "The floor is open to responses."

Lights signaling the desire to speak blinked on all around the room, sending holodroids zipping in a dozen directions at once. Senator Anib Ney of Sullust rose first, the vocoder translating his words: "Senator Organa's life was put in danger by the vigilante actions of a Centrist politician, and we are expected to simply ignore this? Can we trust a major investigation to a renegade?"

Thunderstruck, Ransolm barely managed not to gape at the senator in astonishment. Renegade? That might have been flattering under other circumstances. But *vigilante*?

Next was a Centrist in a gaudy suit, Senator Mortan of Comra, who bellowed, "Senator Organa withheld critical information from Senator Casterfo! She recklessly endangered her life, and perhaps that of the entire delegation!"

Princess Leia tried to respond. "I fully admit that I made certain errors in judgment—"

"As did I." Casterfo wouldn't let her take the blame alone, even though he remained pretty sure it *was* hers alone. They were moving past this and concentrating on what really mattered.

But the Senate could concentrate on nothing. The droids kept cataloging debate after debate, with countless senators shouting into their amplifiers but listening to not one word.

Ransolm glanced at his console screen to see Princess Leia standing with her hands clasped in front, her face completely composed. In her calm stillness and the pale blue of her robe, he could almost believe her painted in frost—but by now he knew her well enough to detect the irritation in her brown eyes, and he suspected she saw it reflected in his. Their understanding was immediate; she might as well have leaned over and whispered, *Can you believe these idiots?*

This is temporary, he told himself. *Only posturing. When the senators have time to review our evidence, they'll take action.*

He refused to give up on the political process, as he suspected Princess Leia had. Although Ransolm had learned to respect her, he would not copy her mistake. Giving up on the government was not an option.

But he so wished his words had been listened to, that he'd actually managed to do some good and make his mark.

Lady Carise Sindian was considered by most who knew her to be vain, shallow, and frivolous. She cultivated this reputation at every opportunity.

Those who underestimated her ambitions would overestimate themselves. That made them vulnerable. Even if she never had to use those vulnerabilities, she would always know the soft belly, the un-healed break, the very place to strike. And when you understood a person's weaknesses, you could figure out anything else about them you needed to know.

Meanwhile, the others would never understand her at all.

(Well, the vain part of her reputation was accurate. Lady Carise had enough self-awareness to acknowledge that. But she felt there were worse faults than taking pride in beauty and rank.)

She sat in her position, listening to the Senate roar its outrage over the mission to Bastatha. Probably most people in this room thought this would be the Senate's main point of controversy for the day. They were very wrong.

To have gone all the way to Bastatha and found so little, she thought as she looked up at Princess Leia and Ransolm Casterfo. Lady Carise liked what little she knew of Casterfo, and as for the princess . . . well, she might have no regard for her own rank, but Lady Carise tried to honor Leia Organa as a fellow daughter of one of the Elder Houses.

One had to respect titles and bloodlines. Without that, royalty would be meaningless.

Finally, the Ithorian representative moved to "table the discussion" of further investigation of Rinnrivin Di. In effect, this meant that no one would take action on it again. Casterfo's shoulders sagged in obvious disappointment, but Princess Leia simply sank back into her place without so much as a frown. Lady Carise knew then that the princess had never expected anything to come of her speech in the first place.

Perhaps the next speaker would prove more effective.

"The floor now recognizes the honorable senator from Arkanis, Lady Carise Sindian."

She rose to her feet, ready for her moment. Her glittering red robes reflected the tiny cam lights of the holodroids, and her long black hair was held in place by jeweled combs from her homeworld. Even those who didn't expect to listen carefully would feel compelled to watch. She had their attention, and now she intended to use it.

"Honorable members of the Senate," Lady Carise began, looking out on the enormous expanse of the chamber. "Only three weeks have passed since the glorious ceremonies marking the dedication of the statue of Bail Organa."

This was greeted with a smattering of applause, snaps, and whistles, the various audience approval of every species. Lady Carise smiled.

"The late viceroy of Alderaan helped to forge an alliance that brought hundreds of worlds together. The unity he inspired in others reminded us of the potential for even greater cooperation within the galaxy. When we looked up at his face carved in stone, we remembered how much can be accomplished by one individual who inspires others. Although it pains me to say it, I must add that the Senate has not been as effective in Mon Mothma's absence, and that her successors in the office of chancellor have failed to match her ability to create consensus. Now the New Republic is beginning to suffer for it. Growing lawlessness is only one symptom of this malaise. There are others, and more will develop the longer we allow this situation to continue."

One of the very few things the Senate didn't discuss in depth was its own ineffectuality. Uncomfortable silence surrounded Lady Carise, but it was a silence she intended to use.

"We cannot wait for Mon Mothma's return to take action. She saved this galaxy once from the dangers of oppression; we must now save ourselves from the dangers of weakness. Therefore I wish to make a proposition, one that some here will consider radical." She let her gaze focus on that Populist rabble-rouser Varish Vicly, but only for a moment. "Others may believe it does not go far enough. But after due consideration and input from the people, I remain certain that my fellow senators will agree that this is by far the best way to restore our government to vitality. Gentlebeings, we must lead again. In order to do that, we need a *leader*."

How she had fought to be the one to make this statement. Her allies in the Senate had been hungry for this glory as well. But she had won, and this was her moment.

"I hereby propose the abolition of the title *chancellor*. In its stead, we will elect a 'First Senator'—and that First Senator will be given *real* authority over economic and military matters. Our troops and politicians will be answerable again. The Senate will have to cooperate." Lady Carise brought her hand up in a fist. "And we can finally move the New Republic forward!"

One moment of silence, and then—pandemonium.

"This is treason! High treason against the core values of the New Republic!"

"How do we know the title of First Senator won't prove just as ineffectual as the title of chancellor?"

"We would have to redraw that entire section of the New Republic's constitution!"

"What if the First Senator turns into another Emperor?"

Lady Carise answered that question immediately. "When we redraw the constitution, we can define the First Senator's authority and safeguard against tyranny."

"Can you?" This came from Princess Leia, whose cheeks were flushed. "Need I remind the honorable members that Palpatine maintained the illusion of the Imperial Senate for nearly twenty years after the Old Republic's fall? A tyrant can make anything seem to be 'the will of the people.'"

Lady Carise held up her hands. The mediator droids obeyed her signal, silencing all the other senators whether they liked it or not. She felt as if she could almost drink the energy swirling in the room, an intoxicating mixture of fury and zeal. "Honorable members, I do not expect this transition to be an easy one. Nor do I expect a vote to be held today. What I request is only that the Senate study my proposal seriously and come up with a plan that would allow us to elect a First Senator at some point within this term."

There. She knew, of course, that the arguments over this would go on for ages. The Senate accomplished nothing quickly, least of all its own improvement. But the idea of finally choosing a powerful leader had been introduced. She, Lady Carise Sindian, had been the one to introduce it. They would remember that, someday. Schoolchildren would learn her name.

One of the mediator droids intoned, "The floor now recognizes the honorable senator from Riosa, Ransolm Casterfo."

Lady Carise would have expected Casterfo to look crestfallen after his failure with the Rinnrivin Di investigation, but instead he stood proudly, hands clasped behind his back. "Gentlebeings, this is *not* the time for debate. Frankly, debate is what is killing this Senate."

A smattering of applause and chirps welcomed this. Frustration might have been the most commonly held feeling in the Galactic Senate.

Casterfo continued, "If we continue to table every discussion worthy of being had, continue to delay every motion that could make a difference, we will only sink ourselves deeper and deeper into the bureaucratic mire that now defines the New Republic. We are failing to lead our citizens. We are becoming *a joke.*"

Silence met this, but it was the silence of assent. Lady Carise's cheeks burned as she remembered some of the vulgar humor at the Senate's expense she'd heard in spaceports and such. At least she had a noble title still worthy of honor, one no government could ever take away.

"What Lady Carise has proposed is radical, yes," Casterfo continued. He had warmed to his subject, and the electricity in his voice had begun to galvanize the crowd. "That does not make it wrong. I for one believe that this Senate does need more authoritative leadership. Others will not. For many of us, no amount of debate will ever change our minds. So I move that we vote *now*. Here, today. Let us see where the majority stands! Let us stand up and say precisely what we believe, and *act* on that belief! If the vote is no, then we do not waste further time and acrimony on the matter. But if the vote is yes, if others among you are hungry for decisive leadership again, then we can spend our energy where it truly belongs, on determining the *best* way to define and elect our First Senator."

The applause returned, louder this time. Lady Carise felt as if the spotlight had shifted to Casterfo entirely. Jealousy prickled at her, but she forced it back. If the Centrists could gain a vote on this question today, regardless of the outcome, that had to count as a victory. Even raising the idea of a First Senator would start the conversation among the peoples of the galaxy, readying them for future unity and greatness. Besides, Casterfo was proving himself to be a worthy ally—a talent worth cultivating.

"I call for the vote." Casterfo's blue eyes were bright, his form silhouetted by the chamber's lights. He looked like a heroic figure on a poster or in a propaganda holo. These images would no doubt be transmitted later. "Here and now. Stop debating. Stop questioning. Don't worry about the details of the procedure, which can be determined later. Only say whether or not you are ready for this Senate to finally move forward again."

"Opposition to the vote?" the moderator droid said flatly. Lady Carise knew most Populists would object immediately, but it was very difficult to avoid a vote on the Senate floor; the government was structured to let everyone have a say, always, which was finally working to Centrist advantage.

Calling a vote was one thing. Winning it was another.

We haven't had time to make people see the benefits of strong leadership, she thought. *The people remain afraid of Palpatine's shadow.*

Yet as the objections to a vote failed to reach veto status and the preparations began, Lady Carise realized Casterfo's true brilliance. He hadn't couched his argument in terms of accepting a First Senator. Instead, he had emphasized the frustration everyone felt about the Senate's inertia. Casterfo hadn't asked them to vote *for* anything, only to vote against a despised, deadlocked bureaucracy.

The votes began to tally on the viewscreen floating above—each individual anonymous, but guessable. The nay votes of the Populists lit up in green, while the yea votes of the Centrists went yellow. Normally the planets not committed to any one faction either split roughly half and half or abstained completely.

This time, however, the yellow marks on the board multiplied until they cast a golden glow. Lady Carise stared into the light, her hand over her heart. She and Casterfo would share the credit for this, and there would be more than enough credit to share. When he caught her eye through the holos, he was smiling, and she grinned back. By now, they both knew.

Through the many speakers and translators came the final result: "The motion carries."

Leia generally refused strong drink at functions with her fellow senators, even purely social ones. That night, when the droid asked what she wanted, she ordered a Corellian brandy. "And make it a double."

"*One vote,* and our entire system of government is wrecked?" Varish Vicly used her claws to pull her golden fur back from her scowling face. "How could that happen?"

"It happened because our government is designed to be flexible," Leia pointed out as she took her seat at Varish's long, enameled table. "We didn't want to be rigid. We wanted to bend. Well, we just bent so far we broke."

She and several other Populist senators had been invited to this dinner several days earlier; Leia had looked forward to the party, not only for the rich banquet that would be presented but also because she had intended to begin informing her colleagues of her plans to leave the Senate at the end of her term. Instead, they would spend the whole evening grappling with the political disaster that had just befallen them.

"But how could virtually all the neutral worlds turn against us like that?" Varish snapped her fingers; Lonerans could snap eight of them at once. "I wouldn't have thought it was possible."

Tai-Lin Garr settled himself onto the long cushions that lined Varish's table, just next to Leia. As a native of Gatalenta, he came across as calmer and steadier than anyone else in the Senate—but today's vote had clearly shaken him badly. "Lady Carise convinced no one. Casterfo convinced nearly everyone."

"He got up there and pretended to cooperate with Leia, then sold out the whole galaxy. That power-hungry snake. No offense!" Varish added as she waved at a Fillithar at the other end of the table. The Fillithar hissed that none was taken.

Leia shook her head. "Casterfo's sincere. Wrong, but sincere. He's also convincing, and he has charm to spare. If the Centrists can muster up a few more speakers like him, or even a candidate, we could be in serious trouble."

Groans and curses filled the room, and the droids began hurrying out the second round of drinks.

Most senators kept relatively modest homes on Hosnian Prime; even Leia, who had no other primary residence, lived in a simple but comfortable apartment close to the main governmental buildings. However, Lonerans believed in opulence as a virtue unto itself, which meant Varish Vicly's suite of rooms was at least four times larger than most people's living spaces. Despite the almost outrageous level of luxury she maintained—abstract artwork blazing across the walls in vibrant color, and crystal arrays hanging from the lights—Varish's home created a sense of welcome and comfort that almost always put visitors at ease, something they all needed tonight.

Yet Leia couldn't relax. She found herself thinking of her mother— the birth mother she hadn't known, Padmé Amidala. After Leia had learned her mother's identity years ago, she'd done what research she could to discover something more about the former queen and senator. She'd learned that her mother had been present at the vote that had given Palpatine ultimate power over the old Galactic Senate, and Leia could imagine the despair that must have been within her heart.

Is that happening again, today? My mother watched the old Republic fall—is it my turn to see the New Republic crumble?

Leia took another gulp of brandy.

Tai-Lin sat up and straightened his scarlet robe. "We cannot now avoid the election of a First Senator. All we can do is make sure that the First Senator will be a Populist, to ensure that this power won't be misused."

Murmurs of assent went down the table, and Leia found herself nodding. No other solution existed.

Varish cocked her head, golden fur spilling over one shoulder. "Are you nominating yourself, Tai-Lin? Not a bad idea."

"I have a better one." Tai-Lin smiled. "Our candidate must be more than a trusted, long-term senator. She must also be someone known throughout the galaxy. Someone whose friends and family are famed for their contributions to the New Republic. A war hero not even the Centrists can accuse of being weak."

Leia's eyes widened. *Oh, no.*

Varish clapped her furry hands together. "Of course! The First Senator of the New Republic must be Princess Leia!"

Damn.

CHAPTER
TEN

———————————————

"But that's amazing." Greer smiled as she set down her datapad, surprised out of professional mode by Princess Leia's revelation. "You'd be a wonderful First Senator."

"You'd win for sure, Your Highness." Korrie hugged her datapad to her chest. Exciting stuff for a girl of sixteen, finding out she might be working for the person on the verge of becoming the most powerful individual in the galaxy. But Greer couldn't be condescending about Korrie's glee when they were equally thrilled.

Politics didn't offer enough excitement, usually—but this? A race for First Senator would be nearly as good as a race in a starfighter. Not quite. But almost. As much excitement as Greer could handle, anyway.

"How very marvelous," C-3PO said. "When will the election be scheduled?"

Princess Leia only shook her head at them before leaning back in her office chair. "I told you guys already. When my term is up, I want to resign."

Greer wanted to protest but didn't dare. Fortunately, what C-3PO lacked in tact, he made up for in enthusiasm. "But, Your Highness, you mustn't resign! Not now when the galaxy needs you."

"Threepio's right." Greer wondered if those words had ever passed her lips before. "You're probably the strongest candidate the Populists could field. That makes you our best chance of winning. If a Centrist wins the election instead . . . bad things could happen."

Which was a weak way of putting things, and Greer knew it. But speaking the truth out loud meant saying words like *war* and *tyranny*. She didn't want to drag the conversation there if it wasn't necessary. Surely it wouldn't be. Princess Leia had to listen to reason, right?

Leia sighed as she got to her feet and walked to the window of her office. The view revealed little beyond shrubs and the reddish footpaths outside the senatorial complex, but at least it let the light in. If it hadn't, Greer would've found the office too claustrophobic to endure.

Sometimes she missed the sky.

"Our mission to Bastatha reminded me of what it felt like to be in action during the Rebellion," Leia said without turning from the window. "To know your entire life depended on your speed and your courage, and the blaster in your hand."

"How terrible," C-3PO said. "Those were indeed frightening days, Your Highness."

"But wonderful, too." Leia looked over her shoulder, not at C-3PO but at Greer and Korrie, whom she probably hoped would understand. "I miss being hands-on. I miss dealing with problems personally. I miss talking to pilots and soldiers instead of politicians all the time. I miss feeling like . . . no. I miss *knowing* that what I was doing really mattered."

Greer had imagined herself in the Rebel Alliance before, playing X-wing pilot as a little girl and pretending to blow up the Death Stars, sometimes both of them at once. But of course that was how a child thought of war: as a great adventure where the good always won and the evil died without shedding real blood.

To hear Princess Leia, who had suffered unspeakable tragedy and danger throughout the war, speaking of those days with nostalgia—maybe it was the ultimate testimony to just how bad the Galactic Senate had become.

If the Senate was collapsing, however, Greer knew who she wanted to remain standing at the end.

"You could at least continue the Rinnrivln DI investigation," Greer ventured. "The Senate would probably give you even more latitude—the Populists because they want you to shine, the Centrists because they want you to screw up."

Leia groaned and laughed as she returned to her desk. "No doubt."

Encouraged, Greer continued, "So it's not like you'd have to give up being in action forever. And if you were First Senator, you could work around the bureaucracy you've hated so long. It wouldn't be the same as just staying in. Everything would change."

"Everything will change with or without me," Leia pointed out.

Greer nodded. "But with you, we have a chance to change for the better."

Princess Leia had a way of looking at people as if she could see straight through them to the bone. She was a hard person to lie to, a harder person to convince. Yet the only terrible secret Greer kept was one the princess knew and kept for her. When Princess Leia fixed Greer in that stare, it wasn't a prelude to an investigation, but her way of calling for absolute, total honesty. "What would you do, if you were me?"

Excitement and freedom versus duty and purpose: Greer had made that call once. Princess Leia was, in effect, asking her if she regretted it.

"I'd stay." Greer lifted her chin. "I'd run. And I'd win."

The princess leaned back in her chair, deep in thought. They'd worked together long enough for Greer to know what that meant: She hadn't chosen to remain yet, but she was no longer resolved to leave.

"An exploratory committee," Princess Leia finally said. "Just to—consider the possibilities. I'll agree to that much."

"How splendid!" chirped C-3PO. Korrie grinned as she got to

work pulling up potential names for the committee. They both thought the debate was over and that they were on the verge of the most exciting political campaign in thirty years.

Greer knew only that, for the first time, she had lied to Leia Organa.

Some regrets could never be spoken aloud.

"Told you—you're never going to leave." Han shook his head and smiled as if to say, *See? I'm always right.* His cocksure grin would've fooled most people.

Leia, however, could sense his disappointment, and it was harder to bear than her own.

"I don't want this," she said. "You know I don't."

"Of course not. That's why you're putting together the, whatsit, 'exploratory committee.'"

She shook her head. "Han, the only thing worse than my becoming First Senator would be a Centrist becoming First Senator. If I walk away now, I could be handing the galaxy over to the next emperor. You know I can't do that."

After a moment, Han sighed. "I know."

Political news spread fast. As soon as Leia had told her staff to set up the exploratory committee, she had put in a comm request to Theron. If her husband had heard news this significant from a broadcast of some kind, it would have been terrible.

Telling him herself? Still not good.

Han had turned out to be on whatever ship he was flying on Theron, literally waist-deep in the wiring on the black-tiled wing with his tools lying around him. He'd pushed his safety goggles up to his forehead so that his gray-white hair stuck up in front. In the background, both droids and mechanics kept working hard, doing something complicated to the ship's rear engines.

"Repairs?" she asked, hoping to leaven the conversation. "I didn't think you would even have started flying in the rounds." The early heats of the Sabers competition could be supervised from platforms on the ground; flight surveillance didn't begin until the lunar relays.

"This?" Han shrugged as if it were nothing, but already he'd begun to smile again. "Actually, thought I might soup this baby up before I take her out again. Give her a little fighting power, and see how far I can push the engines. She's a good ship—fast, handles well—but she needs that little something extra."

Han had said virtually the same thing about every ship he'd flown since the *Millennium Falcon*. He kept hoping to re-create that magic. But Leia knew he never would, no matter how much speed or maneuverability any other spacecraft might have. Some loves came only once in a lifetime.

"The work would be going better if I didn't have to deal with a rookie crew," he continued. "If I still had Greer on my team, we'd be finished by now."

"I'll tell her you said so."

"She doing okay?" Han frowned in genuine concern.

"I think so. Greer's more excited about the political campaign than I am." Leia smiled ruefully. "Which isn't saying that much, really. But still."

"Well, tell her hello from me."

This was Leia's cue to ask whether Han had heard from Ben or Luke (though she knew he wouldn't have), or to inquire about how Chewbacca was doing. Their conversation would trail off into something simpler and easier, and they could both pretend everything was all right.

But it was important to be honest at moments like this, even if it was hard.

"Han? I'm sorry about the campaign. I really wanted something different for us." She thought of her daydreams about the two of them flying through the galaxy together, carefree at last. Already those dreams were fading to shadows. "But nothing ever changes."

"Hey." Han looked up from his work, more solemn than he'd been at any other point in the conversation. "Don't apologize to me for taking this seriously, okay? You put duty first. Drives me crazy sometimes, but that's who you are. It's also probably why the New Republic is still in one piece."

Leia couldn't quite smile. "Someday."

"Someday."

The words sounded like a promise. But Leia couldn't make herself believe that day would ever really come . . . and she knew Han couldn't, either. *Someday* was the sun disappearing behind a cloud, a morning lost to darkness long before night should have come.

Lady Carise Sindian walked through the hallways of the senatorial complex, her pink cloak rippling behind her as if in a breeze. She paced herself for speed and disdained the moving sidewalks that ferried around so many other senators. Passivity was a habit Lady Carise did not intend to acquire.

The past day had been one of her greatest triumphs—*so far,* she thought. Yet victory demanded more of a person than defeat did. Instead of exulting in the successful vote, Lady Carise had spent hour upon hour receiving calls from countless Centrist senators, balancing them in such a way as to show favor to the most important without alienating the others. To her surprise and relief, Senator Casterfo had obeyed protocol by promptly coming to her offices.

Had she been in his place, would she have been as quick to cede the main credit for the vote? Certainly not. But Casterfo understood the importance of authority, which meant understanding the need for hierarchy. That made him an asset rather than a threat. Lady Carise had summoned him back to her offices only an hour before to suggest that they attend the gatherings of potential Centrist candidates together, the better to avoid even a hint of factionalism. Casterfo had agreed to everything—had even been quite charming—until the moment she had called their meeting to a close, and explained why.

"Going to see Senator Organa?" Casterfo had smiled as if they were discussing a mutual friend. "I imagine she's not best pleased with me today. But do give her my regards."

Ransolm Casterfo cannot be such a fool as to think he could make a friend of a Populist senator, Lady Carise thought as she passed under the shadow of Bail Organa's statue, scattering a flock of Toydarians that had been dawdling ahead of her. *Nor should he assume the princess is naïve enough to take his pleasantries at face value. So what game is he playing?*

It bore further observation. However, Lady Carise set the matter aside for now. She was visiting Princess Leia not as a fellow senator, but as a fellow sister of one of the Elder Houses, which deserved its own weight and importance.

After the princess's doddering protocol droid had seen her in, Lady Carise took her seat before Leia's desk, folding her hands in her lap. "You must realize why I'm here."

Princess Leia shook her head. She wore a plain gray dress more befitting a commoner than a senator. "I'm afraid you have me at a loss, Lady Carise. Unless this is about yesterday's vote—"

"Of course not. No politics today." Lady Carise beamed. "You and I have the luxury of considering more high-minded issues, don't we?"

Instead of responding, the princess stared at Lady Carise in what seemed to be total incomprehension. Was she well? Possibly senility had begun to set in. Of course Princess Leia was rather young for such troubles, but one never knew.

With what she considered gracious good manners, Lady Carise did not force the princess to guess. "I wished to discuss the governorship of Birren. Your staff must have been researching the matter for weeks now. When will you be traveling there for your inauguration?"

"Oh. Yes. Right." Princess Leia acted as if she hadn't thought about the matter once since their last discussion. How disingenuous. "You know, Lady Carise, I'm not actually of the bloodlines of any of the Elder Houses. Bail and Breha Organa adopted me—"

"You were a war orphan." Lady Carise had always found this story extraordinarily touching. "And yet they raised you as their own. Through their actions the Organas showed that nobility is not merely a matter of blood."

Princess Leia smiled at the kind mention of her parents. "My point is, I shouldn't be the person inheriting the governorship of Birren in the first place."

"But of course you should! None of the Elder Houses adjudicates succession through strict bloodline inheritance." Privately Lady Carise held some reservations about this. Bloodlines had to matter somewhat, otherwise the very concept of royalty would be discounted. However, she believed that inner nobility could be demonstrated through action, and despite her political disagreements with the princess, Lady Carise felt nobody could deny Leia's courage was the equal of any monarch's. "You must succeed Lord Mellowyn, just as your son must someday succeed you."

For a moment Princess Leia looked weary, as if she had aged between one sentence and the next. "I can't see Ben taking much interest in the governorship, either. Really, it would be better for everyone concerned if I were to remove myself from the succession. Wouldn't it then fall to you? Birren was settled by both Alderaanian and Arkanisian explorers, after all."

Lady Carise managed to reveal no reaction beyond surprise. Inside, however, she felt as if every firework from the dedication ceremony had exploded again in the sky above, even brighter than before. *She's giving it to me. To me! A planetary title of my very own! My standing in the Elder Houses would rise immeasurably, overnight.*

But her dedication to the nobility remained even stronger than her ambition. "Princess Leia, you do me great honor by even suggesting it. Yet I could not possibly usurp your throne."

"You're not usurping it if I'm giving it to you." Princess Leia waved her hand as if shooing something off. "Honestly, I can't see the point of spending weeks away from the Senate just to claim an honorary throne nobody else cares about filling, not even the people of Birren. If you don't take the governorship, I'll send an emissary there to see about officially abolishing the position. But if you're willing to take it, and the citizens don't object—please, Lady Carise, be my guest."

"Thank you." Lady Carise could no longer keep her smile inside, and she beamed at the princess. "I promise that you'll be proud of my service as supreme governor."

Princess Leia smiled back, but crookedly. "See? Now everyone's happy."

"Of course I'll travel to Birren immediately. It's *so* important for someone to be hands-on."

The phrase seemed to strike Princess Leia strongly. She straightened as her gaze sharpened back to full intensity, as if she had only just woken. "I agree completely."

For most of the next half hour, Lady Carise felt as if she were floating on a cloud of delight. But as she strolled back toward her own offices, head filled with thoughts of herself in a golden gown to match her throne, it suddenly hit her: *Weeks away from the Senate.* Spending that much time on Birren now—at such a critical point, with the candidates for First Senator likely to announce themselves within the month—could she possibly afford it? Was she sacrificing her real work as a senator for the sake of the supreme governorship of Birren?

She would simply have to find balance. Duty demanded that she fulfill both of her roles to the best of her ability. The winds of politics shifted by the day, but nobility was forever.

Joph had meant to take only a short nap, but instead he'd nearly blown through his whole down shift. He swore when he saw the time and dashed to the hangar, where a dozen or so other X-wing pilots had gathered around a holotransmitter. "Did they start?" he shouted as he ran toward them.

Temmin Wexley, aka "Snap," gestured for Joph to join the group. "About to! Move your boots, Seastriker!"

The second Sabers run was about to begin: orbital sprints. While the final three stages of the Five Sabers were best watched through edited footage later—because they lasted hours, then days, then weeks—the first two were the best racing you could watch. Joph had shouted himself hoarse cheering on the pilots in the initial starfighter atmospheric dash, and he expected the orbital sprints to be just as exciting. More, even, because only after the second race could you begin to identify potential winners.

Joph hurried toward the group—but paused as he saw one pilot working on her ship without even glancing at the races. "Greer?"

She glanced over at him from her place beneath the *Mirrorbright*. The sleeves of her grease-stained jumpsuit were pushed above her elbows. "Hey, Joph."

"Aren't you going to watch?"

"Nah." Greer shrugged with one shoulder and bent closer to her work. The glow of her handheld scanner etched her profile in the hangar's shadows.

"But one time you *won* the Sabers!"

"Exactly. Been there, done that." Greer didn't look away from the *Mirrorbright* again, not even once. "Anyway, I only won the Junior Sabers."

Which was still completely awesome. Joph opened his mouth to protest, but—in a rare flash of tact—realized it might be smarter not to say anything.

The thing was, Greer had another job back in the Senate offices. Given the maintenance she'd run on the *Mirrorbright* right after their mission to Bastatha, the ship couldn't possibly need any more work done. So Greer had come here without any real need, knowing the other pilots would be watching the Sabers. She wanted to watch; she just wasn't allowing herself to do it.

Joph loped toward the others and accepted a cup of the engine room jet juice, which burned going down but lit you up pretty quick. Even as he settled in to watch, though, he couldn't keep himself from glancing over at Greer. *Is she doing this to punish herself?* He wondered. *If so, for what? Or does she figure it doesn't count if she just listens to the Sabers run?*

"Looks like a good race today," Senator Organa said from behind them, which made all the pilots straighten at once. Joph turned with the others to see her standing there in a dark-blue jacket and trousers, a smile on her face. Although she couldn't have missed the group's consternation, the senator acted as if she hung out in the hangar all the time. "What's that in the jug?"

"Oh, this?" Wexley's broad bearded face turned red. He swallowed hard before venturing, "Uh, it's—caf. Definitely. So we can stay alert on duty. Ma'am."

"Too bad." The senator folded her arms as she leaned against the nearest X-wing. "In *my* day, starfighter pilots knew how to brew quality hooch."

In the following pause, several of the pilots began to smile. Snap ventured, "Would you believe that this caf happens to taste a whole lot like that? With, uh, similar effects?"

She grinned and held out one hand. "Let me be the judge."

Somebody had the good sense to offer the senator one of the chairs, and before long she was in the heart of the gathering, talking with them about the Sabers like she was just another pilot. "Don't count out the team from Sullust," she confided as everyone settled in. "They didn't do much on the starfighter round, but they shine at longer distances. Trust me—I know a guy."

People chuckled at the reference to Captain Solo. From the corner of his eye, Joph saw Greer drawing closer. When the senator waved her forward, Greer joined them at last—still averting her eyes from the holo, but accepting a cup of jet juice and at least starting to smile.

Was this all about getting Greer to watch the race? Joph wondered. He sensed it wasn't. But Senator Organa was doing something besides just hanging out for the races; that much, he knew for sure.

"I hear the team from Pamarthe is likely to be a contender, too," Leia said.

"Of course they are," Joph said. "They always are. Everybody knows that if you're from Pamarthe, you're good at flying, fighting, or—" He realized he shouldn't finish that phrase just in time. Anyway, everybody understood without him saying it. For generations, Pamarthens had enjoyed a reputation for courage, skill, and gusto.

Senator Organa gave no sign she'd noticed Joph's careful omission. "Are you rooting for the home team, Greer?"

"I don't have to." Greer finally cracked a smile. "They'll win with or without me."

She was from Pamarthe? And she worked in an *office*? Joph always thought of Pamarthens as tromping around in their fields, working on their ships or guzzling tankards of ale. Which was ridiculous, because of course they couldn't do that all the time, even though most people from Pamarthe seemed committed to trying. It was hard to imagine one of them handling senatorial bureaucracy with ease.

The race began, as did the cheering from the pilots—but Joph remained quiet, listening to the senator and Greer. "So many people recruit pilots from Pamarthe," Princess Leia said quietly, her words almost lost in the din. "Particularly in that area of the Outer Rim, so close to Daxam Four. Neighboring worlds recruit Pamarthe's fliers for racing, for the military—for all sorts of things."

Daxam IV. Joph had been privy to enough mission data to know Daxam IV was somehow connected to Rinnrivin Di.

Greer got the message, nodding slowly. "I really should go back for a visit sometime soon. It's been a while."

"You're sure you can handle it?"

"Of course I can. It's home. I know exactly where to go."

A mission. This is a mission! Greer's going to go find out whether Rinnrivin Di's hiring pilots from Pamarthe. Envy and excitement prodded Joph to blurt out, "You know, I always wanted to see Pamarthe."

Both the senator and Greer stared at him, which was the first moment Joph realized he'd been eavesdropping—and on a conversation about a secret mission, which was probably bad. Definitely bad. When was he ever going to learn to keep his mouth shut?

But then Senator Organa nodded. "I think that if I check with your superior officers, we'll find you're due for some time off, Lieutenant Seastriker. Greer, you wouldn't mind having a little company, would you?"

Joph took a deep sip of his drink to hide his excited smile. A secret mission? Now, *that* was more like it.

CHAPTER
ELEVEN

———————————

Pamarthe's rugged islands clung close to one another in the vast, choppy ocean that covered much of its surface. Despite the modern spaceports carved into the basalt cliffs and the array of sturdy small craft that flew and floated among the islands daily, the Pamarthens maintained many of the old bridges of wood, stone, and rope, restoring them as needed without ever replacing them. They said this was to make sure their people still had courage. Privately Greer thought they just wanted to scare offworlders.

Anyway, it worked on Joph Seastriker.

"This goes on for another *kilometer*?" Joph said, both hands gripping the rope railings on either side. His gaze darted down to the swirling water far below. "What sadist built this bridge in the first place?"

"A true Pamarthen." Greer used her grandparents' thick accent, letting the burr of it settle in around the *r*'s. She drew her woolen drape over her head and tucked it in more securely around her neck amid the swaddle of robes and wraps her people wore on her home-world. "Which is what you're pretending to be, remember? If you show up at the cantina pale and queasy, you'll blow our cover in a heartbeat."

Joph gulped. "I don't think I can help the queasy part."

"Then just keep moving. Get a flush in your cheeks." The kid's skin was nearly as pale as Princess Leia's, which would mark his family as relative newcomers to her world, but that could be generations back. And the island they were walking to lay at the far northern tip of the archipelago, where most such newcomers had settled. "Besides, the faster you get to the next terminal, the sooner you can take a break."

"Okay. *Okay.*" Joph took a deep breath, eased his grip on the ropes, and started moving forward. Although the bridge swayed beneath his feet, he resolutely kept going. The same heavy woolens that Greer wore so easily made him look half as broad as he was tall. "Why didn't we just land on this island instead of the other one?"

"We restrict landings here. To keep out the invaders who haven't shown up in about three hundred years." Greer shook her head. Sometimes she thought the local clans were still hoping for villains to come running over the next hill, spoiling for an old-fashioned sword-fight.

"I guess it works," Joph said. "Nobody would ever invade this place if they knew it meant crossing these bridges all the time."

"You fly a starfighter. How can you be afraid of heights?"

"When I'm in a starfighter, I'm in control, piloting a ship I main-tain myself, so I know it's as good as anything else that flies. Here? It looks like nobody's repaired one of these bridges in years. The ropes could give way any—any second." His face paled as they swayed in the wind again.

Amused despite herself, Greer said, "I thought you wanted excite-ment, Seastriker."

"I do. But my idea of excitement doesn't involve throwing up. At least, not until the day after."

Greer shook her head. "Hang in there."

To her, the rope bridges' sway felt almost comforting, like being a ship on the sea. Like most Pamarthens, Greer had had to learn how to handle watercraft before anyone would teach her how to fly. *If you cannot conquer the sea, you will never conquer the air:* That was what they all said. Some of the happiest moments of her young life had been spent on a boat, winching a sail into place or looking for a good cove in which to anchor.

At that moment, facing the wind and the sea spray, she felt good. *Really* good. Maybe she'd been too cautious lately.

Greer turned forward again, gazing toward their destination. The island, half shrouded in fog, jutted up from the ocean as if defying the waves. When she saw the soft glow of lights from the coastline buildings, the sense of homecoming that swept over her was too powerful to deny. Just a couple hours' flight away, friends of her grandparents would be cooking enormous kettles of fish stew and coming together—if she were there, they would welcome her in a moment, smiles wide and arms wider—

You're not here for happy reunions, she reminded herself. *And this only works if nobody recognizes you.*

Fortunately, pilots were known more by ship than by face. When they walked down the steps into the old cantina, nobody who looked at Greer showed even a flicker of recognition, though Joph's pale-blond hair drew a couple of glances. They slid into an empty space at the end of one of the benches for the long tables, which was when the tavern-keeper came over. "Haven't seen you two about before."

"Been gone awhile," Joph said.

His tone sounded casual enough to Greer, but the tavern-keeper must not have liked what he heard. From his apron he pulled a flask of something reddish amber that made the nearby patrons start to laugh.

Port in a Storm. Greer would've known it at twenty paces.

The tavern-keeper set a squat glass in front of Joph. "If you've been gone too long, you're not a real Pamarthen any longer. Gone soft like an offworlder?"

Joph tried, "No, I—"

"No? Best prove you've still got your choobies, then." The tavern-keeper poured a full glass of Port in a Storm, then scooted it in front of them. "Let me see you take that down."

"He's just a kid. Leave this to me." Greer reached past Joph to take the glass, tilted it back, and drank deep. The fire seemed to zoom to the top of her head and the core of her gut simultaneously—but she knew how to take it. Three gulps, and she was done. Greer smiled at the tavern-keeper, turned the glass upside down, and banged it on the table. "How's that for choobies?"

"And *that's* a woman of Pamarthe!" the tavern-keeper yelled as cheers filled the room.

Just like that, they were accepted. After a few congratulations and handshakes, the hubbub faded, and Greer and Joph were only two among dozens of hardened pilots and fighters, waiting for their next tankard of ale. The chatter flowed freely, unchecked by suspicion.

"Too many patrols around Kessel these days. Might as well put a net over the whole planet and be done with it."

"—mark my words, the whole Imperial fleet is out there, just biding their time, mark my words, we've not seen the last of 'em—"

"And then he says, I don't care if you like my friends, and I say, well, you share all your opinions about *my* friends, and he says—"

"Could you believe the Sullust team took the orbitals?"

Greer barely glanced over as she interjected, "Word on the ground has it Sullust's the one to beat, this year."

"Sullust? Get on with ye. They'll be sent home crying by the Coruscant team!"

"And our team? You'll count the Pamarthens out already?"

"After the way they fell apart at the orbitals? They've no chance any longer. Flew like a pack of offworlders."

So the conversation went, swirling and eddying all around them. Greer spoke up often enough for it to seem natural, no more, and otherwise kept listening intently without appearing to listen at all. She'd learned how to do this with senators; she could manage it with pilots, who had worse language than the politicians but better manners. Joph got *too* involved in a conversation about pie, a subject apparently very close to his heart, but that was harmless and distracting to those around them.

Greer took it all in without reacting until the moment a few hours in when she heard the exact kind of thing they'd been listening for, "—not enough pilots who understand discretion, these days."

" 'Discretion'?" she repeated, turning to the pilot who'd been speaking, a grizzled old woman who wore some of her smaller tools on leather cords around her neck.

But the pilot had been doing this too long not to be wary. "What's it to you?"

"We're between jobs." Greer nodded toward Joph, who turned out to be very good at looking innocent. "We're looking for work in this area, and we need money fast. So we're not asking too many questions. If anyone asked *us* questions . . ."

Joph finished for her. "We wouldn't answer."

"There's work to be had," the pilot said. Her milky-blue eyes studied them, looking for signs of trouble and apparently finding none. "That is, if you've got a good ship and the nerve."

"Nerve? Listen, we've got—" Joph's indignation was easily silenced by Greer patting him on one shoulder. His performance was so convincing that not even she realized he was faking it until he settled down again easily.

Greer leaned closer to the pilot. "Listen. We could really use a good run or two. If you've got any leads, we'd appreciate them. Risk is no object."

The pilot shrugged, perhaps deciding that if they weren't what they seemed, it was someone else's problem. "Lots of runs to and from Daxam Four these days. They pay well for speed and silence. Quick money to be made there, if you've got the nerve. Slide into orbit and signal the central hangars; seems like the Amaxines have some sources there to tell them about passing cargo ships. Chances are, you'll get a call about a job before you've got time to take off your flight suits."

"Daxam Four," Joph repeated with a grin. They'd hit the jackpot. "Thanks, ma'am. You have no idea how much you've helped."

Although the pilot seemed pleased to be thanked, she made a scoffing sound. "Thank me after you've dealt with the Amaxines. Not before."

Greer and Joph exchanged looks. *The Amaxines?*

The pilot chuckled as she lifted her ale. "Oh, you'll see."

Greer had successfully shifted the conversation to other topics, and had made sure to remain in place for a good while after the old pilot departed. This meant drinking more ale, and while she and Joph were careful to pace themselves, by the time they walked out of the cantina, dawn had begun to lighten the eastern horizon. But it was still only a faint pale line near the line of the sea.

Joph walked onto the bridge without hesitation. Liquid courage seemed to help him. Greer followed along, looking down without fear at the waves breaking white against the stony coastline. Although she didn't turn around, her ears were sharp enough to know that they weren't being followed. Another good thing about these rope bridges: They remained resolutely low-tech, meaning there would be no record of their visit here. They would be able to fly out clean, unnoticed, and with a promising lead.

"I could've drunk that stuff," he insisted.

"I'll bring you a bottle sometime and let you try. But trust me on this—we didn't want our whole mission riding on your first taste of Port in a Storm."

"Fine, then." He sighed. "Hey, can I ask you something?"

"Of course. But there's no guarantee I'll answer." Greer said it lightly, assuming he just wanted some distraction from the pitch and roll of the rope bridge.

"How come Senator Organa asked you about this in the hangar? You're her assistant; she could've brought it up at work."

Greer had understood this from the moment Princess Leia had first spoken. "The senatorial oath demands a promise that they 'will not use the Senate offices for purposes of espionage.' Probably the oath means 'office' more in terms of the senator's overall position, less in terms of the actual room where political business is done. But the oath doesn't specify that. So if Princess Leia is ever asked whether she violated her oath, she can truthfully promise no . . . on a technicality."

Joph turned to grin at her, openmouthed. "We're involved in *espionage*."

"Only if you don't keep saying it out loud."

He mouthed *espionage* again before adding, "Wait. Why isn't it, you know, just like Bastatha?"

"The Senate authorized that. They didn't authorize this."

"Unauthorized. I like how that sounds. Now, this is more like it." Joph started forward again, then made the mistake of looking down. "Oh, brother. Is the bridge . . . did it get higher while we ate?"

"No. But the tide's going out. So you'd have farther to fall." When Joph blanched, Greer laughed and took his arm. "Come on. Walk faster. I've got you."

When a wave of dizziness washed over her, too, she ignored it and kept going. Probably just the Port in a Storm.

If being the Populist candidate is half as irritating as being suspected *of being the next Populist candidate,* Leia decided, *this campaign is going to be unbearable.*

She doubted Tai-Lin Garr or any of the other senators at Varish's home that night had spoken a word to a soul beyond their closest advisers. They didn't have to. Tai-Lin had been correct when he said that Leia was the obvious candidate; everyone had seen this coming except Leia herself.

"Your Highness?" C-3PO came shuffling into her office. "Yet more visitors. We have leaders from the Association of Small Craft Manufacturers eager to see you!"

Leia looked up from her list of communiqués, which was at least three times longer than usual. "Did they give any particular reason?"

"Why, no, Your Highness. I would imagine it is normal lobbying activity. Well within regulations." The droid was never happier than when citing rules. "Therefore it is highly appropriate for them to visit, though I suppose the lack of an appointment is irregular. I could ask them to schedule—"

"Never mind, Threepio." Leia set her communiqués aside for the moment. "Show them in."

"Right away, Your Highness!" Threepio chirped as he shuffled back into her main office. *At least the droid's enjoying this,* she thought. *Someone ought to.*

Leia made polite small talk with the small craft manufacturers, then with the ore traders of Gad, then with a group of junior senators from Populist worlds on the Outer Rim. None of them could yet come out and say that they were hoping for her favor if she was elected First Senator; they could, however, hint at the kinds of campaign promises they thought would make that election more likely. Unsurprisingly, all these promises benefited her visitors' pocketbooks.

She forced herself to think of Tai-Lin, whose intentions in nominating her she knew to be pure. If Leia was obliged to run for First Senator, she intended to win—and if she won, she intended to do the job well. Setting the right precedent would be important. A few years of strong, disinterested, fair leadership might finally show the people how government ought to be run.

But how many years?

The term length and limits were still being debated by the committees, but a seven-year term seemed most likely. Seven years—almost twice as long as the main campaigns in the war against the Empire. Those years had been the most terrifying, heartbreaking, meaningful, and exhilarating of Leia's life. Was she going to spend twice as much time trapped behind a desk?

Once the final visitors for the day seemed to have left, Leia leaned her chair back so far she was practically reclining. When Korrie came in and saw her, the girl smiled. "Want me to bring in a cushion so you can put your feet up?"

"If you do that, I'll fall asleep. And if I fall asleep, that means I'll go a whole day without leaving this place. No thanks."

"It's been a big day, I guess."

"The first of many to come. Are you sure you're ready?"

"If you are," Korrie replied, obviously meaning it as a sign of solidarity. But Leia again had to ask herself if she was ready for this, or if she even could be.

Yet she knew in her heart that the war only seemed wonderfully thrilling in retrospect. So many of the exploits she now thought of as "adventures" had, at the time, been terrors. The Empire's discovery of the Hoth base—the ambush on the forest moon of Endor—the attack run on the first Death Star: Leia wouldn't give up her memory of any of them, but she wasn't sure she would've relived a single second.

(Well. Maybe the time Han had run through the ice tunnels of Hoth to rescue her.)

She told herself that what she had been doing then would be very much the same as her role as First Senator were she elected, because she would be doing her duty. If you only did your duty when it suited you, then you weren't actually putting duty first at all. Leia knew that, believed it and accepted it.

Didn't make her duty any more enjoyable.

"Your Highness?" C-3PO peered through the door. Leia was about to tell him to ask any more visitors to come back tomorrow when he added, "Lady Carise Sindian to see you."

"Right. The documents about the governorship on Birren. Send her in." Leia straightened just in time for Lady Carise to sweep in wearing her latest ornate gown. "Lady Carise. Leaving already?"

"As you said, Princess Leia, the inauguration takes some time. So, better to begin early." Lady Carise set out the holos to be verified with Leia's thumbprint, her self-satisfaction so obvious it made Leia itch.

Might as well have a bit of fun with this, she decided.

"It's probably as good a time as any to be away from the Senate." Leia spoke idly, almost absentmindedly, as she went through the verifications. "Looks like the Centrists won't have a candidate to field for quite some time."

Lady Carise's deep-golden skin did not blush easily, but the faintest reddening of her cheeks was enough to tell Leia she'd struck home. "I feel confident our senators will soon reach consensus."

"I share your confidence. It's not as if five or six or even ten Centrists were fighting it out to be the candidate." Leia knew the number was at least that large and likely to grow. The Centrists were so power-hungry that none of their leaders could pass up the opportunity to wield the greatest power for themselves. "After all, yours is the party that values control. What better proof of that can there be than self-control?"

This time, Lady Carise couldn't even reply, either from embarrassment or from exasperation. Surely even she saw the irony, though. The bickering Populists had, instantly and wordlessly, agreed on a candidate, while the Centrists couldn't find their own center.

"The more I think about it, the more I think a First Senator might not be a terrible idea," Leia concluded as she verified the final document, pushed it across to Lady Carise, and smiled. "Otherwise, our fellow senators could run around in useless circles forever. Couldn't they?"

"Certainly it's time for a change." That was as much as Lady Carise could manage. "Thank you, Your Highness."

"My pleasure." Leia gave her a little wave as she went out the door.

"Destination, ma'am?" asked the pilot. This was a courtesy, not a necessity; he would have filed his charted course days ago. Lady Carise approved of the formalities.

"Birren, the capital city spaceport."

"Aye, ma'am."

Lady Carise would normally have gone directly to her cabin, but today she followed the pilot to the control room. If her presence surprised him, he was too well mannered to reveal it. He flew a top-of-the-line vessel, befitting a royal journey, and as such every area of the ship displayed streamlined elegance. Even in the control room, the piloting controls had been tapered down to thin, shining panels. The transparent bubble around them revealed a full hemisphere of the starry sky beyond. She could imagine stepping into air, into space itself, and floating free.

If I weren't royal, and a senator—I might have enjoyed being a pilot.

But Lady Carise caught herself. What a silly thing to wish for. Anyone who could be royal would be.

Anyone, that was, except for Princess Leia Organa.

How could the princess value her position so little? Given that she'd been adopted into the nobility to begin with, should she not be more grateful, more honored, not less? Certainly her behavior had turned common, mocking the perfectly ordinary political process of choosing a candidate. The Centrists weren't behaving badly; they were behaving *normally.*

So how had the Populists managed to behave well?

By having no other leaders worth the naming, of course. The Populists had realized their benches were filled with the petty and the fractious and promptly seized upon Leia Organa as their only viable option. The Centrists, however, had a wealth of potential candidates. Soon the strongest would assert himself, and the race could begin in earnest.

Her transport eased deeper into space, freeing itself from the pull of Hosnian Prime's gravity. As the far moon passed out of view, the pilot said, "Prepare for the leap to hyperspace on my mark. Three, two, one, and—"

The ship shuddered. The stars elongated. Lady Carise caught her breath as they slipped into hyperspace and left everything else behind. No matter how often she traveled through space, that thrill never left her.

Cheered, she nodded toward the pilot and headed to her luxurious quarters, where her droid would already be preparing tea. Not even Princess Leia's attitude would ruin this glorious journey for her, nor her love of the political process. Let the Populists have their day to laugh and point. Another day was coming, brighter and better. A day when the galaxy would again be rightly governed, and the strength of the Centrist worlds would be revealed like a sword finally being pulled from its scabbard.

And Lady Carise would be one of those who brought that day to dawn.

CHAPTER
TWELVE

No espionage in the Senate offices, *check.*

So Joph acted mildly surprised when his superior officer told him Senator Organa had requested him for a routine flight on the *Mirrorbright,* perhaps to train as a backup pilot. More surprising was when he and Greer actually took the ship into orbit—but of course that made sense. Their story had to check out.

As soon as the *Mirrorbright* had entered the upper atmosphere, however, the princess said, "Okay, let's hear it." Joph had thought they'd go into the main room, but instead Senator Organa took the auxiliary chair and sat with them at the controls. "What did you find?"

The words gushed from Joph before he could even think about checking them. "Daxam Four is the place for sure. On the Outer Rim. There's some group there called the Amaxines who are mixed up with all of this somehow, and . . ." His voice trailed off as he realized that in his enthusiasm he had just stepped all over Greer's report. She raised one of her angular eyebrows at him, and he thought, *You have got to stop trying so hard.* "Um, you explain the rest, Greer."

"There's not much else to explain," Greer said drily, "except that whoever these Amaxine guys are, they're bad news. Pilots who have spent their whole careers running spice don't like to tangle with them. They oversee shipments coming in and out of Daxam Four—couldn't get confirmation on the likely cargo, but it's definitely illegal, and operating on a scale that suggests Rinnrivin Di is involved. How many people could be moving that much cargo through a backwater like Daxam Four?"

"Amaxines," the princess said thoughtfully. The lights from the control panel illuminated her from beneath in gold and green. "How strange."

Caught off guard, Joph said, "Wait. You've heard of them?"

"I've heard of the legend of the Amaxines. It's an old story—one my mother told me, dating back to the dawn of the Old Republic." Princess Leia's eyes gazed into an unseen distance. "Supposedly they were a warrior people, their entire culture based on battle. Instead of currency, they traded weapons for goods and services. The tale has it that they refused to make peace with the Old Republic but knew they could never defeat such an enemy. So instead they pointed their ships at the galaxy beyond ours and left forever, searching for yet another war to fight."

"Which means they spent eternity wandering around in the void of space," Joph said. "Who names themselves after those guys?"

"Not many people, which is why I was able to track this down pretty quickly."

Greer punched a few buttons on her main monitor, and the green arc of their orbit above Hosnian Prime disappeared, replaced by a chart that looked like a cobweb—numerous connections all leading toward one central point. He leaned over Greer's right shoulder as the princess leaned over the left, and Greer began tracing the paths with her finger. "There's no record of such a group, at least not in any public informational grid. However, I was able to track mentions of the word *Amaxine* above any typical count."

Fascinated as he was by this, Joph couldn't help asking, "How did you figure out a 'typical count' for this one obscure word?"

Greer sighed. "I asked Threepio."

Joph had only worked with the droid once, but he already knew that C-3PO would have searched exhaustively through months' worth of galactic communication just to answer Greer's question. "Okay, then, the count's accurate."

"The Amaxines, or Amaxine warriors, only get mentioned in a few specific areas. Certain worlds, mostly clustered in one section of the galaxy, had a much higher-than-average hit rate. And the world with the most hits of all was, you guessed it, Daxam Four." Greer pointed her finger into the center of her holographic chart—the section of the web where the spider could be found.

"Do we have any information about these Amaxines?" The senator folded her arms. "Any mention of exactly what business they're operating that requires so much 'discretion'?"

"Not much," Greer admitted. "Apparently they pay enough to keep people's mouths shut. But from what I've gathered, they're a kind of local planetary militia."

Planetary militias weren't unusual. However, Joph knew it made no sense for Daxam IV to have one; it wasn't a criminal target or bordered by known enemies. And the amount of money the Amaxines seemed to be collecting from Rinnrivin Di—that was more than any militia could possibly need to defend a planet from raiders. Senator Organa said, "What kind of world is Daxam Four?"

Joph could answer this one, but he waited for Greer to nod before he began. "Outer Rim, subarctic desert climate, still primarily self-reliant—they limit offplanet commerce, which is kind of weird, seeing as how it's a Centrist planet. Usually they're the ones who want everyone to be able to buy and sell everywhere. We could've picked up cargo there—we learned how to get those jobs—but we kinda figured that would take our mission from 'unauthorized' to 'illegal.'"

"You're learning caution, Seastriker." Senator Organa smiled at him, just for a moment.

"Speaking of Centrist worlds," Greer continued as she gestured at the chart, "what do you want to bet almost every one of these planets has in common?"

Joph's eyes widened. "These are all Centrist worlds?"

"Not all, but most. The others are mostly neutral planets known to be major vectors in the spice trade." Greer leaned back, obviously satisfied with her conclusions. "I think some Centrist senators might just be taking kickbacks in return for hiding what looks like the biggest drug cartel of the past twenty years."

But the princess shook her head no. "That's not what I sense."

Joph frowned. *Sense?* What did that have to do with anything? He knew better than to ask out loud.

Greer, however, seemed to understand. "Really? You don't think this is a Centrist plot? That's the most obvious interpretation."

"Which is why we can't afford to jump to conclusions now," Senator Organa continued, and she sounded logical again. "We only have a small piece of the puzzle, so we can't assume we already see the solution. Besides, I don't trust a lot of the Centrists, but most of their leaders are too stodgy to ever think about skimming money off the spice trade—if that's even what's happening here."

"You'd be surprised what people will do for money," Greer said darkly. She looked up from her chart to gaze through the transparency. The view beyond was the black of space above, pale atmosphere blue below. It was as if they were suspended between ground and sky.

"Not much surprises me." The princess frowned as she studied the chart again. "This may be less a matter of shared political beliefs, more a matter of the Amaxine warriors being active only in this area of space."

"So do we investigate there?" Joph couldn't wait for another mission. Maybe she'd say they could start today.

"Perhaps, but I want to get someone else's advice on this first," Senator Organa said.

Greer gave her a look. "Do you mean Casterfo?"

Joph wondered how that guy had moved so quickly from obstacle to ally, but apparently he had, because Princess Leia nodded and said, "He's the only Centrist I trust at all. Besides, he's an up-and-comer in their faction. That means he has connections and influence on those worlds I don't, and he can ask questions without attracting as much attention as I would. Also, if he had anything to do with this, he wouldn't have jumped into that situation on Bastatha and nearly gotten us both killed."

"Just weird to hear you approving of a Centrist," Greer said, but by now she was smiling. "Never thought I'd see the day."

Senator Organa sighed. "Honestly, neither did I."

When Ransolm Casterfo received Princess Leia's message, he quickly agreed to another meeting—and to her request that they meet offsite from the Senate. If he went to her office, that would mean signaling his lower rank; such behavior was appropriate but not conducive to the kind of partnership he hoped to build with Leia Organa.

And obviously we'll never meet here *again,* he thought as he looked around his office, smiling slightly at his newest acquisition, a TIE pilot's helmet in such good condition it still gleamed. *My collection agitates her past the point of reason.*

Instead they arranged to meet at the hanging gardens, one of the genuine delights Hosnian Prime had to offer. An enormous building of sandstone had been constructed in the shape of a staggered pyramid, each floor hollow in the center. It stood at the edges of the vast capital megalopolis, so visitors could enjoy the glittering skyline or the distant horizon, depending on where they sat. Beautiful plants of all varieties sprouted from boxes both inside and out, and on the inside, tall, willowy trees grew, often blossoming into pale-blue flowers. They received the light they needed from the ample spaces between each floor, which let the sun's rays slant through. The serenity within the hanging gardens contrasted with the activity outside, a constant swirl of low-flying air traffic.

"And that area, down there?" He pointed as he settled into the chair next to Princess Leia. His gesture took in a few dozen craft that hovered near the ground, positioned to get a good view of both the gardens and the sunset. "I imagine that's where young lovers go when they claim to be somewhere else."

Princess Leia smiled down at them—but sadly, Ransolm thought. She said, "They're taking time to be young. Good for them."

At first he wasn't sure what to make of her melancholic mood, but when she showed him the datapad with Greer Sonnel's findings, Ransolm thought he understood. "You suspect a Centrist conspiracy?"

"No. In fact, I'm almost sure that's not it." Princess Leia shook her head. "But I think that these Amaxine warriors, whoever they are, seem to be hiding out in Centrist territory. They're handling almost all the cargo going in or out of that planet. And the only person we know doing business there on a grand scale is Rinnrivin Di."

Ransolm was pleasantly surprised by her measured, rational response. So many Populists seized on any sliver of evidence, no matter how flimsy, for their implausible theories of corruption and scandal. However, he was beginning to learn that Princess Leia was her own person, one worth listening to. "Thank you for bringing this to me. You're quite right; the links to Daxam Four cannot be mere coincidence. We must look into this right away."

"Agreed. And you're better placed to do it than I am. You know what questions to ask, and who to put the questions to."

"I shall ask questions," Ransolm promised, "but I also intend to look into the matter personally."

Princess Leia grinned at him; the sunset painted her white gown nearly gold. "I think you're developing a taste for action."

He leaned forward, smiling conspiratorially. "You're a bad influence."

That made her laugh out loud. "Do you know, that's the best compliment anyone has paid me in a long time?"

"Then you aren't being paid enough compliments." Ransolm decided to risk the next. "Of course, the Populist candidate for First Senator could expect a great deal of flattery in the future."

She held up her hands as if she could ward off the election. "Nothing's official. Not even close. And please, let's concentrate on the matter at hand. I need a break from the Senate for a while."

The princess was keeping her cards close, Ransolm figured. After seeing how skillfully she played sabacc, he should have anticipated as much. "Then I repeat my thanks. You've given me valuable information I can act on without delay. The incursion of such criminal elements threatens these worlds, and as you know, we Centrists believe in law and order."

"Do you ever," she said wryly, but her good humor seemed to have been restored.

"I've actually just lent my support to a campaign to restore the death penalty on Riosa. More systems are leaning toward it, you know."

"More Centrist systems, you mean."

"Yes," he said, "most Populists are too soft for such measures. But I've watched you strangle a Hutt to death with satisfaction. You're not one of the soft ones, Senator."

"Two compliments in one day? If you're not careful, they'll throw you out of the Centrists."

"I'll take my chances." He realized, somewhat to his surprise, that their meeting wasn't merely useful; when the princess wasn't being combative, she was enjoyable company. The Senate needed more cooperation between Centrists and Populists, and surely cooperation could be furthered by good relations . . . even by friendship. Ransolm asked, "As long as we're here, shall we have dinner?"

To judge by her raised eyebrows, the invitation was a surprise, but a pleasant one. She gestured to a nearby server droid. "Why not?"

In quieter moments during their dinner, Leia tried to imagine Varish Vicly's consternation if she saw Senator Leia Organa willingly sharing a meal with "the enemy." Her fur would probably spontaneously curl. Tai-Lin Garr would take it quietly, but harder, shaking his head in sorrow. And the Centrists? Oh, their reactions would be *priceless*.

But there were few quiet moments. Leia found Ransolm Casterfo surprisingly easy to talk to. He was intelligent, cultured, and even witty. Also, he was young enough that she didn't have to worry about any misunderstandings of the romantic variety—but not so young that she had to feel guilty about appreciating the view.

"We're working hard to restore Riosa as a galactic center of manufacturing," Casterfo said earnestly. His aquamarine cloak turned his eyes an even more vivid shade of blue. "It's been difficult, of course, but with the new factories, the economy is finally taking an upward turn."

Leia wondered whether to chance her next question. She might shut Casterfo down completely, but she decided it was worth the risk. If she was to continue working with him, she had to get to the bottom of this. "Riosa's economy was wrecked by the Empire, wasn't it? That makes it hard for me to understand your—let's call it fascination."

To her surprise, Casterfo nodded. "Yes, we were wrecked. Deliberately, even maliciously. Our factories and our people were pushed to the limit and beyond to manufacture components for both Death Star stations, and when we could supply them with nothing more, they cast us aside to starve." He took a sip of the pink juice they'd been served. "My belief in an empire is not belief in *the* Empire. It never could be, not after what happened to my world."

"I guess I can't get around the contradiction."

"It's not a contradiction." Casterfo remained silent a few moments, weighing his words. Dusk had fallen, and the ships zooming by were shooting stars in the cobalt blue of early night. "You know, I assume, that the manufacturing efforts on Riosa were often overseen by Lord Vader himself?"

Leia tensed. It seemed to her that she could hear that heavy, metallic breathing, as though the mere mention of his name had resurrected him. When she trusted herself to reply, she said, "No. I didn't know that."

"Vader visited Riosa often. Each time, he tightened his fist even more." Casterfo's gaze had turned distant. "The quotas rose higher. The hours grew longer. What had been paid employment became mandatory service, then slavery in all but name. Workers with manufacturing experience were herded into labor camps with pitiful living conditions. Not enough food, only the bare minimum of shelter—and always, always more work. You could keep going until your fingers bled and still, it wasn't enough."

She stared at him in dawning comprehension. "You were in one of those camps."

Casterfo breathed out sharply. "Technically, yes. It was my parents who had the more wretched experience, my parents who were herded behind the camp walls to work themselves to the bone." He tried to laugh, but the sound came out strangled. "Would you believe that bringing me with them was a 'special privilege' my parents were given? That they were *lucky* to be allowed to bring their child to suffer by their side? Others had to leave their children behind to starvation or slavery or who knows what other torment."

Leia had heard such stories from other worlds, other survivors. That didn't make it any easier to see Ransolm Casterfo struggling for control as he thought of his parents. She laid her hand on Casterfo's forearm, hoping he would take it as comfort rather than pity.

He didn't even notice. "My parents survived the war, but only just. They'd been forced to work without proper safety filters; the toxicity in their lungs killed them both less than a year into the New Republic's rule. All because Lord Vader thought they could work harder." Casterfo looked into Leia's eyes again, and he didn't even try to disguise the rawness of his pain. "I believe in strong leadership by good men. But I know the damage evil men can do. I learned that from Darth Vader's example. I saw him cut down innocent people with my own eyes. So trust me when I say that I can admire the Empire's core structure and still condemn Palpatine, Vader, and all their works."

"I do. I trust you." What moved her as much as Casterfo's story was the faith he had shown in her by telling it. "What happened after?"

Casterfo took a deep breath, then smiled as if he'd entirely thrown off his dark mood. He hadn't, but he was making a valiant effort. "I had a rough few years, but then I was taken in by a couple that had some offworld wealth. They didn't exactly adopt me as a son, though I was one of several children they housed, fed, and educated. But for them, I might have starved."

"No wonder you got angry when I called you spoiled," Leia said. "I'm truly sorry."

"You didn't know. Whereas I did know about Alderaan, and I

threw the insult back at you anyway. It wasn't our finest hour. Let's leave it at that." He lifted his glass for another draught of the juice, then saw it was empty. A droid zipped over immediately. "Did you ever see Darth Vader with your own eyes? I suppose, in the Galactic Senate, you must have."

"I   yes, I did."

Casterfo frowned. "Princess Leia?"

He had dared to tell her his most painful truth. She could never reveal hers, not to anyone who didn't already know; Leia understood that. But perhaps she could find the courage to match his honesty with a measure of her own.

"At the beginning of the war against the Empire, just as the Imperial Senate was dissolved—" She swallowed hard. "My ship was captured by the *Devastator*. That was Darth Vader's flagship at the time. He personally brought me to the Death Star, where he—where he questioned me."

Comprehension dawned in Casterfo's eyes. "You mean . . ."

Just say it. "I mean he tortured me, for hours. While a couple of his Imperial stormtroopers watched." Sometimes that got to her when nothing else did. The troopers had been soldiers of the line. Some of them had honestly believed they were doing the right thing, or so she told herself.

But how could you believe that after you watched a nineteen-year-old girl writhing on the floor and screaming for mercy that never came? How could you stand there and watch that girl convulse in helpless agony without doing something, anything to help?

Apparently some people could.

"Then he brought me to witness Alderaan's destruction. Vader's hand gripped my shoulder just after I watched my planet die. He made me suffer in every way a human being can suffer, all for the love of the Emperor."

Casterfo slipped his arm from under her hand—she had gone utterly motionless—and grasped her fingers in his. As old as she was, as cynical as she'd become, Leia would never have guessed that such a gesture could still move her, but it did.

"I hated him so much," she whispered. The breeze blew past them, rustling the blueblossom trees within the hanging gardens. It was as if they were helping to hide her painful words. "Sometimes I felt as if the only thing that kept me going in the aftermath of Alderaan was the strength of my hatred for Vader."

For my father.

As always when Leia thought about this, she called upon what Luke had told her of their father's last hours. He had renounced darkness, saved Luke, and become Anakin Skywalker again. Whenever Luke told the story, a beatific smile lit up his face; his memories of that event gave him a level of comfort and even joy that sustained him. Those were memories Leia couldn't share.

"Then we have that in common," Casterfo said. "We both know what a monster Lord Vader was, and we have no desire to see his like gain power in the galaxy ever again. But you think he will emerge from order, while I think he will emerge from chaos."

Leia couldn't muster the nerve for another debate. "Let's hope we never find out."

"Hear, hear."

They let go of each other at the same moment and leaned back, but Leia knew the connection they'd forged wouldn't be broken that quickly. Only a few short hours before, Ransolm Casterfo had been her uneasy ally. Now, for better or for worse, they had become friends.

When the server droid rolled by them again, Casterfo snagged two glasses of Corellian ale for them without asking whether Leia wanted one; it seemed he had the good sense to know she needed it. After the first couple of sips, and too many moments of silence, Leia decided to change the subject. Awkward, but surely any topic of conversation had to be more pleasant than Vader's evils. "Any bets as to who the Centrist candidate will be?"

Casterfo shook his head. "There are a dozen possibilities at least, Senator—"

"I think we're on a first-name basis by now, aren't we, Ransolm?"

He acknowledged this with a quick nod. "As I was saying, Leia, at least a dozen potential nominees so far, and more may arise."

"Who knows?" She managed to smile. "You might wind up voting for me yet."

"I'll vote with my party, of course, but I'll say this much: You're the only Populist I'd ever trust with the job."

"Too bad Riosa isn't a more influential world," Leia said. "I'd feel a lot better if you were the Centrist candidate."

Ransolm tried not to smile, but the result only made him look mischievous. "That makes two of us."

"I think we can drink to that," Leia said. They lifted their glasses and clinked them together, and the darkness in their pasts seemed farther away than it had before.

CHAPTER
THIRTEEN

The next morning, Leia wondered whether she'd had too much of the ale—but she hadn't. Her weariness and bad mood were the natural result of reliving memories so dark she rarely allowed herself to think of them, much less speak them aloud.

Think of your conversation with Casterfo as practice, she told herself. One day she would have to reveal all this to her son. The truth of Vader's identity had shattered her; she could not imagine what it might mean to Ben. At least Luke could tell Ben the most important part—that Vader had, in the end, been redeemed. Anakin Skywalker had returned; the dark side had been defeated by the light.

Leia knew this. She believed it. But she still did not *understand* it.

"You're unusually quiet this morning," said Tai-Lin Garr, who walked with her across the grounds of the senatorial complex. "And not in high spirits, I think."

"I'm . . . grumpy. In a bad mood. That's all." She cast about for a plausible reason, and found one in the early hour. "What kind of sadist plans a meeting at breakfast?"

Tai-Lin, ever patient, shook his head fondly. "You've never been one to mind early hours. And you know how busy our schedules are."

"If the alternative is a breakfast meeting, I can find the time." Leia took a deep breath and tried to let it go. "Well, if I do wind up becoming First Senator, I know the first thing I'm going to outlaw."

Chuckling, Tai-Lin said, "You'll change your tune when we sit down to eat and you get a little caf in you."

"Caf usually helps," she agreed.

Tai-Lin Garr had been inaugurated into the first Senate of the New Republic alongside Leia; he was one of only a handful who had served from then to now. Although he possessed the preternatural calm of most people from Gatalenta, in Tai-Lin that serenity was anchored even more deeply. In all these years, Leia wasn't certain she had ever heard him raise his voice, despite the ample reason Centrist politicians had given him. He was an attractive man only a year or two younger than herself, with only the temples of his black hair turning silver. In the distinctive scarlet robes of his planet, he cut a striking figure. A figure one could imagine in, say, a campaign holo.

"You know, there's still time for you to try for the nomination yourself," Leia ventured. "You'd make a better First Senator than I ever would."

He shook his head. "Let's be realistic. You are the only Populist candidate who could win—and if you lose, this entire experiment is doomed to disaster."

Leia paused, and he stopped alongside her. They stood in the middle of the complex square amid an intricate pattern of tiles in blue and white, as if it were the board for a game of strategy. "Doomed? Even with another Populist as First Senator?"

Tai-Lin nodded, his expression grave. "The Centrists are forced to respect you because of your role in the war. Even then, they'll be intransigent; they'll fight every step you try to take. But at least we'll have some modicum of civility. You'll be able to push some things

...ough. With anyone else in the position, we'll be even more dead-locked than we are now."

As little as Leia thought of the concept of a First Senator, she couldn't believe she was the only one with any chance of making the role effective. Yes, the Centrists could be difficult, but so could the Populists, and the Centrists would at least respect the idea of a hier-archy.

He's basically declaring that galactic-level politics can't work, she re-alized. Uneasiness stirred within her. *If too many Populist senators agree with him, it's going to become a self-fulfilling prophecy.*

Tai-Lin clasped his hands in front of him and stepped closer just as a few civilian vessels sliced through the sky above them, as if he wanted the silvery sound of their engines to conceal his words. "Leia? You don't intend to drop out of the race? If you abandon the Populist cause—"

"I'm not dropping out." Technically, she wasn't even officially *in* the race yet, but it made no difference. Leia thought again of her dreams of flying around the galaxy with Han, without responsibili-ties or cares, with all the time in the worlds. "But before all this, I had been seriously considering retiring. I've wanted to spend more time with my family."

"Of course." Tai-Lin inclined his head. "You would wish to join your brother and son, I imagine."

"I miss them, yes. Still, I imagined living with my husband again. It's been a while since we were together more than half the year."

Tai-Lin hesitated before he came closer. "There's something I've been meaning to ask you for a long time, and finally I feel I know you well enough to dare. If I overstep my bounds, please, tell me."

Uh-oh, Leia thought. Was this some kind of romantic overture? Surely not. She seemed to have a case of paranoia this morning. But she understood why an outside observer might believe she was avail-able, which was proof Han had *definitely* been gone too long. "I'll tell you, Tai-Lin. Go ahead and ask me."

"Did you never consider following in your brother's path and be-coming a Jedi?"

Leia found herself caught short. "Why do you ask?"

"They say on my world that the Force sometimes runs strong in certain families."

So much of the lore of the Jedi had been lost—but on Gatalenta, the old religion had remained strong. History had become legend, but some of the legends were still told. Gatalenta had been one of Luke's first destinations when he began his research into the Jedi Knights of old. Tai-Lin continued, "If that is true, then you might have the potential, just like your brother."

And my son, she thought but did not say.

"If you have that ability, then I cannot imagine why you would not become a Jedi as well," Tai-Lin finished. "Surely I've known few people who would make a finer Jedi Knight than you."

Leia inclined her head in gratitude for the compliment, but she could not answer right away, because she could not tell the full truth. The Force was too important a subject to be shared lightly, even with Tai-Lin, her ally and friend.

Her safe, sensible, and, as far as it went, honest reply: "My duty has always been here, in the work of creating a new and better government."

He sighed, as if in regret. "You alone can determine your rightful destiny."

Could she? To Leia it felt as if her destiny had been out of her hands for a long time.

Together they walked the rest of the way to the conference building in silence broken only by the cries of migrating snowbirds overhead and the murmurs of the ever-increasing foot traffic around the Senate complex as staffers arrived for the day. Somewhere, probably not far away, Greer and Korrie would be arriving; C-3PO was probably already in the office happily sorting communiqués. Bail Organa's statue sparkled translucent in the sunlight, watching over her. The pleasant weather and bright sky made Leia feel as if she might have enjoyed the morning if it weren't for the breakfast meeting. And Tai-Lin's probing questions about her past. And the memories stirred up by her conversation with Ransolm the evening before . . . maybe they were to blame for the increasing sense of dread welling inside her . . .

I need caf, Leia thought. Everything else she would deal with later.

The conference building of the New Republic senatorial complex contained multiple rooms appropriate for every kind of auxiliary function imaginable, from memorial concerts to awards ceremonies. Leia and Tai-Lin headed toward one of the smallest banquet rooms. The breakfast meeting had been organized by Varish Vicly, who couldn't imagine a bad time for a party.

Varish came loping toward them now on all fours. "There you are! I was worried you'd be late."

"We're still early," Leia protested as both she and Tai-Lin were wrapped in quick, long-limbed hugs.

"Yes, but I worry. You know how they get."

"They" meant prominent representatives of both the far-left and far-right branches of the Populist faction. The far-right branches wanted to dissolve the Senate so each world would again become a totally separate entity; the far left hoped to open voting to the general populace, so that instead of thousands of senators refusing to agree, they could have countless citizens refusing to agree. The only thing these senators had in common was, it seemed, a willingness to support Leia's candidacy for First Senator.

"Now come along and be introduced to everyone," Varish insisted. Soon Leia found herself shaking hands and paws, murmuring greetings; thanks to some review holos Korrie had prepared for her, she recognized each senator in attendance and could even ask a few pertinent questions about their families and worlds.

In other words, Leia thought as she listened to someone cheerfully talk about his grandchildren, *this is going wonderfully for everyone but me.* Though not until now had she realized how much she dreaded her candidacy—or maybe just discussing her candidacy—whatever it was that made her so ill at ease.

They entered the banquet hall together, the entire group walking two by two. Leia knew the seat at the far end of the table would be hers, guest of honor as counterpart to the host. So she walked the length of the room, attentive to the senator at her side, before glancing down at the arrangements—sumptuous even by Varish's standards, with a velvet runner stretching along the table and delicate paper streamers lying across the tables, beneath elaborately folded napkins. Leia had to laugh. "Honestly, Varish. For breakfast?"

This won good-natured chuckles from the room; Varish Vicly's lavish tastes were well known, a foible she herself joked about. Today, however, she shrugged. "I didn't request this. Maybe the serving staff heard my name and assumed that meant to go all out for glamour." Varish smiled as she took her seat. "If that's my reputation . . . you know, I can live with it."

Leia settled into her chair, picked up her napkin—and stopped.

Something was written on the paper streamer on her plate. Actual writing. Virtually nobody wrote any longer; it had been years since Leia had seen actual words handwritten in ink on anything but historical documents.

But today, someone had left this message on her plate, only one word long:

RUN.

Leia shoved her chair back, instantly leaping to her feet. "We have to get out of here," she said to the startled senators at the table. "Now. Go!"

But they didn't move, even as she dashed toward the door. Varish said, "Leia? What in the worlds—"

"Didn't you hear me?" These fools who had never been in the war, who didn't know an urgent warning when they got one. Leia held up the paper so they could see it. "Run! Everyone get up and run!"

With that, she took off, running as fast as she could, finally hearing the others stir behind her. Maybe they thought the note was only a prank, but Leia knew better. The inchoate dread that had swirled inside her all morning had solidified; *this* was what her feelings had been warning her about.

As they dashed through the hallways of the conference building, Leia glimpsed an alert panel and swerved sideways to hit it. A robotic voice said, "No detected hazards at this—"

"Override! Evacuation alert *now*!" Leia resumed running just as the warning lights began to blink and the siren's wail sounded. Immediately people began filing out of various other rooms, mostly grumbling but at least moving toward the exits—and when they saw her, they, too, started to run. The sense of urgency built behind her like a wave cresting, preparing to crash.

Leia's breath caught in her throat as she pushed herself harder, running full out toward the doors, so fast they almost didn't have time to open for her. In the square beyond, security droids had begun herding people away from the building, but too many continued to mill around, staring in consternation at the scene. The others evacuating flooded through the doors behind and around her, but once they were clear of the structure, half of them stopped, remaining stupidly within range.

Within range of what? She still didn't know. But every instinct within her—the Force itself—screamed that disaster was near.

Leia didn't stop. She kept running as hard as she could, never looking back, until . . .

Brilliant light. A roar so loud it resonated in her skull. And hot air and debris slamming into her, knocking her down, rolling her over, erasing the world.

Greer knew only that, in one moment, she was walking through the Senate grounds not far from the conference hall, Korrie by her side, trying to come up with an excuse to cover her afternoon trip to the medbay—and in the next, she lay dazed amid smoldering debris, her thoughts fuzzy and her body aching.

What the— She sat up, but too quickly, and her head whirled. Greer put one hand to her forehead, took a couple of deep breaths, and forced the collage of devastation around her to make sense.

Half of the senatorial conference building had vanished, leaving rubble behind; the other half smoked ominously, stained black. All around her, people either lay on the ground or stumbled around nursing injuries; skin, scales, and fur were all marked with blood. The acrid smell in her nostrils testified to the explosives that had been used.

Somebody bombed the Senate building, Greer thought.

That first moment of concrete knowledge snapped her brain back into focus. Greer looked around, searching for a glimpse of the spring-green robe Korrie had been wearing. "Korrie? Can you hear me? Korrie?"

"You're okay!" Greer turned to see Korrie hurrying up to her, curly hair disheveled and gown torn, but otherwise all right. "I couldn't see you for a second. It was like—like the explosion stole all the light for a moment. The world went blank, and then it was turned upside down—"

Korrie's voice cracked in a sob. She was still only a girl. Greer took her hand, hoping to provide some comfort. But she saw then that she'd lost a fingernail—ripped out at the root—and the blood trickling onto Korrie wasn't helping at all.

A triage droid zipped through the air, dropping down to hover just beside Korrie, extending a scanner bar; blue rays swept over Greer's body. "Mild concussion without internal bleeding. Negative for broken bones. External injuries and preexisting medical conditions only. Noncritical." It scanned Korrie next, finding nothing even worth reporting aloud. After that, it took off, searching for someone more badly hurt.

"Help me up," Greer croaked. Korrie slid one of Greer's arms over her shoulder and got them both back on their feet. Now that Greer could see more of her surroundings, the full impact of the disaster hit her. Although security staff and med droids moved through the crowd with urgency and purpose, dozens if not hundreds of people had to be injured, and they lay amid an enormous scene of devastation.

"The breakfast meeting." Korrie swallowed hard. "Princess Leia was in there when it blew."

Greer's whole body turned cold, save for the one finger hot with flowing blood. "We have to find her. Now. Go get someone to help us search. Joph Seastriker, maybe—the barracks would've been out of range—"

"Greer, everyone's already looking."

Of course the troops would have been called in immediately. But she couldn't sit by and do nothing. "Not everyone is looking, because we're not looking. I don't care if we have to go through this brick by brick. *We find Princess Leia.*"

Korrie nodded. Having a concrete task to perform helped.

Within another minute, Greer could stand on her own. Her dark-blue tunic and skirt had been shredded by debris, rips and tears revealing the skin of her belly and thighs. Grayish-white dust coated her hair so thickly that every turn of her head shook forth a few more flakes. But she kept going, checking out each injured person, summoning med droids where needed, ignoring her own dizziness. She wouldn't stop until she found Princess Leia and made sure she was all right. Greer refused to consider any other possibility.

As she went, she recognized other people she knew: Count Jogurner's chief of staff, blood staining her white-blond hair as Dr. Kalonia helped her to stand. Andrithal Robb-Voti of Taris, leaning against an intact wall in a daze. Ransolm Casterfo helping a wounded Togruta woman toward the medcenter. Zygli Bruss of Candovant being lifted onto a stretcher. This was unquestionably the single biggest attack on the government since the final battles with the last surviving ships of the Empire more than twenty years before.

It was Korrie who finally called, "Over here!" Greer turned to see Princess Leia getting to her feet at the far edge of the square, one hand in Korrie's, the other at her temple as though her head hurt badly. Greer limped to their side, only to have Princess Leia immediately embrace her.

"Thank goodness," the princess said. She sounded as though she had been screaming, or crying. Terror and the ash in the air were stealing all their voices. "I was so worried about you both."

"What happened?" Greer didn't expect Princess Leia to know, but her mind kept returning to the question, worrying it over and over, as if this time an answer would come. "Who would have wanted to destroy the building?"

Princess Leia's gaze turned upward, toward the statue of Bail Organa. Despite the sunlight, it showed as gray due to the coating of soot and dust, and his outstretched hand had been broken off halfway to the elbow. Greer realized she could see the shattered fingers lying amid the rest of the debris.

The princess said, "This bomb destroyed something far more important than a building. It may have destroyed the Senate itself."

Who could have done this? Greer thought. Too many candidates sprang to mind: Organized crime, whether minions of Rinnrivin Di or a desperate attempt by the Hutts to reclaim their former power. Extreme Populist factions angry that the Galactic Senate even existed. Centrist radicals attempting to create a climate of fear that would justify their grab at absolute authority. Some wild-eyed loner with a grievance no rational person could ever understand.

She was sure of only one thing: As soon as the immediate shock had dissipated, accusations would fly in every direction. The Senate's torpor would inflame into turmoil—and the fate of the galaxy itself could follow.

CHAPTER
FOURTEEN

Leia refused to accept a healing treatment for her concussion until everyone more seriously injured had been attended to. At one point, Dr. Kalonia told her to stop acting so noble and get help already, but nobility had nothing to do with it. Healing treatments usually included sedatives, which meant she'd pass out within an hour of receiving one and probably not wake for at least half a day. Leia wanted to remain clearheaded as she tried to comprehend what had happened.

First thing, she recorded a voice-only message for Han, telling him that she was all right and that he didn't have to come to Hosnian Prime on her account. Although she would have taken comfort in his company, she also knew that, as soon as she was able, she had to get to the bottom of who was responsible for this bombing. There would be no time left for sentimental reunions.

To her amazement and gratitude, no one appeared to have been killed. Although a few hundred people had been injured, some seriously, the med droids reported that nobody was in critical condition. But there certainly would have been a death toll—a high one—if not for the warning Leia had received.

The paper streamer had still been clutched in her hand when she came to, and she had given it to a security supervisor as soon as she found one after the explosion. *RUN.* Obviously it had to have been planted by someone who knew about the bomb, presumably the bombers themselves or a mole in their organization.

There were reasons to plant a bomb and ensure it only did property damage. Normally, Leia knew, this was the act of a terrorist organization seeking respectability or at least propaganda value; such bombings were intended to demonstrate both lethal power and respect for life—however disingenuous.

But no one had claimed responsibility, a necessary element for propaganda purposes. This crime remained anonymous and bewildering.

"Tomorrow, maybe," Greer said as they finally took their turn in the medcenter. Her hand rested in a shallow dish of bacta, just enough to allow her fingernail to regrow; she'd been given a round of serum injections first thing. "We'll probably get a message claiming responsibility tonight or tomorrow."

Leia, meanwhile, had stripped down to her basics and already sat at the top of the tank, breathing apparatus in her hands. "I don't think so. If they wanted us to know, we'd know by now."

"Do you think the warning could have come from someone else?" Korrie ventured. She sat cross-legged on the floor, somewhat distracted by the synthskin patch quickly fusing the cut on her forehead. "Or maybe one of the bombers changed her mind at the last minute, and all she could do was give us a warning?"

"Possible. But unlikely. Whoever this is, they wanted us to be confused and angry. They're going to make sure we stay that way." Leia sighed as the doctor approached. "You're going to tell me I need to stop talking immediately, aren't you?"

"Indeed not." Harter Kalonia's coolly precise speech did little to disguise either her compassion or her sly humor. "I'm going to tell you that you needed to stop talking quite a while ago."

"All right, all right." Leia tucked escaped strands of hair back into her braid, slipped the breathing mask on, and dropped into the bacta.

Disgusting stuff, bacta—its viscosity seemed to mark the exact halfway point between "liquid" and "slime." Leia's eyes remained tightly shut, and the fluid's temperature was warm, but she couldn't escape the feeling that she'd been swallowed alive.

Many bacta patients reacted this way, which was why doctors injected sedatives first. Sure enough, as Leia floated in the tank, one lock of her hair swaying around her like seaweed, she felt the first wave of relaxation overtaking her.

Stay focused, she told herself. *You need to think this through, step by step. Do you remember seeing anyone suspicious?* But the tranquilizing pull of the drugs was stronger than gravity. Leia felt as if she were drifting into a realm without pain, without fear. Maybe this was what it was like to be in the womb. *I wasn't alone there, though. Luke was with me. Where's Luke?*

She remained conscious as they lifted her from the tank, wrapped her long hair in towels, and eased her onto a hovercot. Leia even remembered looking up at Dr. Kalonia and a med droid as they loaded her onto a transport. And if her memory served, she managed to get to her feet and walk into her own quarters with only a little assistance from the doctor.

Next had come the moment when she flopped down onto her own bed, and after that, she knew nothing at all, not for a very long time.

Leia woke with a dry mouth and fuzzy thoughts. Her body felt light, completely free from pain, and the sedative had not entirely released its hold on her mind. In the first few instants she simply enjoyed the experience of lying in a trance where fear could never touch her.

But memory demanded its due—that, and the red flashing lights on her comm panel.

Groaning, she pushed herself onto her elbows and looked at the nearest screen. Projected onto it was the information that she had suffered a concussion, moderate damage to her internal organs, and a few broken ribs, all of which the bacta had repaired. For the next few days, she would be restricted to limited physical exertion only. A med droid would return that night to confirm her successful treatment.

"Great," Leia muttered. "But that's not the damage I'm worried about."

Next she brought up the holos she'd been sent. Her filters had been preset to sort them by her specific priorities, which meant the political messages would be at the bottom. The first image that flickered into being was Han's face, and he looked more stricken than she had seen him in years. "Leia, sweetheart, Greer tells me you're sleeping the bacta off. But when I heard somebody bombed the Senate, and saw those pictures . . ." He shook his head, as if trying to cast the images out of his mind. "If I hadn't gotten your message, I would've gone out of my head. I'm just glad you're all right. Contact me when you're up and around again, and if you change your mind about me coming to Hosnian Prime, just say the word." Han gave her the smile that had never failed to stop her heart. "I love you."

Han's image faded. Leia hoped the next message would be from Ben, or Luke, but instead Chewbacca appeared, growling his wishes for her recovery and his plans to deal harshly with whoever was identified as the culprit. Leia smiled at the Wookiee's typical bluster, trying to overcome her disappointment. The next few dozen all appeared to be from political figures repeating stock phrases about shock, outrage, gratitude for her survival, and hopes for her recovery. Leia clicked through them as speedily as she could, pausing only for the updates that told her Varish's broken limb would be like new tomorrow, and Tai-Lin had escaped with no more than a scratch. Ransolm Casterfo had sent one of the final messages, and his was the only one that seemed to have come from a human rather than a politician. "I try to make myself believe it, and I can't, even though I was there. Thank the Force it was no worse. Your staff says you'll be well in the morning, but if you need anything, let me know."

He had offered as a friend rather than as a political favor. Leia couldn't help being amused by the thought of asking him to fetch her some soup, but she suspected he'd actually follow through.

Next she dipped into the informational channels, sampling news both official and organic. At this point, most people were expressing genuine shock and concern. How long had it been since she'd heard Centrist and Populist worlds saying the same thing? How long since they'd been unified by shared feelings?

If only we could use this incident to build unity between our planets, Leia thought. But she knew they wouldn't be so lucky.

Within a day, the accusations would begin.

"Isn't it obvious?" said Orris Madmund, the junior senator from Coruscant, as he walked along the halls of the main Senate building beside Ransolm Casterfo. "Yesterday's bombing was the Populists' work."

"I beg your pardon?" Ransolm stared at Madmund, who puffed up in indignation at even having been questioned.

"The Populists set the bomb themselves in order to paint themselves as heroic victims, and to throw suspicion on us. A crime as vile as it is transparent. Really, Casterfo, you must stop being so naïve."

Had everyone gone completely mad? "Don't be absurd. Aren't the Populists supposed to be the conspiracy theorists? The risk was too extreme to everyone involved for anyone in the Senate to have done this. It can only be some unknown terrorist faction."

Madmund retorted, "Tell that to the Populists who are already blaming us! They're pointing fingers at us even now. Open your eyes."

Throughout the Senate that day, fear and distrust ruled. Security alerts went off five times before lunch. Staffers looked wild-eyed and hurried between offices as if the corridors were somehow inherently more dangerous. Messages filled Ransolm's queue during every call he took, and no sooner could he return one of them than the queue would promptly double.

He remained shaken by Madmund's accusations all day. Not because he believed them; it was ridiculous to think that even extremist

Populists would go to such lengths. Ransolm did not assume their innocence out of naïveté, but because of two unquestionable facts: One, the Populists wouldn't have endangered the life of their likely candidate for First Senator; and two, Populists were too fractious and argumentative to manage a conspiracy. Sometimes he found it miraculous the Populists could even agree on where to sit.

I can work on reasoning with my own side, Ransolm decided, *but the Populists will only listen to one of their own.* And there was no question in his mind as to who that person should be.

So, shortly after leaving his offices for the day, he visited Princess Leia's home for the first time.

"What's that?" Leia asked as she stood in the doorway in a simple blue gown, her hair in its usual loose braid.

He held out the box he'd managed to procure. "A dozen buttersweet puffs. To heal what ails you."

She laughed as she looked down at the small box of pastries. "This is even better than soup."

"Beg pardon?"

"It's nothing." Leia took the box from him and nodded toward her rooms. "Please, come in."

Ransolm already knew that Princess Leia didn't stand on ceremony or demand luxury. Even so, the simplicity of her quarters caught him by surprise. She owned little, all of it attractive but functional, and nearly everything in soft shades of white and gray. On the wall hung the room's one ornament, an elegant painting of Gatalentan origin, bold in brilliant swaths of red.

She noticed him looking at it. "A birthday gift from Tai-Lin Garr a few years ago. Maybe my favorite gift ever—at least, until these." Settling the box of baked goods on the table, she motioned for Ransolm to sit as well.

"You have a lovely home," he said.

Leia chuckled. "You say that now. Come back sometime after my husband's been home for a few weeks. Socks everywhere." Although she made a joke of it, Ransolm recognized in that moment that she missed her husband greatly.

In one corner played the official broadcasts of at least a dozen worlds, cycling in rapid succession; Leia must have preprogrammed the selection, and an auto-translate projected dark letters of text beneath the images.

Suspicion Mounts as Investigation into Senate
Bombing Continues

So-Called Napkin Bombing Alleged to Be Work
of Centrist Leaders

FRAME JOB? How Far Will the Populists Go to
Discredit the Centrists?

The litany ran on, paranoia upon paranoia, mostly blame being batted back and forth between the two political parties save for the Ithorian news service, which inexplicably seemed to be convinced the Hutts were behind it all.

"I trust you have the good sense to know this," Ransolm began, "but so many foolish people are speaking today, I must be clear. This was not the work of the Centrists."

"I believe you," Leia said, never glancing away from the newscasts as she opened the box he'd given her. "It wasn't the Populists, either. We have some fools in the ranks, but nobody's this big a fool."

"Do you think you can convince the Populists of our innocence?"

"Not through logic, or good sense, or even common decency, if that's what you were hoping for. The only way we can bridge this gap is by figuring out who's really responsible." She sighed and took a bite of her puff.

Ransolm felt his spirits sink. It wasn't as if he hadn't known this even before speaking to her; he had simply hoped her greater experience and connections might point to a solution he hadn't yet seen. But no, the quagmire was just as deep as he'd feared. "I suppose investigators have yet to come up with any actual evidence."

"You didn't see? Hold on." Leia cycled through the holos more swiftly, until they hit upon one showing security footage of a Twi'lek woman darting into a door of the conference building, then swiftly out again. Her dark coverall resembled that of the catering staff; the sunshades she wore would have struck no one as peculiar, not on so sunny a day as yesterday.

"Ryloth? It can't be. They haven't the resources or the motive." Ransolm folded his arms as he considered the possibilities. "Anyone could hire a Twi'lek mercenary."

"Agreed. This footage only emerged in the past couple of hours—but I still expect Ryloth to be accused on the Senate floor. And then the Hutts, and who knows who else. But the brunt of the suspicion will be focused on extremists in our own parties. Count on it."

Ransolm could imagine the endless debates that would result. Could it even endanger the coming election? Only a First Senator could shepherd them through this crisis; the galaxy needed leadership more than ever. "Who do you think did it?"

"I don't know," Leia said, expression thoughtful. "Still . . . doesn't it strike you as peculiar that this happened just as we began investigating a massive criminal cartel?"

"You suspect Rinnrivin Di?" The idea had never occurred to Ransolm, and he did not find it persuasive. "His sort try to avoid government attention, not provoke it. He would have little to gain by bombing a Senate building, and much to lose. Also, if he were to set a bomb, he's not the type to warn anyone."

"Agreed. It's not Rinnrivin Di. But whoever it is making all that money, whoever set him up in the first place . . . *that* might be a different story."

The holo flickered, showing images of the alleged Twi'lek bomber over and over again. Her face was unrecognizable from the footage, and undoubtedly she had traveled to Hosnian Prime under false ID. Yet it would be broadcast into infinity because it gave the illusion of discovery, the shadow of an answer they might never find. "That's possible," Ransolm finally said. "I admit the timing would be rather convenient. But we're still only guessing."

Leia gave him a look. "Good thing we're investigating this anyway, isn't it?"

"So it is." He began to warm to the idea of the hunt. Perhaps the cartel they sought had nothing to do with this bombing, but Ransolm had rarely felt so helpless in his life as he had yesterday when he heard the explosion. Running out to see the rubble, breathing in the acrid, chemical-tinged air—it had brought back terrible memories of Riosa after the Empire had emptied his world out and thrown it away. For an instant he had been a young, scrawny boy again, newly orphaned, lost and hungry amid the devastation.

At least this investigation let them do something meaningful, something useful. And if they got to the bottom of the bombing plot in the process, so much the better.

"I should arrange a trip to Daxam Four immediately," Ransolm said; he had read her latest communiqué about Greer and Joph's intel only shortly before the explosion. "Search for these Amaxine warriors, whoever or whatever they are. In fact, I already have a convincing pretext for a personal visit."

Leia tilted her head. "What's that?"

"It touches on a sore subject—"

"Now you *have* to tell me."

"My collection of historical artifacts." Leaving the word *Imperial* out of it seemed to do the trick; at any rate, Leia didn't react. "Recently, someone in collectors' circles began advertising a very rare object for sale, and it caught my attention . . . not least because the seller lives on Daxam Four. I opened some preliminary discussions, and I believe I can arrange to purchase the item in person."

Nodding, Leia asked, "Do you think the seller could be connected to the Amaxines? There's nothing that specifically connects that old legend to the Empire."

"I have no reason to think so—but if this individual isn't connected, perhaps they can provide information we can use. At any rate, it should prove a convincing cover story for me to snoop around on the planet's surface." He smiled. "I think I'm catching on to this espionage thing."

"Be careful," she said. "When you think you've finally figured things out? That's usually when your plans go to hell."

Ransolm had found this held true for things far beyond espionage. He nodded in assent.

Then Leia added, "Do me a favor. Take Greer with you."

Just when he thought they were becoming friends. "Do you really feel the need to have me watched? Still?"

"What? No." Leia looked genuinely indignant. "Would you rather go into a dangerous situation without backup? If so, feel free. Besides, I think this is the kind of assignment she could handle and enjoy."

The paranoia of the day must have begun to infect his brain. "My apologies. A fellow traveler would be welcome. You must need your assistant, though. I could ask Seastriker—"

"Actually, Joph Seastriker's coming with me to Ryloth, once the Senate sends someone to investigate there." Leia's smile was thin. "Neither he nor the Senate knows that yet. But give it a few days."

Ransolm shook his head in wonder. "Always a step ahead, aren't you?"

Her gaze turned back to the holos, which were now showing the smoldering rubble of the Senate building again. "I only wish."

CHAPTER
FIFTEEN

––––––––––

Ransolm Casterfo had believed Leia when she told him Greer was coming along to Daxam IV as backup, not as a sign of any mistrust. However, no one seemed to have informed Greer of this.

"Coming out of hyperspace in five," she said coolly—the first words she'd spoken since shortly after they'd left Hosnian Prime. Her thick black hair flowed free down her back, the only element of her body or personality that didn't seem to be under strict control. "Strap in."

Greer had the helm of the vessel they'd rented for the journey, a small Jeconne courier. After some deliberation, Ransolm had chosen this ship because it was modern and stylish—he was traveling under his true identity, after all, and had to look the part—but also commonplace, unlikely to attract attention on its own. He had expected an experienced pilot like Greer to have some opinion on the matter, but he had the distinct sense that she wouldn't have cared whether he'd brought a two-person orbit-hopper or a Super Star Destroyer.

"I suppose it's beneath you," he said.

That earned a swift sideways glance. "What do you mean?"

Ransolm gestured around the sleek black cockpit with his long-fingered hands, clearly referring to the whole ship. "The Jeconne. Too mundane for someone who used to be an elite racer?"

"It's fine," she said shortly. Another few moments of silence passed, during which Ransolm gave up on any attempts at conversation. But then she added, "I was hardly 'elite.'"

"Nonsense. Senator Organa shared your bona fides before this mission began, you know." If Greer Sonnel assumed she was the only one Leia talked to, time she learned otherwise. "Junior Sabers winner, a professional racer on the Crystal Cairn team for two years, until you retired suddenly three years ago. A short career, but an illustrious one, given the races you competed in—and you retired undefeated."

Greer contested none of this, but she stared at her panel with unshaking attention, even more than required when leaving hyperspace. "Two years doesn't make you elite."

Although Ransolm didn't consider himself a vain man, he had learned during his hardscrabble childhood on Riosa that he had to use every asset he had. That was the only way to get ahead; weak people could not expect admiration or assistance, and so he would prove he was not weak. He bought the best clothes he could afford, made influential connections and let others know about them, and played up every skill he could honestly claim.

So why would someone discount her own skills? Abandon her own fame? It made no sense to him. Weary of trying to get through to Greer, Ransolm leaned back in his seat. "As you like."

Her hand closed over the handle for the hyperdrive. "Slipping out in three, two, one—mark."

The courier shuddered as the stars froze in their proper places again. Beneath them lay Daxam IV, vivid amid the blackness of space with its orange deserts and small teal-blue seas. Almost no cloud cover shielded the world, or offered any promise of rain. Yet in this stark, largely uninhabited area of space, the rough terrain of Daxam IV had to count as an oasis.

"Okay." Greer punched a few controls, including the one to send an automatic signal requesting a berth at the capital city's spaceport. "How are you going to play this?"

"You're actually interested now?" Ransolm could hear how priggish his voice sounded, and on one level he loathed himself for it. But by now he knew Greer Sonnel wouldn't respond to friendliness. She would have to be the one to initiate the thaw.

His comment earned him an arched eyebrow, but she did at least swivel her seat to face his. "I'm your backup. If I don't know where you're going or when, then I won't be much good at keeping you alive."

"But if you follow me, you're likely to scare off the types of people we're looking for." Ransolm reached into the pocket of his dark-red cloak and pulled out his comm device to show her the messages he'd sent and received. "Collectors of Imperial artifacts tend to have a . . . jaded view of New Republic officials."

Greer took the comm device in her hand, staring down at the screen. "You're going to buy one of the helmets of the Emperor's personal guard?"

"Exactly." Which was actually very exciting—Ransolm had already mentally selected a place of honor for it on his wall, assuming of course it was genuine—but beside the point. "I'm already known in these circles and was able to arrange a potential transaction. A seller who goes by the name Crimson Blade—"

"What?" Greer frowned. "Is that his real name?"

"Ah. No." Ransolm wanted to hedge. "In the collecting scene, we often operate under names not our own. *I* go by my real identity, but others prefer more . . . colorful terms."

Emperor's Wrath. Interceptor Fire. Avenger of Jakku. Ridiculous, the lot of them. Ransolm knew this to be merely role-playing, the assumption of a part they might take on in reenactments, but he didn't trust an outsider to understand that.

Fortunately, Greer showed no interest. "So you have no idea who this seller really is."

"It hardly matters, because he turned out to have one of these helmets, a prize more than valuable enough to warrant a personal visit.

He may well be tied to the groups we seek; if not, he should know some individuals who are. Once I've established a connection with him, I can build on that."

Greer considered that in silence for a few moments before she handed back his device, pursing her lips as if to say, *Not bad.* "And I guess I'm your pilot?"

As though he needed one. "Let's pretend you're a member of my staff, rather than Senator Organa's. If they check, we can make it seem as if I just hired you out from under Leia's nose a couple of weeks ago, and the Napkin Bombing kept records from being updated in a timely fashion."

Greer nodded as their console began to blink with their approved landing time and coordinates. "Smart."

"Was that a compliment? No. It couldn't have been. You spoke the words out loud without bursting into flames."

"Spare me," she said. Was that the hint of a smile on her full lips? Surely Ransolm had imagined it.

Daxam IV somehow managed to look even more forbidding from the surface. The deep-orange sands stretching out for kilometers made Ransolm think of other desert worlds he had visited, where the sun beat down mercilessly. At the time, he'd loathed the heat, but he almost missed it now.

Despite Daxam IV's two suns, the planet orbited at the very edge of its solar system, far enough that the chill ran deep even at twice-noon. Ransolm had felt somewhat ostentatious packing a fur cloak, but at the moment he couldn't have cared less whether anyone else found his clothing grandiose. He might have frozen stiff by now without it.

Greer, of course, showed no sign of discomfort even though she wore mere woolens. But Pamarthen robes were famous for their warmth, and she had layered beige and blue ones, belting them close and draping both hoods over her head. Together they walked through the streets of the city—

—correction, he thought. *Through what passes for a city on this bar-ren rock.*

Only a few streets formed the town center, each one lined with low, scrubby houses or shops. He found it difficult to tell one from the other, since most structures had been cast from the same mold: square, squat cubes of adobe or stucco, with their whitewashed sur-faces stained reddish by the sand.

"One question," Greer said. "This guard's helmet is expensive, right?"

"Rather." As much as Ransolm longed to add it to his collection, he could never have justified the expenditure were it not part of this mission.

"So whoever owns it has to have serious money." Greer's gaze went up and down the desolate street. "If I had serious money, I'd live somewhere else."

She had a good point. This "Crimson Sword" had wealth, and yet chose to remain on Daxam IV, a planet that had only one possible advantage Ransolm could see: It was obscure, rarely visited, and therefore out of sight. Also—"Large sums of the money from Rinnrivin Di's cartel are being funneled onto this world. Hard to imagine what they're spending it on."

Greer nodded. "Not on the nightlife, that's for sure."

Were there spice warehouses here? Vaults of valuable goods wait-ing to be sold for quick, laundered credits? If you hid such things on a world like this, you could be fairly certain they would stay hidden.

Until now, he thought with some pride.

His appointment was at a teahouse, which proved to be a small, run-down establishment with poor lighting and cheap booths. Small lanterns hung from the ceiling, casting a dim gold light that didn't penetrate the shadows. Ransolm scanned the room and recognized his target at first sight.

She would have stood out in any room. Perhaps sixty years of age, she had long, wiry hair that curled halfway down her back, black streaked through with silver. Thin and angular, she gave the impres-sion of someone who had been carved by time into her purest, simplest form—as if all softness had been stripped away. Small white scars marked areas of her forehead, left cheek, and throat. Her dark eyes were already focused on him, and she sat in a corner that allowed no one to approach her from behind. But none of this was the reason Ransolm immediately knew her.

This was the woman from the casino on Bastatha, the one who had not wanted to be noticed.

Ransolm glanced at Greer and nodded toward the counter across the room, where lone patrons could sit on low wooden stools and take their tea. Although he could tell Greer bridled at being so casually ordered around, she knew her obedience was necessary to their cover. As she walked off, he turned back to "Crimson Sword."

He knew better than to lie outright. "Have we met before?" he said as he took his seat opposite her. "You look very familiar."

"I am Arliz Hadrassian, and no, we haven't met." Her low, husky voice sounded like that of someone far older, or a spice fiend who had been at it too long. But Ransolm suspected that rasp had more to do with the scars on her throat. "However, we visited Bastatha at the same time, not so very long ago. I took note of the senatorial delegation."

Careful, Ransolm told himself. She had to know that he'd been investigating Rinnrivin Di, and would be on her guard. Yet Hadrassian had agreed to sell to him even knowing his real identity—which meant she thought he might prove friend rather than foe. He would have to tread a very cautious path to decrease her suspicion, and increase her hopes.

"When we were running errands for Ryloth," he said darkly. "Hardly the proper business of a senator. But we flushed a few local mobsters out for the authorities, so I suppose it wasn't a total waste."

"You think little of mobsters, I take it." Hadrassian said this as if she did, too.

Ransolm decided to be completely honest in his answer, since he could think of no fib that would serve him better. "Grubbing for credits, making money off addicts—what kind of business is that? What kind of *life*?"

"I agree, Senator Casterfo. We are meant for better things." Hadrassian's smile sliced across her face like a blade. "A few rounds of sabacc in a casino may serve one night's purpose, but real rewards do not come from mere games of chance."

"Agreed." *I set up this purchase to assess her. She could only have agreed to it in order to assess me in turn. What is it she hopes to find?*

He nodded at the server who had approached the table—an actual human instead of a droid, evidence of this planet's poverty—and chose one of the teas from the cart at random. It proved to be fragrant and sweet, and the ceramic cup warmed his hands. Ransolm was grateful, not least because it gave him a moment to collect his thoughts.

"So," he began. "How did you come about the helmet?"

He expected the usual sort of story: collected from another collector, on and on, back to the usual foggy tales about a heroic friend or ancestor who had personally taken Imperial artifacts as trophies of war. But Hadrassian surprised him again. "I served in the Imperial Starfleet, Senator Casterfo. So did many members of my family, and many friends. The helmet belonged to my elder brother." She cast her eyes down at her cup of tea, the first time her attention had been anything less than razor-sharp. "He became seriously ill the day before Palpatine left for the second Death Star, and so lost his chance to accompany the Emperor on that final journey. Had he gone along— who knows? Perhaps history would have been rewritten."

How precisely would a lone Imperial guard have thwarted the entire rebel fleet? But people convinced themselves of stranger things than this in order to believe they could have altered fate. "Your brother agreed to part with the helmet? I should've thought he would treasure it forever."

"He returned to regular service after Palpatine's death, and was one of those who fell at Jakku. This helmet is one of the few things I have left of him."

"Then I'm even more surprised you're willing to sell such a keepsake," Ransolm said.

"I wouldn't have sold it to just anyone. You were exactly the sort of customer I hoped for." Her eyes crinkled at the edges, hinting at the smile she suppressed.

All this time, I thought I set up this sale. But this isn't my snare. It's hers.

Normally Ransolm would have been chagrined to have strolled so easily into a trap. Instead relief washed over him. Hadrassian would be less likely to suspect his agenda because she had orchestrated their meeting for purposes of her own.

He asked himself how he would have acted if he really were here only as a buyer. Leaning across the table, he said, "Tell me—what did you do in the Imperial Starfleet?"

Hadrassian smiled easily this time. "You want to hear some war stories? Your interest in the Empire's history is well known, Senator Casterfo, but I doubt such an important man has the time."

"I'll make the time."

The next two hours were filled with tales of the Imperial Starfleet, particularly Hadrassian's youthful duties as a TIE pilot. Later she had become an ISB officer—"More interesting," she confided, "but only in the moment. Not in the retelling."

Ransolm took note of that; anyone admitted to the Empire's internal security force had been considered loyal to the core. But he kept the conversation focused on her days chasing down spicerunners around Kessel and Kerev Doi.

He didn't have to pretend to be fascinated. Hadrassian's stories were amazing.

They parted well, with an appointment the next day for the actual purchase of the helmet. "Not here," Hadrassian said. "I'll send the coordinates for my territory in the Western Wastes. A quick hour's flight, no more. But please ask your staffer—" She nodded toward Greer, who remained in place at the counter. "—to remain behind. I prefer to keep my transactions confidential."

Was this the same sort of setup Leia had faced on Bastatha? Ransolm doubted it. Hadrassian had taken this meeting to sound him out, and he felt sure he'd passed her test. Whatever trust he'd earned could only be spoiled by insisting on Greer's presence. "Understandable," he said. "I look forward to it. Will you have more stories for me?"

Hadrassian inclined her head. "Many more, Senator Casterfo."

Although he managed to hold on to his elation until he and Greer were well away from the teahouse, once they were in the clear Ransolm recounted every detail of his conversation with Arliz Hadrassian. Greer didn't seem to share his enthusiasm, but he kept going, talking the entire way back to the spaceport hangar. "—and still completely loyal to the Empire. As though she'd taken her oath yesterday, I swear."

"Must be nice for you," Greer said.

It took Ransolm a moment to process that. "Excuse me?"

"Meeting someone who shares so many of your interests. Like, say, worshipping the Empire."

He would have been less offended if she'd slapped him. "I do not *worship* the Empire. Haven't you been listening? Don't you realize this means we're on the right track?"

"I realize we're getting closer to finding out what's happening on Daxam Four," Greer said. "But I'm still not sure which track you're on."

Ransolm refused to dignify that with an answer. He stalked past her, determined to grab what he needed from the ship and head to the rooms he'd rented for the night. All his careful conversation, all his planning, and still, he won only sneers. Was nothing he did ever going to be good enough for Leia's self-righteous team?

That night, long after dark had fallen, Greer took the Jeconne courier out for a spin.

I wonder if Casterfo will see it and think I'm ditching him, she thought. By now the man was almost certainly asleep. But she couldn't shake the idea, largely because she felt guilty.

Snapping at the guy did no one any good. Princess Leia had chosen to trust Ransolm Casterfo; that made it Greer's job to help him. He'd done some quick talking today, and quicker thinking. If he hadn't, Hadrassian might have realized she wasn't playing them as smoothly as she'd hoped. Besides, he'd shown courage when he went to "rescue" Leia from Rinnrivin Di, and apparently he'd even visited the princess in the aftermath of the bombing.

But Casterfo still rankled Greer on every level. The one thing she couldn't shake was something Princess Leia had said on Bastatha: *Can't you just see him in an Imperial uniform!*

Pamarthe's relationship with the Empire had been a complex one. In the earliest years of Palpatine's rule, its citizens had flocked to join the Imperial Starfleet as pilots and gunners, funneling their martial spirit into the Emperor's armies. No one at Pamarthe had ever been able to understand the Republic's use of clone soldiers to replace citizen-warriors, and they were eager for new battles, new conquests.

But all that changed after the Death Star destroyed Alderaan. The idea of firing upon civilians and soldiers alike, from a distance, without taking the slightest personal risk in return—every true warrior of Pamarthe knew that to be the foulest kind of cowardice. Many deserted immediately, and within the year hundreds had joined the Rebel Alliance, including Greer's parents. She had grown up listening to their stories of battle against the Empire.

Casterfo said he was no admirer of the Empire, but he acted like one. Surely that was what irritated her about him so.

Or maybe, she admitted to herself, *you're just jealous of how carefree he can be. How optimistic. How he gets to lead a life with no limits, while you're . . .*

Greer breathed out sharply in frustration as she banked the courier, soaring upward into the night. With every meter she rose from the ground, she felt freer. Daxam IV's near-cloudless atmosphere meant a broad vista of stars stretching out before her, so that she could hardly tell whether she was in space or the sky. Gradually she relaxed, easing into a high flight that would trace a wide circle around the city.

Low winds, light atmosphere—the flying was easy, and Greer's thoughts had begun to wander when signals at the far western edge of her flight plan began to blink at the rim of her viewscreen. Frowning, she focused more tightly on them to get a good read. According to her records, she was well outside the main air traffic lanes, and Daxam IV was so deserted she wouldn't have expected to see many craft at all. *Maybe they're cloudsowers, or standard sentries,* she mused.

But these ships were too fast for any of that; they could only be starfighters. Which meant she'd found the Amaxine warriors.

Greer quickly damped down her own signals and swooped lower, so she'd be harder to detect. Soon she skimmed only meters above the ground, dust swirling beneath the courier as she studied her read-outs. Fifteen—twenty-two—no, nearly thirty starfighters flew over the far Western Wastes, and in military formation. She set her scanning range to maximum, and her eyes widened as she realized at least five other squadrons were practicing identical maneuvers.

Few militias were so large. Even fewer flew with such precision. And almost none had a fleet of starfighters as fast and well armed as those of the New Republic fleet.

That settled it. The Amaxines were far more than a group of over-enthusiastic patrollers. They were a paramilitary organization, one with significant funds, ties to organized crime, a leader who would no doubt turn out to be someone close to Arliz Hadrassian if not Hadrassian herself—

—and an appointment with Ransolm Casterfo, first thing in the morning.

Greer muttered, "We'd better hope he's on our side."

CHAPTER
SIXTEEN

"Senator Organa, welcome to Lessu, and to Ryloth." Emissary Yendor strode toward the *Mirrorbright*, his walking staff in one hand. Although he wore the long tan cape that marked him as an official, he had abandoned his formal robes for a simple brown jacket and pants. Leather straps twined around his lekku. His casual dress meant that he had complied with her request to keep her arrival low-key—that, and the broad grin on his blue face.

Leia smiled in return. "It used to be Princess Leia back on Hoth."

"We're not on Hoth now," Yendor said in good humor. "Thank goodness. If I'm never that cold again, it'll be too soon. And I only washed off the last of the tauntaun stink about a year ago."

"They didn't smell *that* bad."

"With all due respect, Your Highness, you never had to muck out their stalls."

"Point taken." Leia held out her hand, and as they shook, she took a quick glance around. This was the only spaceport for Lessu, Ryloth's main capital city, yet almost no other activity seemed to be taking place. Ships remained inert; cargo was neither loaded nor unloaded; foot traffic seemed minimal. Normally Leia would have attributed this to a senator's arrival, but as per her instructions, no ceremony had been arranged. Only the emissary and a small group of local security had come to greet them. Lessu's spaceport was this quiet because there was simply not enough traffic to fill the area.

Ryloth's trying hard to rebuild from their centuries of oppression, she realized, *but they've got a long way to go.*

To Emissary Yendor she said only, "Princess Leia is fine now, too. Any friend from the Rebellion is a friend for life. You flew with Corona Squadron, didn't you?"

"Yes, Your Highness." Yendor's smile became less formal, more proud. Every old soldier liked to be remembered. He glanced past her to the others coming up behind. "Please, introduce me to the rest of your team."

"See-Threepio, human–cyborg relations." C-3PO performed a little bow. "Though we have met before, Emissary Yendor. We worked together on recalibrating the thermal units for Echo Base one afternoon precisely five days after our arrival on Hoth. May I say it is a pleasure to see you again?"

"How could I ever have forgotten that day?" Yendor said, managing to sound sincere.

Leia introduced the rest of her party. "This is my intern, Korr Sella, and my pilot, Lieutenant Joph Seastriker."

"Good to meet you both," Yendor said, "even if you have absolutely no right to be so young."

Korrie and Joph gave each other a look. Leia managed not to react to their dismay, but it struck her again how youthful they appeared—younger even than Ben, with their puppyfat cheeks and unlined faces. Yet somehow Leia had been a senator at Korrie's age, and not even as old as Joph when the Rebellion won the Battle of Endor. Yendor could only be five or six years older than Leia herself.

And if Joph and Korrie looked so young to her, how old must she look to them? They had to feel as if they were shepherding a museum piece around the galaxy. To judge by Yendor's expression, he was having the same thoughts. *We belong to another age*, she thought with a sigh. *But we have to make our way in this one.*

However, the rest of their day felt like living through an era so far distant it ought to have predated the Old Republic.

"Is it *all* written on paper?" Korrie said in despair, about three hours into their work in the Ryloth archives.

"Except the stuff that's written on tanned hides." Leia put the ancient vellum to one side, wrinkling her nose. "Or on wooden tablets or rolls. But yes, it's all either written or printed."

Only Joph Seastriker's thick shock of golden hair showed behind his high stack of leather-bound volumes. "Could they seriously not afford regular holograms or computers or anything? Ever?"

"No, Lieutenant Seastriker, they couldn't." Leia kept her voice civil—but her staffers needed to understand this. "Ryloth has never had much in the way of resources, and whatever they had was traditionally taken away from them by either the Niktos or the Hutts. They learned that if they wanted to preserve their own version of their history, this was the only way they could do it. We have to respect that, even if it makes our jobs harder."

Which it did. Immensely. But nobody ever said being a member of the Galactic Senate was fun.

She, Korrie, Joph, and C-3PO were clustered around a long sandstone table in the heart of the Ryloth archives—a vast, cavernous basement area in which all the planet's records were kept, going back to what seemed to be the beginning of time. Candledroids floated close by, giving Leia enough light to work by, but making the rest of the space feel even colder and darker by contrast.

"Here's more to add to the dossier, Your Highness!" C-3PO tapped his metal hand on the page of an open book. "Another mention of Rinnrivin Di, this one from approximately fifteen years ago."

Korrie leaned toward the page, her eyes narrowing as she tried to

make out the handwritten words. "It's a list of the Hutts' spice bro-
kers. Rinnrivin was on the lowest rung of the operation—at least as
far as anyone on Ryloth knew."

"I'd be willing to bet that was accurate." Leia folded her arms across
her chest as she sat back in her chair. She'd worn a lightweight jumpsuit for the journey—appropriate for Lessu's moderate climate, but
inadequate to the damp chill of the archives. "To judge by what we've
seen from Rinnrivin's dossier so far, up until seven to ten years ago he
was no one. Little money, less power, hardly any independent organization of his own. And now? We've turned up enough information to
know Rinnrivin has one of the largest criminal enterprises in the galaxy."

C-3PO swiveled his torso to her, tilting his head as if in human
curiosity. "Perhaps our information is inaccurate, Your Highness. It
comes from humans and other sentient creatures, not machines, and
could therefore be faulty."

Leia shook her head. "No. Though we don't know everything about
Rinnrivin's operations yet, we've seen too much to doubt that he's at
least as powerful as the Twi'leks told us, probably more."

"Well, what about this?" Joph pushed the books in front of him to
one side so he could make eye contact with the others again. "Maybe
another cartel collapsed around that time. One of the Hutts died
without an heir, something like that. Rinnrivin could have seen an
opportunity, stepped in, picked up wherever the other cartel left off."

Leia weighed that idea for a long moment before saying, "That
would be plausible. The only problem is, we have no records of any
such cartel. Not here, not on Hosnian Prime, nowhere."

"Rinnrivin stayed out of sight long enough," Korrie pointed out.
"We might not have known the other cartel existed. Surely there are
others out there we haven't heard about even now."

"True. But if Rinnrivin were merely stepping into a power vac-
uum, by now we'd have run across traces of whoever it was he was
replacing. We haven't." She wished they had. The more she thought
about the mysterious origins of Rinnrivin Di's operations, the more
deeply they unnerved her.

As she and Casterfo had speculated, someone else had sponsored Rinnrivin Di. Her lone meeting with the Niktos had taught Leia that the man was no fool, and not the type to readily accept second-tier status from just anyone. Whatever the real power was behind Rinnrivin's cartel, its reach had to go almost past anything Leia could imagine . . .

"Are you still sure this isn't connected to the Centrists?" Korrie ventured, gesturing at the piles of ledgers on the table. "Because all of this suggests Rinnrivin's money goes to Centrist worlds. That makes me think the original money must have come from there, too."

"Just because a planet politically aligns itself with the Centrists doesn't say anything about what any individual citizens might do or believe." Leia said the words, and she meant them, but inside she felt the inexorable tug that told her *something* was very wrong here.

Centrist worlds pride themselves on law and order, she thought, remembering Ransolm Casterfo's words about the death penalty on Riosa. *They'd be more likely to pick up on large-scale criminal enterprises operating in their midst. Could every single Centrist world touched by Rinnrivin's cartel truly be ignorant of his power and reach?* Possibly. Few peoples had as much reason to track the Niktos as the Twi'leks did. But Leia now sensed the shape beneath the surface—the immensity of the danger lurking just out of sight, but growing closer all the time.

Piloting a top-of-the-line ship like the *Mirrorbright* to an independent world like Ryloth as part of a secret mission: High-quality adventure. Top grades. Excitement score of . . . seven, maybe seven and a half.

Spending hours sitting in a musty basement reading words written on actual paper, trying to trace financial records: Zero adventure. Excitement score so low it had actually drained excitement out of other parts of Joph's life, like a black hole engulfing all light and heat.

"This stinks," he confided to his one companion on the ship that evening.

"I detect no strong chemical components in the onboard atmosphere," C-3PO replied, "though of course that's not part of my primary programming. We could locate an astromech unit for a more thorough scan of the ship's ventilation systems—"

"I didn't mean literally." Joph kicked back in the pilot's seat, staring glumly out at the silent stillness of the spaceport. "I meant that this is boring."

"I see, sir." The droid's politeness never flagged. Joph wondered if the droid's programming kept him from ever being bored—or maybe, to C-3PO, humans were so slow and dim-witted that boredom was all he knew.

Princess Leia had been invited to some kind of dinner. If the event were a grand state banquet, Joph would probably have been asked to attend as well. However, this was a humbler affair, a private gathering that Emissary Yendor had put together for the princess and some others who had known one another during the war. Korrie, meanwhile, was finishing up work in the archives. Until she returned, Joph had nothing to do but "guard the ship."

Hey, at least you got a chance to fly this, Joph reminded himself as he looked at the *Mirrorbright*'s sleek console. Not much consolation, but he had to take what he could get.

Just then, the communications unit began to blink with the pattern of lights that meant "top-priority message." Joph sat up straight. Only someone from the Senate or another high official in the New Republic could send that kind of message. It happened so rarely that his training had never covered how to handle it. Did he answer for Senator Organa? Or would he be violating security protocols even seeing it?

He had to try. Joph punched in the appropriate signal. "*Mirrorbright* receiving. Lieutenant Seastriker here."

"Joph?" Senator Casterfo's face took shape onscreen. "I take it Leia's not aboard, then."

"Banquet." Should he have phrased that more carefully? Didn't matter. Joph continued, "I can, um, take a message—or go get her, if it's that urgent—"

"Not quite that urgent, though we should act soon." Casterfo leaned closer to the projector screen, so that his holo seemed to hover in the cockpit itself. "Greer's turned up evidence that the Amaxines are far more than a militia; they seem to be a substantial fighting force in training."

"In training for what?" Joph asked. Behind him, Korrie walked in, the *Mirrorbright*'s door swishing shut behind her. She frowned as she came closer, listening to the call.

Casterfo continued, "That's the question. But here's the thing: We need to conclusively link Rinnrivin Di to the Amaxines, posthaste. If we can't bring them down along with Rinnrivin, this could be more than a mere criminal matter. The Amaxines might defend him, or avenge him. Given the scale they're operating on, it could even mean open conflict between systems."

Joph straightened in his chair. "All right. What can we do here?"

"Greer suggested that Rinnrivin would scarcely leave such a large fighting force unmonitored. We performed some scans that turned up spy satellites sending periodic updates from Daxam Four to a few worlds—including Ryloth."

"You think Rinnrivin Di is hiding out here?" Korrie said.

If Casterfo found it odd that Korrie was now a part of the conversation, he gave no sign. "No. I think Ryloth is a relay station of some sort. Rinnrivin has enough influence there to bribe local officials into simply 'not detecting' his satellites orbiting Ryloth. What we need to know is where the Ryloth satellites are sending their signals."

The final puzzle piece snapped into place. "Because that's going to tell us where Rinnrivin Di is."

Senator Casterfo nodded, or Joph did; the signal wavered, distorting the image of his face for a moment. "Very likely. We're transmitting the specs you should search for right now. If you can find and splice those satellites, this investigation will take a big leap ahead."

"We're on it," Joph promised as the computer began processing the received data.

Anything else Casterfo might have added was lost when the holo signal blanked out completely. After a moment of silence, it became clear that he would not re-signal, or could not.

Joph drummed his hands against the bulkhead. "We've got a mission. No. We've got a secret mission. Now, that's more like it."

"Wait, you're going now?" Korrie said. "As in, right this moment?"

"Hey, you heard the senator. It's important."

"We haven't even told Senator Organa!"

"She's busy, and another member of the Galactic Senate just gave us orders."

Korrie sat in the copilot's seat, datapad clutched to her chest, her loose curly hair framing her worried face. "Do you want to do this now because you think it's so critical that we shouldn't wait, or because you're just bored?"

Joph grinned. "Yes."

"But sir!" Threepio shuffled out of the back, where he'd been powered down for too brief a time. "This is highly irregular. Princess Leia would undoubtedly wish to be consulted."

Probably. However, the more Joph thought about this, the more he was sure this was the right time—and he hoped that wasn't just his own wishful thinking. "If Rinnrivin has spies here on Ryloth, and he probably does, he's most likely to be watching Senator Organa herself. Not us. Which means our best chance of doing this without being observed is acting now, while the senator's somewhere else."

Although Korrie's expression still looked dubious, she finally nodded. Threepio said, "I'm sure we're making a terrible mistake."

"Only if I screw it up." Joph brought the engines online and felt the *Mirrorbright* shiver around them, ready for action. "And I'm not going to screw it up."

They soared away from Ryloth, a bright streak in its night sky, leaving the hazy blanket of the planet's atmosphere to just skim orbit. Normally vessels stayed clear of the narrow bands of satellites circling the equator, but Joph pulled in close as Korrie double-checked each against the specs that would help them identify likely targets. Within minutes, the viewer began to ping with multiple red dots— satellites that might be working for Rinnrivin.

Joph skimmed closer to the first one, feeling as if he were threading the ship through an asteroid belt. Silvery satellites dotted the space around them as he matched orbital speed. "Threepio, you can process the data coming in from one of these if I hijack the signal for a few seconds, right?"

C-3PO cocked his golden head. "I function primarily as a protocol droid and translator, advising Princess Leia on matters of higher diplomatic importance—"

"But you speak to other machines, so you can understand these satellites." If not, Joph's day was about to get a whole lot more difficult.

If the droid could have sniffed, he would have. "If you so require, sir."

"I do." Joph slipped in even tighter, until the satellite was practically close enough to touch the *Mirrorbright*'s gleaming white hull. Just as he was about to tell C-3PO to get started, however, an idea took shape in his mind.

The satellites have to be sending information to Rinnrivin regularly. But there's no way Rinnrivin's staying in one place—not while he's wanted like this. We don't need to just retrieve the data; we need to tap into it permanently.

Thinking fast, Joph said, "Hey, Threepio. If you can get the satellite to give us the data now, can you reprogram it to keep sending us the data going forward? Including the primary destination for the signal?"

"I could, sir, but that will be far more time consuming."

Korrie broke in, "If we take too long up here, we could be detected. That would blow the whole thing."

"Yeah, but that's the only way to be sure we're tracking Rinnrivin Di."

She nodded, but her expression remained troubled. "Senator Casterfo gave us specific orders."

"That's just because he hadn't thought of this yet!"

"We should stick to the plan for now and ask Senator Organa about your idea later—"

"Interacting with the satellites twice would be way more likely to trip any alarms, right, Threepio?" Joph turned toward the droid.

"Yes, sir, but Senator Casterfo's orders were quite clear," C-3PO insisted. "We shouldn't disobey them."

Joph would've thumped C-3PO upside his metal head, if he wouldn't have bruised his hand in the process. "We're not disobeying his orders. We're . . . *improving* them."

"Joph, don't," Korrie pleaded. He'd gotten into the habit of thinking of her as someone closer to his own age, but the alarm in her voice reminded him that she was only sixteen. "It's too big a risk."

"It's too good a chance to waste." Joph made up his mind. "We're doing this. I'm noting for the record that I proceeded over both your objections. If something goes wrong, it's on me."

C-3PO looked as though he were about to blow a circuit. "If we're captured by Rinnrivin's thugs, we'll be doomed!"

"They're not going to fly up here and grab us in the act," Joph said, mentally adding, *At least I doubt it.* "Is there some kind of—sleep mode, something like that, you can put the satellites into? That would slow down any alarm activation."

Resigned, the droid said, "I'll try my best, sir."

The work turned out to be at the edge of C-3PO's capabilities, but he could manage it. Over and over, Joph wheeled the *Mirrorbright* toward a satellite, flying with the precision necessary to bring them close enough for signal range, and let C-3PO coax the satellites into sleep mode. Then, while the data was being downloaded, they could input codes suggesting that the satellites do a little extra work the next time they broadcast their signals. Although they worked as quickly as possible, the delicate flying and C-3PO's complex task meant that every single satellite got within seconds of activating automatic alarms before they were able to detach. The suspense made Korrie look seasick, and Threepio's complaints were interrupted only by his panic, but Joph enjoyed himself immensely.

A challenge to his skills, a mission with some meaning to it, and following his gut to come up with a better idea than he'd had before—*this* was what Joph had dreamed about on Gatalenta. He hadn't had this much fun since he'd piloted his X-wing down into the caverns of Bastatha.

That feeling of exhilaration lasted until later that night, after they'd landed, and Princess Leia found out what they'd done.

"Let me get this straight." Leia paced in front of Joph, who stood rigidly at attention in front of the ship's cockpit. In the far corner of the main room, Korrie and C-3PO stood by silently. Korrie's worry and sympathy were as obvious as the droid's unspoken *I told you so.* "You took it upon yourself to improve Casterfo's orders."

"Yes, ma'am. The idea came to me in a—a moment of inspiration. I felt you would have okayed my actions if you'd been present."

The princess stopped mid-step and gave him a steely stare. "But I wasn't present, Lieutenant Seastriker, and you shouldn't presume to guess what I would and wouldn't approve."

"Yes, ma'am. I know. But—" Maybe she hadn't quite figured out what they'd managed to do up there. "We're going to get updates on Rinnrivin Di's location from now on. That's got to be worth the risk, right?"

"That's not your call to make, Lieutenant. You could've exposed this entire operation."

"Yes, ma'am." Joph wondered just how many demerits he was going to receive for this. Surely she wouldn't bust him back down to ensign, would she?

She continued, "You're here to work with me, on this mission, as I command. Have I made myself perfectly clear?"

By now Joph's spirits had sunk down to the soles of his boots. "Yes, ma'am."

A few moments of silence passed, during which Joph awaited his orders to get his butt back in the cockpit—until Princess Leia said, "It *was* a good idea."

Joph grinned as he lifted his head. While the princess had folded her arms across her chest, her expression had changed from stern to intrigued. He ventured, "Yes, ma'am. I mean, thank you."

"Next time you have a similar 'moment of inspiration,' you run it by me first. You've got good instincts, but they won't help you much if you don't learn to work as part of a team." Princess Leia nodded toward the cockpit. "You strung the net for us, Seastriker. Let's see if you've caught anything yet."

Joph eagerly sat down in the pilot's chair and brought up the satellite signals. Princess Leia took the navigator's position, and Korrie and C-3PO came up behind. A few lines of small green type began to appear on the screen. "Not a whole lot yet—but we can pinpoint the location the signal's being sent to."

"Excellent," the princess said.

"Oh, it was nothing. Merely some complex programming per-formed very quickly indeed," C-3PO said with obvious pride. "I'm always happy to have been of service."

Throwing a dirty glance over his shoulder, Joph forced himself to concentrate on the work at hand. When he had the data, he fed it into the navigation computer to see which location it would spit out. Within moments a planet came up, one Joph had never heard of be-fore. "Sibensko. Expansion Region, in largely Centrist space. Do you know it, Senator?"

"No," Leia said. "But I have a feeling we'll all get to know it before long."

CHAPTER
SEVENTEEN

—————————

Ransolm Casterfo was relieved to find Daxam IV's weather warmer on his second day. The bright sunlight helped ease the slight nervousness within his gut—nervousness Greer Sonnel seemed determined to increase.

"You shouldn't have agreed to a meeting without me," Greer said, not for the first time that morning, as they walked across the spaceport toward the speeder bike rentals. "I'm supposed to be your chief of staff, remember? Why not throw your rank around? Insist on taking someone along? You don't strike me as the type to forget your senatorial privileges."

"Arliz Hadrassian doesn't strike me as the type to approve of anyone 'throwing their rank around' in a situation where she considers herself to be the highest authority." Ransolm glanced backward toward their Jeconne courier. "Fly far away enough for them to miss you, close enough to reach me quickly if I call for you. That's precaution enough."

Greer's dark eyes searched his face—for what, Ransolm couldn't guess. "Do you really trust these people so much?"

"I don't trust them at all," Ransolm said. "But I believe that I can get them to trust me."

"And if you're wrong?"

"Then you get to be smug and I get to find out just how fast these speeder bikes fly."

He'd rented a top-of-the-line model again, this time choosing a sporty one painted brilliant red. Ransolm wanted to attract attention today; he wanted to come across as young, successful, enthusiastic, guileless—and someone who would look at acquiring an Imperial artifact as reason to celebrate. And if that meant he got to drive a very flashy speeder bike?

Duty, he thought with a wry smile. *Always duty.*

As he slung his leg astride his bike and adjusted his goggles, Greer said, "If the pilots I saw last night are tied to Hadrassian's organization, you could be getting in over your head."

"How else can I learn to swim?" Ransolm sighed. "I don't mean to be glib. It doesn't matter if I'm getting in over my head or not. I intend to follow this mission wherever it leads."

"All right." Greer's tone sounded different then—respectful, almost—but Ransolm had no time to assess that. He had an appointment to keep. He gunned the motor, leaned forward, and zoomed toward the Western Wastes, orange sand swirling in his wake.

Hadrassian's compound stood alone in the wastes, a set of buildings at least forty kilometers away from any other human structures. Several dozen people were working on personal spacecraft—starfighters, apparently modern and sophisticated, unlike the average militia fleet. Everyone wore matching black coveralls, and none of them took particular note of his arrival . . . or they all tried to seem as if they didn't. As Ransolm parked his bike, Arliz Hadrassian walked from the largest building, her silver-streaked hair drawn back in a tight bun that accentuated the sharpness of her features. Her smile showed the bared teeth of a predator with prey between its jaws. "Senator Cast-erfo. You honor us with your presence."

"The honor is mine, Ms. Hadrassian—as long as the helmet is, too." Ransolm gave her his most winning smile. It was, he knew, a good one, highly effective on most women and more than a few men. Although he was no womanizer, he understood very well how to be charming when necessary.

Hadrassian laughed. "Greedy for your prize. Well, come and see it, then."

As they stepped into the building, Ransolm's eyes required a moment to adjust to the relative darkness. Inside, on the far side of a long black table, stood another dozen people, all apparently waiting for him. In the center of the table sat the helmet.

Ransolm approached it with awe. The brilliant red was only a shade too light to match the color of blood, and it shone as pristinely as it must have in Palpatine's royal chamber. He tugged off his riding gloves, but he didn't reach for the helmet. Hadrassian had to be the one to hand it over; this had belonged to her late brother. The transfer had to seem as sacred to him as it must feel to her.

She stepped to his side, hands clasped behind her back. "Magnificent, isn't it?"

"Breathtaking." Ransolm could already see it on his office wall.

"Imagine how often this mask was in the presence of the Emperor himself."

Palpatine had been near this mask, had seen it with his own eyes. Ransolm felt an unpleasant, seasick stirring within him. He preferred to think of the officers of the line, the common soldiers whose valor could not be questioned even if their cause was unjust. When he thought of the Emperor and Vader at all, he thought of them not as the Empire's backbone, but its pollution. Its downfall.

"Here." Hadrassian took the helmet into her hands and held it for one silent, reverent moment before turning to Ransolm. "Put it on."

Ransolm paused long enough to feel the heft of the helmet, its surprising weight. Then he slipped it over his head to see the world through it.

His first thought was that the eye slits were deceptively narrow; visibility was far better within the mask than any observer would first think. Perhaps the designer hoped to instill a false sense of security in those who sought to do the Emperor harm.

"Imagine it, Senator Casterfo." Hadrassian's voice had become low and sweet, like a mother encouraging her child to daydream. "You stand at the right hand of the Emperor. Lord Vader himself is with you, and all the moffs. You stand aboard the Death Star, and this time there will be no errors, no accidents, no disloyalty. You will share in the Empire's power and glory forever. How does it feel?"

The high stone walls surrounding the labor camp. Air thick with soot and smoke from the factory chimneys. Ransolm's small hands raw and chapped from polishing the blaster casings, the stink of the chemicals absorbed into his skin. Hunger clawing inside his belly. His father trying to explain to Lord Vader the impossibility of the quotas set for them.

That harsh, metallic breathing. The mortal terror that made Ransolm vomit, right there, on the floor—and he'd thought that was it, for sure, now Vader would kill him.

But Vader didn't care about a small boy's fear. He only cared about the quotas.

His hand around Papa's throat. The way he made Ransolm watch his father gasp and gag and plead. How Vader had thrown Papa down like trash.

How he had hated Vader then. If he'd had a force pike like one of the Emperor's guards, he would have swung it with all his might and claimed Vader's head for his own.

"Glorious," Ransolm whispered. "It would have been glorious."

"Ah, yes." Hadrassian's smile widened. "I see my brother's helmet has found a true home."

"Indeed it has." He slipped the mask off again, grateful to be liberated of its weight. "If I only had a force pike, the picture would be complete."

Hadrassian arched an eyebrow as she looked around at the others gathered before the table; by now, most of them were smiling, too. "If you'd like a force pike, Senator—"

"You have one of the Royal Guard force pikes?" Ransolm could scarcely believe such a prize could still exist.

Hadrassian shook her head no. "Would that I could offer you something so fine. But we have other force pikes. We train with them here, my fellow Amaxine warriors and I—as part of our reenactments, you see."

"Fascinating." Ransolm knew some people met for Imperial drill and battle reenactments, but he also knew real weapons were forbidden at such events. If Hadrassian was speaking of an operational force pike, not a mock-up—then the Amaxine warriors weren't reenacting battles.

They were training for them.

"Come," she said, gesturing toward the door. "If you're not in a rush to take your helmet back to Hosnian Prime, we have much to show you."

"No rush whatsoever." His heart thumped harder. The situation had begun to shift around him, and he could not yet guess what form it would take.

When he and Hadrassian walked out into the clearing at the center of the Amaxine warriors' camp, the others all gathered around, any pretense of inattention abandoned. Amid all the utilitarian black coveralls, Ransolm's tailored green jacket and pants seemed gaudy, frivolous, citified. Certainly some of the Amaxine warriors thought so. Their gazes were more amused than sharp.

Hadrassian walked to a long corrugated metal locker and flipped open the top. "Force pikes," she said, taking two from the locker. "At their strongest setting, capable of cutting through durasteel. At their lowest, capable of causing excruciating pain."

She tossed one of the pikes toward Ransolm, who caught it in his dominant left hand. Fortunately, the pike hadn't yet been activated, but he remained vividly aware of its power and its dark legacy. Force pikes had been used for torture. Their shocks could cause paralysis or even death; researchers were unsure whether the deaths were caused by electrical voltage or from the intensity of the pain alone.

"Do you know how to fight with force pikes, Senator Casterfo?"

Hadrassian handed the other pike to a young man with tan skin and close-shorn hair.

"I've studied techniques in old holos, that sort of thing. But I've never had the opportunity to hold one before."

"Then let us be the ones to teach you." With that, Hadrassian nodded at the other young man, who immediately activated his pike. Ransolm did the same. The low hum of the force pike seemed to thump its way into the sand beneath his feet as Hadrassian said, "Begin."

And now he's going to get himself killed.

Greer cursed under her breath as she saw the scene via the speeder bike's holocam, which she'd patched into the courier's comm systems. As she punched the engines, zooming toward the Amaxine camp, she kept one eye on the holocam images. Casterfo was being led to the center of a broad enclosure, along with someone who seemed likely to be his opponent, or his executioner.

I thought he might be taken hostage. I thought they might try to brainwash him. But I never thought he'd get himself challenged to a duel. *The guy has a rare talent for suicide.*

She could get there within five minutes, fly in low, spray the perimeter with what little defensive fire the Jeconne courier could muster. Would the strike team she'd seen practicing the night before scramble to defend their camp? If so, they'd have her outnumbered and outgunned. Her heart raced in her chest. Greer would die rather than abandon the senator she was sworn to protect, but her sacrifice wouldn't save him. She'd have to count on taking the Amaxine warriors by surprise. Hopefully Casterfo could keep himself alive long enough for her to reach him . . .

The holoscreen continued to flicker. As she watched from the corner of her eye, Greer realized that Casterfo held himself straight. His chin was high. And his hands were in ideal fighting position on the force pike's grip. He actually wanted to see this thing through.

That left her with a decision: Get over there and save his life whether he wanted it or not—or let him try, preserve the cover he'd managed to create among the Amaxine warriors, and run the risk of getting a senator killed?

Did he have it in him? Was there even the possibility that Ransolm Casterfo could survive?

Greer eased off the engines and turned the courier back toward her original cycle. She might be a fool, and a fool who would soon have senatorial blood on her hands, but she'd give Casterfo what he so obviously wanted: the chance to save his own skin.

Surrounded by a ring of spectators with black coveralls and killers' smiles, Ransolm shrugged off his cloak, passing his force pike from hand to hand while he did so. As his grip adjusted to the hum of vibration, he took stock of the field of battle. *Sand, hard-packed, rather dry. Topography nearly completely flat. Sun coming from almost directly overhead, so neither of us can use the glare to our advantage. Opponent three or four centimeters shorter than I am—excellent.*

Hadrassian clasped her hands behind her back, like a mother proudly watching her children win their games. "Only to the first landed blow, I think. We wouldn't want either of you to hurt yourself."

One blow from a force pike would be enough to fell a man. But it would be over quickly. Already Ransolm sensed that the purpose of this fight was not to threaten or kill him—only to test him. If he proved he wasn't soft, if he could simply hold his own, he would have won the respect and trust of the Amaxine warriors. It didn't matter whether he won or lost.

So he decided to kick the guy's ass just for the fun of it.

Ransolm had studied old holos of force pike battles; that much of what he'd told Hadrassian was true. He simply hadn't mentioned his lessons in Hosnian martial arts and in quarterstaff combat. Nor did he speak of the year between his parents' death and his adoption, during which he'd learned how hard you could fight for a crust of bread when that bit of food might mean the difference between your life and death.

He took dueling position, eyes locked on his Amaxine opponent as he thought, *Now you will know me.*

Hadrassian said, "Begin."

The Amaxine leapt forward, a foolish attempt at intimidation. Ransolm sidestepped him easily. Although the force pike hummed insistently in his hand, he held back. *Watch his movements. Learn his tricks.*

A high, slashing stroke toward Ransolm's shoulder was parried with one brute thrust, enough to throw the Amaxine back but show him nothing else of how Ransolm fought. Electrical sizzle drowned out the reaction of the crowd, if there was one. Ransolm cared nothing about them, only about the person he was fighting. His opponent appeared simple to read. This man was impulsive, inclined to show off.

Why not give him a chance?

Ransolm stepped back into another of the formal dueling positions—one knee forward, the other leg extended backward—and held his force pike out in a horizontal line in front of his chest. The Amaxine grinned, following suit.

The next step in formal dueling technique would lead them into some low spiral sweeps, a way of judging finesse and aim. As Ransolm had expected, the Amaxine went straight into it, eager for his chance to show how much he knew.

And *that* provided an opening.

The very moment the Amaxine finished his move, Ransolm swung his pike up hard, a crude move that nearly knocked his opponent's force pike from his hand. The Amaxine compensated quickly enough to hang on, but he had been startled, thrown off his form. So Ransolm kept going, rough hit after rough hit, not giving his opponent one moment to readjust. The younger man was trapped, on the defensive. Ransolm knew what to do when you had an opponent in this position: Show no mercy.

Again. Again. Ransolm kept the blows coming in underhanded, never opening up his torso to the assault. He struck the other force pike so hard the clash of vibration jarred his bones, but he would not stop. As he always had during his training, Ransolm called up the faces of those he wished were in front of his blade now.

The supervisor at the labor camp—

That boy who had stolen the tiny box of meat jerky Ransolm had been hiding in the lean-to where he slept—

Darth Vader, always Lord Vader, if only fate had given him a chance to take that villain's head—

His last blow came up so hard it knocked the force pike from the Amaxine's hands. Ransolm slashed forward, almost blinded by the haze of anger and the past—but he caught himself. His last thrust stopped perhaps one centimeter short of his opponent's neck.

"You said, to the first blow, Ms. Hadrassian." Ransolm did not take his eyes away from the Amaxine, who stared up at him with obvious dread. "But I would prefer not to cause harm to any of your warriors. I believe they have another purpose to fulfill."

With that he stepped back, deactivated the force pike, and bowed. After a pause long enough to make Ransolm wonder if they'd insist on a blow after all, Hadrassian began to applaud. The others followed her, their grins widening, and even the defeated Amaxine nodded in apparent admiration.

"You continue to surprise me, Senator Casterfo." Hadrassian stepped forward and put one hand on his shoulder. "They claim that the air on Hosnian Prime is thin, that it weakens the blood. But not yours."

"No." Ransolm took a deep breath and looked up into Daxam's pale sky. "Not mine."

"Hadrassian says they've got at least fifty starfighters at this location alone, with at least two pilots fully rated to fly each one." Ransolm Casterfo sat in the cockpit of the Jeconne courier, going through the preflight checklist for Greer, while she hurriedly logged everything he was saying. He'd insisted he had to get it out right away or the details might escape him. "She gave no exact numbers, but to judge by the exercises she mentioned, the maneuvers and drills they've performed, I would estimate approximately one thousand Amaxine warriors are linked through the Daxam Four base. But they are only a fraction of the whole."

Greer swore under her breath. "How many bases can they have?"

It was a rhetorical question, but Casterfo had managed to uncover the answer. "Only a handful, five or six, all but one of those even smaller than the base on Daxam Four. But one base is their true center, the hub of their activity—and the place from which they'll strike."

Until then, Greer had hoped her misgivings from the night before were no more than paranoia. But she had seen true, and Casterfo knew it as well: The Amaxine warriors meant to draw blood. Whose blood did they want? "Did you get the base's location?"

"Some obscure planet in the Expansion Region called Sibensko. I've never heard of it."

"I have," Greer said. Casterfo looked up from the console at that, his hand paused on the fuel gauge. When he raised an eyebrow, she continued, "Free traders from Pamarthe used to fly through there sometimes. It's a water world, no landmasses to speak of, but there are large areas where the ocean isn't very deep. Traders built under-sea cities as bases for the kind of commerce you'd rather keep secret."

Casterfo drew himself upright, seemingly prim once more. "Criminal activity, you mean."

"Not originally. Unless you're counting any business not monitored by the Empire as 'criminal.' I'm pretty sure a few rebel pilots stocked up there from time to time; it was a place where you could be sure of remaining hidden." Greer racked her memory for any more details, but what little she knew came from old fireside stories. "Since the Empire's fall, legitimate traffic moved out of Sibensko."

"Leaving the scum behind." Casterfo leaned back in the high, narrow pilot's chair, clearly deep in thought. "Sibensko sounds like the sort of place where a would-be mobster might encounter a would-be warlord."

"Exactly."

Casterfo rose from the pilot's seat, motioning for Greer to reclaim her position. "Princess Leia's team remains on Ryloth, do they not?"

"So far as I know," Greer said. "But we haven't been able to raise them again, and they haven't sent us any information about the spy satellites yet. The radiation interference must still be too strong."

"Then we'll wait." He nodded at her and turned back toward his cabin. Meeting over.

Greer couldn't let it go at that. "I saw the duel."

Casterfo stopped, his hands on either side of the doorway that led to the rest of the ship. "You did?"

"I watched it begin via the holocam monitor. Thought about flying in to save you, but then you looked like you knew what you were doing." Greer realized she was smiling. "And you did. Casterfo, that was one hell of a fight."

He looked over his shoulder at her, unexpectedly vulnerable to such simple praise. "Do you think so?"

"You fight like a man of Pamarthe." That was the highest praise Greer could give, though probably Casterfo wouldn't get it. "I'd spar with you if I could."

He got it. His grin was more genuine than she'd seen from him before. "I'm honored."

First priority: to inform someone in the Senate of what he had learned. Leia deserved to be the first person to hear the truth, but she remained incommunicado on Ryloth.

Besides, Ransolm reasoned, as he sat down in his narrow courier bunk, another Centrist senator needed to hear about this. To judge by the star charts he'd just pulled up, Sibensko also lay within an area of space with mostly Centrist worlds. When the Populists heard about this, the mass of them would not be as judicious as Leia; they would begin crying conspiracy, and the political situation could disintegrate rapidly. But if he could form a small coalition of Centrist senators who would back these findings, then this could become an opportunity for union rather than dissent.

But whom should he reach out to? Anyone much more powerful than him might well attempt to claim the investigation himself—

unlikely, given Princess Leia's role, but far from impossible. Anyone much less powerful than him would be of no use. He needed a peer, one he could convince. Preferably one who owed him a favor . . .

Lady Carise Sindian. Of course. Ransolm smiled as the idea registered. His speech in support of her motion to elect a First Senator had helped to carry the day, and he felt certain Lady Carise knew that as well as he did himself. Her planet, Arkanis, was wealthy and influential. She had every reason to support and believe him, and the ambition to see this through.

Resolved, he put through a communication request. Assuming it would be hours at least before a return signal came in, he began readying himself for some much-needed sleep, kicking off his boots and peeling off his socks—and then the light began to flash. When he answered, Lady Carise's face appeared. She wore an elaborate tiara and a frown. "Senator Casterfo?"

"Lady Carise! I wouldn't have dreamed I would reach you on Hosnian Prime so quickly—"

"I'm not on Hosnian Prime. I'm on Birren, and rather busy at the moment." She gestured behind her, where the glint of precious metals outlined elaborate grillwork over arched windows. "The third stage of my inauguration is about to begin. The anointing will commence any moment!"

Ransolm asked himself if he wanted to know, decided he didn't, and pushed on. "I'll keep this brief, then. Our investigation into Rinnrivin Di's cartel has led us to suspect a connection to a paramilitary group known as the Amaxine warriors, one that might represent a real threat."

"A paramilitary group? A few bellicose men making themselves feel courageous by shooting at inanimate targets that will never shoot back? Senator Casterfo, do you hear yourself?" She shook her head as though in pity. "I'm sure some people are willing to break the law to buy themselves a beat-up old X-wing or some such. There were always a few who resisted the demilitarization efforts after the war, but never so many that they warranted any concern. To claim this group of toy soldiers forms a threat to the New Republic, an organization of thousands of worlds—you sound ridiculous. Hasn't anyone else already told you as much?"

When she put it that way, it sounded worse than ridiculous, but Ransolm trusted his instincts. "You're the first I've spoken to."

"Well, Senator Casterfo, I'm truly flattered—and to be quite honest, relieved. I'd hate to see you sabotage your political career before it's even properly begun. And If you waste any more time on this, you'll never get anything else done. Need I remind you we have an important election coming up?"

"No, you needn't." He gave the words just enough emphasis to remind her that the election wouldn't be happening without him.

But Lady Carise seemed too caught up in whatever ceremony was beginning to take much notice. "Here come the wardens of the sanctum with the anointing oils. I must go. Do try to move on, won't you? People like that never act. They only talk." Her gloved hand skimmed across the screen as she cut communication.

When the screen went dark, Ransolm sighed and flopped down on the thin mattress. Would any other Centrist senator respond more effectively? He had begun to doubt it. Apathy and inaction had infected both sides of the Senate. Only he and Leia seemed to see the potential disaster looming on the horizon.

CHAPTER
EIGHTEEN

———————————

The *Mirrorbright* slipped free of Ryloth's gravity, and Joph could feel the increased liberty of the wings, the lack of atmospheric friction holding them back. He loved that moment, when a ship knew itself to be in space again.

And the *Mirrorbright* was a beauty of a ship. Joph knew he'd probably never get another chance to fly her again—Greer would reclaim this chair the first chance she got—so he wanted to enjoy it while he could.

"We're clear of Ryloth, ma'am," he called back to Princess Leia. "Ready to lay in a course back to Hosnian Prime."

The princess said, "Not yet."

"Not yet?" C-3PO toddled closer to the cockpit. "But, Your Highness! We've promised to attend Senator Vicly's next gala, and of course your impending campaign will require due preparation—"

"I said, not yet." Princess Leia stepped around C-3PO to stand beside Joph, the many lights on the console illuminating her features in faint shades of red and gold. "Run a scan on the satellites you hijacked the other day, Lieutenant. Let's see if Rinnrivin Di is still on Sibensko. I suspect he stays on the move, these days."

Joph tuned in to the satellites' signal, trying hard to keep his pride under wraps. Yeah, okay, he should've cleared things with her first, but what really mattered was that he'd had a good idea, she *knew* it was a good idea, and this investigation was finally getting somewhere. "We're getting something—okayyy, he's definitely changed locations already—the last signals went out to—wait. That can't be right." He frowned. "Harloff Minor?"

"Surely you must know Harloff Minor!" C-3PO insisted. "Why, it's very near Coruscant. A center of commerce and culture—"

"I know Harloff Minor," Joph said. "It just doesn't seem like the kind of place where the head of a cartel would hang out."

Princess Leia shook her head. "Actually, it makes perfect sense. Rinnrivin Di still hasn't been charged with any major crimes. Large, heavily traveled worlds like Harloff Minor? The officials there won't be on the lookout for him. The alerts about my near-abduction on Bastatha won't even register on their scanners." She tapped her fingers on the console, deep in thought. "That's not where Rinnrivin does business. That's where he goes when he wants to seem respectable. Legitimate."

"So as long as he's there, he's not doing anything illegal?" Joph said. When the princess nodded, he shrugged. "Guess we have to wait until the satellites tell us something more interesting."

"That's interesting enough." The princess got to her feet. "Lieutenant Seastriker, lay in a course for Harloff Minor."

This mission was even better than he'd dared hope for. It was all Joph could do to keep from grinning.

"Harloff Minor?" C-3PO protested. "Whatever are we to do there?"

Princess Leia smiled back at them both as she returned to her cabin. "We're inviting Rinnrivin Di to dinner."

Harloff Minor offered a variety of climates and cities for the discern-
ing traveler, which meant that any number of galactic guides could
recommend good restaurants. Leia selected a sophisticated yet informal place in one of the larger equatorial cities, both because of its
excellent cuisine and because it offered private tables on small ter-
races. Any guest would be impressed by the view.

"Splendid," Rinnrivin said as he strode onto the terrace that evening, wearing black garments so exquisite Lady Carise Sindian might
have asked for the name of his tailor. "Utterly splendid. Your taste is
impeccable, Huttslayer."

"I'm glad we agree—on this, at least." Leia rose from her chair to
greet him, the breezes tugging at the soft layers of her long green
gown.

Rinnrivin took her offered hand, bent, and kissed it. What Niktos
had for lips were rather rubbery, but he was doing the best he could.
"On more than this, I hope."

"I suppose we'll see."

"Such a relief to know you weren't harmed in that terrible
incident—they're calling it the Napkin Bombing, I hear. Dreadful."
Oddly, Rinnrivin didn't only sound sincere. He sounded angry, as if
the bombers had insulted him personally. "Such a reckless, childish
act. One should never use force when persuasion is adequate."

Leia raised an eyebrow. "And what is it you think the bombers
wanted to persuade us of?"

"Their own might," Rinnrivin said with disgust. "Their determination to seize power by first destroying the Senate. And in the end, was
it anything more than a nuisance? The greatest damage was to a mere
statue."

His attitude toward the bombing and those responsible bore consideration, but Leia needed to steer him toward other matters now.
"Let's change the subject. Don't you think it would be a shame to
waste such a beautiful evening?"

"You're right, of course." He gave her his thin, polite smile, the one
that so reminded her of Tarkin. "Such people aren't worth worrying
about."

Leia gestured toward their table. "Please, sit down."

The restaurant terrace overlooked much of the city, its ornate architecture almost golden in the warm moonlight. A wide river snaked through the scene, capturing that light and reflecting it. Night had fallen, and the illuminated windows of the nearby buildings seemed to hang in the darkness like lanterns.

"I chose the menu," Leia said, "though I have nothing to offer you as exquisite as the Toniray wine."

Rinnrivin inclined his leathery head. "Should I ever come across another bottle, I promise you, it shall be yours."

"No. The one glass was enough. You can't dwell on the past." Leia had always known this, had always been aware that she could never, ever look back.

The server droids presented the meal: tender meats cooked in delicate sauces, salads crisp as cool air, and soups thickened to savory perfection. She had arranged for a few kebabs of Nikto beetles, which she knew to be one of their favorite delicacies, but trusted Rinnrivin wouldn't insist she try it.

Other topics interested him more. "To what do I owe this unexpected pleasure, Huttslayer?"

"There are so many topics we should discuss, Rinnrivin. I hardly know where to begin." Leia knew the precise fraction of a second she needed to time her pause. "You realize, of course, that I had no idea Senator Casterfo would be arriving that day."

"You looked as astonished as I felt." Rinnrivin's chuckle didn't disguise his irritation. "But I know the type. Young. Hungry for glory. Not caring who gets in their way."

A few weeks ago, I would've agreed with you, Leia thought. *Apparently we never age out of making fools of ourselves.* "He's still attached himself to the investigation like a mynock—except mynocks are easier to scrape off. So I thought I should seize the chance to speak to you without, shall we say, senatorial interference."

"Very prudent of you." Rinnrivin nodded.

"You've risen to prominence very quickly. So quickly that some would say you must have had help."

She'd decided to spring that one question on him—accurate enough to put him on edge, but still so far removed from what they'd learned to date that Rinnrivin would feel secure. The obvious response would be a protest that he was an enterprising man, cunning and capable, someone who could build his empire as swiftly as he chose.

Instead, he shrugged fluidly and helped himself to another glass of the Corellian brandy. "What can I say? Many wish to become rich, but few are willing to take the risks necessary to do it. For those of us who do not fear risk, opportunities await. Opportunities given to us by those more timid, who will happily accept less than they might have had, only to keep themselves safe." He pronounced the last word as though it were an obscenity.

"So you . . . reached out to like-minded individuals. Found enough to get started."

"It wasn't so simple as that. It took time, Huttslayer. Time and care. What seems like a quick rise to you was, for me, the culmination of many years of work."

His explanation was logical and plausible. He delivered it easily, even with charm. Under certain circumstances, Leia might have wondered if he were telling at least a partial truth. Instead she knew he had rehearsed this many times, beginning long ago—well before she had ever begun her investigation.

I wonder who helped you rehearse?

Rinnrivin held his goblet in one leathery hand, as if letting the moonlight sink into the wine. "My work bears benefits for all my partners, Huttslayer, whether old or new. Dare I hope that this invitation hints at a potential new partnership?"

"I don't take bribes," Leia said. The next pause was even more delicate than her last, but she knew how to spin it. "Yet—I question whether the Galactic Senate will continue to survive in its present form. The Napkin Bombing has been profoundly destabilizing. When I left, the Senate had degenerated to chaos."

"Oh, we know the Senate is poised at the brink of change." A Nikto grin was a fearsome thing, fanged and too bright. "A First Senator is to be chosen. A single person with true authority. And rumor has it that you are the most likely victor."

"Don't put too much stock in rumors, Rinnrivin. I haven't even officially said I would run."

"We both know your candidacy is inevitable."

"Perhaps, but my victory is not."

"Ahhh. Now I see. We all need powerful friends, do we not?" Rinnrivin's beady eyes glinted. "Maybe more than one kind of influence will be needed to win this election?"

Leia hadn't even thought of bluffing about that. But she seized on it as a good excuse, one Rinnrivin would believe in completely because it was the conclusion he'd hatched himself. "We're getting ahead of ourselves. That's a discussion for a later day. Tonight is simply a matter of . . . rebuilding bridges."

He nodded in satisfaction. "Excellent. I have one point of curiosity, though. However did you find me here?"

This question she was ready for. "You're not the only one with contacts, you know. I knew you to be a man of refined preferences, so I put the word out in a few likely places that I'd love to hear when you were next visiting. To have this happen so quickly, however—well. It proves we have similar tastes in some things, at least." She held out her hand to gesture toward the view.

Really, it was spectacular. She'd always meant to bring Han here, but they'd never made it happen. *Someday,* she promised herself. *Someday soon.*

"You gave me a gift when we last met," she continued. "I appreciate your thoughtfulness, and hope you will understand why I feel the need to return it to you."

Leia reached into her pocket and pulled forth the holocube documenting her murder of Jabba the Hutt. She flicked it on, activating the scene for the very last time.

Rinnrivin cocked his head as if scenting prey. "Surely you cannot give up such a treasure."

"As I said before, Rinnrivin, you can't dwell on the past. At least, I can't. And I would hate to deprive you of the sight of your worst en-

emy's death." As the translucent images writhed above the cube—
Jabba's tail thrashing, her arms straining—Leia set it in front of
Rinnrivin Di. "Besides, I don't need the hologram. I have the memory."

"I envy you that, Huttslayer." Rinnrivin leaned closer, avidly watching Jabba's death all over again.

Leia suspected that was the first wholly honest thing Rinnrivin had said all night.

In her mind she replayed what he'd said about "powerful friends." Rinnrivin's ego wouldn't allow him to admit he'd been sponsored into his current position, but with those two words, he'd admitted he had help. Now to find who helped him.

He continued, "Thoughtfulness is the sign of a good ally."

"Yes, it is." Silently she added, *and the sign of a terrible enemy.*

Leia had known the Galactic Senate would still be recovering from the terror, anger, and suspicion ignited by the Napkin Bombing. But she hadn't prepared for the situation to be even worse.

"I've been going through communiqués ever since we entered range of Hosnian Prime, but I can't get them sorted." Korrie's fingers flew over her datapad, but she lacked Greer's absolute efficiency. "As soon as I get them prioritized, another dozen come in."

"I fear Ms. Sella is correct." C-3PO sounded as close as a droid could come to mournful. "The competing requests are cross-referenced upon so many vectors, why, there's no telling which is of primary importance."

"Don't worry about it." Leia settled onto one of the long padded benches of the *Mirrorbright.* "Just start sending some of the higher-priority ones my way. Make sure we have date and time stamp. We'll figure out the rest as we go."

First Tai-Lin's face appeared, his usual serenity marred by weariness and doubt. "Princess Leia, I realize that you consider the mission to Ryloth of the highest importance, but this is a time when the Populist candidate for First Senator should be visible. The people would be reassured by your presence. They need to know that you are the rock we can rely on in such troubled times. Please, return as soon as you can."

He'd sent this within two days of her departure. Well, so much for being the rock of the galaxy. Leia sighed and moved on.

Next came Varish, who was propped up in what appeared to be a medcenter bed, albeit one that had been decorated with velvet pillows and a silk coverlet. "Leia! Three days in and I'm still regrowing my arm bones. Still! They keep talking about improvements in bacta therapy, but I have to say, I'll believe that when I see it, and I am most decidedly not seeing it." Varish sank back onto her sumptuous cushions, revealing only then some of the pain beneath her cheery demeanor. "Do come and visit me as soon as you get back, won't you? I'm bored to tears."

After this came a set of news files from various sources around the galaxy, arranged in one of the auto-sort sequences Leia had pre-programmed. The sequences rotated at random, ensuring that she would always review a broad spectrum of galactic information and opinion.

At least, that was how it had always worked before. Now there were two sides, two theories, two diametrically opposed opinions, and no middle ground to speak of.

Coruscant: "Although no concrete links between the bombing and the Populist faction have been firmly established, sources report several clandestine meetings between Populist senators in the weeks leading up to the Napkin Bombing. Experts have noted that the warning was given only to a single Populist—"

Gatalenta: "Conflict and discord have long divided the Senate, but few issues have been more injurious than this current bombing. Centrist efforts to assign blame to those very Populist senators most endangered by the explosion continue, in defiance of all logic."

Arkanis: "How long must we act out the charade of cooperation with people so depraved that they would risk the lives of thousands only to cast themselves as victims?"

Naboo: "The Centrists refuse to content themselves with arguing for greater militarization. No, they commit acts of violence in order to scare the populace into voting them ultimate power."

Leia cut that off. She knew now how polarized the issue had become; beyond that, nothing any of these broadcasts said was likely to be intelligent or useful.

Bringing up the next message made her smile as Han's face took shape. "Leia. Looks like you're not back from Ryloth yet—hope that means your 'side project' is going well." This was their way of referring to her current investigation. Han knew only the basics, both for his safety and for that of the mission. "You probably know we're headed to the fourth stage of the Sabers. The sublight relay round means I'm out of comm range for a while."

Now Han would be as incommunicado as Luke and Ben. Leia felt a pang of loneliness that she hoped didn't show on her face.

"Make sure you're taking care of yourself, all right? It's gonna be a while before I can be back to take care of you, and I know how good you are at getting into trouble." Han's lopsided grin made him look, just for a moment, like the dashing young smuggler she'd first met. "That's what I like best about you, you know."

His message faded away to be replaced by more broadcasts, which Leia rapidly flipped through with increasing irritation, several formal Senate notices of debates called and canceled and called again, and another message from Varish, now back home but in a sling and eager for company. Instead of distraction, Varish now wanted to talk about the iniquity of the Centrists; she seemed sure the two of them could single-handedly find the perpetrator.

C-3PO piped up. "Your Highness, we have an incoming message from Senator Casterfo. A recorded one, rather than live—"

Leia's discouragement melted away in an instant. "Bring it up now."

Bluish static shifted into the image of Ransolm's face. "Princess Leia, our mission has proved successful beyond our wildest hopes. Details should wait until we can meet in person, or at least speak via a secured channel, but I wanted to let you know immediately that our investigation has taken a dramatic leap forward." He sat on the edge of his seat, energized to the point of exhilaration. Whatever had happened on Daxam IV hadn't only been useful; Ransolm had enjoyed himself immensely. At least someone was having fun.

As his image faded, Leia murmured, "We're going to have plenty to talk about."

"Shall I queue more messages for you, Princess Leia?" C-3PO asked. "There are—oh, my—nearly four dozen more."

"I've heard enough for now." She got to her feet, aware of every aching muscle in her back. All she wanted was to return to her bunk and sleep most of the way back to Hosnian Prime.

Yet she realized that Joph and Korrie were sitting in the cockpit silently. Korrie hugged herself; Joph kept fiddling with instruments he must have already set and checked. Their youthful confidence seemed to have been drained from them.

Leia went to the doorway. "Everything all right in here?"

"Yes, Your Highness." Korrie sounded even more expressionless than a primitive droid, and Joph simply nodded.

"Hey," Leia said. "Come on. What's the matter? If something's bothering you about our findings—about any part of this mission—"

"It's not that, ma'am." Joph had never sounded so grave to her before. "It's just that listening to those news reports, well, things sound bad."

Korrie added, "They were bad before. But now—Princess Leia—do you think the New Republic could collapse?"

Leia had asked herself if the Senate would break down, whether they would come to a constitutional crisis. She'd wondered whether the Napkin Bombing would provoke some kind of conflict on a smaller scale. But she had not consciously believed total governmental collapse could come to pass—

—and if it did, war would come along with it. Only now did Leia understand that she'd been calculating that risk all along, moving it closer and closer to the realm of the possible within her own mind.

Korrie's fear did not shock Leia as much as the realization that she'd been coming to this conclusion herself.

"I won't lie to you." Leia looked down at Joph and Korrie, recognizing anew how young they were. If she could not act as a mother to her own son right now, she could at least help these two through the difficult days to come. "If the two factions within the Senate continue tearing each other apart like this, schism is a possibility. But just because it's possible doesn't mean it's probable. We still have time to work things out."

"But will we?" Korrie asked in a small voice.

"I hope so," Leia said.

What she truly felt was closer to determination than hope. The devastation of the war, the countless lives lost in combat, the sheer terrible waste of it: They couldn't let that happen again. Surely the other senators from the rest of the galaxy felt the same way.

Surely.

There has to be a way out of this, Leia thought. *And it's up to me to find it.*

CHAPTER
NINETEEN

Leia watched the force pike duel play out on screen, the image bright in her darkened office. Ransolm stood by her side, and although he was obviously attempting to be modest, she could almost feel self-satisfaction radiating from him.

But if he could fight like that, Ransolm had every reason for pride.

As the recording of the duel ended, Leia looked up at him over her shoulder. "I'm glad we're on the same side."

He couldn't entirely suppress his smile. "Now you know how I felt when I saw you taking down Jabba the Hutt."

Even though they'd each arrived on Hosnian Prime late at night, they'd wanted to meet at once. The Senate buildings were closest to the hangar they both used, so her office it was. Despite the urgency, Leia had been famished and eager for something besides the rations aboard the *Mirrorbright,* so she'd stopped at a take-out Ivarujari place for some boxes of spicy noodles. Ransolm had turned out to be a fan of Ivarujari cuisine as well, so they'd turned her office desk into a sort of picnic table, eating while they worked by the light of a few candle-droids. Each of them wore simple traveling clothes in gray or tan, and Ransolm hadn't bothered wearing his usual sweeping cloak. All of the useless pomposity of the Galactic Senate had been swept away, leaving her and Ransolm to get down to real work.

"The Amaxine warriors trust you. They even think they've recruited you." Leia picked up her box of noodles. "We have to use that."

Ransolm took his seat again. "Agreed. But how, and when? If we move too quickly, they'll become suspicious."

The timing of all this confused Leia nearly as much as it intrigued her. "When you met with the Amaxine warriors, they were confident. Even triumphant. But Rinnrivin Di had traveled to a world where he's almost entirely separated from his criminal activities, and the Napkin Bombing made him angry. He prides himself on keeping his temper, but this got to him."

"You mean you believe the Amaxine warriors and Rinnrivin Di are at odds? We were so sure they were conspirators."

"The two aren't mutually exclusive." The various bits of intel they'd gathered swirled around in her thoughts like moths. Leia had to pull together the strings of the plot, to weave a cobweb that would catch them all in their proper places. "We know Rinnrivin Di's cartel is connected to the Amaxine warriors. Either the Amaxine warriors set Rinnrivin up in the first place, or the same entity is funding them both."

Ransolm weighed her words, utensil and noodle box in his hands. "The Napkin Bombing affected each in different ways. The Amaxine warriors were emboldened, while Rinnrivin felt threatened. Do you believe the Amaxine warriors themselves were responsible?"

"The timing is right. And it *feels* right." Leia could sense herself being tugged in that direction as surely as a compass needle was pulled by a magnetic pole. Still, she needed to back up her instincts with logic. "But what do the Amaxine warriors have to gain by the bombing? And why go to the trouble of planting a bomb and then warning the victims when they didn't even claim responsibility? They risk exposure even though they want to stay hidden."

"Hidden *for now*," Ransolm interjected. "I doubt Hadrassian would have gone to the trouble of luring me to Daxam Four had she not envisioned finding other allies in the Senate for her group, and soon. Still, even if the Amaxine warriors are nearly ready to emerge, I can't think what they had to gain by the bombing. The only result has been property damage and a great deal of confusion."

The strands came together, weaving their cobweb pattern at last. Leia sat up straight. "That's it. Confusion. That's what they were after."

Ransolm swallowed. "What do you mean?"

"Our investigation of Rinnrivin Di was official, public. The Amaxine warriors would have been watching closely from the beginning. Rinnrivin tried to bribe me into complacency on Bastatha, and he failed."

He was catching on, nodding as he said, "It was no coincidence we first saw Hadrassian on Bastatha. She was there to watch us. Maybe to orchestrate Rinnrivin's kidnapping attempt."

"Exactly. Then you and I addressed the Senate jointly—a Populist and a Centrist. Even though we could hardly get anyone to listen, we were both publicly pushing for a wider investigation. Finally, word gets out that I'm probably going to be the Populist candidate for First Senator, which would give me the authority to get to the bottom of this in no time." Leia attempted to imagine herself as Arliz Hadrassian, an Imperial loyalist watching a hero of the Rebellion on the brink of taking power. "They needed a distraction. Something that would paralyze the Senate completely. And they sure got one."

"It would explain Rinnrivin's anger as well." Ransolm leaned forward, one forearm on her desk. "His cartel only thrives if it remains hidden. If the Napkin Bombing is linked to the Amaxine warriors, Rinnrivin will be dragged into the light along with them."

She breathed a sigh of both relief and resignation. "I think we've hit on the strongest possible suspect. The question is, how do we prove it?"

Until this point, Ransolm had been completely with her, but now his gaze drifted down to the table, awkward or ashamed. Leia couldn't understand his reaction until he quietly said, "We also have to know whether the Amaxine warriors have help. The ties to Centrist worlds could be coincidental, but perhaps not. If anyone in my own faction is abetting this kind of violence, we must be the ones to expose them."

Leia took care with her next words. "So I try to steer the official investigation into the bombing in the right direction, while you make sure no Centrist senator is involved."

She could not show any suspicion of the Centrists herself, not without solid proof. If she did so, Ransolm's defensiveness might take over. He put integrity over party loyalty—she knew that about him now—but she also knew how easily his pride could be bruised.

Her words had been well chosen, because Ransolm nodded. "A good plan. In the meanwhile, I take it, we both find out as much as we can about this mysterious planet that's so important to both the Amaxine warriors and Rinnrivin Di."

"Exactly," Leia said. "Soon we'll need to find out what's on Sibensko. What, or who."

Several Centrist senators were avid acquirers of Imperial artifacts; Ransolm's collection was far from the most impressive in the Senate offices. However, a mask of the Emperor's Royal Guard would be considered a prize by anyone in collecting circles.

That gave Ransolm an excuse to throw a party.

A reception, really—Ransolm supposed a gathering of a few dozen or so senators in his own office hardly counted as a party. A few glasses of Corellian brandy passed around while people looked at historical artifacts: That didn't live up to the wild indulgence of Hosnian Prime's most famous hosts, such as Varish Vicly. But it served Ransolm's purpose, bringing a good thirty Centrist senators together, and loosening their tongues.

"Like new," said gray-haired Senator Apolin of Kuat, with great satisfaction. He held his second glass of brandy in one hand. "I remember seeing the Royal Guard in person, once, when I visited Coruscant. Imagine how imposing this looked in life."

Ransolm murmured the right things while noting, *Visited Coruscant during Imperial rule. Got close enough to Palpatine to see the Royal Guard. His connections to the Empire have to have been stronger than he publicly admits.*

Senator Fatil of Orinda, a blond woman roughly Ransolm's own age, wasn't content with admiring the helmet; she had to inspect and praise every single item in his collection. "Even the uniforms suggest power," she murmured, standing very close to Ransolm as she traced her fingers over a TIE pilot's black mask. "They command respect. Awe. Submission."

She wants to either bring back the Empire or take me to bed, Ransolm thought. *Possibly both.*

The brandy continued to flow, and conversation became more candid:

"You didn't hear so much complaining in those days. Worlds knew they were responsible for their own messes. Didn't come whining to the Emperor about every little cyclone or drought."

"The Academies on Populist worlds? They've become jokes. Poor imitations of what the Academies were like a generation ago, where the best and brightest trained to serve their leader. Now, on Centrist worlds, we're rebuilding the old programs of study. Reestablishing standards. About time, too."

"If the will of the galaxy were truly so anti-Empire, there's no way so much of the Imperial fleet could have escaped. No way they wouldn't have been hunted down no matter where they tried to hide. There are still friends of the Empire out there."

"To this day, they've never adequately explained what happened to the first Death Star. Yes, we all know the big story, Luke Skywalker single starfighter blah blah blah, but honestly, does that sound credible to you? The Empire had the greatest engineers in the galaxy, and the Death Star was their finest achievement. There's no way it could've been vulnerable to that kind of attack. The Emperor had to have been betrayed by someone on the inside."

Ransolm heard nothing that pointed directly to the Amaxine warriors, or any general knowledge of a pro-Empire militia. If any of these senators were linked to Hadrassian's organization, they were too clever to speak of it, even indirectly, even when slightly drunk.

Yet what he heard troubled him even more.

These people—his political allies—weren't merely interested in greater centralization and efficiency. They waxed nostalgic for the Empire itself. For Palpatine. For the fear and obedience planets showed in the aftermath of Alderaan's destruction. The worst aspects of the Empire, the very things Ransolm hoped to wipe away in a new order, were the elements of control these people most wanted to bring back.

One man, who served as chief of staff for Lady Carise Sindian, even said, "Lord Vader was nearly a second Emperor. One totally loyal to Palpatine yet capable of exercising ultimate authority in his own right. Can you imagine any leader today commanding such obedience?"

Ransolm turned as if to refill his own glass, because he knew he could not disguise the contempt on his face. *To talk about Vader as if he were* admirable. *To praise the way Vader followed orders, even when those orders were to work people to death in his factories while their starving children watched—*

He took a deep breath, composed himself, and returned to the gathering with a smile on his face. The small hypocrisies of politics had to be mastered.

Once everyone had departed and the cleaning droids were hard at work, Ransolm sat at his desk for a while, staring at his collection. It looked so handsome now with the red Royal Guard mask at the center of the far wall. He'd worked for years to bring all the pieces together, and he still felt proud of them.

But he was no longer proud to be counted among the others who valued these artifacts. To him, the Imperial relics stood for strength. To the others, they stood for domination.

At last, Lady Carise thought as the cloth-of-gold mantle was settled on her shoulders. *At last I have a title of my own.*

She knelt in the Great Hall of Birren, at the head of a crowd of hundreds, before their Arbiter. After weeks of ritual and ceremony, she was finally being given the symbolic tokens of leadership—mantle and scepter, to show that she would both shelter and defend her people.

In spirit, at least. Lady Carise had no intention of removing herself from the central position of the Galactic Senate to administrate on a backwater world like Birren. But the Birrenese didn't expect her to; in fact, they seemed to regard the ceremonies almost as a nuisance. Insolent, she thought, but irrelevant.

When she strode through the Great Hall with the mantle on her shoulders and the scepter in her hands, applause rang out, and the new governor had finally completed her rituals. She had planned a grand fête for the evening with plenty of fireworks and music, and she intended to arrive in style.

"No need to do this today, milady governor." The Warden of the Treasures was a stout woman of middle years, respectful but puzzled by Lady Carise's insistence. "You've plenty of time to go through Lord Mellowyn's things."

"The ball doesn't begin for another few hours." Lady Carise's shoulders ached under the weight of the mantle. "We might as well begin."

With resignation, the warden consented, switching all the locks to align with Lady Carise's fingerprints and retinal scans. The older woman bowed as she backed out, leaving Lady Carise alone.

Leaning forward, Lady Carise let the scanners check her eyes and her hands, though impatience made it hard for her to stand still. Birren's connections to the Elder Houses went back for centuries. Who knew what priceless items awaited inside? She wouldn't have taken any of them away from Birren; she took her role as governor seriously, and would not have abandoned her honor for a few jewels or a little gold. But she could use any of these things while on this world. If there were an exceptionally alluring gemstone necklace, or a sparkling tiara, here in the chamber—wouldn't it be a shame to let them sit neglected when she could instead wear them tonight?

Heavy gears turned and clicked within the enormous lock, whining like whalesong. The tall bronze doors swung open at last, and in the darkness only vague shapes could be seen. Enthralled, Lady Carise motioned the candledroids forward, dashed in after them, and stopped.

This is it?

The treasures of Birren added up to no more than a couple of moldering old chests, some gilded furnishings that had seen better days, three or four obsolete droids waiting to be reawakened, and a few bits of jewelry that had more shine than substance. Lady Carise picked up one of the bracelets, sniffed, and let it fall again. So much for her hopes of grandeur.

Annoyed and bored, with nothing to do until she readied herself for the ball, Lady Carise began poking around amid the "treasures," trying to guess why any of it would have been kept. Did the droids have sentimental value, perhaps? Did someone think that atrocious style of furniture would come back into fashion? Not likely, in her opinion.

Just when she began to think she might as well leave, she lifted a carved wooden box and saw that it had been engraved: FOR PRINCESS LEIA ORGANA OF ALDERAAN.

Lady Carise perked up. Lord Mellowyn must have wanted to give some sort of present to his successor, whom he would have assumed would be Princess Leia. By delivering this box to the princess, Lady Carise would fulfill her sacred duty as governor and, perhaps, finally win some respect from Leia. It was about time.

And if there happened to be jewelry in there worth the wearing—well—the princess wouldn't mind if Lady Carise borrowed it just once, for a special occasion.

She sat in one of the gilded chairs and opened the box. Wrinkling her nose, she began to paw through the useless things there: a tiny doll no taller than her hand; a small, soft blanket of fine gillendown; a hexagonal, mirrored music box; a ring sized for a tiny finger; and a lock of dark-brown hair tied at either end with ribbon. These were childhood mementos, no more.

So much for the jewelry, but after taking a moment to think it over,

Lady Carise decided this was even better. Princess Leia would no doubt become emotional upon receiving these. She would be even more grateful to Lady Carise. Yes, this would work very well.

Idly, Lady Carise picked up the music box and opened it. She recognized the song immediately; it was a traditional Alderaanian lullaby, one Carise's grandmother had sung when she felt sentimental about her homeworld. The words welled in her memory:

> Mirrorbright, shines the moon, its glow as soft as an ember
> When the moon is mirrorbright, take this time to remember
> Those you have loved but are gone
> Those who kept you so safe and warm
> The mirrorbright moon lets you see
> Those who have ceased to be
> Mirrorbright shines the moon, as fires die to their embers
> Those you loved are with you still—
> The moon will help you remember

It was a sadder song than Lady Carise had realized. What a thing to sing to children. Nor had Alderaan ever had a moon. Probably it was symbolic, she thought. Poetic. The sort of nonsense Alderaanians put so much stock in.

The music dropped slightly in volume, which usually meant a voice would start singing along. But instead a man began speaking.

"*My beloved daughter,*" he said. "*The supreme governor of Birren, whom I trust completely, said that he would keep this here for you when you someday inherit this title. My hope is that this recording contains no new information, that I have had the chance to explain everything to you myself.*"

Lady Carise realized the speaker could only be Bail Organa. She covered her mouth with her hand, eyes wide, as she listened to the voice of a man now dead nearly thirty years, speaking for his daughter's ears only.

Organa continued, "*However, I make this recording during a time of increasing danger for our Rebellion. I know too well that I may not survive the war that is surely to come. By hiding the information here, on a world of no significance to the Empire, I hope to keep it out of the wrong hands and deliver it into yours. For this is knowledge you—and only you—have the right to possess.*"

Probably he would now start going on about war secrets, no longer secret, about a war that had ended decades ago. Lady Carise rolled her eyes, deciding Princess Leia would probably like this even more. She loved nothing so much as reminding the galaxy what a great war hero she'd been. A recording like this from her father would be marvelous propaganda fodder. How long before it was played for the public as part of Princess Leia's campaign to be First Senator?

"*You've never expressed much interest in knowing about your birth parents,*" Organa said. "*So many times, you've told your mother and me we are the only father and mother you've ever needed—and never doubt how much that means to us both. But Leia, the story of your origin is one you must know. You were hidden with us, for your own safety, and for that of your brother. Yes, you have a twin brother, though you must not seek him until the war has ended, and both Palpatine and Lord Vader have been defeated.*"

Princess Leia's brother was the Jedi Luke Skywalker. Why would Bail Organa have forbidden his daughter to seek Skywalker out? And what was this mysterious origin story? Lady Carise leaned closer, and the glinting light from the mirrored surface of the music box reflected on her face.

Organa said, "*Obi-Wan Kenobi took your brother for safekeeping, and I took you. We hid you both from each other, and from your father, who could not know that any child of his had been born alive. You see, Leia, I always told you the truth about your mother and how she died. But I never told you that she was Padmé Amidala, former queen and senator of the planet Naboo.*"

A war orphan and yet a royal by birth? Surprised as Lady Carise was, she decided that made sense. Leia's nobility was indeed in her blood.

But Bail Organa continued, "*Nor could I share that your father was Anakin Skywalker, one of the last Jedi Knights and a great hero of the*

Clone Wars. But now I must tell you the worst, and you must be strong. I must tell you what became of Anakin Skywalker."

Lady Carise's hand gripped the music box more tightly as she listened to the next few seconds, her astonishment coalescing into dread as Bail Organa spelled out the entire truth of a man's descent into darkness—and yet she was unprepared for the moment she heard the words.

"Your father has become Darth Vader."

She snapped the music box shut, silencing Organa's voice. Then she dropped the music box back in the small chest, after which she shut it, too. Lady Carise put the chest on the floor, kicked it farther from her, decided that wasn't far enough, and got out of her chair to back away from the thing until her shoulder blades collided with the chamber's stone wall. Dazed, almost faint, she kept staring at the small wooden chest that held a secret with the power to change the course of the galaxy.

Darth Vader was the father of Princess Leia.

Of Luke Skywalker, too, but this detail was nearly irrelevant to Lady Carise. Skywalker had been so long away on his strange quest for the lore of the Jedi that he no longer had much influence outside his own acolytes. He was a figure of myth more than one of flesh and blood.

Princess Leia, however—she had power. If she were elected First Senator, she would become the ultimate authority in the entire galaxy.

But the child of a figure so widely hated as Darth Vader could never win that election.

Lady Carise realized she had been given the one thing that could ensure victory for the Centrists. The untouchable, unimpeachable heroine, Leia Organa, could be toppled off her pedestal forever merely by playing this recording in public.

Yet she had taken all the sacred oaths of the governorship of Birren. Those oaths matched the ones shared by most of the Elder Houses, which included keeping any secret under the royal seal— and the entire chamber of treasures was under such a seal. If Lady

Carise exposed this recording and let Princess Leia's true parentage be known, she would have broken her sacred vow. She would have betrayed the royal seal. It would be the same as saying that nobility meant nothing.

But Princess Leia is a liar and a fraud! She's kept this secret from everyone all these years. Didn't we deserve to know?

Then again, perhaps the princess didn't even know the truth. Bail Organa had probably never had the chance to tell his daughter any of this, since the recording made it clear he thought it would be dangerous for her to seek her brother before the end of the war. Somehow Princess Leia had learned his identity, and her mother's, too—which implied she knew the truth about her father as well—but that implication was far from proof.

It took only a few moments for Lady Carise to make her decision. Nobility was more important than rabble-rousing. A royal seal had to remain inviolate. She could fulfill her oath and keep this secret, maybe even from Princess Leia herself.

However, she intended to hold on to the chest and its contents.

Just in case.

CHAPTER
TWENTY

"I could get used to this," Joph said.

Greer gave him a sideways glance as she brought their ancient Y-wing into orbit around the space station. "Running around under assumed names? Not telling anyone where we're really going? Following orders Princess Leia might not actually have the legal authority to give?"

"*Exactly.*" He folded his hands behind his head as he leaned back in the chair, his thick golden hair the least convincing halo imaginable. Sometimes, despite his youth and sunny disposition, Joph Seastriker's yen for trouble made him come across more like a potential smuggler than a New Republic pilot.

"You still crave excitement." Greer shook her head as she began signaling for a docking berth. "Wait until you get some."

"Come on! We're on a secret mission, we've already saved the princess from kidnapping once, and I even rigged a mobster's satellites.

That absolutely, one hundred percent counts as excitement." His blue eyes narrowed, momentarily less innocent, more searching. "You know, there's something I don't get. At this point, you've proved a thousand times that you don't like playing it safe. So why do you keep pretending that you do?"

Greer remembered the day she'd walked away from her racer, the way Han Solo's hands had closed over hers as he said a gruff goodbye to her that would allow them both to pretend there weren't tears in her eyes. "You're still a kid, aren't you? You still think recklessness is a virtue, or that you can only prove you're brave by risking your life. Staying alive as long as you can to do some good in this world—" The word caught in her throat, but she pushed on. "That's not playing it safe. That's our *job*."

Joph sat up, suddenly serious, his expression gentler than she'd known it could be. He'd finally glimpsed some shadow of the truth she tried so hard to hide. "Hey, if there's something I ought to know—or something we need to talk about, whatever—you know you can tell me, right?"

"There's nothing worth telling." A green light on the console began flashing: docking clearance granted. "Let's go in," Greer said, focusing on the task at hand and, she hoped, changing the subject.

She and Joph had scrounged up the cheapest used ship they could find, one so battered that buying it was less expensive than renting anything else. Greer thought it might have been banged up in the Clone Wars and patched back into service every few years since. Any two young pilots flying around in a ship this rickety would obviously be hungry for work of any kind, at any price.

When they'd gone to Pamarthe, they'd wanted to come across as pilots looking for a job. Now they needed to actually *get* a job—one that would take them to Sibensko.

Space stations generally served as military outposts and had for generations; some planets kept their own civilian stations operational, primarily for the use of pleasure craft. But this station, adrift in deep space, was unique. Abandoned by asteroid miners more than a century earlier, it had been taken over by smugglers, slavers, and others who valued a place to do business where no planetary laws applied. Any repairs and updates to the station had been undertaken by individual spicerunners and low-life pilots, when and if these individuals happened to notice something that required fixing, when and if they had the time, money, and inclination to actually do something about it.

As such, the space station Chrome Citadel looked like it might fall apart at any second.

The various repairs appeared to have been piecemeal at best. Chrome Citadel's rough conical hull had been patched with different shades and types of metal—its namesake shiny surface long since buried beneath layers of duller stuff—and many sensors that would normally be shielded within station atmosphere had instead simply been bolted on wherever they would fit. Although the work was inconsistent and shoddy, it had somehow been enough to keep the thing going despite its dilapidation.

Only desperate people would come here, Greer thought as she brought their ship in for docking. *Anyone else would stay far away.*

Joph looked askance at a particularly dodgy bit of patchwork near one of the main vents. "Are we sure about the atmospheric controls in there? Because this thing seems like it might vent all its air any second."

Greer shrugged. "Only one way to find out."

Inside the Chrome Citadel, chaos ruled. As Joph and Greer walked from their docking port, they merged with the busy foot traffic of a few dozen species, each one a pilot or a trader, several of them familiar from WANTED holos in respectable spaceports, most of them probably very dangerous. Every corridor was lined with makeshift stalls selling everything from dehydrated deep-space rations to fashionable headscarves. Greer bought a red one and knotted it around her thick black hair as she saw some of the bush pilots do. While both she and Joph had worn loose, rumpled coveralls, they still looked too tidy and respectable for the rough crew in this place.

Joph, also, had noticed that they stuck out, and they quickly stopped at one of the nearest stalls. "What do you think they'd do if they knew?" he murmured as he strapped on the leather tool harness he'd just bought.

After taking a long look at the motley crowd of humans and non-humans, every one of them armed, Greer said, "If they knew, we'd be thrown out of the nearest air lock."

He nodded toward one farther down the corridor, which looked as though it had been painted and enameled over dozens of times since it was last opened. "At least it looks like most of the air locks don't work."

Greer sighed. "We've got that going for us, then."

A group of Ottegans swaggered past, smelling faintly of spice. Humans with their red hair plaited in ropes bickered with a droid shop-keeper about the cost of a new welding torch. A Hassk woman kept her furred hand on her blaster, eyes darting toward every passage and corner, never relaxing her guard for a moment.

"Hey," Joph murmured, nudging Greer's shoulder. "Check that out."

She followed his gaze toward a stall near the far curve of this corridor. Amid the booths hawking flasks of counterfeit Corellian brandy and scan-proof shipping containers was one that sold decorative trinkets—flags, holocubes, good-luck charms, decals, and such.

And hanging amid the flags, front and center, was the banner of the Empire.

Other Imperial emblems showed up as well: a holo of a benevolently smiling Palpatine, taken from some old propaganda message, and decals in the shape of the Imperial insignia. But they were only a handful of the items on display, crowded in among popular characters from holocomedies or galactic folklore, colorful abstract patterns, and even the insignias of the New Republic and the old Rebel Alliance. Greer tried to put things in perspective. "They're kitsch. The stuff our parents and grandparents owned, so people buy them ironically. More a joke than anything else."

"I dunno." Joph shook his head. "It makes the Empire look like—like something out of a story. Something that wasn't real. If you ask me, buying stuff like that and showing it off like it's no big deal—it disrespects the old rebel pilots, you know? They went up against the

Death Stars in *X-wings.* And we're repaying them by treating Palpatine like he was only a bogeyman out of a kids' story?"

On most worlds, the seediest cantina was where the most lucrative, least legal jobs were to be found. On the Chrome Citadel, the cantina was nearly the one place people *didn't* seek work. It was only for drinking, dancing, and checking the room for any member of the genders and species you found attractive. Work was instead traded openly at the station's highest point, the tip of the cone, via an open message market.

"Look sharp," Greer murmured as she and Joph walked into the room, where various electronic display boards shone with rapidly scrolling messages, rows and rows of them, each promising work at a certain level of pay. Pilots crowded around, standing near small, waist-height consoles with quick key-in controls; Greer remembered these from some of the less upright areas of Pamarthe, where people sought her homeworld's famously daring fliers. "These jobs go to whoever punches in fastest."

Joph frowned. "Who'd post work here instead of vetting the pilots themselves? This is supposed to be sensitive stuff, right? The kind of things you don't want to get caught doing?"

"Exactly." She kept her eyes focused on the board, scanning as many messages simultaneously as possible. "The kind of thing you don't want to get caught hiring people for, much more likely to be illegal than anything they'd advertise for on Pamarthe. Message rooms like this transfer the risk to the pilots, which pretty much guarantees the work here is the most dangerous of all."

In other words, precisely where they were likely to find work connected to Arliz Hadrassian, Rinnrivin Di, or the Amaxine warriors.

LIVE CARGO TO NAL HUTTA NO QUESTIONS ASKED—that would be a call for a slaver. Greer's lip curled in disgust.

200 KILOS GS FROM KEREV DOI TO TATOOINE—no doubt *GS* stood for "glitterstim."

BOUNTY ANNOUNCED FOR LIVE CAPTURE OF SMUGGLER IN ARREARS, IDENTITY AND IMAGES OF QUARRY ON ACCEPTANCE ONLY—*bounty hunters, too?* Greer shuddered.

Joph's hand shot past her to hit the console, tagging one of the jobs.

Only as the message faded from the scrolling screens and appeared on the console in front of them did she see its words: TRANSPORT MATÉRIEL FROM DAXAM IV TO SIBENSKO, DISCRETION VALUED.

"Quick eye," she said to Joph.

"Thanks." He was trying hard not to sound too proud of himself, and failing.

The console's glow shifted to red as another message appeared at the bottom of their screen. ACCEPT OR DECLINE TO RE-RELEASE JOB. Swiftly Greer hit the button that said ACCEPT.

After hours of debate at the Populist meeting that night, most of which had been spent blaming the Centrist ministers for the Napkin Bombing with much invective and little proof, Leia had a headache, a prickly temper, and a strong desire to do nothing more strenuous than laying her head on her pillow. But just after she'd changed into her nightgown, the very moment she reached for her bedcovers to pull them back, her comm unit blinked with a new message.

She thought maybe it would be from Han, but instead found the message was encoded. After C-3PO had been roused from his re-charging station and translated it for her, whatever disappointment Leia felt at not hearing from her husband had evaporated in a blaze of excitement.

"We couldn't have asked for anything better," she said as she paced the floor of her main room, the long hem of her nightgown swirling around her feet. "This gives us a direct link between Daxam Four and Sibensko."

"Yes, Your Highness." C-3PO, ever eager to please, had to serve as sounding board. "Do you think Mistress Sonnel and Lieutenant Sea-striker will be taking on cargo that is, shall we say, incriminating?"

"The job specified *matériel*. That almost always means armaments, explosives, items necessary for military action." Leia paused, thump-ing her hand against the back of her long sofa. "It's possible the work may be entirely legal. The Amaxine warriors might be hiring like this only because they hope to keep this secret. Still, it doesn't matter. We don't need to catch them committing a crime . . . at least, not yet. We only need to get ourselves into Sibensko, and this job should do that."

"I beg your pardon, Your Highness, but it sounds as if—" C-3PO's pause was broken only by the sound of his internal gears whirring as he turned toward her. "—why, rather as if you intended to accompany Mistress Sonnel and Lieutenant Seastriker on their mission."

Leia hadn't realized that. Hadn't consciously made a decision one way or the other, and had hardly even acknowledged there was a decision to be made. Yet the droid's programming analyzed human conversation so thoroughly that he sometimes pointed out subtleties she'd missed.

"I guess it does sound like that," she said slowly. "I guess I do."

"But, Princess Leia!" C-3PO's voice rose in alarm. "You can't! The mission sounds terribly dangerous."

"Threepio, in the quarter century you've served me, have you ever known me to run away from danger?"

"Well. No." The droid considered this a moment before adding hopefully, "Yet you might eventually develop a stronger instinct for survival."

Leia couldn't help laughing. "Don't count on it."

C-3PO never thought faster than when he was trying to keep himself out of the latest round of trouble. "Captain Solo would no doubt be highly concerned."

"Captain Solo once piloted us into an asteroid field, remember? He doesn't get to lecture anyone on taking risks. Anyway, I outrank him."

"But you cannot leave Hosnian Prime at this point in the political process! Your candidacy will be officially announced within a few weeks. Then your presence within the Galactic Senate will be crucial. Surely there will be appearances to coordinate on other worlds as well."

He had a point. Once she became an official candidate, the demands on Leia's time would increase exponentially. She would be expected to give speeches on planets from the Galactic Core to the Expansion Region. Broadcasters would clamor for interviews; Greer would have to schedule studio time for holos to be distributed galaxy-wide, showing Leia speaking about her policy proposals. Above all, she'd need to be active in the Senate, demonstrating that she was engaged, dynamic, and committed.

In other words, as soon as she became a candidate, Leia would have time for nothing else—especially not secret missions that might take down what looked likely to be the biggest spice cartel in the galaxy.

She shut her eyes and took a deep breath. "You're right. As soon as my nomination as First Senator becomes official, I won't have time for this."

C-3PO practically preened. "I am glad to have been of service—"

"Which is why we have to get to Sibensko *before* the announcement."

"Oh, no," the droid said. "If you'll pardon me for saying so, Your Highness, won't any absence from the Senate be seen as a potential lack of commitment? Appearances are so important."

She shook her head. "I've given my life to duty since I was fourteen years old. Anyone who doubts my 'commitment' at this point is a fool whose opinion I can safely ignore."

"Of course, Your Highness."

"So my trip to Sibensko is *on*."

C-3PO paused again. "This means danger, doesn't it?"

"You'd better believe it." Leia flopped down on her sofa, smiling. "Bring up my calendars, will you? I want to start thinking about the best time to do this."

Shuffling toward the nearest information bank, C-3PO wistfully said, "It's enough to make one wish to go back to programming binary loadlifters."

The duel on Daxam IV had gone well, but it had also reminded Ransolm Casterfo that he had to keep his skills sharp. Since it appeared he had a use for this sort of thing even now that he was a senator, he didn't intend to let himself get rusty.

In the stark-white training chamber, he remained stock-still, poised with the quarterstaff in his hand. His formfitting gray work-out gear had been drenched with sweat for a long time now, but Ransolm remained determined to press on. Most people neglected training with non-powered weapons; these were the same people who got themselves killed because their blasters ran out of charge. He intended to be able to fight with whatever was at hand, whether as sophisticated as the latest model of vibroblade or as brutish as a long stick.

The projectors in the corners of the training chamber shimmered, creating the illusion of a Mandalorian warrior with a blaster in his hand. Instantly Ransolm swung upward, striking the blaster's muzzle with his quarterstaff. The holographic bolts shot uselessly over Ransolm's head. Although the pre-programmed Mandalorian attempted to compensate, skidding back into a crouch, Ransolm was ready for him. With one savage thrust, he plunged the end of the quarterstaff through the Mandalorian's head—even faster than the man would've been able to fire. The holo shimmered into nothingness.

Ransolm smiled. He'd won again.

After another few rounds, once his muscles were quivering and his empty belly demanded food, Ransolm finally headed back to his quarters. A swift ride on the border monorail took him to his apartment, which was a fairly humble one by senatorial standards. But what was the point in spending a lot of money on a place where he lived alone, and that he used only to sleep? His was a bachelor apartment, with utilitarian furnishings that had come with the place, in a combination of the gray and orange colors so in vogue at the moment as to be completely generic. Stashing his quarterstaff in his equipment closet, Ransolm began settling in for the evening. He rubbed his sweat-damp hair with a towel, slung that around his neck, and began searching through the kitchen to see whether anything edible remained.

His comm unit blinked; someone was calling. Ransolm quickly went to the unit to answer. As he hit the panel, a holo of Princess Leia took shape within his living room.

"Leia?" He smiled as he sat heavily on his sofa, spreading his weary arms across the back. "To what do I owe the honor? It's rather late for a social call."

Her lips quirked, evidence of the excitement she was trying to hold back. "Would you consider an invitation to Sibensko 'social'?"

"You're joking," he breathed. "However did Greer and Joph manage it?"

"They went to the right place, snagged the right job. They'll be transporting matériel. Schedule is somewhat flexible, it seems, but they'll need to act soon."

"*Outstanding.*"

"I intend to go with them."

She grinned at Ransolm then in unconcealed anticipation. In that moment, it occurred to him that, in her zeal, she'd contacted him wearing only a housecoat tossed over her nightgown. How the gossips would talk if they knew he and Leia spoke like this late in the evening. But gossips were fools, and Ransolm valued her lack of artifice. Leia hadn't held the truth back from him for a moment.

After his first flush of enthusiasm, however, came doubt. "I hesitate to point this out, Leia, but our first mission to Bastatha was fully endorsed by the Senate. Our work on Ryloth, Harloff Minor, and Daxam Four was either authorized or, technically, unofficial and entirely legal."

"True," Leia said with an eloquent shrug. "Anyone can have a dinner guest on Harloff Minor. Anyone can buy a Royal Guard helmet if he wants."

Ransolm gave her a look. "But using New Republic pilots and ships to take on potentially illegal work—traveling to a world known for criminal activity, under what I assume will be false identification—you may well be overstepping your authority as a senator."

She remained unfazed. "That's also true."

"I feel the need to point out that such a mission will no doubt be extremely dangerous."

"I can't deny it."

Ransolm leaned closer to his comm unit. "*I want in.*"

Leia's smile would have turned the night to day. "You know, I had a funny feeling you were going to say that."

"You know me so well."

She became more serious then. "If by some chance you hadn't of-fered, I would have asked you along. If a Populist senator on her own went out of bounds and came back with proof of a conspiracy based on Centrist worlds? At best I'd be laughed off the Senate floor. At worst, I'd be censured, In either case, no one would believe me. But your presence on the mission gives us credibility. If we're able to prove the connections I think this trip to Sibensko will prove, and you and I present our evidence to the Senate together—we might just have a chance to make them listen."

"We will," Ransolm said. "I'm sure of it."

Leia raised an eyebrow. "You have more confidence in the Galactic Senate than I do."

Sometimes she sounded so jaded, so cynical, even though she had been an idealistic revolutionary in her youth. Maybe a quarter century of politics did that to a person—at least, politics the way it had always been played in the New Republic.

Ransolm Casterfo intended to change the game.

CHAPTER
TWENTY-ONE

The mission to Sibensko had to be kept secret, which meant that their meetings to plan this next adventure had to be disguised in some way. Ransolm thought the most effective thing to do would be to hide in plain sight. So he reserved a pavilion along the riverside for the Equinox Day sunsail races, one of the traditional amusements on Hosnian Prime.

In ancient times, it seemed, the equinox had been marked with boat races, and to this day racers traversed a course that followed the river's winding path. People had gathered along the banks of the river, whether in verdigris-tinted pavilions or on blankets spread upon the grass; the massive capital city skyline seemed more distant than it was, contrasted with the simpler pleasures on offer here. Picnics were brought out by droids that rolled unevenly across the soft ground, or on hovertrays owned by the wealthier or wiser. A few floating pods bobbed in the air only a meter or so above the water, each holding aloft a dozen or more spectators eager for the race. Autumn had officially begun, but on this day the sun still shone warmly. In every sense the day felt like a celebration, and soon the preliminary air show would get started.

"How did you get out of the show?" Ransolm asked Joph Sea striker, the first of his guests to arrive. "Aren't you one of their star pilots?"

"You'd better believe it." Joph's blue eyes scanned the sky wistfully. "I told the truth—said Senator Organa wanted to discuss some of my work for her. You know, I don't think my commander even checked. You say her name, and people straighten up."

"Woe betide anyone who doesn't," Ransolm said, but fondly. "When will Ms. Sonnel and young Korr Sella be joining us?"

With a shake of his head, Joph said, "Korrie's not coming. The mission's too dangerous for her to take part in, and Greer and Princess Leia figured they shouldn't stick Korrie in a position where she could be accused of hiding information from the Senate."

"Sensible." Then his gaze caught a familiar figure approaching in a coral-colored dress. Greer was almost unrecognizable—because of both her unexpectedly festive clothing and the wide smile on her face. It had not occurred to Ransolm before this moment that even when Greer Sonnel was satisfied or enthusiastic, she rarely seemed *happy . . .*

"Hey there." Greer came up the pavilion steps, her shining black hair swaying behind her. In her hands she held a small bag containing something that seemed to be cylindrical and heavy. "Are we talking strategy right away, or do we first pretend to have a party?"

"I imagine we'll mix the two." In the distance, Ransolm could now see C-3PO toddling toward them; Leia couldn't be far off. "Is this your offering for the celebration?"

Greer's smile had turned positively sly. "A little something Joph was curious about on Pamarthe." She reached into the bag and pulled out a heavy glass bottle filled with reddish-amber liquid. "Here you go, fellas. Genuine, high-octane, Pamarthen Port in a Storm."

Smugly, Joph said, "You finally realize I can handle it, huh?"

She arched one thick, wing-shaped eyebrow. "Let's say I want to watch you try."

Ransolm took the bottle into his hands, surprised at its heft. He'd heard of Port in a Storm—the famous fortified wine of Pamarthe that had a reputation for taking even the strong to their knees. But many worlds had such stories; people from every single planet in the galaxy bragged about having the most powerful intoxicants, the spiciest food, or the worst weather. Everyone needed to stand out as the toughest of all. In reality, however, it was a big galaxy, which meant true extremes were hard to come by. "If Lieutenant Seastriker is bold enough to sample it, I'll have a glass myself."

"Brave man," Greer said with a smile. "Who brought the glasses?"

The pavilion had been duly stocked with a set. Ransolm placed glasses on the table, and Greer filled them approximately halfway—maybe three fingers' worth. He lifted his and held it out toward the others. "A toast. To Princess Leia."

"To Princess Leia," Joph and Greer replied. In unison they tipped back their glasses. He felt the sweetness and burn in his mouth, and then—

Ransolm had never asked himself what it might feel like if fireworks were set off within a human body. Now he knew. His eyes widened as the fireball expanded within him, like a yellow dwarf star becoming a red giant. Noise seemed to fade for an instant, though he could hear Joph's sputtering cough. Ransolm's dazed brain decided red giants weren't hot enough to describe what was happening inside him. Maybe this was how supernovae got started.

When he could speak again, Ransolm rasped, "That cannot be meant for human consumption."

Greer shrugged, sipping her glass of Port in a Storm as though it were fruit juice. Meanwhile, Joph had lowered his head onto the table, face down, hands bracing either side of his head. Ransolm put down his glass and pushed it away; even the smell of it seemed likely to ignite his nose from the inside out.

"Sorry I'm late." Leia came up the pavilion steps, C-3PO just behind her. But she stopped short when she saw what was on the table. "Port in a Storm? You're actually drinking that?"

"Not any longer." Ransolm grimaced but was able to keep back a shudder.

Joph whispered, "I think my skull is melting."

"This is dangerous stuff." Leia gave her chief of staff a stern look, which cowed Greer not one jot. "I've only ever known one person who could tolerate this who wasn't a native of Pamarthe."

"Captain Solo?" Joph said, without lifting his face from the table.

Leia shook her head. "Chewbacca—a Wookiee friend of ours. Han would never touch this."

"On the contrary, Your Highness," C-3PO interjected as he stiffly made his way up the steps. "Captain Solo has been known to use Port in a Storm on a few occasions."

"Really?" Leia's expression was so startled Ransolm might have laughed, if his throat hadn't felt like it would burst into flame at any moment. "Han actually drinks Port in a Storm?"

The droid put one metal hand to his chest as though begging her pardon. "Oh, no, indeed. However, Captain Solo has sometimes employed it during ship repairs as an emergency solvent."

"Figures." With that, Leia pointed at Joph, who was only now sitting up again, expression dazed. "No more of this until we're done. A glass of wine is one thing—but we need to stay sharp."

"Agreed," Ransolm said. Anything to avoid drinking the deadly stuff again.

To Leia's relief, everyone proved able to concentrate on the task at hand despite the drinks—even if Joph's eyes remained slightly unfocused, and his first questions were hesitant. "Shouldn't we go right away, before Arliz Hadrassian or Rinnrivin Di can catch on?"

Leia breathed a small sigh of thanks for the sonic neutralizer she'd tucked into the pocket of her mauve tunic. Even if any of the merry picnickers around them were inclined to pay more attention to this conversation than the sunsail races wafting by overhead, they wouldn't be able to hear a word spoken by anyone within the pavilion.

Greer explained, "We have to follow the timetable we were given along with the job."

"But they're smugglers," Joph said hoarsely. "Or gunrunners, or whatever. They're not exactly people who do stuff by the book."

"Which is why they're so quick to get suspicious." Han and Chewie's stories had told Leia this much. "If a legitimate pilot turns up early, it's a minor inconvenience at most. If an illegal pilot turns up early—they're trying something. And everyone involved knows it."

Greer nodded. "For whatever reason, the Amaxine warriors don't even want us to pick up the matériel until next week. If we show up early, we'll tip them off."

"Speaking of tipping them off," Ransolm said, "Arliz Hadrassian could potentially be on Sibensko when our team arrives, and by now she's seen every single one of us. She believes Greer is my staffer, and she'll recognize Joph from Bastatha. If Hadrassian's present when they arrive to pick up the shipment, we've got trouble."

"That's where the disguises come in." Leia smiled, reliving old memories. "An Ubese bounty hunter's mask for Joph, maybe, and some kind of armor for Greer? With false IDs, tints for their hair, and the right clothing, they'll pass easily enough."

"That works." Those two hoarse words set Joph coughing again; Greer patted his back.

Let's hope he recovers in time, Leia thought. Overhead the sunsails swooped by, their brilliant red sails capturing the heat and transforming it to energy that would keep a skillful pilot aloft. Amid the crowd's cheering, she added, "Besides, I have a feeling Hadrassian won't be handling the transfer personally. She needs some plausible deniability."

"So do we," Ransolm pointed out. "You and I stood before the entire Senate and announced the need to investigate Rinnrivin Di in depth. I suspect a few tongues have been wagging about our simultaneous journeys offworld recently. If we take off together again, suspicions will be raised publicly. Assuming Rinnrivin or Hadrassian has a source within the Senate, we'll be tipping our hands."

"A source in the Senate?" Joph gaped at him. "Nobody would do that. Come on. Being a senator gets you all the power and prestige you'd have to kill for as a smuggler, without risking your own skin."

"No, Ransolm's right. I'm almost certain they have someone." Leia had come to this conclusion on her own. She had dreaded having to convince the idealistic young Casterfo of this, but once again he had outpaced her expectations. "If the Amaxine warriors are linked to the Napkin Bombing, they had to have intel from someone who understood the Senate inside and out, both physically and organizationally. Maybe any skilled slicer could've exposed the plans of the building, but finding out that a meeting of Populist ministers was taking place at breakfast? Even knowing which place setting was likely to be mine? That's inside information, and only someone at a high level could get it."

Greer hugged herself as if against a chill, even as the afternoon sun made her black hair shine almost blue. "So not only are we up against some Empire-worshipping group of zealots, but we also have to deal with their ally inside the Senate—in other words, some Centrist senator who has the power to take us all out."

"At least that's what it looks like." Leia kept her attention on Ransolm, who had pressed his lips together tightly and glanced away when Greer spoke the word *Centrist*.

They talked through the rest of the plans: how to get to Sibensko, how Leia and Ransolm would manage to accompany them, and the likeliest sources on Sibensko for the information they would need. Even after the meeting ended, however, they lingered to watch the races, the sunsail gliders dipping closer to the water as the afternoon's light began to fade.

When darkness fell, the fireworks began. Joph excused himself to hang out with some friends; Greer declared she needed to go to bed early. "And why don't I take you by the lubrication baths?" Greer said to C-3PO while she put the Port in a Storm back in its bag. "You're overdue."

"That does sound festive. How very courteous of you, Mistress Sonnel."

"I try." Greer gave Leia a farewell smile. As she walked away, the coral of her dress and C-3PO's golden sheen fading into the crowd, Ransolm said, "She must have a lover, then."

Leia gave him a look. "I wouldn't have taken you for a gossip."

"I'm uninterested in rumors. I only meant—early to bed? It's a rather transparent excuse for leaving, and why leave a gathering so pleasant? Something far more enjoyable must await her."

"Greer's entitled to her personal life." Leia considered Ransolm's profile for a few moments as the fireworks blossomed gold and white behind him. "You were unhappy with her, earlier. When she said Centrist senators had to be linked to the Amaxine warriors."

Ransolm stared resolutely at the fireworks even as he answered. "I recognize that it's someone within the Centrist party—or claiming to be—who has to be behind this. But one rogue shouldn't be allowed to stain our entire philosophy. What I resent is the implication that all Centrists would be sympathetic to the terroristic acts of a paramilitary group."

"Obviously that's not true, or you wouldn't be here." Although Leia felt more optimistic about the potential for growth within the Centrist philosophy since getting to know Ransolm Casterfo, he remained an outlier within his party. "But I suspect more than 'one rogue' is sympathetic to the Amaxine warriors' aims."

His waspish temper had been provoked. "You still think we're all bloodthirsty for power."

"I think the desire for power can make people do terrible things. Walking away from power can be its own kind of strength."

"You fear authority," Ransolm said. More fireworks popped overhead, sending sprays of scarlet shimmering across the entire sky. "The government needs authority. But I cannot fault you for your caution, Leia. What you lived through at the Empire's hand—at Vader's hand—no wonder you're suspicious. During the war, I imagine paranoia was the only thing that kept you alive."

"And friendship, and love." Leia knew that Luke's selflessness in coming for her on the Death Star, and Han's unspoken devotion in saving her on Hoth, had not only kept her alive but also changed the entire course of the galaxy for the better. "Those things matter, too, maybe more than all the rest."

Ransolm's smile turned wistful. "I thought I was supposed to be the idealist."

Lady Carise had timed her return for Equinox Day on Hosnian Prime. What would make for a better entrance than appearing unexpectedly at one of the most fashionable parties? However, a problem with her transport's hyperdrive had ruined these plans completely. Although she had been delayed only half a day, that delay made the difference between her attending a gala and arriving as she did now, late at night, all celebrations winding to an end, wearily making her way through the shadowy corridors of the Senate offices after hours.

The astromech droid towing her belongings behind it on a hoverflat beeped inquisitively. Lady Carise snapped, "Of course I'd rather go home first. But one item should go straight to my office." She didn't intend to leave Bail Organa's wooden chest in an unsecured location for even an instant. Her home was safe enough, ringed with electronic sentries, but Lady Carise knew it was not invulnerable. However, the durasteel safe in her office probably couldn't have been crushed even by a black hole, and its retinal and fingerprint seals would make it very difficult for anyone else to ever gain access.

I'll present the box to her tomorrow, Lady Carise decided, one hand lifting the hem of her red-violet dress as she stepped onto one of the moving sidewalks. *As soon as that wild-eyed assistant of hers can arrange an appointment.* Lady Carise had already decided to absent herself before Princess Leia inspected the contents of the box—long before the music box was opened—but she also wanted to somehow make it very clear that she knew absolutely everything hidden inside. Princess Leia had to understand exactly how much Lady Carise knew, or else she would not be nearly as grateful. She would not realize that Lady Carise had the power to destroy her in an instant . . .

Which I won't. Violating a royal oath is unthinkable. Lady Carise nodded, impressed with her inner nobility. Yet with no sense of contradiction, she also remained completely aware that Princess Leia was more useful to her in the Senate, still in power but personally indebted to Lady Carise Sindian forever.

If Princess Leia became First Senator, Lady Carise could position herself as the one Centrist able to sway their leader. The one person who got things done. She liked the sound of that.

"Lady Carise?" Hearing her name startled her from her reverie. She looked up to see Ransolm Casterfo near the end of the sidewalk, not far from his own office door. "I hardly expected to see you here at this hour."

"I could say the same." She stepped nimbly off the sidewalk, neatly dodging her obedient astromech with a swirl of her long skirts. With a smile intended to charm, she added, "In my case, my transport from Birren was unaccountably delayed. Now, what's your excuse?"

Casterfo seemed charmed enough, leaning in closer to confide. "I decided to drop by and put in an order for some Riosan liqueur, and those orders travel faster via official channels, as I'm sure you know."

"You need to order liqueur in the middle of the night?"

"Oh, it's on my way, and I had a sudden whim after the sunsail races. You see, Greer Sonnel—that's Princess Leia's chief of staff—she treated all of us to some Port in a Storm tonight, which by the way is deadly. Stay clear. Well, I thought I'd present her with a little of our home brew. It's not nearly so noxious, but it's strong enough that I might recover a little of my pride." Casterfo sighed ruefully.

Lady Carise made sure to keep her smile on her face, just as pretty, just as bright. "My, but you seem to have become very friendly with Princess Leia's staff." She knew instinctively whom "all of us" referred to. "Is this some effort at bipartisanship? Or are you getting in good with the Populist candidate for First Senator while you can?"

Casterfo frowned. Her comment had irritated him. Good. "As you know, Princess Leia and I have worked together quite a lot recently."

"Chasing after phantoms, as I recall."

"We shall see." He politely inclined his head in a bow. "Good evening, Lady Carise."

"Good evening, Senator Casterfo."

Lady Carise watched him go, busying herself with the items on her hoverflat, her mind entirely fixated on one single, disastrous fact:

He knows.

As soon as she got to her office, the wooden chest went into her safe. Then Lady Carise shooed out the astromech droid with instructions for returning her property to her house. Once she was alone, she opened the most secure communications line she had—an unofficial one—and sent a call at highest urgency.

It was answered within seconds by the appearance of a hologram revealing the face of Arliz Hadrassian.

"Senator Sindian. To what do I owe the pleasure?"

"Pleasure! You've practically ruined our plans over and over again, and now you've tipped off Ransolm Casterfo as well? What I'm feeling at this moment is nothing remotely close to 'pleasure.'"

"*Our* plans?" Hadrassian's husky voice sharpened. "For years I have raised my army in the desert—for years I have worked and struggled and dreamed—and you call them 'our plans'?"

Lady Carise could have sneered. "Yes. Because I do not speak for myself alone, Hadrassian. Or have you forgotten your loyalties? Do you no longer wish to restore what we lost with the Empire? *Have you abandoned the First Order completely?*"

Never before had Lady Carise spoken those words out loud in her office. *The First Order.* Someday, the entire galaxy would shout them with pride, but for now they were too secret, too sacred, to be taken lightly. That dream was so close to becoming reality—only a few years away, if even that—and protecting it required discretion.

However, discretion did not appear to be one of Arliz Hadrassian's talents. "I will *not* be lectured about the Empire by a child who can't even remember it."

"Nor will I be lectured by someone careless enough to spill her secrets to Ransolm Casterfo. He knows there's more to Rinnrivin Di's operations, and he's still working to trace them to their source, which is why he went to Daxam Four in the first place. When you said the two of you were meeting, I thought it was on *your* terms—"

"It was." Hadrassian's large dark eyes narrowed. "Casterfo is a potential ally. I've been working to recruit him."

"He's playing you," Lady Carise snapped. "He's still working with Princess Leia—socializing with her, even! There's no way he's not a part of her investigations as well."

"I'm not convinced." Hadrassian lifted her chin. Her years had given her the look of someone scoured clean by the sands, down to the strongest stone. "I've seen his love for the Empire. When the time comes for the First Order, Casterfo will be the first to champion its cause."

"The time will never come if you keep ruining everything with your impatience!" Hearing her voice rise nearly to a shriek, Lady Carise paused and took a deep breath. "Was the attack on the Senate not enough for you?"

Hadrassian shrugged. "You said a distraction would be appropriate."

"I meant a scandal, or some remote wreck or crash. Not *bombing a Senate building.*" The Amaxine warriors' audacity knew no bounds. Their political savvy, however, was not nearly so expansive.

Lady Carise knew how to play the game. She portrayed herself as pretty and frivolous, a woman as interested in celebrity as power, and she did it well. So no one suspected the critical role she played in preparing the galaxy for the return of meaningful authority through the government she and other like-minded people already whispered about as the First Order. It was Lady Carise who had searched for former Imperial officers and their sympathizers among the various subcultures where they might congregate, helping to create the contacts that connected them to the surviving ships of the Imperial fleet. Lady Carise who had encouraged them as they organized from mere malcontents into the burgeoning paramilitary force known as the Amaxine warriors. And it had been Lady Carise who convinced the Centrist leaders in her faction to use the criminal front they'd already established through Rinnrivin Di to hide their funds in order to arm and train the Amaxine warriors. With weapons and training, they could, in time, serve as the shock troops in the initial battles of the great war to come.

Once the Amaxines had caused enough damage and confusion, the First Order itself could finally emerge from hiding to claim its rightful place, with the lost vessels of the Imperial fleet as its true fighting force. But paramilitary leaders turned out not to be as easy to manage as senators. Arliz Hadrassian was no politician; she was a zealot. The fire of certainty blazed in her eyes, incapable of diminishment or doubt. Sometimes Lady Carise thought the woman had arranged the Napkin Bombing less to create a distraction, and more for the sheer pleasure of destruction.

If Hadrassian's zealotry came any closer to exposing the Centrist plans for the First Order, the Amaxine warriors would have to be taken down—and Lady Carise knew she'd be dragged down with them.

"If you're so uncertain about Casterfo's loyalties," Hadrassian suggested, "take steps to ensure he remains on our side. Convince him. Convert him."

"How am I supposed to do that when he's practically become friends with Princess Leia—" Lady Carise stopped herself.

The Empire's rule of Riosa was difficult. Wasn't Casterfo orphaned? Something like that. At any rate, he's always been very clear about his contempt for Palpatine . . . and for Vader.

Hadrassian frowned. "Lady Carise?"

"I'll take care of it. For now, stick to our plans." With a flick of her hand, Lady Carise snapped the holographic connection off. She turned toward the safe, and it seemed to her that she could see through its impregnable surface, through the wooden chest of mementos inside, straight to the music box with a secret that could change the galaxy.

I cannot betray the royal seal, she thought. Lady Carise still felt that as powerfully as she had ever felt anything else.

But if it came down to the royal seal versus the rise of the First Order, what would she choose?

CHAPTER
TWENTY-TWO

If you wanted to be an ace starfighter pilot, it wasn't enough to love flying. You had to love everything that went with it, from flight pattern protocol to basic maintenance. Some guys who could fly like zephyrs washed out of the Academies because they couldn't bring themselves back down to the ground long enough to take care of their ships.

Joph Seastriker loved his X-wing down to the bolts. He relished the smell of grease and the echo within a hangar that picked up every clank of metal. And he even enjoyed plunging his arms elbow-deep inside his starfighter's workings, all because it was an indispensible part of flight.

At the moment, he lay on a mechanic's creeper beneath the X-wing's nose, peering inside an open panel to work on a tricky conduit that had been interfering with maneuverability. Amid the snarl of wires, he saw a slightly frayed connection. That wasn't necessarily the problem, but he'd take care of it and see.

"You sure you're doing okay over there, Seastriker?" shouted Ledaney, who was fixing up his own X-wing a few meters away. "Or do we need to fetch you some soda water and a fan?"

Guffaws echoed from every pilot in the place. Joph had made the mistake of being honest about his reaction to Port in a Storm, which meant he was going to spend the whole day hearing about it from guys who'd never once tried drinking the stuff.

So he shot back, "I'm good, Ledaney. But what about you? Word has it you've been hitting the Corellian stuff pretty hard lately."

This time the laughter was louder. Anybody who didn't know Ledaney would assume Joph was talking about the famed brandy, but every pilot in the squadron knew Ledaney's new man was from Corellia.

Zari Bangel, who had been strolling by, paused with hands at her tool belt, just beside Joph's repair platform. "You sure have gotten to know Senator Organa's staff pretty well, seeing as how they're sharing their intoxicants with you. Been flying all over the galaxy these days."

Joph shrugged before realizing that gesture meant nothing when you were lying down. "You know how it is, Zari. Senators pull rank, you run errands, and once they get used to you, you're pretty much along for the ride."

"Actually, that's not how it usually is," Zari replied. She leaned against the metal side of his platform, arms folded across her chest. "You've really been on the go."

"Take it up with Senator Organa," Joph said as casually as he could manage. His heart had begun to thump a little faster. If his fellow pilots became too curious about where he'd been—and why—rumors would start to spread, and the mission to Sibensko would be blown before it had ever begun.

Ledaney spoke up again. "Whatever it is you're doing is probably a lot more exciting than performing in the air shows."

Joph peered more intently into his machine, hoping to project a sense of intent concentration that would discourage chitchat. "Hmm. Guess it depends on what you'd consider exciting."

"Traveling all over the galaxy like that, taking care of business—" Zari's tone had become wistful. "—it sounds *important*."

"More important than an air show, that's for sure," added Ello Asty in his low, sonorous voice.

They're not suspicious, Joph realized. *They already* know *something's up, and they want in.*

His first impulse was to come up with an excuse, any excuse, to get out of the hangar as fast as he could. But if he'd been in their shoes, aware that adventure and purpose were out there waiting, would he have been put off that easily? Hell, no.

Joph couldn't start recruiting people for the Sibensko mission. He wasn't authorized, extra people would endanger the secret, and besides, getting even four people and one droid down into the underwater cities would be a job of work. A dozen extra pilots would only hold them back.

But if these Amaxine warriors were as dangerous and well funded as Princess Leia and Senator Casterfo seemed to think, the day might come when more pilots would be needed to go up against them. Lots more pilots. And some likely volunteers were standing here in this hangar.

"Me, I like performing in the air shows." Joph kept working on the panel, not looking at anyone, but aware his listeners would have detected a shift in his tone. "That's exciting enough for anyone . . . right?"

"Not for me," Zari said quietly.

Ledaney added, "Me either."

Others spoke up. Joph talked idly with them, all the while silently making a list of names. He'd share that list with Princess Leia soon. Might come in handy, someday. You never knew.

Under normal circumstances, Ransolm Casterfo would have had to serve another two full terms in the Galactic Senate to be senior enough to conduct troop inspections. However, he could always be invited along by another, higher-ranking senator—which was why he and Leia Organa were walking along the white-tiled corridors of the transport ship *Rieekan.* Officers lined the way, standing stiffly at attention, their facial expressions ranging from nervous to businesslike to vaguely amused.

Everything was correct, in accordance with regulations. But in Ransolm's opinion the scene lacked a certain sort of grandeur. These troops' uniform jackets and trousers weren't so far removed from daily wear; their helmets were tethered with a simple leather strap. How could such soldiers inspire awe? How could they defend others when they looked so poorly defended themselves? Proper armor such as the Empire's would have been so much more appropriate. The white helmet of a stormtrooper must have made a man feel invincible . . .

"You know, Ransolm," Leia said as they walked toward the bridge, "now that I think about it, I'm surprised you didn't join the military yourself."

"I considered it. Instead I served on Riosa's planetary security force for two years, starting when I turned eighteen." He smiled as he remembered the thrill of his first starfighter, his first blaster. "In my imagination, I saw myself chasing down smugglers and slavers every day in one brilliant battle after another."

Leia clasped her hands behind her back as she gave him a sidelong look. "And in reality?"

Ransolm sighed. "Reality involved far fewer battles, and many more citations for violating docking procedures."

Although Leia chuckled, she said, "Come on. Planetary defense forces see some action from time to time."

"We did, but not much. The fact is, Riosa's manufacturing facilities stagnated in disrepair after the Empire wore them down. Our natural resources were depleted and our banks empty. No one came to steal from our world because there was virtually nothing left to steal." They came to the bend in the corridor that would take them to the bridge, where no soldiers stood and waited. Ransolm found he was relieved; while he felt no shame talking about his world's ruin, he nonetheless was more comfortable sharing this with Leia alone. "By the time I would have either signed up for a new tour of duty or gone off to enlist in the New Republic armies, I'd decided Riosa needed political and economic help more than it needed soldiers."

"So you gave up your dream to do your duty." Leia spoke softly, as if moved.

Ransolm looked over at her. "Is that what you did?"

"No. I was raised knowing I would lead a life of service, first through my royal position and then in the Senate. By the time I turned fifteen, the Rebellion had already begun to take shape, and I knew I wanted to be a part of it." Her smile was rueful, even sad. "So I never even got around to having a dream besides my duty."

Impulsively he asked, "What would it have been? Your dream."

He wasn't sure he'd ever seen her at a loss for words before. "I— who knows? The way I saw things back then was so different from the reality I see now."

"Just guess. Or ask yourself what you'd do right now, this moment, if duty didn't stand in your way."

Leia's smile widened, became genuine. "I'd run off to traipse around the galaxy with my husband."

Naturally Ransolm knew of the famous Han Solo, and yet somehow he found it difficult to imagine Leia married to such a man, a former smuggler. "You mean you'd join him as a racer?"

"Maybe." Mischief glinted in her brown eyes. "Or maybe we'd become professional gamblers. Make our fortune at the sabacc tables."

"After the way you broke the bank on Bastatha? I believe it." They laughed together, and Ransolm was relieved that his question hadn't turned into a conversation too personal for the occasion.

Yet he knew that Leia hadn't minded his asking. Their partnership— despite its rocky start—was one he thought would outlast their investigation into Rinnrivin Di's cartel and the Amaxine warriors. More than that, Ransolm knew they had truly become friends. He'd learned as a child to keep his emotions inside; although he'd never lacked for company, he'd rarely let anyone get close.

But leave it to Leia Organa to knock down any wall in her way.

"We should say our goodbyes to the captain and head back down to the surface," Leia said. "Then again, we haven't taken a look at the main engine room yet."

"If I didn't know better, I'd say you were procrastinating."

"You wouldn't be wrong." When Ransolm frowned at her in surprise, Leia explained, "This afternoon's session is the point of no return, I guess."

"But you must have agreed to be the Populist candidate for First Senator almost as soon as the motion passed. Today's nomination on the Senate floor is only a formality."

Leia squared her shoulders like a fighter walking onto the field of combat. "I did, and you're right, it is. Like I told you before, though, I'd just as soon this honor went to someone else."

"No other Populist could do the job so well," Ransolm insisted. They stood together in the arch-ceilinged corridor, seemingly alone in the vast ship. "Given that the Centrists still haven't settled on their candidate, you may wind up winning by fiat."

"Don't remind me."

He kept his voice soothing as they resumed their stroll toward the bridge. "Look at it this way. The entire afternoon will be nothing but senators getting up to sing your praises. We'll hear about every battle, every accomplishment. In other words, this is the fun part. Try to relax and bask in the glory, hmm?"

With a sigh, Leia said, "You know, I needed to hear that. Thanks."

"Pleased to help."

Ransolm remained in a contemplative mood as they finished the official inspection and took the *Mirrorbright* back down to Hosnian Prime. He returned to the Senate complex immediately in order to prepare for the session, while Leia headed to Varish Vicly's for some sort of pre-celebratory luncheon of Populist politicians. Idly wondering whether Leia would keep the *Mirrorbright* as her official vessel after her election, Ransolm walked into his office . . .

And stopped short.

"Forgive the intrusion, Senator Casterfo." Lady Carise Sindian sat in the chair in front of his desk, wearing an elegant pearl-gray dress. "But I heard that you went to inspect the troops this morning, alongside Princess Leia."

"What of it?" Ransolm had begun to tire of Lady Carise's pretensions. "It's entirely within protocol for me to do so."

Lady Carise folded her hands in front of her chest, as if in pity. "You've become close to her. Loyal to her."

"I remain a committed Centrist, if that's what you're worried about." Even now, Ransolm planned to vote against Leia in the coming election. Unless, of course, the Centrists nominated someone completely abominable . . .

"No. That's not what I'm worried about. What frightens me— upsets me, *angers* me—is that Princess Leia is lying to you. That she has betrayed you."

A flicker of doubt stirred within him, fanned by memories of Leia's disdainful attitude when they'd first begun to work together. But that was quickly extinguished. "Forgive my bluntness, but I suspect you're being underhanded. I'm certain you're being manipulative. And I must ask you to leave."

"Not yet," Lady Carise insisted, almost tenderly. "I can't leave you like this, unaware of how you're being used. I struggled over whether or not to tell you this, more than you can ever comprehend, but in the end I knew I had to speak. You see, there's something about Princess Leia you don't know. Something she has deliberately kept secret from the Senate—from you and from me—for decades. And this secret proves beyond any doubt that she cannot be trusted."

Melodrama rarely moved him. "There's literally nothing you could say to convince me of that."

Lady Carise shook her head. "Only one thing, Senator Casterfo. And now you must hear it."

With one hand she gestured toward his desk, and Ransolm realized something had been placed there: a small wooden chest, hand-carved, the sort of thing people used to store sentimental mementos. "What's that?"

Rising to stand beside him, Lady Carise said simply, "The truth."

"When the first Death Star was built, even before the galaxy at large had learned of this monstrosity, Princess Leia received the station's plans—the very ones that revealed the weakness leading to its destruction!" Varish's voice, carried by amplifier droids, rang out through the entire Senate chamber. "As the Star Destroyer *Devastator* closed in to capture her vessel, it was Princess Leia who had the presence of mind to extract the plans from the *Tantive IV*'s main computer core and hide them within a droid that could be jettisoned to the nearest planet undetected. Had she not, we would no doubt be living under Imperial tyranny still."

Cheers and applause rose up from the Populists; even most of the Centrists clapped politely. Leia sat in her place, her face a perfect mask of serene acceptance, as she listened to this version of her life story. In this one, she always made the right choice the first time. She never felt fear or despair. She rushed on courageously toward victory. Nothing in the speech was inaccurate, but nothing hinted at the long, cold nights on Hoth, the hours she'd wept for Alderaan, or the many times she'd argued with a general or admiral who'd turned out to have the better idea after all. The human side of fighting a war—the human cost—none of that was acknowledged, as if it had never been.

Let it go, she told herself, trying to follow Ransolm's advice and enjoy this. *Besides, you* did *figure out that trick with Artoo-Detoo.*

Varish kept going, describing acts of valor and heroism that Leia remembered as moments of pure terror. But she took pride in hearing about Luke and Han's heroism at the Battle of Yavin, about her own bravery on Vrogas Vas, and about how she, Han, and Chewie had taken down the shield generator on the forest moon of Endor. Yes, Leia had given her entire life to her duty, but at least she'd given it in a good cause. Thanks to her husband, brother, son, and many friends, nobody could say she'd sacrificed all her happiness or love. If she'd managed to create some stability for the galaxy, and if she could continue to do so in this new role, then wasn't it all worth it?

Varish tossed her silky mane as she concluded, "And so it is with the greatest confidence and pride that I hereby nominate Senator Leia Organa, hero of the Rebellion, to stand as First Senator of the New Republic!" The Populists cheered wildly, rising to their feet all around the wide amphitheater. Leia rose for only a moment so that they could take in the finery she'd donned for the occasion—the

snowy-white gown, the heavy necklace—and nodded to acknowledge the cheers.

As she took her seat again, the moderator droid flatly went through
the next point in the process. "Does any person present know of any
fact that would disqualify Senator Organa from higher office?"

Nobody, including Leia, even bothered to look up until a voice
rang out, "I must take the floor."

In astonishment, she lifted her chin to see Ransolm Casterfo rising
to his feet, his image projected on every screen and holo. Shock made
her flush hot and then cold, though Leia recovered herself in an instant. This had to be some kind of stunt—a backhanded way of pretending to object to Leia while actually acknowledging her fitness for
the position—surely that was it. But it was so tactless, so showy, so ill
advised . . .

"The First Senator of the New Republic can only be granted supreme authority if we, the citizens, feel that person deserves our
trust." Ransolm looked terrible. His face had gone pale, and he braced
one hand against his console as if otherwise he might fall. Yet his
voice did not falter. "To my deepest regret, I have learned that Leia
Organa does not deserve that trust."

Murmurs welled around the room. Tai-Lin had half risen from his
seat, scowling, and Varish's fur stood on end. Leia could hardly believe this was really happening. What could Ransolm possibly be
talking about? What could have angered him so much just since this
morning, and why in the worlds would he be declaring it to the entire
Senate?

Ransolm continued, "Princess Leia's lies have protected her long
enough. Her deception cannot be permitted to endanger the entire
galaxy. If people are considering electing her as First Senator, they
have the right to know exactly who they're voting for."

Leia's confusion crystallized in an instant around one of her most
terrible fears: *He knows.*

No. Impossible. Nobody had ever known this besides her, Luke,
and Han; she wasn't even sure whether Han had told Chewie. They
hadn't even told *Ben* yet. So Ransolm couldn't have learned the most

horrible truth of her life. There was no way. He had to be talking about something else.

But what? There was nothing Leia could think of, nothing besides . . .

Ransolm pointed at her and declared to the entire Galactic Senate, "Senator Leia Organa is none other than the daughter of *Darth Vader himself!*"

CHAPTER
TWENTY-THREE

Uproar swirled around Leia, surrounded her. She could hardly hear the shouts, stamps, whistles, and pounded desks from the senators over the rushing of blood in her own ears. Her breaths came shallow in her chest, as if Ransolm Casterfo's revelation had wound itself so tightly around her that she would soon suffocate.

"This is a lie!" Varish howled over the din. "A filthy, outrageous lie, and one Senator Organa will rise to deny!"

Will I? Leia's thoughts filtered through a daze. Her limbs had gone so watery and weak from shock that she wasn't sure she could get to her feet.

"I do not come without proof," Ransolm said. "I will now present my evidence for everyone to hear, so that they can all know how close we came to allowing Lord Vader's daughter to rule over us all."

Proof? What possible proof could there be? Leia stared at Ransolm, aware that she should feel angry or betrayed, but unable to summon any emotions besides horror and confusion.

Then Ransolm held up a box—not just any box, a keepsake chest. Every child on Alderaan had one. Parents and grandparents carved the designs, but only the child decided what would be put inside. Placing one of your possessions inside the keepsake chest meant that you had outgrown it but recognized its importance to you. In adulthood you could open the chest, look back, and see how you had chosen to tell your own story.

Leia thought that keepsake chest looked like hers. But she hadn't seen it in at least thirty years, and surely it had been destroyed with Alderaan.

Nobody was ever supposed to open a keepsake chest without permission, but Ransolm opened this one now. From within he pulled out a music box, one Leia recognized so instantly that the memory pierced her heart like an arrow. She had no time to wonder how it had survived or come into Ransolm Casterfo's possession; Ransolm had already opened it, and the tune began to play. *Mirrorbright shines the moon—*

—and then Bail Organa began to speak.

Just the sound of his voice brought tears to her eyes, but every word revealed her deepest secret. In despair Leia thought, *They are using both my fathers against me.*

Bail Organa, who had so often spoken out in the Old Republic and Imperial senates, who had possessed the courage to stand against Palpatine when nearly every other planetary leader had bowed to the Emperor's power, uttered his last words to the public from the music box, played on every speaker, to be reproduced by every news source around the galaxy within moments. "*Your father has become Darth Vader.*"

The shouting rose again, even louder than before. Leia bit the inside of her cheek, struggling to keep some small measure of her composure. Her father—her *real* father—had had the foresight to store this somewhere offplanet. He had given Leia the truth in the only way he could. And the Senate had repaid his service and his love by using it to humiliate his daughter. She felt a moment of dull gratitude that at least Bail had never known this; he'd never had to face just how terribly his message had been used against her.

Tai-Lin Garr had somehow managed to claim the floor. His imposing height and scarlet cloak, plus the powerful gravitas he projected, brought the room nearly to silence. "We have no proof that this object is authentic. No evidence at all. Given that Bail Organa was a well-known public figure, any number of recording devices or droids could have captured and synthesized his voice to say anything the programmer wished. Surely a mere music box cannot be allowed to slander one of the most illustrious members of the Galactic Senate."

"I have every reason to believe it is genuine," Ransolm replied. "But if it is not, let Senator Organa pronounce it false."

And for all the anger in his voice, all the desperation in his eyes, Leia could tell that—deep down—Ransolm still hoped this would all turn out to be untrue.

She could lie. She could get to her feet, angrily denounce the music box as a forgery, and walk out of the Senate with her head high. No biological samples marked either ANAKIN SKYWALKER or LORD VADER had ever turned up in the Imperial registries; no doubt Palpatine had made sure none could ever be collected, lest his dangerous apprentice be cloned. So nobody would ever be able to prove beyond any doubt that Leia was Vader's daughter.

But the doubt would linger. The whispers would follow her for the rest of her days. No denial could be strong enough to outweigh an accusation so sensational and so damning—particularly when it was correct. She could fall now, as if at the stroke of an ax, or endure being diminished cut by cut, rumor by rumor, year by year.

Leia got to her feet. Although she feared her knees would buckle under her, she managed to face them straight and strong. The amplifier droids swarmed around her like moths, ready to project her next words to the world.

She said, "Senator Casterfo's accusation is true. My father was Darth Vader."

"How did you find it?" said Senator Giller, only one of the throng of Centrist politicians swarming around Ransolm Casterfo as he walked from the fast-emptying Senate chamber back to his office. The pandemonium around him had scarcely stilled since Leia's confession. "This was a masterstroke, I tell you, a masterstroke!"

"She won't even win reelection to the Senate, assuming she isn't forced to resign immediately," said Senator Madmund, who grinned up at Ransolm as if they were both in on a good joke. "Haughty Princess Leia, defanged at last."

"And just in time!" a staffer hastily added. "Can you imagine if she'd been elected? How long would it have been before we were all bowing down before another Vader?"

Senator Giller clapped his broad hand on Ransolm's shoulder. "You've saved us all, Casterfo. No one will ever forget that."

No, they wouldn't. Undoubtedly Ransolm had just taken a huge step forward in his career. Within a day, he would be one of the most famous members of the Senate, if not *the* most famous next to the disgraced Leia Organa. He would be invited to every party with the movers and shakers, asked to join all the most important committees. It wasn't even impossible that he might be called upon to serve as the Centrist candidate for First Senator now.

Yet he felt no pride. Instead, his stomach churned, his replies were short and meaningless, and he wanted nothing more than to get away from the people praising him. Since he'd first heard the information in the music box, Ransolm had not had a single moment alone; Lady Carise had remained with him almost until the moment they entered the Senate chamber. Not one moment to deal with the fact that his friend had in fact been his enemy. He had to escape all this and think.

Finally, when Ransolm reached his Senate office suite, he was able to rid himself of the others. His staffers and droids, glowing with newfound importance, shooed them off. "Senator Casterfo has important business—you can imagine—yes, yes, we'll be setting up meetings with everyone immediately—"

Ransolm went into his private office alone. As soon as the door slid shut behind him, he sealed it. Then he fell to his knees, clutched his rubbish bin, and was violently, noisily sick.

Darth Vader's daughter. He had fallen under the sway of *Darth Vader's daughter.* She had heard his secrets. Touched his arm. Drawn

him into intimate late-night conversations via holo. Ransolm had
made himself vulnerable to the child of the person he hated more
than any other in the world—

He vomited again, his body rebelling against the ghastly knowledge of what Leia really was, wringing him out until he had nothing
left inside.

Wiping his mouth on his velvet sleeve, Ransolm sat heavily on the
floor, resting his back against the wall. The Imperial artifacts mounted
all around seemed to mock him with their empty black eyes. *Just
imagine,* he thought with the darkest possible humor, *the ultimate
remnant of the Empire stood right here in this office, and you didn't
even know it.*

Ransolm knew he would never get over the revulsion he felt at
having unwittingly trusted Darth Vader's child. How might she have
used his secrets against him? She might still try, though now surely
she lacked the political power to accomplish much. He kept trying to
figure out why she had targeted him, why she had pretended to be his
friend.

Yet in the eye of the storm of anger and betrayal Ransolm felt, one
image refused to fade—the sight of Leia's face as he had denounced
her.

He'd looked her in the eyes as he said it. Never had Ransolm been
given the chance to truly look Vader in the eyes, so he'd taken this
opportunity to prove his courage. The entire time the Populists had
been proclaiming Leia's heroism, he had been envisioning that moment. In his imaginings, Leia's smile had turned contemptuous as she
lifted her chin high. He had expected her to sneer at his ignorance, at
all of them who had so foolishly believed in her, secure in the power
of darkness she no doubt commanded.

Instead Leia had only looked pale and small. It was easy to forget
what a tiny woman she was, given the force of her personality. But
Ransolm had seen her standing there, white and stricken, so little
that it had seemed the cacophony of the Senate could blow her away
as easily as the wind moved a leaf.

Ransolm's gut rebelled again, but his stomach was empty. Once the racking heaves had ended, he closed his eyes and tried not to think. Not to feel. He tried to pretend he was in a galaxy where neither Leia nor Vader had existed at all.

Leia made it to her office without being torn apart by a mob. Under the circumstances, that had to count as a win.

"Refuse all calls," she said to Greer, pretending not to notice how Greer failed to meet her eyes. "Don't let anyone in unless it's someone I know extremely well. I trust your judgment. Threepio?"

"Yes, Your Highness?" He shuffled forward, eager to serve. Leia felt as though she had never been so grateful for his golden, unchanging face, which could never show contempt or disgust.

She said, "Get the holocam ready. I'll be sending priority messages very shortly, and I want to start the recordings as soon as possible."

"Right away, Your Highness." C-3PO hurried off to work.

Korrie emerged from the back storage room, tearstains evident on her cheeks. Gently, Leia said, "You don't have to stay here if you don't want to."

"That's right. I don't." Korrie grabbed her satchel and began dumping in everything from her desk, all of it in a jumble. "Because I quit."

The sting made Leia suck in her breath. Once she'd walked into her own offices, she'd felt—not safe, because at the moment she doubted she'd ever feel entirely safe again—but as if she would at least be surrounded by friends instead of enemies. Instead, she had to watch even more people she cared about turning their backs on her.

But surely things didn't have to end on such a terrible note. "For what it's worth, Korrie, I'm sorry you found out like this."

"No, you're not. You're sorry we found out, period." She buckled her satchel shut, slung it over one shoulder, and added, "And just for the record, I haven't gone by Korrie since I was a kid. My name is *Korr.* You should have used it." With that, Korr Sella stormed through the door, disappearing into the angry crowd that still shouted and cursed.

"Goodness me," C-3PO said. "If she had specified a preferred form of address, I could of course have ensured it was used in our offices."

Leia put one hand to her throbbing temple, forcing herself to hold it together. She had messages to send, one of them among the most important messages she would ever send, and she couldn't afford to fall apart until that task was done.

And after that—what? Leia couldn't imagine. She *wouldn't* imagine. She simply had to keep putting one foot before the other, never looking any farther ahead.

As soon as C-3PO had readied the holocam, Leia went into her office and shut the door. What she was about to say was deeply private, even though it was about news that at this moment was no doubt racing to the very edges of known space. She needed to explain to Ben that they'd kept from telling him because they'd wanted to find the right moment. She realized now that she'd been fooling herself. Luke, too. There could be no good time to learn news this devastating—

The door chimed, and Greer's voice came through the speaker. "Senator, it's Tai-Lin Garr to see you."

Tai-Lin was virtually the only person Leia thought she could bear talking with at the moment. His serene bearing would comfort her tremendously—unless, of course, he'd come to permanently break ties. Either way, Leia had to know, even with the weight of that unsent message hanging over her. "Send him in."

As the door swished open, Tai-Lin walked in, neither as unruffled as Leia had hoped nor as indignant as she'd feared. "Leia. How are you?"

"Rotten. But thanks for asking. You might be the last person in the galaxy who cares." Leia turned her chair away from the holocam, toward the small couch where he'd taken a seat. "Or maybe I've underestimated the Senate. Is anybody out there standing up for me?"

"Varish Vicly read out the entire constitutional passage declaring that no person should have to answer for the crimes of a parent. I've put forth a motion to the entire party that, regardless of your standing in the Senate, we owe you our respect and loyalty for your individual accomplishments." Tai-Lin paused. "No one else has had time to summon a response."

Meaning that out of the thousands of senators, exactly two had defended her. That was two more than Leia would have expected. Under the circumstances, both Varish's speech and Tai-Lin's visit were acts of great courage. "Thank you," she said. "I appreciate that more than I can say."

Tai-Lin shook his head sorrowfully. "You should have told some of us the truth, Leia. Me or Varish, if no one else."

Leia gestured toward the far wall of her office suite, through which the angry rumble of the crowd could still be heard. "I'd think it was obvious why I didn't want to share this news with the whole galaxy."

"I didn't speak of the entire galaxy. I spoke of your closest friends and allies in the Senate." Tai-Lin rarely took people to task, which made the subtle sharpness in his tone hard to bear. "Even if you felt the need to keep that secret, you should never have allowed us to put you forward as the Populist nominee. By doing so, you've robbed us of our credibility. I'm not certain any Populist candidate could win now."

She nodded miserably. "You're right. I know you're right. But it had remained secret for so long. I guess I hoped it could stay secret forever."

"For your sake, and the galaxy's, I wish it had." Tai-Lin rose to leave, but he briefly rested one broad hand on her shoulder. "You still have friends, Leia. Remember that."

"Thank you," she whispered. Nothing else Tai-Lin could have said could possibly have comforted her more. And yet the terrible wound within her was too vast to be healed even by friendship.

Strangely, Leia felt as if she ought to tell Ransolm about this; her brain knew what he had done to her, but her shock-numbed heart continued to call him friend. The person who had betrayed her on the Senate floor seemed like another person entirely from the dashing young man who had come to rescue her on Bastatha. The bridges they'd built between them had collapsed, but she still felt the urge to step out onto the thin air where they had been.

But now Leia had no one else to talk to. Her message to Ben would be about comforting him, not finding any consolation of her own. She couldn't even bring herself to record a message for Han. He would still be in the heart of the sublight relay round of the Five Sabers, meaning he was cut off from any possible contact. Han might wind up being the last person in the galaxy to know her secret had been exposed; nor was there any chance he would learn about it from her. And at the moment, she couldn't even bear to speak about it any longer. But she knew that he, too, would suffer blowback from being married to a child of Vader.

The door swished open again, and this time Greer stood there, awkwardly holding the wooden keepsake chest in her hands. "I put in a requisition order, because all of this is legally yours. They handed it over quicker than I'd expected."

Leia hadn't even thought of getting her keepsake chest back again. "Thank you, Greer. That helps."

Greer set the chest on Leia's desk, then hesitated. "Can I ask you a question? Just one?"

Would Greer now storm out just like Korr Sella had? Leia braced herself. "Of course."

"Does Captain Solo know? When did he find out?"

"Han's always known. I told him the day after I learned the truth from Luke."

Greer nodded—still wary, but not on the brink of bolting any longer.

But now Leia's memories were claiming her again, taking her back to the forest moon of Endor in the aftermath of the tremendous celebration that marked their victory. Han had held her so tenderly as they rested on soft mosses, the scent of cedars and pine all around them. When she'd told him the whole story, she'd been terrified that Han would immediately abandon her. Their romance had been so new then. Only the day before, he had offered to step aside if she wanted Luke instead. Would he be even quicker to leave once he knew she was a part of Darth Vader himself?

But Han hadn't flinched once. He had simply rocked her in his arms, giving her what comfort he could. If she could only be in his embrace again now, maybe she would feel as if this were something she could bear.

The keepsake chest on her desk seemed to loom larger by the moment. Leia rose to her feet and gently lifted the creaky lid. Although she felt a pang at the sight of her doll and other mementos, she reached for the music box first. Leia opened it and immediately heard the strains of the song: *Mirrorbright, shines the moon—*

Alderaan had possessed a moon for only one day of its existence. When the Death Star appeared, little children must have looked up in awe, believing the moon from their bedtime lullaby had come to their skies at last. They would've smiled up at it, pointed their tiny fingers, sung the song. Leia squeezed her eyes shut, trying not to imagine it.

Those who loved you but are gone, those who kept you safe and warm—

Bail Organa's message restarted from the beginning. Leia walked to the nearest sofa, sinking down onto it to hear him explain everything again. At times she'd wondered how her father could keep such a secret from her; it helped to know that he had always intended to give her the truth.

His initial words had been played in the Senate, so Leia concentrated on the loving tone of his voice and the simple comfort of hearing her father speak once more. But soon they reached the end of the message, words Ransolm Casterfo had not shared with the rest of the Senate.

"*I hope to have told you all this myself,*" Bail Organa's voice said. "*I hope we have enjoyed many more happy years as a family, that we have seen the Empire fall, and that we have gone forth together to find General Kenobi and your brother. If so, this recording can serve only one purpose. You must be listening after my death, so let this be my chance to say once again how much I love you. No other daughter could ever have brought me more joy.*"

Tears welled in Leia's eyes, but she fought them back. If she began to sob, she wouldn't be able to hear her father's voice any longer.

He concluded, "*Please know that my love for you, and your mother's love, endures long past our deaths. We are forever with you, Leia. In your brightest triumphs and your darkest troubles, always know that we are by your side.*"

She could resist no more. At long last, Leia put her head down on her desk and allowed herself to weep.

CHAPTER
TWENTY-FOUR

One day after Princess Leia's parentage had been revealed on the Senate floor, Joph Seastriker and Greer Sonnel sat inside the *Mirrorbright,* waiting for her. Neither of them made eye contact with the other, and for a long time, no one spoke.

Finally, Joph said, "I don't know about this."

Greer turned her head toward him, a lock of black hair falling over her shoulder. "You don't trust her anymore? Because she turns out to be Darth Vader's daughter?"

"It feels weird." Joph had heard the nightmarish stories of Vader's evil deeds his whole life. Yeah, he'd known Darth Vader had really existed; he wasn't stupid. But to Joph, Vader had seemed almost like some folktale creature from stories told to frighten little children so they wouldn't run away from home. He could hardly wrap his mind around the idea of Vader as a man like any other, who must have once fallen in love and fathered twin children.

Then again, the story could be far darker. "Do you think Darth Vader assaulted Queen Amidala?" he ventured.

"I thought of that last night," Greer said heavily. "But no. I've helped the senator research Queen Amidala, so I plugged in some of the data last night. The queen died before the first records of Vader ever appear."

So, a man named Anakin Skywalker had become a Jedi Knight, fought courageously in the Clone Wars, and won the love of a senator-queen . . . and had still chosen to become a monster. Joph shuddered.

Greer murmured, almost to herself, "Captain Solo always knew. He knew and he married her anyway. If he didn't turn his back on her, we shouldn't, either."

Although Joph hadn't met Han Solo, much less actually been mentored by him the way Greer had been, he'd hero-worshipped the guy from afar. So did virtually any other pilot who loved racing. But Solo's trust in his wife didn't reassure Joph as much as it did Greer. Anybody who'd watched Han Solo fly a race knew the man loved taking risks.

Big risks. Crazy risks. The kind of chances that got other people killed.

The *Mirrorbright*'s door remained open to the hangar, so Joph and Greer could hear the faint crackle of a welding torch and the chatter of nearby pilots and mechanics. He'd paid the noise no attention until suddenly, as if on a well-rehearsed cue, it all fell silent.

Princess Leia must have just arrived.

He and Greer exchanged glances before getting to their feet. Joph went into standard at-ease posture, hands behind his back, heart thumping as if the footsteps on the gangway were those of Darth Vader himself.

But then Princess Leia entered the *Mirrorbright*. Her pallor shocked him; overnight, Leia's skin seemed to have turned as pale as the white jacket and trousers she wore. Joph noticed, as he had not before, how much gray had threaded its way through her brown hair, and the fine lines at the corners of her mouth and eyes. It was not that she looked older, but the powerful vitality that had always been a part of her seemed to have drained away overnight. He wondered if she'd been able to sleep at all. Probably not.

Answer suffering with kindness. That was what his mothers always said, one of the tenets people on Gatalenta tried to live by. Joph had always found the saying trite, when he'd bothered thinking about it at all. But that was his first instinct now—not to shun Princess Leia, but to help and protect her.

"Lieutenant Seastriker." The princess's voice sounded thick and rough, as if she had a cold. "Greer. Thank you for coming today. I . . . realize it can't have been easy."

"It's a pretty quick trip from the barracks." Joph kept his tone light; they all knew the terrible truth that hung over them like a storm cloud, but he figured acknowledging it would just drag everybody down. "Made it here even faster than usual. No big deal. I mean, no big deal, ma'am."

The ghost of a smile passed over Princess Leia's face. "All right, then."

Greer said, "We're ready to do whatever you need done, Your Highness. If you're planning on—on leaving Hosnian Prime, maybe traveling to rendezvous with Captain Solo in the Theron system, just say the word."

"Same here." But Joph wondered whether that was a promise he could keep. He'd been assigned to Princess Leia's detail by his superior officers. Would they belay those orders now?

Princess Leia shook her head. "We're not going anywhere until our voyage to Sibensko—which, as far as I'm concerned, is still on. I called you both here today simply to make sure you both remain willing to take on the mission."

"Of course I am, Your Highness, but—" Greer paused, gaze drifting to the floor for a moment before she looked back up at Princess Leia. "—are you sure you can take this on? The fallout from all this . . . forgive me, but it has to take a toll. Maybe this isn't the time."

"Rinnrivin Di is moving large amounts of spice and larger amounts of money around the galaxy, funneling it to Centrist worlds," Princess Leia replied. Some of the light had returned to her eyes. "A paramilitary organization has begun arming and preparing itself for war, and may already be responsible for a terrorist attack on the Galactic Senate. What's happening to me, personally, doesn't matter. We have to act now. If it's not the ideal time, well, it's the only time we've got."

"Yes, ma'am." Greer straightened, her uncertainty gone. "The *Mirrorbright* will be ready to go as soon as you say the word."

Joph added, "And so will we."

"I always thought I could count on you two, but it means a lot, knowing that for sure." Princess Leia's voice sounded like her own again. Joph wondered if this was the quality that had won the loyalty of her troops during the war against the Empire, her ability to press on even in the face of disaster. "Now if you'll excuse me, I have some unfinished business to take care of."

With that, she walked out. Once again, silence followed in her wake, but Joph paid it no attention. He and Greer were sticking with the princess, and he intended to make sure that was enough. "So what do you think she means by 'unfinished business'?" he said to Greer.

Shaking her head, Greer replied, "I wouldn't want to be Ransolm Casterfo right now."

Calling the meeting had been the right move for Princess Leia; Greer knew that. After the princess had sent that message to her son yesterday—the Force alone knew what she'd said, but her red-rimmed eyes testified to the tears she'd shed. No wonder she'd needed to realize she wasn't completely alone. And it was good for Greer, too, to discover that Joph Seastriker would come through for them; beneath his youth and his daredevil attitude lay the kind of decency that could stand up to the ugliness of the world. On Pamarthe they called that quality bedrock. A warrior of bedrock was one on whose loyalty a kingdom could be built.

Yet Greer had spent the meeting only half concentrating on the incredibly important things happening around her. It took so much of her will to remain still and steady on her feet.

As soon as Joph left the *Mirrorbright,* Greer slumped onto the long padded bench. She lay on her side, feet still brushing the floor, cheek pressed against the cushions, as she struggled to even out her breath.

She couldn't inject again. Not so soon. Dr. Kalonia had warned her about relying on the stuff too much, and Greer knew where dependency led.

But how else was she supposed to keep going? The princess's words still rang in Greer's memory: *What's happening to me, personally, doesn't matter. If it's not the ideal time—well, it's the only time we've got.*

"All right," she said to herself. "Once more."

Pushing herself to an upright position, she waited for the rush of dizziness to subside, then got to her feet. Although a few of the pilots watched her walking out of the hangar, clearly eager to discuss what she'd known about Princess Leia and when, Greer ignored them all. Luckily, a wheeled transport making its way through the complex turned out to be headed in the general direction of the medbay, so she could catch a ride most of the way there.

She walked in to find the place deserted, no patients, and Dr. Kalonia taking her break. Good. The 2-1B medical droid turned its half-blue, half-transparent torso toward her. "May I assist you with your illness or injury?"

"Yes, you can." Greer eased herself onto one of the beds. "I need another dose of hadeira serum."

The 2-1B remained stationary, its circuits whirring in consideration. "Your use of hadeira serum already exceeds suggested limits."

"But I'm not in danger of an overdose, am I? That means you're able to give me the medication." She rolled up the sleeve of her coverall, exposing the tender crook of her arm and the barely visible latticework of veins just beneath her coppery skin.

"I can administer the serum, but I am required to remind you that you are now considered high risk for hadeira toxicity."

"I know." Greer sighed. "Believe me, it's impossible to forget."

Sometimes at night the muscles in her legs would spasm painfully, leaving her to swear as she rocked back and forth on her mattress.

The day before, when the stress of Casterfo's explosive revelation had rocked them all, Greer's pulse had quickened far past human norms, pounding so hard she could see it through the fabric of her shirt. If she went over the line that separated "dependency" from "toxicity," those symptoms would stop being occasional nuisances and turn into her constant state of being.

But if that was the price of going on, of remaining by Princess Leia's side for the duration of the mission, then Greer would pay it.

To the undoubted consternation of most members of the Senate, not to mention the public at large, Ransolm Casterfo had refused to give any interviews or take any meetings to discuss the revelations about Leia Organa. He had instead busied himself with the other work of a senator. He found it easier to concentrate on that sort of thing: reading up on the proposed new water purification systems for New Republic ships, or doing research for the upcoming debates over shipping-lane restrictions. When calls came in from Lady Carise Sindian, the senior senator from Coruscant, or other high-level officials, Ransolm simply requested that they all leave messages for later. He did not intend to answer any of these messages for several days. His staffers kept asking him about each one, however, their consternation obvious; after a while, Ransolm could stand their presence no more and gave them the rest of the day off. The droid could handle what little administrative work had to be done, and he preferred to spend the day alone.

Everybody wanted him to expound on his role in bringing down Princess Leia. They wanted him to step up, take credit, and emerge as the Centrist leader he had long dreamed of being. Even a few short months ago, he would have been unable to imagine passing up such a golden opportunity for advancement.

But he had not exposed Leia's parentage for his own personal gain. Exploiting the situation now would cheapen his actions.

I acted in the interest of the truth, he told himself as he kept staring at the purification-system schematics, his brain refusing to make sense of the tangle of pipes and filters. It would be a long time before anyone else believed that his motives had been pure, if they ever believed it at all. But he clung to the knowledge within his own heart, as if it were the only thing keeping him afloat in a stormy sea.

By lunchtime, he'd centered himself enough to concentrate on the work in front of him. He sent the droid out to fetch some Ivarujari food that could be eaten at his desk and was determinedly working out the manufacturing specs for the pipes when he heard the door chime—then open without any cue from Ransolm himself.

And he knew, just *knew*, who the next visitor had to be.

Ransolm took a deep breath and got to his feet, just before Princess Leia stormed in.

"What, all alone? Except for your creepy Imperial mausoleum, I mean." Leia gestured at the artifacts around her. "I would've thought you'd be throwing the party of the century, celebrating your success. You pretended to be my friend and then betrayed me to the entire galaxy. A political masterstroke. So where's the wine?"

"Pretending? You accuse *me* of pretending?" The horror and nausea Ransolm had struggled against since hearing the news vanished in an instant, replaced by pure rage. "You, who hid your true identity from everyone for decades?"

"This *is* my true identity! The person I've been all this time—the battles I've fought, the work I've done—that's who I am. My birth father has nothing to do with any of that."

"How can we be certain? How can we trust anything you say from now on?" Ransolm had lain awake all night, running through the various ways their understanding of history might be altered through this one critical fact. "The Empire found rebel bases time and time again. The Battle of Endor was nearly lost because it was all an elaborate trap. Could it be that they had a highly placed source inside the Rebel Alliance—a daughter who would obey her father?"

Leia's eyes widened, and for one instant Ransolm thought she might hit him. "You're accusing me of being a spy? Did you forget the parts where I nearly died along with the rest of the Rebellion during those battles? If so, you're dumber than I thought."

"Yes, you must have thought I was a fool." The words tasted bitter in Ransolm's mouth. "Because I trusted you so quickly. Because I told you the most personal and painful stories of my life, never guessing that they revolved around your father."

"Only my birth father," she insisted. "My *real* father—the only father I ever knew or wanted—was Bail Organa of Alderaan."

What could Organa have been thinking, taking in the offspring of someone so corrupt and monstrous? Ransolm had wondered about that, too, but knew he would never be able to fathom the answer. "Well, Bail Organa himself thought the connection mattered, didn't he?"

"That was a message recorded out of love." Leia's voice broke, but only for a moment; anger had eclipsed almost everything else inside her. "And you used it against me. How could you? We were friends, or I thought we were. When you found out—however you found out—did it never occur to you to come to me, to ask me about it personally?"

"Why? So you could lie to me yet again?" Ransolm again felt the pent-up, useless fury of the child he'd been, watching Darth Vader reach out with his hand to strangle the life from another helpless prisoner. "You knew how I hated Vader! You knew what he had done to me! How could you still keep your secret, knowing that?"

Leia shook her head in disbelief. "What Vader did to *you*? Do you think that can even begin to compare with what Vader did to *me*? He made me watch my planet die. He froze Han in carbonite and sold him to Jabba the Hutt. He cut off my brother's hand and nearly took his life. And he tortured me, Ransolm. He tortured me until I screamed and shook and thought I would die just from the pain alone. Did you bother to ask yourself how it might feel, to realize the person who'd done all that to you was *your father*? Can you imagine how terrible it is to realize all you'll ever know of your birth father is how much he enjoyed making you suffer? That's what I have to live with."

Ransolm had assumed Leia had lied about not only her relationship to Darth Vader but also her feelings about the man. It shocked him to see that her anger was real. "It's all the more reason you should have told me."

"I hadn't even told my son. Now he has to find out in the most horrible, public way imaginable, all because of you." Leia's hands were clenched in fists at her sides. "Obviously I overestimated our friendship. But you owed it to me to come to me with this information first. Even if you still felt you had to shout it out to the entire galaxy, you could have talked to me privately first. Given me a chance to speak with my son. Not even out of friendship—just out of common decency. But I guess you didn't think I even deserved that."

"You had your chances to speak to your son," Ransolm insisted. "He's not a child any longer, is he? You could've told him at any point before this. Do you think you'd ever have had the courage to tell the truth?"

"What I kept from Ben, I did for his own good—or what I hoped was his own good. Now we'll never know. But what you did to me, you did for your own benefit. Well, congratulations, Senator Casterfo. May you enjoy all the power you bought by betraying me. And keep on condemning *me* as the heir of the Empire while you sit in here surrounded by all of this." Leia grabbed the Royal Guard helmet from the wall and hurled it toward the nearest display case; the glass shattered with a crash, slivers and splinters scattering all around. "Goodbye, Casterfo. May you get absolutely everything in life that you deserve."

She turned and marched out, shoulder colliding with the droid that had returned in the middle of all this and stood mutely just outside the doorway of Ransolm's office. The impact sent the lunch carton tumbling from the droid's hands, spattering noodles onto the carpet. Leia never even paused. A moment later the door swished again, and he knew she was gone.

"Senator Casterfo, are you unharmed?" The droid tilted its head.

"I'm fine," Ransolm answered, the words no more than automatic. His empty stomach churned; the smell of the food on the floor now sickened him.

"Cleaning and repair crews can be summoned. If Senator Organa caused the damage, she can be reported for assault upon the property and person of a senator—"

"No. Don't do that. No reporting her, no repair crews, nothing. I'll handle this." More than anything, Ransolm wanted to be alone, to process everything he'd heard in the past several minutes. The droid hesitated, obviously unable to understand why a human would refuse necessary services, then rolled back to begin cleaning up the spilled food. It went far enough away for the door to slide shut and seal Ransolm inside again.

For a few breaths he simply stood there, shaking from pent-up adrenaline. Then, nearly numb, he got to his knees to begin picking up the shattered glass. He misjudged an edge, however; a hot sliver of pain sliced across his skin. Ransolm put his thumb to his mouth and tasted blood.

CHAPTER
TWENTY-FIVE

The moderator droid's words rang out through the vast chamber: "The Senate recognizes Senator Leia Organa."

Leia stood, aware of the spotlight heat as she hadn't been in years. Yesterday's applause lingered only in memory; now her fellow senators greeted her with stony silence, except for a few faint hisses from the back. She gave no sign she'd heard them, or that the thousands of faces staring at her showed only disgust and disbelief.

This might be the last time she ever addressed the Galactic Senate. For her family's sake, she had to make the most of it.

"I come before you today to withdraw my nomination for First Senator." Someone in the far distance laughed disdainfully, but Leia paid it no heed. "That's simple to accomplish—merely by speaking the words before you all, I've already ended my candidacy. But I would be doing the Galactic Senate a disservice if I did not take this opportunity to discuss yesterday's revelations about my birth father.

The citizens of the New Republic have the right to hear exactly what I knew and when I knew it."

No one stirred. Even the most hostile listener would want to learn every detail. Leia might not have their support any longer, but at least she had their attention.

"It has always been known that I was adopted by Bail and Breha Organa of the royal house of Alderaan. I was described as a war orphan—a story I myself believed until adulthood. As you heard yesterday, Bail Organa had not shared the truth with me when I was younger, and sadly, the Empire's destruction of our world meant he never had the chance to speak of it later.

"My brother, the Jedi Knight Luke Skywalker, was the first to learn that we were twins and that our father was the man who later became known as Darth Vader." Vader's name seemed to darken the room. "He told me on the day preceding the Battle of Endor. As you can imagine, I was shocked. Horrified. I had never guessed that the truth behind my birth could be so tragic, or that my birth father could be a man I had such strong personal reasons to hate. My efforts to accept this lasted a long time. In a very real sense, I still struggle with this knowledge, and I expect that I always will."

Whenever she'd talked with Luke about their birth father, this was the part where he'd refuse to use the name Darth Vader. *He was Anakin Skywalker when he fell in love with our mother,* Luke would say, taking her hand gently in his. *And he became Anakin Skywalker again in the last hour of his life. He came back from the dark side, Leia. They said it could never be done, but our father did it. He made that journey because of his love for us.*

Leia believed Luke. She could feel that truth within him. But it was difficult for her to find solace in this the way Luke did. How could Vader torture her without mercy if he had that good inside? He'd still had the power to make the right choice, but had instead forced her to suffer.

The Senate, of course, would not be open to hearing that Darth Vader hadn't been so evil before he died. Even introducing the topic would turn her into an apologist and probably get her thrown out of the building. Leia had to stick to the truths that would help her and her family the most.

"As many have known for a long time, and as you heard on the recording yesterday, my birth mother was also well known. Padmé Amidala Naberrie served the planet of Naboo first as queen, then as senator. She was among the few who stood up to Palpatine during his rise to power, one of the only people who warned against the evils to come." Leia thought of the holos she'd seen of a delicate young woman in the ornate regalia of the Naboo throne; they shared the same eyes. She continued, "My mother is every bit as much a part of me as my father. Her courage in her own political career has always informed my own role as a senator. And as for my father . . . I can think of no more powerful example of the dangers of ultimate power. That is why I have always identified as a Populist, why I have always warned against the concentration of political authority, and even why I agreed to run for First Senator—to keep such authority from ever being so poisonously misused again."

People were listening to her now. *Really* listening. Leia knew she hadn't won back their loyalty, but she thought they recognized her honesty. Hopefully, when Ben heard this someday, he would understand, too.

She began to breathe a little easier. For now, at least, the worst seemed to be over.

Then the moderator droid said, "The floor recognizes Lady Carise Sindian."

Screens and spotlights shifted to reveal Lady Carise, overdressed as usual in glittering blue. She gestured upward, as if toward space and the great galaxy beyond. "On behalf of my fellow senators, I first wish to say that I appreciate Princess Leia's honesty . . . however late it was in coming. Yet something in her speech today has given rise to other, potentially more dangerous concerns. Princess Leia spoke of her brother, the famous Luke Skywalker, who has been little seen in the public sphere for many years now. Perhaps Her Highness learned virtues from her father's example, but can we say the same for her brother? If he uses his rumored strength in the Force for evil, how could we ever defend against him?"

Leia had been prepared for boos. For insults. Even for rocks or rotten fruit to be thrown at her. Whatever attacks they could aim at her, she could take.

But she couldn't bear hearing them turn on Luke.

"How dare you question him?" Leia knew her voice sounded too sharp, too shrill, but her temper had gotten the best of her. "After everything Luke's done for the Rebellion and the New Republic? Maybe Lady Carise has forgotten that he was the one who destroyed the first Death Star—or that he was responsible for ridding the galaxy of Palpatine—"

"So Skywalker claims." Lady Carise put on her cocktail-party smile. "But we have only ever had his word for what happened on the second Death Star, and if his word is worth no more than yours has been these past several decades—well, Your Highness, we hardly know what to believe."

Murmurs began, welling louder by the second. Leia felt her breath catch in her throat. *No, no, not this, don't let them drag Luke down, too . . .*

"The floor recognizes Tai-Lin Garr," said the moderator droid.

Tai-Lin's mere attention calmed the room; sometimes Leia thought he would be able to turn a cyclone into a breeze. His scarlet robe looked like a badge of office, and he was the only one that day, Leia thought, who seemed to be above the political fray.

"I would first say to the honorable Senator Sindian of Arkanis that we have no reason to question Luke Skywalker." Tai-Lin let his grave tone, rather than his words, condemn Lady Carise's insinuations. "Since the Rebellion, Skywalker has lived a private life. He has asked no more of the New Republic than any of its other citizens, nor have we just cause to ask more of him than the substantial service he has already given. As Senator Vicly of Lonera reminded us yesterday, the New Republic does not blame children for the sins of their parents, and this is no time to begin."

Leia took a deep breath, regaining her control. Luke couldn't escape unscathed from this—no one in her family could—but at least Tai-Lin would keep a senatorial inquisition from getting started.

Tai-Lin continued, "On behalf of the Populist faction, we accept Senator Leia Organa's withdrawal of her candidacy. But I wish to state that Senator Organa's exemplary record remains unsullied, and that she retains my personal friendship and political support."

Still no applause, not even from the other Populists, but Leia could feel the tension in the room diminishing. Undoubtedly she would remain persona non grata for the duration of her term, and there could be no question of running again now. But her speech and Tai-Lin's had dulled the edge of the Senate's anger.

Instead of being hated, Leia would be ignored. She supposed that eventually she would feel grateful for that. It could've been worse.

The moderator droid said, "One piece of business regarding Senator Organa remains on the schedule of events, namely the approval of her brief leave of absence from her duties."

Leia had put in the request weeks earlier in order to cover her mission to Sibensko. The mission that exceeded her senatorial authority and went to the verge of being illegal.

The mission Ransolm Casterfo knew everything about.

She'd avoided looking at him all day, but she did so now. Ransolm sat in his place, wearing a green cloak that clashed badly with his blue shirt and trousers. His complexion was so wan he might have been a figure carved of wax. He wasn't watching his monitors, the moderator droid, or Leia herself. It seemed as if he were staring into space.

One of the Centrist senators jumped at his chance for attention. "I see this little vacation was requested before any of the latest unpleasantness, but I wish to be the first to say that this absence could not come at a more opportune time."

Other voices rose up, people falling all over themselves to say Leia should leave, though her few defenders framed it as necessary recovery time, while most senators seemed to feel they needed to recover from ever having been near her. She paid no attention to any of it, focusing only on Ransolm.

He said he'd put in for an emergency leave after mine was approved.

That way we'd avoid suspicion. But now he's in the clear. He can call me out, maybe have me ejected from the Senate completely, and I don't have one bit of proof that he planned this mission along with me. Leia could have cursed aloud. Now, on top of everything else, Rinnrivin Di, Arliz Hadrassian, and the Amaxine warriors were going to get away with it all.

But Ransolm said nothing. He never showed the slightest sign of acknowledging the debate. His eyes never focused on Leia for an instant.

She realized that what probably meant, but didn't fully believe it until her leave was approved and the Senate moved on to other subjects: Ransolm intended to let her go.

That evening, as they all congregated in the *Mirrorbright* again, Greer said, "Casterfo could just be setting us up. Waiting until he can send New Republic troops to catch us in the act."

"It's a possibility," Princess Leia admitted. She sat in one of the chairs, as informal as Greer had ever seen her: facing the wrong way, folded arms atop the chair's back, legs on either side. Essentially, the princess looked like somebody who no longer gave a—

"Can he even do that?" Joph asked. "Casterfo couldn't report on us without admitting he had advance knowledge of our trip. Since he didn't turn us in right away, that makes him an accessory or something. Right?"

"A smart politician could find a way around that, and he's not dumb." Princess Leia's gaze had turned inward in a way that meant she was considering every possibility. "But my instincts tell me that he'll stay quiet. If he were going to blow the mission, he would've done it right away."

"But you can't be sure." Greer felt profoundly ill at ease, even queasy. She hated the idea of being at Ransolm Casterfo's mercy.

Princess Leia shook her head. "No, we can't. We just have to try it and see. So let's stop worrying about the not-so-honorable senator from Riosa and start working out our strategy."

Greer nodded. "Well, the plan's pretty basic. Joph and I dress the way we did on the Chrome Citadel, take our junker ship to Sibensko. Probably the most believable reason for you to be aboard is if you're traveling as an indentured servant, booking the cheapest possible passage on some errand for your boss."

"I can do that." Princess Leia obviously didn't mind traveling incognita for a while. "And Threepio?"

"We're bringing Threepio?" Joph said in quiet dismay.

That won him a sharp look from the princess. "We'll want to slice into the central computer core. That's not Threepio's specialty, but his programming is more than adequate for the task. There are other droids we could bring, but I'd rather stick with the one I know and trust."

Resigned, Joph said, "Okay, but even as old as he is, Threepio looks too nice for pilots as broke as we're supposed to be."

Privately Greer doubted this; C-3PO had been antiquated for decades now. But it wasn't a point worth arguing. "Maybe he can be traveling with the indentured servant. Helping her perform whatever task her boss requires, and keeping tabs on her, too."

"I guess we could grub him up a little." Joph began to warm to the idea. "Add some dust, a few dings here and there. That would help, right?"

"It's a good plan," Princess Leia said. "And you know Threepio's just going to love getting dirty."

Greer laughed at the thought of C-3PO's dismay, but even that small motion of her head made her slightly woozy. Her last dose had hit her hard, she realized. Usually it was smarter to take a break for the rest of the day after a serum treatment, but she had work to do. "Once we get there, we broadcast the access codes we received when we took the job. That should get us into Sibensko, and we'll have to play it by ear from there."

"Oh, hey, I forgot to mention—we got a new data packet from the Ryloth satellites today." Joph looked sheepish at not having shared the news earlier, but Greer figured they'd all been distracted by Princess Leia's predicament. "Turns out Rinnrivin Di's paying one of his visits to Sibensko right now. So is that good news for us or bad?"

"Bad if he recognizes us, good if he doesn't." Princess Leia rose to her feet. "Which gives us all more reasons to work on our disguises. Whatever you need, make sure you've got it by oh six hundred hours tomorrow. Understood?"

"Absolutely," Greer said. Already the doubts she'd briefly harbored about Princess Leia seemed far away and nonsensical. "We're ready."

Princess Leia nodded and headed out of the ship. Joph grabbed a nearby datapad, eagerly searching for something. "Remember how the princess told us about the time she disguised herself as a bounty hunter? I'm going for the same kind of thing. Same species, even."

"Should work." Greer had acquired her armor days ago. She got up to leave—

—and the entire world spun and swayed, then went black as it vanished entirely.

Joph had dived toward Greer so quickly that he'd been able to break her fall to the floor. Instantly he cradled her head in one hand as he reached for his comlink with the other. "Medbay, emergency! We need medical assistance on the *Mirrorbright* in the main hangar, registry number 22061270. Repeat, we need a medic here immediately!"

"No," Greer whispered. Her faint had lasted only a few seconds. "It's okay."

"Like hell it is. You nearly smashed your face into the floor, you know that?" Joph hooked his free arm under her knees, propping them up slightly so more blood would flow to her head. "Maybe it's not a big deal, but you have to get that checked out."

Greer shook her head. "Wrong on both counts, Seastriker."

On the gangway came the thump of footsteps. Joph turned to see Dr. Harter Kalonia, medkit in hand, wearing an expression so gentle it belied her words. "Ms. Sonnel, how many times must we review the proper procedures for a hadeira serum treatment?"

"At least once more," Greer said wearily.

Dr. Kalonia raised one of her angular eyebrows. "And will you finally listen to me then?"

". . . probably not." Greer tried to smile.

The doctor tsked as she knelt by Greer's side. She wasn't rushing to begin treatment; Joph realized Dr. Kalonia agreed with Greer about this not being an emergency. "You've been sneaking around to see my Too-Onebee when I'm away, haven't you? I thought so. I see I shall have to ask maintenance to install a restraining bolt. In the meantime, we need to run a blood scan to ensure nothing more serious happened because of your dosage."

Greer pushed up her sleeve, and Joph saw an array of small scars all along her veins. "Sure."

Joph backed up to let the doctor do her work. As soon as possible, he reached for the datapad, removing the image of the Ubese bounty hunter and searching for information on hadeira serum. Instantly the answer popped up, and as the light from the screen played across his face, Joph felt the shock hit him as surely as a blow.

"Well," Greer said. She lay on the floor looking over at him, paying no attention to Dr. Kalonia's ministrations. "Now you know."

"Greer—you have bloodburn?"

"Diagnosed three years ago. So you finally found out why I quit racing."

Bloodburn was a syndrome that sometimes befell space travelers, particularly those who had begun extraorbital flights young, as Greer had. Nobody knew precisely what caused it, but bloodburn remained rare enough that people didn't let it stop them from flying. Every space traveler knew it could happen, though: One day your own blood could turn on you and begin the long, slow process of stoking fevers higher and higher until finally your brain was fried, and you were gone.

Hadeira serum treated bloodburn. It didn't cure it. No cure had ever been found.

"There, now. It's not so bad." Dr. Kalonia spoke more softly now. It occurred to Joph that the doctor had to have been keeping this secret, too, because Greer probably wouldn't even be allowed to fly the *Mirrorbright* on official missions if the higher-ups knew. Bloodburn got you kicked out of starfighter duty, for sure. "You need hydration and rest, Ms. Sonnel. Will you at least try to do that much?" When Greer nodded, the doctor glanced over at Joph, then got to her feet. "If I see you out and about tomorrow, young lady, I'll have to report you."

"*If* you see me," Greer added.

This seemed to be a standing joke between them, because Dr. Kalonia smiled slyly. "I'm rather good at not seeing things I'm not supposed to see, aren't I?" With that she tucked her medkit under one arm and walked off the *Mirrorbright*.

Joph couldn't wrap his mind around it. Greer, who flew and fought like a champion racer when she got the chance—Greer was *dying*.

"They say it helps if you avoid physical stress." Greer stared up at the ceiling. "So I quit racing. Gave up visiting home, even when I missed it so much I hurt, because if I couldn't live like a warrior of Pamarthe any longer, what was the point? Captain Solo felt so bad when I got the news that he asked Princess Leia if she had work for me here on Hosnian Prime. That's why she took me on."

"Oh." Joph felt too numbed to come up with any coherent answer.

Greer continued, "Being her chief of staff and flying the *Mirrorbright* once in a while—that, I can handle. I could live an almost normal life span if I stick to an office job and a regular schedule. If I eat right and exercise ever so gently. But you might have noticed that things have gotten a little livelier around here lately."

"That's why Princess Leia always wants you to stay behind with the ship." Puzzle pieces Joph hadn't even recognized before began to lock together, revealing the whole picture. "That's why she gives you a chance to back out, every time."

"I tell her I know my limits." Greer's expression turned rueful. "She believes me. And don't you tell her anything different."

"Greer, come on." Joph sat on the floor next to her. "This mission is about ten times more dangerous for you than it is for the rest of us."

"I can take it. I'll be staying behind with the ship, remember?"

And what if you collapse in the middle of everything? What happens then? Joph could think of another dozen objections, but he couldn't bring himself to argue with Greer while she lay there, still weak. Still dying.

"You'll get some sleep, right?" Joph tried to remember everything

Dr. Kalonia had said. "And you need, uh, hydration. We'll just get you to your quarters, let you nap and drink as much water as you can—"

"I will. I promise. After all, I've got to be in shape for my big day tomorrow."

Greer slowly sat up. Joph couldn't look her in the eyes. He braced his arms against his knees and bit his lip.

But he didn't fool Greer. "Oh, Joph. Don't."

"I can't help it." Crying openly was considered a virtue on Gatalenta—proof of a caring heart. Joph had learned the rest of the galaxy tended to prefer it when people tried to hold it together, and he'd gotten pretty good at that, but he had his limits, too. "It's just, you know, you're great. And this shouldn't be happening. It's not fair."

Her expression crumpled. "You know, thank you for saying that. Nobody's ever said it before, but it's *not* fair. It's not."

Joph wasn't sure which one of them hugged the other first, but they hung on for so long it didn't matter.

Just when he thought he might completely lose his composure, Greer let go, stepped back, and mock-punched his shoulder. "That's the last time you ever feel sorry for me. *Ever.*" Her smile wavered, but her voice got stronger with each word. "Got it?"

Pity would kill Greer faster than any disease or serum toxicity. It was the one pain he could protect her from. "Got it."

The next morning, Leia stood in front of the holocam in her apartment. She wore a simple black coverall; there would be time to change into the rest of her ragged disguise after she was aboard the junker, where nobody on Hosnian Prime could see her. Through the windows she saw a night sky only just beginning to be brightened by dawn.

She took a deep breath and began. "Han, it's me. By the time you receive this, I'll have left Hosnian Prime for what the rest of the world thinks is my hiding away to contemplate my disgrace."

Leia could be wry about it now. She'd poured her heart out in a more heartfelt message yesterday, one so grief-stricken she had hesitated before sending it even to her husband. But if she couldn't have Han with her to help her through it, at least she could tell him how she felt. And that meant she could focus on other things this morning.

"I'm not going on any sabbatical. What the rest of the Senate doesn't know is that I'm traveling to Sibensko, as part of the 'project' you and I already discussed. Sibensko can be a dangerous place, I know, but don't worry. I'm not going alone, and I know what I'm doing."

Over and over, Leia spoke into the void, not knowing when or if the people she loved most would hear her. She knew why it had to be this way, but never before had her separations from Han, Ben, and Luke been more difficult to bear. Only once in her life had she felt so lonely—without her father, or her fellow Rebellion officers, or Mon Mothma, or these three men she loved so dearly to support her. That had been on the Death Star in the wake of Alderaan's destruction.

Luke and Han had saved her then. Now she would have to stand alone.

Leia smiled into the holocam, trying to envision her husband's face. If the mission to Sibensko went wrong, her next words might be the last Han would ever hear her say. The first time she'd had to ask herself what to do in this situation had been at Cloud City, and she said the same thing now as she had then. "I love you."

Then she snapped off the holocam, slung her bag over one shoulder, and walked out of her apartments, into danger.

How was it that danger felt more like home?

CHAPTER
TWENTY-SIX

The junker ship came in low over Sibensko's southern axis. Stretching out in every direction, as far as the eye could see, was nothing but dark, choppy water.

"Are we completely certain these are the correct coordinates?" C-3PO had become peeved as soon as they'd dirtied him up, and it amused Leia that his mood had only worsened since then. "Rinnrivin Di and his associates are rather low sorts of people, exactly the type to send us in the wrong direction altogether."

"They may be lowlifes," Leia replied, "but they're lowlifes who want a job done. This has to be the place. Ready, Greer?"

Greer wore full Mandalorian armor in gray and black; the helmet hung on a hook in the back, awaiting her departure from the ship. "Sending the codes now."

Joph's voice sounded high-pitched and metallic within the Ubese bounty hunter's mask. "So how do you let someone into an underwater city?"

Leia pulled her ragged cloak more tightly around her. "Let's hope we're about to find out."

The comm unit on the main console erupted into static, through which a low voice said, "Codes confirmed. Prepare to land."

"How are we supposed to land without land?" Joph muttered.

As he spoke, however, the waters churned. From the depths emerged a broad, circular platform, ringed by red stripes. Greer swiftly brought the ship around, swooping in and landing with such lightness that Leia hardly felt the runners make impact. The moment they touched down, the red stripes at the platform's circumference glowed brightly and the air around them took on the strange, iridescent sheen of a force field.

Then the platform sank under the seas again, and the force field kept the water at bay. Within moments they were plunging into depths almost untouched by sunlight above. In the murky ocean, Leia caught glimpses of movement—enormous sea creatures unbothered by the activity on Sibensko, or used to it. To them, Leia supposed, all the smugglers and thieves that came to this place were only a small, irrelevant part of the vast ocean.

"Here it comes," Greer said.

Beneath them floated what first appeared to be a cloud of green light. As the ship got closer, the light took shape, forming itself into a kind of glass labyrinth. Tubes and tunnels connected undersea domes, fuzzy with algae, but still glowing. Leia looked down to see huge mechanized plates opening wide like a blooming flower, surrounding them.

The platform finished its descent with a small shudder and thud. The mechanized plates rose again, closing into a secure dome, and then the roar of water pumps began. As Leia watched, the water level descended until only a few puddles remained on the floor.

"Atmospheric levels outside normalizing." Greer looked up from her console and smiled. "We're in."

Joph could hardly contain himself. "Okay, I know these people are pure scum, but I have to admit—this is incredible."

"Criminals can be as ingenious as the rest of us. More, sometimes."

Leia pulled up the hood of her cloak, then pulled a thin veil over her nose and mouth. She thought that would disguise her, though the cloak was shabby enough to ensure few people would give her more than a glance in the first place. "But I have to admit, this setup is a whole lot larger and more sophisticated than I would have expected. The Hutts could've financed something like this at their height, but virtually no one else."

"It's been expanded dramatically, from what we know. This is at least four times the size of the outpost it used to be." Greer went for her helmet. "And we're supposed to think Rinnrivin Di put this together in only a few years?"

She was right. This was bigger than criminal money, Leia realized. Even though the Hutts could've built something so extravagant, would they have bothered? Jabba himself had been content to build his palace on a world as obscure and dull as Tatooine. Whoever had built this had deep pockets and high ambitions. *The only groups who build on this scale,* she thought, *are governments. Or would-be governments.*

Maybe the Amaxine warriors aren't as far out on the fringe as I believed.

"First things first," she said, half to herself. "Let's find Rinnrivin Di." Their satellite data only told them what planet he was on; she wanted to know his location down to the millimeter.

Joph turned toward her. "I've been wondering how we were going to do that."

"Easy." Leia took the tracker out of her cloak pocket and activated it; sure enough, within moments a sensor began to blink. "He's not far away. A klick, maybe two?"

"You put a tracker on him?" Joph said. "How did you manage that?"

"The first time Rinnrivin Di and I met, he gave me a certain holocube that meant a lot to him." Leia thought again of the small image of her younger self, seemingly vulnerable, actually preparing to commit murder. "I inserted a microscopic tracker into the cube, then returned it to him. It's one of Rinnrivin Di's prize possessions. I knew that if he ever got it back, he'd never let it out of his keeping again."

"But the tracker only tells us where the holocube is," Greer pointed out. "Not where Rinnrivin is."

Leia nodded. "True. He may be storing it in a ship or in his quarters here. Still, if we don't find the man himself, we find a place he's sure to return to. If we can record him here, particularly dealing with anyone we can trace to the Amaxine warriors, then we'll be able to link his cartel with the paramilitary group even more closely."

"What made you so certain he'd never give it up?" Joph asked.

She allowed herself one moment to relish her memory of Jabba's desperate gurgling just before he died. "I was sure. Let's leave it at that."

Greer settled the helmet on her head, and when she spoke again, her voice sounded slightly metallic. "The door's opening. Let's get out there and hustle like two pilots desperate for their next meal."

"You got it." Joph clapped his gloved hands together.

"Are we entirely sure this is safe?" C-3PO asked plaintively. Everyone knew better than to pay him any attention.

Greer led the way, with Joph at her elbow. Although this worked for their cover identities, she suspected he was staying so close in case she collapsed again.

Part of her wanted to be irritated by his concern. But mostly it touched her. She had told so few people about her condition, precisely because she didn't want to be treated like some delicate trinket that could shatter at the slightest touch. Captain Solo and Princess Leia had known better than to do that, which meant Joph was the first person to hover around her so protectively. It turned out the hovering was actually kind of sweet.

At the moment, however, they didn't need "sweet." They needed to come across as tough and hardened, ready for anything. She strode ahead of Joph, gaining the lead, just as a man in a black jumpsuit greeted them. His shaggy beard and hair didn't disguise the sharpness and hostility in his eyes.

Greer remembered that jumpsuit. It was identical to the ones worn by the Amaxine warriors on Daxam IV.

"Welcome to Sibensko," he said with a bow, his elaborate politeness almost mocking. "I'll need your work codes now."

As though exasperated, Greer took out her datapad and sent him the code. *Come on,* she thought. *Come on.*

He nodded in satisfaction. "Good. We've been expecting you. My name is Padric; I'll guide you through pickup and transfer." Padric's attention drifted toward the droid and hooded figure behind them. "We hired two. Why have four come?"

"She's an indenture we picked up for a few extra credits. The droid keeps her tagged, makes sure she does her master's bidding. I have her indenture codes if you need to see them." Greer had found a real set of indenture codes for a woman who almost matched Princess Leia in age and height, but who had recently been freed.

Sure enough, after another moment, Padric relaxed slightly. "Fine. But she and the droid remain in public areas only. They aren't to play any part in your work here. Understood?"

"Understood," Greer said. "Our passenger's not asking any questions." Behind her, apparently feeling he needed to play some role in the drama, Joph nodded. She turned back toward the princess and C-3PO, inclining her head only briefly before she and Joph followed Padric out of the docking station into Sibensko at large.

If anything, the tunnels were even more impressive from inside. Braced with elaborate arches and struts, they carved enormous spaces out of the water. A crowd nearly as rough as the one on Chrome Citadel mingled about, evidently at ease this far away from any legitimate authorities. Greer even caught a glimpse of a young Hutt slithering disconsolately in the distance.

"We'll load your shipment as quickly as possible," Padric said as they walked along, so swiftly that Joph practically had to jog to keep up. "Which will take some time, actually. You know how it is with delicate cargo."

"Of course." Greer didn't like the sound of this. What did "delicate cargo" refer to? Surely not slaves . . .

"Once we're loaded, you'll rendezvous with our contacts at the destination point and help transfer the cargo to them. That's it. Job done." Padric had an oily smile. "Though if I were you, I'd get off-world in a hell of a hurry."

"I usually do," Greer said as they moved out of the main corridors, through a secure door Padric opened with a transdermal signal key implanted in his wrist. "Doesn't pay to stick around after a job."

"With an attitude like that, you won't stay broke for long." Padric said this with genuine approval. "You're a go-getter. We'll have need for people like that, once things have changed."

Greer turned toward him. "What do you mean?"

"You'll see. Everyone will see before long."

Padric punched in an elaborate code, and yet another door opened into a small inner sanctum. Greer was grateful for the helmet she wore, which hid the shock on her face at the sight of thermal detonators—*thousands* of them—all piled high in pallets, ready for transport.

Her voice remained steady as she said, "I see what you mean about delicate cargo."

Smugly, Padric nodded. "Exactly."

"We'll take our time loading." Greer addressed this to Joph, who stood so still she thought he might be in shock. She turned back to Padric. "So where are these headed?"

Padric's smile widened. "Straight to Hosnian Prime."

Through the thick cowl of her hooded robe, Leia took in the high, arched tunnels of Sibensko. The expanses of glass or whatever transparent material was in use stretched for enormous distances—far longer than she would've thought safe.

For once, she and C-3PO were on the exact same page. "It's a wonder this entire city hasn't broken down completely under the weight of the water," the droid said.

Her sharp eyes picked out the details that revealed some of the arches to be more than arches. "Look up there. See the mechanism hidden in the framework? They've installed watertight doors, probably every couple hundred meters or so. This place is fortified against tunnel collapse."

C-3PO seemed to brighten. "How very reassuring."

"Maybe," Leia said. "Though it makes you wonder about the strength of the supports down here." The central joining seemed to be held together in only one place—capable of carrying the weight, but also capable of failing. "Maybe criminal masterminds aren't the world's most cautious architects."

"Oh, dear."

Together she and C-3PO made their way through the twisting maze of Sibensko. Leia went unrecognized—both a relief and a novel sensation. Computer terminals lined many hallways, and linkup stations were nearly as common as bars. But the work she needed to do required a terminal connected to Sibensko's computer core, which none of these commercial setups would provide.

She took to wandering in and out of various stores, on the lookout for a lazy shopkeeper or an unlocked door. Nobody paid her any attention, but that did her no good if she couldn't find an in.

Finally, she and C-3PO reached a crowded cantina where the barkeepers appeared to be as intoxicated as the patrons. Leia bought an ale, held it for a long time while only taking a few sips, and slowly edged her way farther inside. C-3PO dutifully followed behind. When someone brought up Ubardian oil wrestling on holo, leading to a wave of cheers, she used the distraction to slip into the back.

"At last." Leia pulled back the hood of her robe as she powered up the house computer. "Threepio, can you get into this?"

"I should hope so," he said primly. "It appears to be a rather primitive system."

"Here's hoping the security system is equally primitive."

Leia was gambling on Sibensko's extremely tight external security to pay off with a less secure internal system. Why worry about intruders when every single person on the planet had to provide approved codes to land? It was just the kind of assumption a self-satisfied mobster might make. Even Jabba had opened his palace doors for each of them, so long ago.

But artificial intelligence had its own ideas, sometimes. "Dear me," C-3PO said as he interfaced with the Sibensko system. "How very backward. It actually wants to try a hard data transfer."

Hard data transfers had their place in security, but at the moment Leia had nothing to transfer the information to. Why hadn't she thought to bring something along? "Can you convince it to just share the data directly?"

"I *am* trying." C-3PO shook his head as if in disbelief. "The system isn't invulnerable, but I must say, it's awfully stubborn."

Leia managed not to thump her head against the nearest wall. "Keep at it."

It took a while—so long that her heart had begun to thump crazily with suspense—but at last, C-3PO convinced the system to open up. Within several minutes, the droid had gotten past the few information locks and was deep in conversation with the computer core.

"We're looking for any information about the Amaxine warriors," she urged. "Any links between them and Rinnrivin Di's cartel."

"Yes, Your Highness. I believe such data is readily available, but now that we're talking, the core is proving rather chatty. It's had no one to speak with in ever so long."

Leia experienced the vaguely guilty sensation that surfaced every time she realized that droid personalities were more than programmed conversational quirks. A computer core could be lonely. C-3PO could take pity on it.

But that was a question for another day. "Download everything you can, Threepio. We need all the evidence we can get our hands on."

C-3PO obtained extensive banking records proving that the Amaxine warriors—or the nameless entity behind the Amaxine warriors—had provided billions of credits in start-up capital to Rinnrivin Di seven years prior. Only then had his cartel shifted from being a minor player to a major power. Arliz Hadrassian's name came up several times, and C-3PO logged each one. Even more important, he found links that could be followed up on later, which might tie Rinnrivin's funding to nameless sources on Centrist worlds.

Are they planning a major military buildup? Leia wondered. *If so, the Amaxine warriors might be a test case. A hint of things to come.* Yet she still resisted the idea that the Centrist coalition of planets wanted war. Surely no one who had lived through the wars against the Empire would ever want to take up arms again . . .

"Goodness gracious," C-3PO said. "Well, that was unexpected."

Leia turned back toward him. "What?"

"The computer core is most fretful about an area beneath the city proper," he confided. "It's rather large, nearly as many square kilometers as the city itself. And it appears to be used solely by the Amaxines."

"Show me the schematics."

C-3PO did so, and Leia gaped when she took in the sheer scale of what they'd found. Her mind began doing the calculations. An area that vast couldn't be reserved for mere meetings. Not even a training arena.

That was a space large enough to contain an army.

"Can the computer tell us what's stored down there?" Leia asked.

"Starfighters, a few transport ships, and—oh, my—a rather large number of armaments." C-3PO swiveled his head toward her. "Perhaps we should have brought a military escort."

She went for her secure comlink. "Are you there? Signal back if you can."

After a moment, Joph Seastriker answered, his metallic-filtered voice down to a whisper. "We're here. Greer's finalizing the shipment, which by the way is explosive. Literally and figuratively."

Leia grimaced. "Then I'm glad we're the ones who got it. What's your timetable look like?"

"I think we'll be fully loaded pretty soon. The hoverdroids are bringing in the last crates now," Joph said. "What about you?"

"We've got everything we need to bring down the Amaxine warriors and Rinnrivin Di. But we've also learned that Sibensko doubles as a military base. We can't leave here without investigating." She made up her mind in an instant. "I'm going to send Threepio back to you with the data. Meanwhile, I'm going to head down to see what the Amaxine warriors are really up to. Maybe I can get some images we can use for additional evidence."

"You shouldn't go alone," Joph said, with unexpected firmness. "Wait, and Greer or I will come to your location. Then we can look into it together."

"No, you won't, Lieutenant." Apparently the kid needed to remember who ranked who around here. "I know this part is risky. Extra people won't make it any safer. We'd just put more lives at danger."

Resigned, Joph said only, "We're expected to take off within the hour."

"And you will—with or without me." Leia took a deep breath. "Threepio will reach you shortly. Get him off Sibensko no matter what. Nothing is as important as getting this data to the Galactic Senate." *Not even my life.*

C-3PO, however, couldn't fathom it. "But, Princess Leia! I couldn't abandon you here!"

"You can and you will, because it's an order." She put one hand on his metal shoulder, reminded of how much she actually cared for the droid. "You're the key to bringing this all down, Threepio. You and no one else. This is one of the most critical missions you've had since you and Artoo escaped with the plans for the first Death Star. Do you understand?"

As usual, appealing to C-3PO's sense of importance did the trick. "Of course, Your Highness. Rest assured that I shall ensure this information reaches the proper persons."

"Thank you, Threepio." Leia glanced into the cantina; people were still thronged around the wrestling holos, paying no attention to the back of the house. "Now get out of here. Get to Greer and Joph as soon as you can."

She remained in place for what seemed like a long while after C-3PO had gone, but what could in actuality have been only minutes. Then Leia raised the hood of her robe over her head and hastily ducked out.

"*And Notea has the advantage!*" the wrestling announcer said, his voice broadcast loudly over the speakers as she threaded her way through the distracted group in the cantina. "*Yes, it looks like it's Notea's day today—*"

Once Leia reached the corridor, she felt as if she could breathe again. She mentally superimposed the schematics C-3PO had shown her over the parts of this underwater city she could see and those she had already walked through. Her sense of direction had always been strong, and within seconds she felt sure that she knew how to reach the lifts that would take her down to the Amaxine warriors' secret underground lair.

Swiftly she walked through the crowds, which were no longer as numerous as they had been earlier. Apparently this was what passed for nighttime underneath Sibensko's ocean. *Good,* Leia thought. *Fewer people to walk around, fewer people who might notice us.* If her luck held, she might be able to rendezvous with the others before very long.

She turned a corner and descended a series of steps into a deeper tunnel both longer and darker than the others. This one seemed to lead to the lift she wanted. Better yet, it seemed to be nearly deserted. Nobody else was walking through the tunnel but three figures not that far away—a Nikto and two of his guards—

Leia's gut clenched. It couldn't be. Surely her mind was playing paranoid tricks on her.

But she hadn't checked her tracker since they'd begun downloading information from the central computer. With every step she took, she became more certain that the Nikto walking toward her was none other than Rinnrivin Di.

Keep your hood on. Don't look at him. There's no reason for him to expect you here. Just stay calm.

So Leia told herself, but she could sense that a confrontation was inevitable.

Rinnrivin's voice echoed through the tunnel. "There you are at last. May I have the privilege of knowing precisely who it is who's been tracking me all this time? Though I must admit, I have an idea."

He held up something in his left hand: the holocube, even now playing her murder of Jabba the Hutt over again.

Pretense would be useless. Leia threw back her hood and veil to face him squarely. "Rinnrivin. Fancy meeting you here. I regret that our reunion is taking place under such unfortunate circumstances."

Cocking his head, Rinnrivin said, "Do you honestly think I'm fool enough not to have sensors that would detect a signal from a tracking device?"

She shrugged. "I don't know. You were fool enough not to check for a tracking device in the first place."

Rinnrivin's leathery face shifted from a thin smile to a snarl. The gentlemanly mask had finally dropped away. What remained was the true man: ugly, violent, and willing to kill.

Leia was outnumbered, alone, beyond her authority . . . and trapped.

CHAPTER
TWENTY-SEVEN

Immediately Leia corrected herself. She was outnumbered, alone, beyond her authority, trapped—and in possession of a blaster strapped just beneath the folds of her cloak.

Her hand stole down toward it as she faced Rinnrivin squarely. Despite the distance, their gazes locked. He said, "I had so hoped we could be friends, Huttslayer."

"No, you didn't. You hoped I'd be your tool." Fast as a flash, Leia pulled her blaster, firing almost as soon as her finger could touch the trigger. One of Rinnrivin's guards dropped instantly. She swung her blaster around just in time to match the other guard; the two of them were now locked in a standoff. Keeping her eyes on the guard, Leia addressed herself to Rinnrivin Di. "All those times you watched me kill Jabba the Hutt, and you never learned from his example. It doesn't pay to jerk me around."

Rinnrivin was not cowed in the slightest. He merely crossed his arms in front of his chest, the gesture wrinkling the fine gray silk of his jacket. "Posture all you like. The fact remains that you've been exposed. You can no longer leave Sibensko—at least, not without my help. Which, at the moment, I am unwilling to give."

"Looks that way," Leia agreed. She took one pace backward, and the heel of her foot hit the lowest of the stairs she had just descended. Cautiously, never losing her aim on the second guard, she took that step.

This won her only scorn from Rinnrivin. "Do you honestly think you can escape that way?"

"You never know until you try." Another step. Then another. Rinnrivin's guard shifted on his clawed feet, uneasy and unsure at what point he should stop threatening and start firing.

"May I point out that you'd be well within the range of my man's blaster all the way to the top of the steps?" Rinnrivin shook his head sorrowfully. A flicker of motion to one side made Leia tense, but it was only a school of glowfish, their blue-white fins briefly bright against the dark waters outside.

"Believe me," she replied, "I've forgotten more about blaster ranges than you'll ever know."

"That may be," he agreed. "Your forgetfulness would certainly explain why you're trying to get away, even though you have no hope of success. Or is the explanation far simpler? Is it merely . . . cowardice?"

"Call it whatever you want." With that, Leia lifted her blaster, losing her sights on Rinnrivin's guard—

—and targeting the central strut of the tunnel support directly overhead.

One bolt held the entire thing together. That bolt was no larger than a child's fist. At this range, in semi-darkness, perhaps one shot in a thousand might be capable of destroying that bolt.

But Leia made the shot.

For one terrible instant, the metal groaned, and she caught a glimpse of blind panic on Rinnrivin's face before she spun and began running up the steps as quickly as she could. Then, with a tremendous roar of water, the tunnel gave way.

Leia didn't have to turn around to know that Rinnrivin Di and his guard had been instantly crushed to death. She had only one priority: running fast enough to save her own skin.

Taking the steps two at a time, Leia reached the top just as she heard the wave surging behind her and saw one of the watertight doors sliding down to seal this corridor away from the rest of the Sibensko complex. Within moments, it would lock into the floor and seal her inside to drown.

She called on all her strength to hurl herself toward the door. Her body struck the floor so hard that pain jolted through every bone, but she managed to land in a roll. Water rushed past her, even over her, in the moment before the watertight door finally snapped shut.

And Leia was on the right side.

For a moment she sat in the tremendous puddle that now covered this corridor, panting, her waterlogged cloak heavy on her shoulders. She stared at the metal door that now marked Rinnrivin Di's watery grave. But she had no time to think on that; bright-yellow alarm lights had already begun to flash. Before long, Sibensko would be in complete lockdown. Should she go for her ship immediately, or should she try to get the evidence they needed first?

One of the hard lessons Leia had learned during the Rebellion was this: Any single life was expendable, including her own.

Shrugging off the damp cloak, Leia got to her feet as she took up her comlink. "Joph? Greer? Are you there?"

"We're here," Greer replied. "Threepio just walked into the hangar, and we've finalized the shipment, but some kind of alarm's going off—"

"I'm afraid that's my fault." Leia took a deep breath as she adjusted herself. Now she wore only a black skimmer shirt and leggings, plus the leather holster strapped to one thigh. Crowds of people had begun rushing from shops and cantinas, panicked by the breach alert and desperate to get to their own ships. "Greer, I'm giving you new orders. You're to take off immediately. Get out of here as fast as you can, and bring the evidence inside Threepio's data banks back to the Senate."

Joph broke in. "Princess Leia, we can't just leave you here!"

"You can and you will." She squared her shoulders and took a moment to reckon her surroundings anew. The path she'd intended to take to the Amaxine warriors' den had been cut off, perhaps permanently, but another lift would get her there if she made it in time. "Once I've checked this out, I'll steal a ship if I can—and trust me, I probably can."

"It's too dangerous," Greer insisted. "You can reach us in just a few minutes if you start right away."

"No. I have to get as much evidence as possible, *now,* because we'll never be able to return to Sibensko. It's worth risking my life, but it's not worth risking yours. Least of all is it worth risking the data inside Threepio."

Again, Joph tried to dissuade her. "After this, the Senate will be all over Sibensko—"

"And the Amaxines will be long gone." Leia knew how to put steel in her voice, and she did it now. "You have orders, Lieutenant Seastriker. That goes for you, too, Greer. Take off as soon as possible. Organa out."

With that, she snapped off her comlink. If her crew couldn't argue with her any longer, maybe they'd finally get around to escaping from this place.

As for herself—Leia intended to take her chances.

Back on the ship, Joph and Greer stared at each other, their hands on the controls, trapped in indecision.

"We can't do this." Every instinct Joph had rebelled against it. "Leaving her behind? She'll die. You know she will."

"If anyone could steal a ship and get out of here, Princess Leia could." But Greer didn't move to obey the princess's orders.

C-3PO offered, "If I might, as loath as we all are to leave Her Highness behind, military protocols are quite clear on this point. We are required to follow her orders. And Princess Leia has been known to escape from unlikely predicaments before."

"Everybody's luck runs out sometime," Joph muttered.

"Trust me, I know." Greer closed her eyes and took a deep breath. Did she feel dizzy or disoriented? This had to count as stress in the extreme. But just as Joph leaned toward her, Greer's eyes opened, clear and focused. "We have to follow orders."

It knocked the wind out of Joph. It took him a moment to respond. "If we do this, and she dies—"

"Are you afraid of taking responsibility for your actions?" Greer snapped.

"No, I'm afraid of getting Princess Leia killed!"

She steadied herself and said, more quietly, "I am, too. But she's right. Getting this evidence to the Senate is more important. Let's go."

Joph did as she said, sealing the ship's doors and readying thrusters. Behind him, he could see the heavy pallets stacked thickly with thermal detonators. If they had a collision at any point—even too rough a ride—one of those detonators might go off. And as soon as one exploded, the others would, too.

He'd been so worried about Princess Leia that he hadn't realized she might well outlive them.

"This is terrible!" C-3PO cried. "Simply terrible!"

"Tell us about it," Joph muttered.

C-3PO kept on: "Princess Leia is in great danger!"

"We *know*, Threepio," Greer said as she fired up the engines.

"No, no, you don't understand!" C-3PO's voice rose to a new pitch of alarm. "I've just analyzed the computers' records of foot traffic within the city against the overall map, and it seems that a substantial portion of the humans within are currently inside the Amaxine warriors' headquarters!"

Joph and Greer stared at each other. He whispered, "She's not just running toward their hideout. She's running toward their *entire army*."

Leia's gut dipped as the lift began its descent. With one hand resting on her blaster, she quickly took stock. *All right, so I don't have Threepio with me, much less any holocams. That means I won't be able to*

fully record whatever I find down here. I'll only be able to testify to
what I've seen.

Would that be enough any longer? After the revelations about
Darth Vader, Leia knew her credibility had plummeted nearly to
zero. However, C-3PO's data would back up so much of what she said
that people might be inclined to believe the rest. Certainly their information would demand a more thorough investigation; if the Senate didn't trust Leia's judgment, they might trust the people sent in to
inspect this place after her.

. . . which meant, really, that she could go for the ship. Maybe she
still had time to make it. By now, Leia knew Joph and Greer well
enough to be certain they'd spend a while bickering before they finally followed their orders. The risk she was taking with her life
might not even be necessary.

But Leia didn't turn back.

It had been a long time since she'd gotten her hands dirty. Too
long. From now on, she intended to be on the front lines, doing whatever most needed to be done, regardless of the cost.

The lift concluded its journey, coming to a stop. Leia readied herself as the doors swung open so that she could begin taking stock of
the Amaxine hideout immediately—

—but she hadn't prepared to come face-to-face with half a dozen
Amaxine warriors.

"What's the meaning of this?" one demanded. "Who are you?"

"I've lost my way." Leia put one hand to her temple as though she
were disoriented. "So many alarms were going off above, and I've
never been here before—the maps are awfully confusing, don't you
think? They should put up better maps, I think. I intend to complain
to the management."

The Amaxine warriors didn't relax, exactly, but they allowed her to
step out of the lift as though to get her bearings. Leia continued to act
confused as she peeked through her own fingers, getting the best
view she could. They stood on the edge of an enormous hangar, one
filled with starfighters of every make and model, from X-wings indis-
tinguishable from those of the New Republic to old TIE fighters.
Were there five hundred of them? A thousand?

However many it was, the Amaxine warriors had undoubtedly amassed a fighting force capable of causing confusion or destruction on a massive scale.

"I don't suppose I could have a drink of water?" Leia called upon her memories of Ben as she smiled at them, hoping they would perceive her as motherly. Most of the Amaxine warriors she saw were precisely the age to treat their mothers with affectionate disregard, an attitude that would go far toward getting her out of this. "That would be so helpful."

The Amaxine nearest her shook his head no, but politely, as he hit the lift controls for her. "You should go, ma'am. As soon as possible."

"Well, thank you just the same." So much for trying to stall. "You're both such nice young men—"

"Hold!" someone shouted from the back. "That woman shows up on our facial recognition system!"

Should've put the veil back on, Leia thought as she swung her elbow back savagely into the nearest Amaxine's belly.

As he staggered to one side, she ran away as fast as she could toward the only open door she could see. The stitch in her side tightened, lancing her with pain. This had been so much easier when she was nineteen . . .

Leia reached the door only steps ahead of her pursuers, barely in time to hit the controls and seal them on the other side. Panting, she looked around to see what kind of room she'd just locked herself into. The first thing she realized was that the circular space had only one door. This had the benefit of ensuring nobody else could get in and the drawback of ensuring she couldn't get out.

"Might as well make myself comfortable," she muttered. "Looks like I'll be here for a while."

But then her gaze focused on the red rings around the perimeter, and the second thing she realized was that this room was no room. It was a landing platform, one that could be raised to the ocean's surface—and at that instant, the floor jerked and began to move.

Alarmed, Leia looked upward at the fast-approaching ceiling; by now she could make out the plates that would soon open, allowing millions of liters of water to crush her long before she'd get the chance to drown.

Force field. There's a force field. Find it! She recognized a small rectangular control at the far side of the floor and dived for it just as she heard the first stirring of the metal gears that would open the plates. Her hand slammed down on the control, hard.

Leia held her breath as she watched the ceiling plates open wide again. The iridescent shimmer of the force field formed a semicircle above her, keeping back the ocean. For a moment, wonder and relief made her smile, but only as long as it took her to wonder what she was going to do when the platform reached the surface. If Joph and Greer had followed orders, and by now they probably had, she had no hope of rescue. The Amaxine warriors were no doubt loading starfighters onto other platforms now, preparing to meet her above the surface. She had no plan, no backup, and only one weapon.

The ocean shifted from black to deep blue as the platform neared the light. Leia got to her feet and put her hand on her blaster. She might be trapped. She might even be doomed. But there was no way she'd go down without a fight.

Surf bubbled around her as the force field cleared the water. Twilight was falling, and the sun still illuminated only one corner of the cobalt sky. She stood amid a churning ocean with nowhere to hide. Just as Leia had anticipated, another platform broke the surface seconds later, and two starfighters—a Y-wing and a B-wing—took to the air, turning straight toward her.

She braced herself. *The force field will protect you at first. No point in firing until the field goes down.*

But the B-wing's bolts sliced through the air with deadly precision. The very first spray of weapons fire hit the force field controls, and with a shimmer it was gone. Leia brought her blaster up into firing position, taking aim at the Y-wing as it approached. Maybe they'd shoot each other at the exact same moment—

Laserfire screamed in from a completely different direction, scoring the Y-wing until it spiraled out of control and plunged into the depths. Leia whirled around to see a ship she'd never laid eyes on before: a sleek, modern, black-tiled racer, onto which someone had hastily added a small weapons array.

The racer came to a stop, hovering above her as a magnetic tow dropped onto the platform. Without hesitation, Leia grabbed the handgrips bolted to each side. No sooner had her fingers closed around them than the tow was activated, jerking her up into the air and into the racer's cargo bay. Its metal doors slid shut beneath her as the racer accelerated again, and the magnetic pull went slack.

Leia's feet slammed to the floor as she let the heavy tow drop. She ran for the cockpit, where the pilot was so hard at work he didn't even turn around.

"Sorry I'm late, sweetheart," said Han.

She slipped into the empty copilot's chair beside him. "Honey, you're right on time."

Her husband had not only received her message, but he'd dropped everything he was doing to rush here to help her in any way he could. Leia let go of all the frustration she felt at Han's long absences, all the bickering they'd never grown out of. In the end, she knew, he would always come through.

The B-wing carved out a wide arc; its pilot had come up here to shoot one lone woman, not to get into a firefight with somebody who clearly knew what he was doing. But the Amaxine warriors must have instilled real discipline in their troops, because he came back toward them at full speed.

"Take auxiliary weapons, will ya?" Han's hands tightened on the controls. "I'm coming in under his belly."

"Got it." Leia hit the console, releasing weapons control to her. A holographic targeting system floated between her and the viewport— silly, all this modern assistance, when all you needed was to take aim—

Han brought the racer in low, skimming the surface as he tilted the ship to maximize their chances with the B-wing. Leia fired, but the B-wing had accelerated at the last minute; she only managed to clip the wing.

"We'll get him next time." Now Han soared upward at such a sharp angle the racer was nearly perpendicular to the ground. When a transmission came in, he flipped the switch and grinned. "Greer! How the hell are you?"

"Captain Solo?" Greer sounded breathless. "What are you doing here?"

"Don't worry," Leia said. "Han's got me. We'll follow you guys out of this system as soon as we take care of a little unfinished business."

With a scowl, Han said, "Looks like we've got company."

Sure enough, another platform had surfaced, this one with two more starfighters. Would the Amaxine warriors send up their entire fleet? If so, the racer didn't have enough firepower to take them out.

One thing at a time, Leia reminded herself.

Without a word passed between them, Han took over primary weapons control, then separated the two laser cannons so he and Leia could fire independently. She knew every move he would make before he made it, and had already seen through the jerky, scattered targeting holos to the shot she wanted to make.

The Amaxine warriors flew closer to one another, no doubt hoping to create a battle formation. All they'd done was create a better target.

She and Han fired as one. Han's cannon took out the B-wing, while Leia sent one of the new fighters screeching downward at high speed, fire trailing behind it. The ship hit the water at incredible speed, with enough velocity to take it all the way to—

The massive explosion was so bright that for a moment the ocean shone like the sun. Almost instantly, tsunamis rose up so high that they nearly swamped the racer, spreading outward in a vast ripple effect that might circle the entire planet of Sibensko. A few lesser explosions lit up the depths for the instants it took the water to extinguish any fire. No one still inside could have had any chance to escape.

"I hate to tell you this," Han said, "but that might have been too good a shot."

"It crashed through the main station structure." Leia slumped back in the copilot's seat. "I think it brought down the whole underwater city. But that shouldn't have happened." Her mind reeled as she thought of the many travelers who had been passing through; most had been smugglers, maybe not so different from Han a few decades ago. They hadn't deserved that fate.

Then it hit her: the Amaxine warriors.

"Explosives," she whispered. "They must have kept a massive amount of armaments down there. The crash set them off, and the explosives did the rest."

"Damn. Sibensko's a rough place. Only came here a couple of times, myself—didn't trust the kind of people who did business here. And this is coming from someone who took work from the Hutts." Han turned toward her. "So how does blowing this place up affect your investigation?"

"We destroyed all the evidence except what's in Threepio's data banks, and even that can't be backed up any longer. But we also destroyed a paramilitary force preparing to attack the New Republic." The Amaxine warriors had been defeated; the enemy was no more.

CHAPTER
TWENTY-EIGHT

"Everything else I'd ever done, everything I've ever been, was erased in an instant." Leia struggled to find the words. "People who had fought beside me in the war, or served beside me for years in the Senate—they didn't even see me as myself any longer. All I'll ever be to them now is Darth Vader's daughter."

Han snuggled her closer against his chest as they lay together in their bed on Hosnian Prime. Moonlight slanted through the bedroom window, but paler now as dawn approached. Leia rested her head on his shoulder and shut her eyes, taking comfort in the tenderness with which he kissed her forehead.

"It's not gonna be like that forever," he murmured. "Not for everyone. Sooner or later, they'll remember who you are."

"For the people closest to me, maybe." Tai-Lin had come through for her, and despite Varish's awkwardness, she had defended Leia from the start. Greer and even young Joph Seastriker had come around within a day or two; a handful of others were likely to follow. A few people from her past, including Ackbar, Nien Nunb, and Lando, had messaged or sent holos that showed their compassion and loyalty. Mon Mothma's message even hinted that she'd suspected for a long while—which meant she'd never allowed it to prejudice their relationship. Leia knew now who her truest friends were, and she would never forget it. "But to the galaxy at large? Everything else is gone."

"Then to hell with the galaxy at large."

Typical Han. "It just hurts, that's all. The rumors, the anger, the sense of disgrace for something I couldn't help. Even the man who outed me to the Senate—Ransolm Casterfo—we'd been working together on the Rinnrivin Di investigation for months, and I honestly believed we'd become good friends. Yet as soon as he heard the truth about Vader, he betrayed me."

"The guy sounds like a jerk."

"I wish it were that simple." Leia would've been able to get over that wound more quickly if she could believe Ransolm had truly been unworthy of any respect. "He's a decent man, mostly. A decent politician, which is rarer. But he hates Darth Vader, and that's reason enough for him to hate me."

"Forget that Casterfo loser, will you?" Han stroked her hair, which spread across her pillow, off the far edge of the bed. "Look at it like this. You wanted out of the Senate anyway. Now you've got your chance. Once your term's up, you're free. You can spend some time flying around with an old scoundrel for a change."

"Han, that sounds like paradise." But she couldn't set aside all her worries so easily. "Has it been bad for you? When the sublight relays ended, and you came out to realize they knew my secret—"

"Everyone assumed I must've had no idea who I'd married. I made it clear that I'd known from the start, that I don't give a damn, and anybody with any sense wouldn't care, either. Nobody's been fool enough to bring up the subject twice."

One of the best things about Han was that he boiled everything down to the essentials and disregarded the rest. Sometimes he simplified things too much, but mostly he helped her center on what really mattered. He'd calmed her down about Ben—more or less—but even Han could only take her so far. Even as Leia tried to push her doubts away, others crept in to take their place. "I only hope I can get someone to listen to what we discovered on Sibensko."

"What do you mean, hope? You've got all the info right there with Goldenrod, right?"

"Yes, I do. And I intend to share the data with the few political allies I have left. But what we've learned about the rise of this paramilitary group and their role in the Napkin Bombing . . . that requires action by the full Senate. I doubt I can make that happen."

Han rubbed her shoulder. "Hey. Come on. Once they hear the whole story, they'll have to do something. Or is the Senate even more useless than I thought?"

Once, Leia would have argued with him about the Senate having no real purpose. That seemed like so long ago. "Oh, they're useless, all right. But you don't understand. Even to speak on the Senate floor, a quorum of senators has to decide that you and your topic are worth hearing. Normally it's not an issue, because the quorum is set at such a low number." She shook her head sadly. "I won't even be able to muster that. Not any longer."

"I'm sorry." His thumb brushed her shoulder. "At least you took those guys out. Rinnrivin Di, the Amaxine warriors—they're history."

"Maybe. But we can't afford to assume there aren't more groups like the Amaxine warriors. And they may still have facilities on Daxam Four."

"Hey. Just now, for tonight, let it go. Not even you can save the whole galaxy before breakfast." Han smiled gently. "You take too much on yourself. Always have. And you've been through too much lately. So let someone else take care of you for a little while."

She felt some of the tension drain away from her. "Do you have any idea how much I love you?"

"Yeah, I'd say I have a pretty good idea." Leia mock-punched him in the arm, and Han chuckled. "C'mon. You know I love you, too."

"Yes," she said as she tilted her mouth up for a kiss. "I know."

Across the capital city of Hosnian Prime, in a far more luxurious home, a much less affectionate conversation was being held via holo.

"Be patient?" Arliz Hadrassian's dark eyes blazed with fury so powerful it seared even through the hologram. "My Amaxine warriors are decimated, most of my best fighters killed, our ships destroyed, and you can only tell me to *be patient*?"

Lady Carise, still in the silk dressing gown she'd been wearing when Hadrassian called in the dead of night, snapped back, "Exactly. Because it was your impatience that led to this in the first place!"

"No, it was your inaction. The Centrists' refusal to stand up and declare themselves separate from the weak, sniveling New Republic!"

"The time isn't yet right. If you were any kind of politician, you'd know that."

"If you were any kind of warrior, you wouldn't be willing to wait for the perfect sunny day. You would take a chance."

"Well, you took one. You set off a bomb in the Senate to create 'confusion' and instead sowed suspicion." Lady Carise reached for her cup of caf, which she badly needed. "Maybe your warriors weren't the ones we needed after all."

Hadrassian's expression shifted from anger to astonishment. "You're abandoning us?"

Coolly, Lady Carise responded, "It doesn't sound like there's much left to abandon."

"Leia Organa—it can have been no other—you will at least avenge my men and eliminate her."

"See? There you go, making it personal when it's political. Leia Organa might well have been the one who destroyed Sibensko, but I neither know nor care. If we're able to use the incident against her to have her thrown out of the Senate, fine, but at this point it's more trouble than it's worth. Politically, she's powerless. She'll never have any more authority. That eliminates her as a threat, and her fate after this is irrelevant. If you were thinking strategically, you'd turn your attention to whoever's likely to lead the Populists next. Keep them confused. Off balance. Aren't soldiers supposed to rely on strategy?"

Hadrassian's smile could be more ominous than her frown. "You will have greater need of soldiers someday. When that day comes, you'll regret what you have done to us. And that day is coming soon."

The holo faded out. Lady Carise eased back on her sofa, took a sip of caf, and grimaced when she realized it had turned cold.

Maybe it was just as well the Amaxines would no longer be an issue. Hadrassian and her militia had always been too much of a rogue element to fit into the Centrists' plans for the future. When the First Order emerged, they would want to establish the new law, not create chaos.

Besides, the Amaxines had already served a useful purpose, one that eclipsed what little good they might have done as an advance guard for the First Order. They had served as a critical distraction when it was needed most. Now that the Amaxine warriors had taken the fall as Rinnrivin Di's funders and partners, no one would look any farther into his finances . . . and trace that money beyond backwater planets to the very heart of the First Order itself. Even now, the riches earned through the smuggling and gambling interests of Rinnrivin's cartel were helping to refit and rearm the former Imperial fleet, bringing them back to their full power and glory so that they would be once again ready to conquer. Oh, there were details she didn't know. Secrets that hadn't yet been shared with her. But she understood how to interpret shadows. Like, for instance, the disappearance of Brendol Hux, her homeworld academy's commandant, after the Battle of Jakku. Some said he had only given up—as if such a hero of the Empire would surrender so abjectly.

So many people lacked faith. But those who still believed—they were the ones who would resurrect the greatest power the galaxy had ever known.

When Lady Carise first got Hadrassian's angry, desperate call— passing on the word from the few survivors of what had happened to Sibensko—it had seemed like a nuisance. Now she realized it was a blessing.

Of course, if Princess Leia was able to share more of her suspicions, trouble could still arise . . . but the princess would never get to address the Senate again.

Ransolm had gone to Senator Erudo Ro-Kiintor's meeting on military appropriations in the hope that he might be asked to join one of the relevant committees soon. As much as he despised the reason for his recent rise in power amid the Centrist faction, Ransolm did not intend to waste the opportunities that the rise had given him.

Surely that was the best way to atone for what he'd done.

He had been right to report the truth. Ransolm still believed that. But now that he'd had time to process the information, he believed he should have gone about it entirely differently. Princess Leia had hidden the secret that she was Vader's daughter from him, which had damaged his trust in her forever—but even if she had not dealt with him honestly, she had dealt with him fairly. The revelation affected not only her but also her son, her brother, and her husband. (Sporting broadcasts that morning had been abuzz with the information that Captain Solo had left the Theron system after the end of the last Sabers round, and rumors abounded as to when or whether he would return for the final championship race.) Ransolm should have contacted Leia, let her know what he'd discovered, and given her a chance to reveal the truth herself.

She'd deserved that much.

Besides, Ransolm had also had the opportunity to ask himself why Lady Carise Sindian had come to him with the information. She had claimed that her sensibilities as a member of the Elder Houses kept her from speaking out, but who took the Elder Houses seriously any longer? Most of the current members saw it as nothing more than a genealogical resource and an excuse for the occasional gala. And Lady Carise could've gone to any member of the Senate with the truth about Leia's paternity.

The only reason for her to choose Ransolm was his partnership with Leia, his trust in her. He did not deceive himself that Lady Carise had done it for his own good.

No, she had intended to manipulate him. The only question was why.

And he did not intend to be manipulated again.

"Forgive me, Senator Ro-Kiintor," he interjected, "but the scale of the appropriations bill seems far in excess of what can possibly be required. The New Republic already maintains a sizable military force for a government largely at peace."

Senator Ro-Kiintor folded his hands together, palm to palm, fingertip to fingertip. "The armies we have now are adequate to the concerns we have now. But we must prepare for future conflicts."

"With whom? The New Republic comprises the majority of worlds in our galaxy. Only small, disconnected sectors stand apart, and few of those represent any military threat whatsoever. None of them shows any sign of declaring war."

"The New Republic is made up of separate systems," Senator Ro-Kiintor replied. "Separate worlds. We haven't supported their individual planetary defenses nearly enough."

This old canard. With difficulty, Ransolm kept himself from groaning. The far-right wing of the Centrist faction never quit harping on this, in the apparent belief that the lowliest moon needed enough firepower to take out a Super Star Destroyer on its own. They managed to be even more annoying than the far-left wing, which pushed for government control of the smallest minutiae of personal and political interaction. Ransolm privately figured Senator Ro-Kiintor looked at the armaments bill primarily as a way to funnel government money to Centrist planets, for whom the largest share of funds was earmarked.

He said, "We can supply extra funds for planetary defense without it costing anything like the amounts you've set out here. This appropriations bill could only be justified if the New Republic were facing imminent, galaxy-wide war."

A brief silence followed, during which Ransolm wondered if he'd gone too far—but then one of Senator Ro-Kiintor's staffers laughed under his breath. When both of the senators turned to look at him, the man said, "I couldn't help it. Believe it or not, Leia Organa is trying to address the Senate again."

She's back from Sibensko, and she's learned something valuable. Ransolm felt an unwilling flash of excitement. He'd done the right thing, then, by not reporting on the mission; he distrusted Rinnrivin Di and the Amaxine warriors far more than he distrusted Leia.

Which was something he hadn't consciously realized, until that moment . . .

"Pathetic," Senator Ro-Kiintor sniffed. "She can't possibly get a quorum to grant her the floor."

The staffer's grin was smug. "I admit, she came closer than I thought she would, but it's more poetic this way. She fell short by one vote. Precisely one. All the Populists and independents already voted, so that's it for her."

Senator Ro-Kiintor shook his head as if in disgust.

As he walked back to his own office, Ransolm reviewed everything he knew about the investigation. He remembered his own battle against the Amaxines in the desert, Joph's daredevil X-wing piloting, Greer bringing the courier down to Daxam IV . . . and Leia, gambling in the casino, firing at their pursuers in the Bastatha caves, helping analyze all the data, and finally, at the hanging gardens, speaking about the torture she had suffered at the hands of her own father.

He still did not know whether he could trust her, but he understood at last that she had trusted him.

When he entered his office suite, his assistant handed over a datapad immediately. "Issues on tomorrow's order of business in the Senate for your votes, sir." At the top of the list was Leia's request for a hearing. It remained one vote short.

Ransolm pressed down on YES.

"You're kidding," Leia said as she sank into her desk chair.

Greer shook her head. "You just cleared it. Casterfo's vote put you over the edge."

Was that his way of saying he was sorry? Or did he just want to hear what finally happened? This might be no more than the ending to a dramatic story, for him.

Leia decided she didn't care. She had her hearing, and nothing else mattered.

She had spent the day in some suspense, wondering if the word of what had happened on Sibensko had gotten out, how firmly she had been tied to it, and whether her enemies in the Senate intended to use this breach of authority against her. Surely people were ready to pounce on Vader's daughter. But nothing surfaced. No one spoke of it. Leia would be able to present her own report first, with what evidence they had been able to salvage.

"See? I told you things would turn around," Han said that evening as they dined at home.

"I don't think Ransolm's starting a trend," she said drily as she tried to eat her dinner without getting it all over herself. Han had brought back Bilbringi food, cheesy meat pies with peppers; she liked Bilbringi, though not quite as much as he did. Tonight, though, it hit the spot. Maybe she shouldn't be so worried about making messes.

Han, who could eat these things in the cockpit while flying, deftly rewrapped his own pie. "Well, don't worry. You don't have to deal with this alone, all right? I'm willing to be here as long as you need me."

Willing. That one word said so much. Leia didn't doubt Han's love for her, but she also knew that he would always be a wanderer at heart. He would stay with her on Hosnian Prime for a year or more if she asked, but she would feel as if she'd clipped a bird's wings.

She set down her food. "Han. It's all right. We both know you want to get back to the Sabers."

"It's just a race, sweetheart."

"Yeah, but this mess I'm in—it shouldn't wreck your life, too. Besides," she added wryly, "I think the galaxy would forgive me for being Vader's daughter faster than they'd forgive me for postponing the hyperspace championship round of the Five Sabers."

Han shook his head in wonder. "You can still surprise me."

"The worst is over," Leia said, trying to convince both Han and herself. "I'll be fine."

Simply knowing he'd soon be back in his ship, flying free, had brightened Han's mood. "I gotta admit—I wouldn't have known what to do with all that political mumbo jumbo anyway. Fighting with blasters is fairer, and if you ask me it probably causes a whole lot less damage."

She sighed in fond exasperation. "Some things never change."

His expression grew more serious, and he reached across the table to take her hand. "That's right," he said. "Some things will always be the same."

"Is that a promise?"

"You better believe it."

CHAPTER
TWENTY-NINE

———————

Maybe being invited back to Varish Vicly's was a good sign.

"You let Han leave Hosnian Prime without telling me goodbye—or even so much as hello?" Varish slipped one of her long limbs through the crook of Leia's elbow, as any hostess might, but Leia could sense the unspoken message as well as anyone else here: *This person is under my protection.* "For shame. I haven't seen him in ages."

"Han has a race to supervise, and I have work to do here." Leia took a deep breath and smiled. "So what's the occasion?"

"Since when have I ever needed an occasion to throw a party? The next time Han's home, I'll have one just for him. If he sticks around long enough!"

Varish's loyalty had not wavered for an instant, for which Leia was deeply grateful. Tonight, however, Varish seemed intent on forcing the other Populist leaders to be loyal to Leia, too.

That was more than a single party could accomplish, even one of Varish's. Although no one said anything rude, and most people smiled politely or at least nodded, a cascade of whispers followed Leia through the crowd. *Can you believe . . . Is she really , , Do you think . . . Who knew the truth?*

She'd known it would be like this. The only way to get through it, she decided, was through a little dark humor of her own—which took the form of the long black dress she wore, cape and all.

If they only wanted to see her as Vader's daughter from now on, why not look the part?

Varish whispered, "You're not going to wear that when you address the Senate, are you?"

"Of course not." This stunt helped her get through the party, but it would work against the substance of her speech. "Just having a bit of fun."

Through the muddle of the crowd she saw a flash of scarlet that could only be a Gatalentan robe. "Tai-Lin!" He might have been the only person left in the Senate she still felt confident to call out to.

Sure enough, he turned and smiled at her as warmly as ever. "Princess Leia. You look—" He paused, then gave her a conspiratorial smile. "—provocative."

"You know me so well."

"Before the party gets too involved, a quick word, if I might?" Tai-Lin looked to Varish for permission to steal Leia away; Varish nodded and let go, loping off to offer wine to the latest arrivals.

Together Leia and Tai-Lin walked onto Varish's long terrace. Other partygoers mingled there, but fewer, meaning they had a chance to breathe. As soon as they claimed a private corner for themselves, Leia asked, "So what's this about?"

"Your upcoming speech."

"But you know what it's about—"

"I don't mean the topic. I mean, why do you think Ransolm Casterfo voted you in?"

Leia had tried to avoid thinking about this too much. "Your guess is as good as mine."

"You must be serious." Few people could sound as grave as Tai-Lin Garr. "Has it occurred to you that he might be setting you up?"

"He did that well enough the first time."

Tai-Lin shook his head. "There's no telling what he might say. What further accusations he might hurl."

"Trust me, I don't have any secrets bigger than that one. I'm not sure that would even be possible." She hesitated before she added, "I think he honestly wants to hear what I'm going to say. Ransolm was deeply involved in the investigation. He took risks in order to see it through. Probably he just wants to know how the story ends."

"You have more faith in his honor than I do."

"Do I?" Maybe that was true. Ransolm's betrayal had flayed her to the bone, but she understood why he'd done it. She trusted her knowledge of the man.

"Attention, everyone!" Varish called gaily, loud enough for the entire party to hear. "As you might have guessed, I've brought you all together for a specific reason, and it's time you find out what it is." She lifted high her glass of bubbling wine. "I want you all to join me in a toast to Tai-Lin Garr—who will soon be declared the Populist nominee for First Senator!"

Cheers erupted throughout the room. Tai-Lin held up his hands, both accepting and encouraging their enthusiasm. Leia applauded, even though her first reaction was shock. How could she not have known about this?

Because you were off chasing Rinnrivin Di on Sibensko, she reminded herself. *And because you don't get invited to meetings of the inner circle anymore.* Never in her life had political power been farther from her grasp. She'd never craved power for its own sake, but she was beginning to miss it now that it was gone.

Congratulations swirled around Tai-Lin for nearly an hour afterward, during which Leia endured several grueling rounds of small talk with people who didn't much want to speak with her. Once she was able to get to Tai-Lin's side again, however, she whispered, "How did you let them talk you into this?"

"They didn't. I meditated on the question and considered every facet of the arguments for and against running." From anyone else, that would sound like pompous faux-nobility. But Leia knew that if Tai-Lin said so, he'd done exactly that. "Finally I realized that duty demanded I run."

She knew how that felt. "You'll be able to accomplish so much. Maybe more than I ever could have done. You're a better peacemaker than I am, Tai-Lin."

He turned toward her, dark eyes bemused. "I would've thought you understood. I don't intend to accomplish anything at all."

". . . I don't understand."

"As I told you a few weeks ago, the very idea of having a First Senator is anathema to me. That power could be corrupted far too easily. I realized that I must claim the position in order to render it irrelevant. By refusing to exercise the tyrannical authority the Centrists would vest in a First Senator, I will be able to maintain the liberty our worlds would otherwise have lost." Tai-Lin sighed. "Only in this way can I keep us safe."

A group of enthusiastic Mon Calamari legislators came up to talk to Tai-Lin, and Leia let him be pulled away into the crowd. Otherwise, she wouldn't have been able to hide her profound disappointment. When she'd believed she might be First Senator herself, she'd hoped to use her authority to cut down on the endless subcommittees that kept bills trapped for years, to come up with a more reasonable format for their debates, maybe even to move that they design a different floor plan for the Senate chamber, because the one they had was a chaotic mess. While she hadn't wanted the government to be headed by a figure as powerful as the First Senator promised to be, she had thought that some change—any change—had to be for the good.

Instead, if the Populists won, the political gridlock and factional fighting would continue. And if the Centrists won, the results might be even darker.

Again Leia felt the approaching danger, and wondered how she could be the only one who knew it.

She was so deep in thought that she didn't even notice that nobody else came up to talk to her for a long time. Amid the whirl of the party, Leia stood alone, a solitary figure in black.

One day later, on the floor of the Senate, she wore shining white.

Nobody else present could or would remember that the dress Leia had on today was very nearly a copy of the one she'd worn at the medal ceremony after the Battle of Yavin. She had purchased it because it reminded her of that day, when victory had seemed so close and, for a few hours, the galaxy had made sense. Now she wore it for courage.

The moderator droid finally spoke: "The floor recognizes Senator Leia Organa."

Leia rose to her feet. The holocam droids swarmed around her like bees, their tiny lights like a cluster of stars; her image appeared on every console and screen. She had braced herself for hisses and boos, but the room instead fell completely silent.

"My fellow Senators," she began. "As you will recall, I answered the request of Emissary Yendor of Ryloth to investigate the Nikto cartel leader Rinnrivin Di. Although our later calls for in-depth investigations were tabled, I took it upon my own authority to look further into the matter."

She did not mention Ransolm Casterfo. If he wanted the credit, he should get up beside her and take the blame, too.

"Each of you is now receiving an extensive data packet from my chief of staff." Leia glanced to one of the staff pools, where Greer nodded quickly, her fingers nimbly working on her datapad as consoles throughout the chamber lit up. "Reviewing it fully will take some time. But when you do so, you will see that Rinnrivin did indeed run an expansive criminal empire—but in the service of others who profited far more from his endeavors. Specifically, I believe that the largest part of Rinnrivin's profits went to a paramilitary organization known as the Amaxines. Even more important, I have acquired evidence that makes it clear the Amaxines were responsible for the bombing of the Senate building."

For the first moment, the only response was silence—but then the voices rose almost instantly into a roar. The Centrists and Populists wanted to blame each other so much that they couldn't stand finding another culprit, Leia thought sadly. But even as some people shouted down her statement and her findings, others were scrolling through the data and seeing the wealth of evidence she'd compiled.

One voice rang out above the others: "How can we be sure this evidence isn't sheer invention? Another of your lies?"

"Not all of this can be proved," Leia admitted. "Most of the data was taken from the Amaxine warriors' secret base on Sibensko when their store of incendiary devices exploded. I will submit visual logs from both the ship we'd appropriated for the mission and my husband's racer confirming that my escape from Sibensko, and the resulting firefight with Amaxine pilots, played a role in the base's destruction. However, I believe they will also confirm that the primary cause was the storage of an army's worth of bombs, thermal detonators, and other explosives."

"Listen to her! Justifying murder, just like her father!" That shriek from the back benches felt like an icicle being stabbed into Leia's chest—but it was one of only many shouts. Most senators seemed determined to remain focused on the loss of their pet theories about the Napkin Bombing.

Before the debate could spin completely off track, Leia spoke again. "If you choose to believe that what I've shown you is no more than an elaborate invention, go ahead. But before you ignore the evidence, consider this. The Amaxine warriors were powerful enough to strike at this Senate. They were arming themselves for full-scale military assault. In other words, the New Republic was on the verge of being attacked by its own citizens. There are those who want the New Republic to fail, and who are willing to bring it down, by force if necessary." Silence had fallen again, as much encouragement as Leia could expect. "We discovered the Amaxine warriors only because an independent world asked us to investigate another organization altogether. Are you willing to bet the survival of our government on the chance that they were the only paramilitary group out there? This group we stumbled across almost accidentally? I'm not. This galaxy's hard-won peace is at risk. We may only get this one warning, this one chance to take action. I implore you to study my findings carefully, and with an open mind. What we've discovered should transcend petty political bickering, or your personal opinion of me. Unless we want another war—and surely, after the bloodshed that ended more than twenty years ago, nobody can want such a thing—we must be on guard. We must come together. We have to act."

Lady Carise Sindian stared down at her screen in growing alarm. She'd known Princess Leia's investigation had cut too close, but she had underestimated just how much information had been dug up. Had there been no security on the Sibensko computer core at all? There were names, dates, amounts, accounts—at least a few layers removed from Lady Carise and her allies, but far too near to the truth for anyone's comfort.

It doesn't matter, she told herself. *Nobody wants to believe Darth Vader's daughter, especially not when they'd rather blame their political enemies. She's presented far too much evidence to be quickly analyzed. Who's going to bother reading through all of this?*

She took a few deep breaths. This would blow over before long. Princess Leia had nothing else to say, and soon the Senate would move on. Lady Carise knew how to start a whispering campaign, how to seed Hosnian Prime with alternative theories for the bombing, how to make sure the Amaxine warriors were framed as a lunatic fringe that should never have been taken seriously. In the end, the Napkin Bombing would go down as an outrage, but a mystery.

Then the moderator droid said, "The floor recognizes Senator Ransolm Casterfo."

Lady Carise looked up to see that Casterfo was indeed on his feet, hands clasped behind his back. She wanted to think he would now decry Princess Leia's evidence, take back the support he had given before, and help set this right.

But she also knew it was Casterfo who had cast the deciding vote to let Princess Leia speak.

"My fellow senators," Casterfo began. "You will remember that I accompanied Senator Organa on her first mission to investigate Rinnrivin Di. I continued working with her for some time after this, exploring the ties between his cartel and the paramilitary group known as the Amaxine warriors. Given what I know, I am bound by honor to say that—despite what I have stated in this chamber about her honesty—on this subject she is telling the truth."

He was siding with Princess Leia. Lady Carise couldn't fathom why Ransolm Casterfo was so hell-bent on committing political suicide, but here she was, watching him do exactly that.

"In addition to the evidence already provided, I can offer visual logs from the ship I personally took to Daxam Four, the site of an Amaxine warrior base. There you will see their training facilities and some small measure of their military might. And I can personally attest that their leaders spoke openly of war, and even of their admiration for Palpatine's Empire."

Again, the senators began to whisper among one another, but this time they actually sounded concerned. They might not have listened to Princess Leia alone, but the weight of Casterfo's testimony gave her back some of the credibility she'd lost.

Aghast, Lady Carise checked her monitors to see that Princess Leia was looking directly at Casterfo, not with gratitude—but with what looked like respect. For his part, Casterfo did something he'd never done for Lady Carise herself, despite her own royal title: He bowed his head.

Anger rushed through her as she thought, *I gave you the opportunity of a lifetime, and in return you betrayed me.*

She pushed those feelings aside as best she could. The long game they were playing couldn't be sacrificed to personal pride. Her allies had hoped to groom Ransolm Casterfo as an ally, perhaps even as a convert, but he'd proved unreliable. Whatever loyalty he still had to Princess Leia was apparently indestructible, which meant that he could, in time, turn out to be a threat.

They couldn't have a well-known Centrist out there sowing dissension. If he couldn't help them, he would have to be pushed aside.

Fortunately, Lady Carise was good at tying up loose ends.

CHAPTER
THIRTY

————————————

Joph thought of himself as a resourceful kind of guy, but he'd never dealt with a situation quite like this before. "So what are we supposed to do with these?"

He and Greer stood in the junker ship they'd bought for the Sibensko mission, currently parked in a low-rent, out-of-the-way hangar well off military property, staring into a cargo hold densely packed with hundreds of thermal detonators.

"This is not the kind of thing we want to get caught with," Joph added.

Greer leaned closer to the pallets, squinting in dismay. "It's not like we couldn't explain," she said warily. "The mission to Sibensko is public now. Still, we have a ton of explosives from a destroyed paramilitary terrorist organization . . . and nowhere to put them."

Initially Joph had figured they'd turn in the detonators to some commander or admiral in the New Republic fleet. But since they hadn't actually been on a military mission, they weren't under military jurisdiction. Their mission had been senatorial—more or less—but the Galactic Senate had no procedure or protocol for turning in destructive devices. Joph had wondered whether they should give them to Princess Leia herself, but what if people got the wrong idea? She was already feared and hated because she'd turned out to be Darth Vader's kid. If the public at large learned she had a massive private stash of weaponry, the reaction could be extreme.

"I don't guess we can sell them," he ventured.

Greer turned back toward him then, eyebrow quirked. "Yeah, let's definitely start working on our criminal record as illegal arms merchants."

"Well, what else are we supposed to do?" Joph flopped down on one of the cargo hold's jump seats. "Hang them up as decorations?"

"I'd thought about taking them back to Sibensko and just dumping them in the water." Folding her arms, Greer leaned back against the metal wall. "But that's only going to set up more potential destruction, either for the wildlife there or for undersea trawlers sent to investigate."

"The Senate's actually sending someone out?" That was swifter and more decisive action than Joph was used to seeing from the government.

But Greer sighed. "No such luck. But you can bet some of the criminal organizations that had interests there will check. The Niktos, the Hutts, maybe even some of the Amaxines' sympathizers? They're going to go after everything they can scavenge and every piece of information they can find."

So what if those guys blow themselves up? Joph thought but didn't say, because immediately he realized it wouldn't be the mobsters themselves who went down to the wreckage in submersibles. It would be indentured servants, or workers too poor to refuse jobs that endangered their lives. They didn't deserve to get killed just because he and Greer couldn't think of anywhere else to stash the detonators.

When Greer put her hand to her temple and winced, Joph felt a jolt of alarm. "Are you okay?"

"I'm fine. I just have a headache." Then she glared and pointed a finger toward him. "And don't ever overreact about my health again. All right?"

Joph forced himself to relax. "All right."

Slowly, Greer turned her gaze back to the thermal detonators. "We need to rent a storage space. Someplace secure and secret."

"And what? Just leave the detonators in there forever?"

"And wait for Princess Leia to give us the word."

Joph wanted to ask what exactly "the word" would be, but he already knew. They'd only managed to take down Rinnrivin's cartel and the Amaxine warriors by stretching the limits of Princess Leia's senatorial authority, and by doing things on their own initiative. If the princess was right, other paramilitary groups were out there, preparing to take the galaxy to the brink of war. The Senate showed no sign of being willing or able to take action against those groups itself.

Apparently the princess thought a day would come when they might have to take a stand against these groups on their own. When that day arrived, they'd need to be armed.

"Storage unit," Joph said. "Check."

Even though Ransolm Casterfo had steeled himself for this visit most of the night and all morning, he still made the walk through the Senate offices with dread in his heart. When he reached his destination, he paused a moment in the hallway to straighten his dark-green jacket and crisp white shirt, took a few deep breaths, then walked forward so that the doors would slide open to admit him.

Greer wasn't in her usual place in the front office. In fact, nobody seemed to be there apart from C-3PO, who looked as astonished as a droid could. "Senator Casterfo?"

"To speak to Senator Organa," Ransolm said in his most formal, correct manner. Then, more quietly, he added, "If she'll see me."

"I shall inquire directly, sir." C-3PO shuffled toward Leia's door, but sideways, as if he didn't think it wise to let Ransolm out of his sight for a moment. Ransolm readied himself for a long wait or a swift rejection, which was why it was so startling when, only moments later, C-3PO reappeared. "It seems Her Highness is indeed willing to see you. Though frankly I can't imagine why."

"Fair enough."

Ransolm walked into her office, relieved that the droid made no move to follow. Leia sat at her desk, wearing the clothes she usually reserved for travel, a tunic and trousers in pale gray. Her hair was tucked back into a messy knot at the nape of her neck. All efforts at senatorial formality and grandeur had been abandoned; this was a woman who no longer gave a damn what anyone thought.

She did not rise to greet him. Her words were even but clipped: "I can't believe you had the courage to face me."

"I can hardly believe it myself." Though Ransolm thought of what he had lacked earlier not as courage, but as understanding. For weeks after learning of her parentage, he had found it hard to even look at her directly, much less try to see her as anything other than Vader's offspring. Yet now when he looked at her, he saw the same person he had come to know and like. Although his actions had ended their friendship forever, he could at least give her the respect she deserved. "You did good work on the Sibensko mission. Once I reviewed the full report, I was all the more impressed. In your place, I doubt I would have made it out alive."

She folded her arms in front of her chest. "I'm so glad to have finally won your approval."

Her sarcasm hurt, but no more than Ransolm knew he deserved. He had not come here to be forgiven, only to belatedly give Leia her due. "Well. I'm glad to know you've been successful and that everyone is all right. Please know that I intend to support further investigations in any manner possible."

He gave her a farewell nod and headed for the door, but then she said, "Ransolm. Wait."

"Yes?"

"I'm not going to thank you for backing up my testimony in the Senate yesterday. Nobody should be thanked for simply telling the truth. But I can tell you that you surprised me—in a good way, this time." A wry smile flickered on her face for an instant, then was gone. "You put the greater good ahead of your own political faction and ambitions. You stood up for what you thought was right, and you told the truth even when those around you wanted you to lie. That makes you the kind of politician the galaxy needs."

"No senator worthy of the office should do any less. As you say, I don't deserve any gratitude for that."

"And you're not getting my gratitude. You're getting responsibility." Leia sighed. "I have no real power in the Senate any longer. I never will again. That means you're going to have to find other allies, both Populist and Centrist, who can honestly work together to get us out of this mess—and maybe even prevent a war."

"Surely it won't come to that."

"I hope not. I still believe we can find a way back to peace. But you, and people like you, will have to be the ones who lead us there. It's going to take a long time to build the kind of movement the Senate needs. You'll have to declare independence, and stop letting yourself be used to do other politicians' dirty work. So you'll also have to get a lot better at learning who to trust. For a long time, you'll have to stand alone." Leia's gaze seemed to look through him, and Ransolm could not guess what she saw. But then she added, "I believe you're strong enough to do it."

Nothing she could have said would have humbled him more, or encouraged him more. Ransolm nodded. "I will always do my duty."

"Yes, I think you will."

They had nothing else to say to each other, perhaps ever again, so Ransolm simply bowed and took his leave. He walked back to his office in a state of melancholy, not for the task before him but for the memory of Leia, weary and isolated, still thinking of the greater good as she learned to accept her political exile.

Ransolm knew the torch had been passed. He hoped he would be worthy of it.

Ten days after her final speech to the Galactic Senate, Leia made her first public political appearance since the galaxy had learned she was

Darth Vader's daughter. She didn't want to face a hostile crowd, but she also didn't intend to spend the rest of her life in fear. Besides, as Varish Vicly had pointed out, this was an ideal opportunity.

"Let me be blunt," Varish had said. "You have a glorious war record and a strong history of service in the Senate, which means we mustn't be perceived as shunning you. People would declare all Populists hypocrites, even if they still despised you. But we can't put you forward as one of our leaders any longer. That means you come to large gatherings focused around other politicians, smile and wave, and give the public time to get used to you again. Once they do, we can start expanding your role. Giving you back a little of your old authority."

Although Leia remained certain that the public would never be fully comfortable with her again, she would follow Varish's advice. She appreciated the show of loyalty, and besides—she wanted to see her old friend Tai-Lin Garr receive the attention he deserved.

His first campaign rally was held in one of Hosnian Prime's largest parks, a popular gathering place for visitors from across the galaxy. Tai-Lin centered the event on a large, fan-shaped fountain that his home planet of Gatalenta had donated at the time of the New Republic's founding. It was a beautiful setting, and a symbolic one: Tai-Lin was silently making it clear that he still thought of himself as a citizen of Gatalenta first.

Leia sat in the back row of the stands behind the new Populist candidate, wearing a simple dress of unobtrusive, olive-green fabric and hoping to pass largely unnoticed. The only ones who seemed to have taken note of her presence so far were the security guards grouped at the gathering's perimeter, one of whom always had his eyes on her. It would have been insulting if it hadn't been so amusing. Leia clapped when the others clapped, and genuinely smiled to see Tai-Lin being cheered by the large, enthusiastic crowd. In his scarlet cloak, he seemed to be wrapped in his own victory banner.

Fundamentally, she knew, Tai-Lin's candidacy for First Senator was deeply flawed. He had the discipline and humility to resist taking advantage of the new authority he would gain if he won. But the strategy he planned to employ was self-sabotaging. It was the equivalent of giving up on galactic politics completely, even on the idea that a single government *could* protect and serve the known worlds.

But Tai-Lin Garr trusted Leia. He had not doubted her when the truth came out, and was one of the very few individuals who understood how it was possible for a man strong in the Force—even the dark side—to have fathered people like Luke and Leia. She didn't think he'd turn his back on her even after his election, if he won.

Maybe I'll never have my own political power again, she thought, *but that doesn't mean I can't still work for what I think is right. If I can convince Tai-Lin to listen to me occasionally, we might be able to redefine the role of a First Senator as something that would work for both him and the galaxy. Instead of a leader, I can be an informal adviser. Maybe I can still help move us forward.*

A small voice next to her said, "Princess Leia?" She turned and was surprised to see that Korr Sella had found her way through the crowds to come here.

"Korr." Leia stopped herself from saying *Korrie* just in time. "I didn't expect to see you."

"Because I quit," Korr said. "Because I walked out after we all learned about Vader. I shouldn't have done that. I've spent all this time thinking about what you were like when I worked for you, and how much I admire you, and I realized that I'm still sure you're a good person. So I shouldn't have turned against you because of something you couldn't help."

Leia had expected understanding from few people, but had thought the wisest and most experienced among them, the ones she'd known longest, would be the first to come around. Instead, they'd been outshone by a sixteen-year-old girl.

"I understand." Leia kept her tone as gentle as she could while still being heard over the crowd. "I always understood."

Korr nodded, blinking fast. In a shaky voice she said, "I know I don't get to be your intern anymore, but if there's ever any way I can help you, or work for you, I just wanted to say I'd do it. I mean—I'd be *proud* to do it."

"Thank you, Korr. That means a lot to me." Leia pressed the girl's hand.

"And—if you want—you can still call me Korrie. It's okay."

"No, you were right. You're not a child any longer. I think you're more grown-up than most of the people at this rally. Korr is better."

Korr finally smiled, and Leia felt sure that someday, if she needed to, she could call on her.

After the speeches, of course, came the pressing of hands, claws, and tentacles. As people thronged around Tai-Lin, Leia began walking away, hoping to slip out of sight unnoticed. But a long golden limb wrapped around her shoulders to keep her near. "Oh, no, you don't," Varish chided affectionately. "You stay right here. Tai-Lin will no doubt want to speak to you afterward."

"If I remember the details of my last election campaign, Tai-Lin will only want to collapse afterward." Leia watched the hubbub for a few moments longer. How could Tai-Lin keep his dignity and serenity even when surrounded by laughing crowds who wanted him to kiss their babies or cubs? "What are his chances, do you think?"

"Good. The polls are promising, though at this stage, when we still don't have a Centrist nominee to test him against, it's hard to say. But we expected the Populist faction to take a hit after your hullabaloo, and it didn't happen."

Leia had to laugh. "You are the only person in the galaxy who could possibly describe what happened as a 'hullabaloo.'"

"And that's why you love me, isn't it?" Varish hugged Leia's shoulders a bit tighter, then began towing her toward the crowd. "At least say goodbye to Tai-Lin before you go."

"He doesn't care about that. And I don't want to cause any trouble."

"You won't. The sooner we start acting like things are back to normal, the sooner things will get back to normal. Besides, I'm not even sure anybody will recognize you in this crowd. It's so packed we can hardly see half a meter in front of our faces!"

That much was true. Leia let Varish lead her into the throngs, taking care not to push or meet anyone's eyes. If anybody within the mob recognized her, they said nothing she could overhear.

Finally, they neared Tai-Lin's side. "Tai-Lin!" Varish called. "We're over here!"

A gap in the crowd opened, large enough for Leia to see Tai-Lin standing there, smiling in welcome as potential voters surrounded him on all sides—

—and one of their faces was familiar.

High cheekbones. Silver-streaked hair. Intense dark eyes. Even though Leia had seen this person only during one night on Bastatha and in Ransolm's holos of Daxam IV, she recognized her instantly: Arliz Hadrassian.

And from her long cape, Hadrassian had just drawn a blaster.

Leia didn't even have time to shout a warning before Hadrassian fired straight into Tai-Lin's chest. Screams erupted throughout the crowd, and people began running in different directions—most trying to get away from the assassin, but a few hurrying to Tai-Lin's side. Leia managed to reach him, falling to her knees beside the place where he lay. Only then did she realize Hadrassian still stood there, completely unmoving, blaster in her hand. The security guards were fighting their way toward them, but they hadn't arrived yet.

"Leia Organa," Hadrassian said. A slow, terrible smile spread across her face. "You're lucky I'm thinking strategically."

With that, Hadrassian lifted the blaster to her own temple. Leia just had time to turn away before the final bolt and the sickening thud of a corpse onto the ground.

"Tai-Lin." She rolled him onto his back in order to assess the wound. "Tai-Lin, can you hear me?"

But of course he couldn't. He had been hit directly in the chest, at close range, by a blaster set to kill. The deep wound where his heart used to be had been cauterized, leaving a blackened crater behind. Arliz Hadrassian had avenged her Amaxine warriors.

This meant disaster for the galaxy, Leia knew. But she couldn't yet think of the political ramifications, the fallout, or anything else besides the fact that her friend lay dead on the ground. As Varish Vicly began to wail, Leia bent forward so that her forehead touched Tai-Lin's. It was the only farewell she could think of.

CHAPTER
THIRTY-ONE

———————

The entire Senate unanimously declared an official period of mourning for the death of Tai-Lin Garr. In her darker hours, Leia wondered if the Centrists had gone along with it only for show, but she thought probably most of the sentiment was sincere. Nobody, regardless of political faction, wanted to see elections decided by radical fringe assassins.

They were all unified in another belief, however, one that horrified Leia: Arliz Hadrassian had been the terrorist, the criminal, and the true threat. Thanks to the data from Sibensko, Hadrassian could be credited for the Napkin Bombing, for Rinnrivin Di's rise, all of it, by Centrists and Populists alike. Now that she had committed suicide, as far as the Senate was concerned the danger was over.

"You can't make an assumption like that," Leia pleaded in a small gathering of Populist senators after Tai-Lin's memorial service on Hosnian Prime. "Rinnrivin's money came from Hadrassian, but where did Hadrassian's money come from? She was an Imperial soldier of the line, then a small-time businesswoman. That's not the individual who bankrolls an entire would-be army."

"Leia, *please*," Varish said sharply. Tear tracks matted the golden fur on her cheeks. "Tai-Lin deserves to be grieved for in peace."

In frustration, Leia had to let it go—at least for the time being. If even one of her very few remaining close friends and allies in the Senate wouldn't listen, no one would. Yet she couldn't bring herself to believe that the investigation into the splinter groups would be tabled forever. People had the data. She'd given them the proof, and Ransolm had supported her findings with his own testimony. Sooner or later, they would see the need to dig deeper, search further.

Wouldn't they?

The next morning, as she walked through the Senate halls, she saw a large group of people clustered around the office suite of the junior senator from Mon Cala. Within, she could hear what sounded like an official broadcast being played at high volume. "Looks like breaking news," she murmured, heading closer to the group.

As she approached, she heard a few whispers: "*Just goes to show you can't trust a Centrist.*" "*Can you believe this?*" "*Looks like Princess Leia got that part wrong—*"

That last one broke off when the speaker saw her joining them, blushed deep green, and stepped aside. Leia only cared that she now had room to angle herself and see the holo being projected in the middle of the senator's front office, and hear what was being reported: "*—expressed shock that a paramilitary group could have received intelligence and assistance from a member of the Galactic Senate.*"

Leia felt relief sweep through her, and vindication. Someone had investigated after all; someone had reviewed the data and dared to follow the trail where it led. And while she hadn't wanted to believe that the Centrists were involved, she wasn't at all surprised to hear that one of theirs had been party to this from the beginning.

Then the broadcast continued: "Senator Casterfo has already been taken into custody and, in accordance with Senate policy, will be taken for imprisonment, trial, and sentencing on his homeworld."

Ransolm? They'd arrested *Ransolm*?

"It can't be," she whispered, nearly numb with shock.

"I know it must come as a surprise," said a more sympathetic listener, a Chandrilan staffer. "But obviously he was good at playing the game."

"No, you don't understand. *It can't be.* It's absolutely impossible for Ransolm Casterfo to be the person responsible for this." Leia knew every moment, every step, of her investigation by heart. Much of the most critical information had come from Ransolm himself. He'd risked his life for her on Bastatha. He'd even called for further investigation on the Senate floor. Did everyone actually think he had done all this just to cover his tracks? Only a fool could believe that.

Then Leia realized—the people who had accused Ransolm *didn't* believe it.

They'd set him up to take the fall.

Greer sat in the front office of the senatorial suite in semi-darkness; the day was too cloudy for much sunlight through the windows, and she hadn't even bothered turning on the main lights. The datapad in her hands illuminated her face as she scrolled through the recordings again, and again, and again. But the images never changed.

The door swished open and Princess Leia hurried in, breathless. "Greer, they've arrested Ransolm—"

"I know." Her voice shook. "I ran here the moment I heard. I thought we could clear him, that we could do it in a heartbeat."

"We can. As soon as they actually watch the footage, they'll know." Leia sat down next to Greer and impatiently took the datapad from her, then stared down in disbelief. "This isn't what happened."

"The footage has been doctored. Thoroughly. Completely." On the screen played an image of Ransolm Casterfo shaking hands with Arliz Hadrassian as he gestured toward her starfighters—two genuine gestures mapped together to create the illusion of approval. Greer remembered well the uneasy line Casterfo had walked with Hadrassian; he had come across as friendly without ever lying about his enthusiasm. This showed him as an enthusiastic backer and, more important, one who had hidden his true actions from the Senate.

Leia shook her head. "A slicer got hold of the footage?"

"Casterfo opened the footage up to everyone. From there, it was easy work for a good slicer to doctor the images and make it look like the original footage was actually the fake stuff." Greer's pulse felt too weak in her limbs, but this once, she didn't think it was the blood-burn. Instead the corruption responsible for this had sickened her to the core. What kind of government could let this happen?

No—what kind of government could *do* this? Because someone in the Senate had to be responsible, and that person was probably going to get away with it. Greer had had her frustrations with the Senate in the past, but she'd always believed there was something there worth salvaging, worth fighting for.

But now she knew the Senate was rotten. Dark and soft like old fruit, grown over with mold. Nothing remained pure enough to save. Although Greer had never fully come around to liking Ransolm Casterfo, she had learned to respect his abilities and integrity. More than that—he was completely innocent of the charges, and no one deserved to pay so dearly for a crime he hadn't committed. And she could only sit here and watch it happen.

Is this the "peaceful life" I have to live if I want to avoid dying from bloodburn? This . . . quiet mediocrity in the service of corruption?

Leia's face paled. "They'll be taking him to Riosa today. On the next transport from the main hangar. When is that?"

Greer shut off the false footage and checked. "In . . . just under an hour."

"I have to go." Leia rose to her feet and headed for the door.

A tiny flicker of hope ignited within Greer. "Can you stop them? Can you save him?"

Leia looked back over her shoulder, already stricken with guilt and grief. "No."

The main hangar didn't see much traffic at this time of day, nor the monorails, which meant Leia reached the designated bay in time—

barely. As she dashed through the door, winded and wobbly, she saw two New Republic soldiers leading Ransolm Casterfo toward a boxy, ominous prisoner transport vessel. Ransolm still wore his usual fine clothes, though they were crumpled now, and his hands were manacled in front of him.

"Wait!" Leia called. All three men turned toward her; the guards looked confused, and Ransolm looked . . . resigned. She hurried toward them, trying to summon some shadow of her old authority. "I want to talk to Senator Casterfo."

The guards turned toward each other for a long moment before one said, "Our orders say we load him now."

Leia drew herself up, allowed her gaze to become cool and commanding. Forget acting like a senator; she was a *princess,* and it was high time these men remembered it. "You'll be able to carry out your orders in due course. Let us speak."

They let go of Ransolm that instant, stepping back several paces. It would do. Leia looked up into Ransolm's eyes, and a pang went through her chest as he tried to smile. "Yours is the first friendly face I've seen all day," he said, his voice steadier than she would have thought. "It may be the last friendly face I ever see. I must admit, at the moment I sorely regret helping reinstate the death penalty on Riosa."

Horror swept through Leia. Worlds with the death penalty usually counted treason as a capital offense. Ransolm would be not only wrongly convicted, but executed, for crimes he had not committed.

"I'll try to do something," she promised. Already her mind was desperately going through the options, finding nothing, but still hoping that somewhere, somehow, she could find a way out of this. "Call in some old favors, ask for an independent investigation . . ."

"And you will fail." He smiled with unutterable sadness. "A rare case of perfect irony. You no longer have the power or connections to save me, precisely because I took that power away through my own actions. I am caught in my own trap."

"Ransolm." Leia shut her eyes for a moment, shocked by the depth of her sorrow and anger. In this hour it was as though he had never betrayed her, as though their friendship were still as strong as it had been the night they shared some of their darkest secrets. "This didn't happen because you outed me. This happened because you defended me."

"Because I saw that my enemy had actually been my one true ally—and now I have learned that my so-called allies were my enemies after all." Ransolm's composure finally broke; he held out his cuffed hands, and she took them, even though his grip was so desperate it ached. "Leia, I'm sorry. I lost your friendship in the worst possible way. I wish I'd never told the Senate about Vader. I wish I hadn't judged you by his actions."

"You hated him. You feared him. You reacted on instinct." Leia still felt that was not an excuse, but it was a reason, one she could comprehend and even forgive.

He continued, "It helps, knowing that you'll go on. Knowing that you'll stand up to the people in the Senate who could be this corrupt. Maybe you don't have the official power any longer, but I've seen you find ways around the rules."

I can't do this forever. Exhausted by her mad dash here, hollowed by her fear and grief for Ransolm, Leia felt every day of her age in her body. They'd been hard years, too. The work ahead belonged to other, younger, stronger people; she had believed Ransolm might be the one. But that dream, like so many others, was being crushed to dust.

One of the guards stepped forward again. "Transport's due to leave. We can't delay any longer."

"But—" Leia couldn't even get the objection out before the guards began hustling Ransolm away again. She ran after them, unashamed to make a spectacle of herself. "One more thing. Just one more thing."

The guards said nothing to her, but they stopped walking. Ransolm looked back at her, and he seemed younger to her then than he ever had. Far too young to die.

"When I first met you, I thought—I said once that you would have served the Empire, if you'd been alive during the war. I said I could imagine you in an Imperial uniform." Leia shook her head. "I was wrong. You wouldn't have fought for the Empire. You would have been with us."

"With you," Ransolm repeated. Once again he gave her that wounded smile. "I hope that's true."

Then the guards continued marching, and Ransolm let himself be led. He did not look back again.

In that instant, her anger rose to a nearly uncontrollable fury. If she'd had a blaster, she might have fired it. Her rage could have driven her to kill others—innocents—just to make sure Ransolm Casterfo didn't have to needlessly die.

She realized, then, something she had never fully understood before. She'd always wondered what had led her father to turn to the dark side, to become Darth Vader. She'd imagined it came from ambition, greed, or some other venal weakness. Never had she considered that the turn might begin in a better place, out of the desire to save someone or to avenge a great wrong. Even if it led to evil, that first impulse might be born of loyalty, a sense of justice, or even love.

Had it been like that for her father? She could never know. But for the first time in a very long while, she had some sense of who Anakin Skywalker might have been before his fall, and of the goodness that must have survived in him through all the darkness, all the years.

Leia stood in the hangar, breathing hard, staring at the transport vessel. She didn't flinch when its engines roared to life, didn't budge amid the gale of displaced air as it lifted off. Instead she remained still and watched the transport rise into the sky until it became so tiny and so distant that she would never see it again.

She remembered this terrible heaviness in her chest from the days of the war, when she'd had to send troops out on missions from which they would never return. Even though she had known the rightness of their cause, she had always found the sense of loss and waste almost unbearable.

But she had borne it then. She could bear it now. And the certainty taking hold in her mind as she watched Ransolm go to his death was one that she already knew would shape her from that day forward.

Only the Centrists could be responsible for this. The Populists had no motive to eliminate nearly the only member of the other faction who would sometimes take their side. That meant the Centrists were eating their own. Not only were they attacking Populists on every side, they were also eliminating the members of their own faction who didn't share their zeal for power. They had no use for moderates, no use for peace. The Centrists actively sought war—had perhaps been planning this for a very long time—and they'd begun removing every obstacle in their way.

Despite her long disillusionment with the political process, Leia only now realized the Senate was doomed no matter what she did.

War had become inevitable.

Lady Carise Sindian was having an excellent morning.

She'd given the right quotes to the right sources about her shock regarding Casterfo's arrest the day before. Like all honest Centrists, she washed her hands of him. They would not let their faction and their beliefs be dragged down by one man's criminal actions. No, indeed, the Centrists would carry on.

Unbeknownst to most, they were moving on very quickly already.

The Senate had resolved on only one motion yesterday, which was to postpone the vote for the First Senator. In the wake of Tai-Lin Garr's assassination and Ransolm Casterfo's arrest, a majority agreed that the political situation was too volatile to support an election in the near future. Lady Carise and her allies had voted for this, because by now they had begun concocting a far superior solution: secession.

It would take a few months to put events in motion. They needed a firm structure before proceeding. But soon, the Centrist worlds would leave the New Republic, tearing themselves from the mire of the Senate's inaction to create and support the First Order. Her heart sang merely thinking of it.

Lady Carise was smiling as she turned the corner that led directly to her office, then froze when she saw who was standing in front of her. "Princess Leia?"

"Lucky running into you here," said the princess, who stood not two meters from Lady Carise's office door. "I've been meaning to have a chat with you for some time."

"As you know, I'm always ready to hear from a member of the

Elder Houses." Lady Carise could afford to be generous in triumph. Maybe Princess Leia would finally turn to her now that she had no other allies, and start behaving with proper respect toward a fellow noble. "Yes, let's catch up. What have you been doing these days?" *Besides being outmaneuvered at every turn, I mean.*

Princess Leia smiled. "I've been getting in touch with some old friends. Including, as it happens, the most senior members of the Elder Houses."

"Oh, really?" Lady Carise had begun to realize just how much anger was hidden by the princess's smile.

"Yes. You see, there was a matter we very much needed to discuss, namely, the sanctity of the royal seal, as applied to the holdings of the supreme governor of Birren." Princess Leia's tone remained cordial, but her gaze sharpened. "I imagine you thought I'd be too distracted to notice—and to be fair, I was for a while—but it didn't take me too long to realize that the keepsake chest could only have been hidden on Birren. Only the supreme governor could have had access to it. And the supreme governor, namely you, had been through weeks of rituals surrounding the inauguration, in which the governor-to-be repeatedly promises to uphold the sanctity of the royal seal, no matter what. You didn't even last a month."

Lady Carise had been prepared for an altercation like this when Casterfo first revealed the truth, but in the weeks since, she'd been lulled into believing Leia would either never notice or simply let it go. So she found herself at a loss for words. "Well. I suppose. But I felt—in such an extreme moral crisis—"

"The oath demands that the supreme governor uphold the sanctity of the royal seal unto death." Princess Leia raised an eyebrow. "Don't worry. I don't intend to pursue this to the fullest extent of the law. It was enough to contact the ruling members of the Elder Houses and convince them to finally pass a resolution, the first one they've bothered to pass in years. To be specific, they've stripped you of your royal titles, forever. The title of supreme governor of Birren will go to the next person in the line of succession, and you are no longer a member of the Elder Houses."

Could she accomplish such a thing? Could it be possible? Lady

Carise felt as if her knees might give out. "You can't. It's mine by right of birth. Nobility is sacred—they wouldn't take it away like that!"

Princess Leia sighed and shook her head. "It's been a very long time since nobility was sacred to anyone but you. It's such a small punishment, both for what you did to me and especially for what I believe you did to Ransolm. But it *hurts,* doesn't it? It has to cut you to the quick. You've never been able to convince yourself you were superior to anyone except through an accident of your birth, which by the way is one of the saddest things I can imagine."

Lady Carise's breaths were coming so fast she might hyperventilate. They couldn't take her titles away. They couldn't!

But apparently they already had . . .

"This is the only punishment I have the power to enact anymore, so I have to content myself with hurting you—for now." Princess Leia smiled. "Goodbye, Carise."

Carise. Just Carise. From this day on, she would only be Carise Sindian. She could imagine no greater humiliation. So Carise could only stand there, gulping for breath, as she watched the princess walk away.

Late that evening, Leia changed out of her senatorial robes into a plain tan coverall and one of Han's leather jackets. It hung big on her, but smelled comfortingly of him, even so long after he'd been gone. She laced up her boots and headed toward a little-used hangar on the edge of the capital city, one she'd signed an exclusive lease on the day before.

The hangar wouldn't serve their purposes for long. She would have to think bigger, hide deeper, and go farther. For now, however, they only needed a place to begin.

When Leia walked inside, she saw that everyone she'd contacted was already there; she'd been early, but they came even earlier. In the back were those who had traveled farthest to help her—Nien Nunb, Ematt, and even Admiral Ackbar, standing straight, ready to serve. To the side was Harter Kalonia, who hadn't hesitated to accept Leia's invitation, and thank goodness; it was always good to have a doctor on hand who knew how to keep a secret. Clustered closer were the young pilots she'd recruited, chosen from either those she had worked with personally—such as Joph Seastriker, who stood at the very front—or those Joph and the other pilots had vouched for, such as Snap Wexley and Zari Bangel.

But one person she hadn't invited came toward her now.

"Greer?" Leia put her hands on her assistant's shoulders. "What are you doing here? I told you, for your own protection, you shouldn't know any more about this than is strictly necessary."

"Exactly," Greer said with a smile. "And since I'm going to be one of your top pilots, it's probably necessary for me to learn everything."

"No. You know you can't—"

"I know, I know. I'm supposed to play it safe and tame and calm, so I can live a long life that's nothing like the one I actually want to lead. And I'm supposed to just stand by instead of supporting a cause I believe in." Shaking her head, Greer said, "I'd rather burn in a better kind of flame."

Even as Leia's heart ached, she knew better than to argue. Instead she simply hugged the younger woman briefly before turning back toward the group, which was falling into an expectant silence.

"Thank you, everyone, for coming tonight," Leia began. "Whether you're an old friend or a new one, you're here because you've shown courage. You've shown initiative. You've seen the coming danger, and you're willing to do whatever it takes to protect the peaceful worlds of this galaxy from war."

"We're ready." Joph's blue eyes were bright with excitement. War would dim that joy too quickly. Leia wished she could keep his youthful enthusiasm safe somewhere, that she could bottle it or tuck it away, but knew it was just one more sacrifice the approaching conflict would claim.

She warned, "Don't speak too soon. Every one of you has to fully understand that this movement, this organization, is not sanctioned by the Galactic Senate. For now, and possibly forever, we operate beyond governmental control. That may mean bending some laws, and breaking others."

"Never stopped us before," Ackbar rasped.

Greer added, "We've already got a few hundred thermal detonators. It's a start."

Leia scanned the room and saw no doubts, no hesitation. These people trusted her. They were ready. Finally she was ready, too.

"The sun is setting on the New Republic," Leia said. "It's time for the Resistance to rise."

ABOUT THE AUTHOR

CLAUDIA GRAY is the author of *Star Wars: Lost Stars,* as well as *A Thousand Pieces of You* and the Evernight and Spellcaster series. She has worked as a lawyer, a journalist, a disc jockey, and a particularly ineffective waitress. Her lifelong interests include old houses, classic movies, vintage style, and history. She lives in New Orleans.

claudiagray.com
Facebook.com/authorclaudiagray
@claudiagray

Read on for an excerpt from

AFTERMATH: LIFE DEBT

by Chuck Wendig

PUBLISHED BY DEL REY BOOKS

The galaxy is changing, and with peace now a possibility, some dare to imagine new beginnings and new destinies. For Han Solo, that means settling his last outstanding debt, by helping Chewbacca liberate the Wookiee homeworld of Kashyyyk.

Meanwhile, Norra Wexley and her band of rebels pursue Admiral Rae Sloane and the remaining Imperial leadership across the galaxy. Sloane, increasingly wary of the mysterious Grand Admiral, desperately searches for a means to save the crumbling Empire from oblivion. Even as Imperial forces fight to regain lost ground, Princess Leia and the New Republic seek to broker a lasting peace.

But the rebel's hunt for Admiral Sloane is cut short after the disappearance of Han Solo and Chewbacca. Desperate to save them, Leia conscripts Norra, Sinjir, Jas, and the rest of their team to find the missing smugglers and help them in their fight for freedom.

The veldt stretches out before them.

The *ki-a-ki* bushes tremble in the warm wind, dark thorny scrubs whose gentle tremors call to mind an animal trying very hard not to be seen. The thirstgrass conspires with the breeze: whispers and shushes and hissed hushes. Red, feathery clouds streak across the open sky, a sky the color of blush and bloom. A lone ship crosses it—some cargo ship, probably, one of the few travelers to this distant world of Irudiru.

Down there, among the grass and the scrub, sits a compound.

The compound has seven buildings. Each sits squat and rectangular, each made of blond brick and bloodred mortar, each with railtop roofs and round porthole windows and water catchment tanks. One of the buildings is different, though: a manse larger and more ostentatious than the other more austere buildings. The house is surrounded by a screened-in porch, a xerioscape garden, and a series of shimmering and shifting holo-statues. A droid with many extensor limbs flits about, tending to the garden and tuning up the statues.

Otherwise, the compound is silent and still.

And it has been for the better part of the last day.

This is the compound of Golas Aram.

What the crew knows about Aram is little, but perhaps enough: He was once employed by the Galactic Empire as an architect. A *prison* architect, in fact. Aram designed some of the Empire's most notable prisons, including the Lemniscate beneath Coruscant, the floating asteroid prison of Orko 9, and the Goa Penal Colony. Aram's reported specialty was making prisons that were self-sustaining and inescapable. He considered it his "art."

Thing is, he didn't work only for the Empire. He operated freelance, too—helping design and build prisons for the Kanjiklub, for the Junihar Cartel, even for Splugorra the Hutt.

Aram is retired, supposedly.

Just the same, Golas is the only Imperial connection out here on Irudiru. He's the one good lead they have. But what happens when they go pulling on that thread? Will they find Han Solo? Or will the whole thing fall apart? Could they be putting Solo in danger?

The narrative they can put together for Solo is shaky, at best. The *Millennium Falcon* got into a scrape not far from Warrin Station. Han had transmitted after that—but whatever he was investigating sure stirred up trouble. Given the presence of that Asp droid and the sheer manic glee of Tashu regarding Irudiru, there's cause to worry. So, if Han was here investigating Aram, then what? After that, the narrative frays. Why look into Aram at all? Did Aram catch Solo sniffing around? Is Solo in prison—or is he looking for someone in prison?

Either way, it's what they have, so here they are.

From their hiding spot atop a gentle hilltop plateau, Norra leans forward, parting the sharp-bladed thirstgrass like a curtain and peering out through a pair of macrobinoculars. Using the dial on the side, she scans through the heat signatures then clicks over to electric and electronic indicators. The binocs highlight a series of danger spots all around the compound; they glow red in the viewscreen. "I see them," she tells Jas—Jas, who lies unseen in the tall grass even though she's only a few feet away.

The binocs highlight that the compound is ringed by an invisible perimeter fence: a barrier of ghosted lasers, impossible to see but sure to cut you apart if you march through them. The ground leading up to the compound, both in and out of the fence, is littered with land mines. Then, located throughout the compound are turret-droids. Each hides in plain sight near vaporators, looking like part of the mechanism. Stealthy buggers, those.

Through the grass, Jas says, "The place is loaded for war. Aram's protecting himself. I get that he's paranoid, given the changes cascading through the galaxy, but this is a whole other level. He's afraid. And he hasn't come out in days." From behind them, Norra hears Temmin working on something—a *tink tink tink* followed by a buzzing twist from a micro-spanner. What is he doing back there? Norra's about to ask, when—

The grass swishes and shakes as Sinjir crawls up on his belly. "Ow!" he says, flexing his hand and popping the knuckle of his thumb in his mouth. "This grass is slicing me to bits."

"It drinks your blood," Jas says, easing closer. "Thirstgrass sustains itself on the creatures who walk through it. Little sips from little cuts."

He frowns. "Lovely. I'm here for my hourly update. And my hourly update is: I am bored. Bored out of my skull."

"That's always your hourly update," Norra says.

"Because it's true every hour."

"It's my update, too," Temmin says, crawling up next to them. "Seriously, this is awful. I want to burn all this grass. And the thorny bushes. And the flies." As if to demonstrate, he swats at the back of his hand. "See? Ugh. I should've stayed on Chandrila."

"Can't we just go back to Kai Pompos?" Sinjir asks. "We'd make it by nightfall. There's a little drinkery around the back of the town, they have a still where they ferment this root, this *korva* root. So we go back, we tip back a few under the Irudiru moons, we reformulate our strategy—"

"This is a fact-finding mission," Norra says, feeling like a mom commanding a child to stay put. "We stay here until all the facts are found."

"Facts are," Temmin says, "the guy isn't coming out. He's dug in like a blood-bug." They'd heard rumors that Aram was a big game hunter, and thought maybe that would afford them an opportunity to get close to him. But so far, no go. Nor has he gone out for supplies. Or even a breath of fresh air. They've seen neither hide nor hair of the man. Just droids. "Here's what we do. We take Mister Bones—" Bones was crumpled up behind them, his skeletal body folded tightly with his head bowed and his arms enclosing his knees. "And we let Bones march down there, find the guy, drag him up here onto the plateau, and we question him. Simple."

"As simple as chasing birds with a hammer," Sinjir mutters.

"Everyone hush," Jas says. "Temmin, did you build my thing or not?"

"Yeah, yeah." He fishes around in his pocket and holds up a pair of devices in the palm of his hand. One looks like a round from a slug-thrower, but it's been modified—the shell casing crimps around a circuit bulb, and the tip of that bulb has four little prongs. Like insect mandibles. The second device is round, no bigger than a button, with a little zigzag antenna sticking out.

"It's a bug," Temmin says, sounding impressed with himself.

"This planet has enough bugs without us adding more to it," Sinjir grouses. "And before anyone corrects me, yes, I know, it's a *listening* bug and not a *real* bug and—oh, never mind. Good job, Jas. Now what?"

"We can't get eyes on, so we need to get ears on. I load this into my rifle and fire it right at his manse. Then—" She grabs the second device. "This jury-rigged earpiece with which to listen in."

"Clever," Sinjir says. "Still not sure what *I'm* doing here."

Jas hands him the earpiece. "*You're* going to do the listening."

"Joy." He makes a face as he takes it and screws it into his ear.

The bounty hunter unslings the slugthrower from her back. Norra again grabs the binocs and focuses them at the compound.

A herd of animals have come up alongside the invisible perimeter—long-limbed, long-necked leathery things, these beasts. They number in the dozens. Some stop to nip at the tufts of *ki-a-ki* bushes, while the others bat at one another with bony protuberances atop their narrow snouts. Norra is pretty sure they're morak. Big things, but herbivores. Though she'd hate to get stomped under those long legs—legs that end in claw-tipped feet.

Jas pulls the slugthrower close and uses her thumb to pop open a bipod at the end of the barrel, giving it stability. She tugs the scope tight against her eye. Norra watches her through the grass—the way Jas draws a breath deep, then slowly exhales it until no breath remains and she is still. . . .

It's surprisingly close to what Luke taught Leia, isn't it?

Shut out the world. Be mindful, but empty.

Like a cup to be filled up.

(Of course, Jas does this in order to kill people more efficiently.)

The bounty hunter's finger coils around the trigger.

But then—

The morak all look up at the same time. A gesture of alarm.

Norra reaches out and touches Jas's shoulder. "Wait."

"What is it?" Jas asks.

"Something's up."

Sinjir plucks the earpiece out of his ear, scowling at it. "This thing is fritzing out. It's making this . . . high-pitched whine. Wretched sound."

Down below, the morak begin to move. All of them at once, a herd movement. They go from walking to galloping, their long, bony legs launching them forward with a swiftness that surprises Norra.

The animals are headed toward the hill where the crew is waiting.

Closer, closer.

The ground begins to vibrate beneath them.

It's too steep, surely. They can't—

The animals reach the bottom of the hill and begin to scramble up the side of it. Their clawed feet make great haste, and now Norra knows what those claws are for. Dust spirals behind them.

They're coming right for us.

"We have to move," Norra hisses. *"Move!"*

She and the others spring up out of hiding and turn tail, bolting through the grass. The morak crest the hill, bleating and blowing mucus from their snouts. The ground rumbles as the herd stampedes.

The grass slices at Norra's arms, but she can't waste time caring. Everyone moves fast—everyone except Bones, who sits somewhere under cover, and is hopefully resilient enough to suffer the knocks and blows of the morak. She's not even sure where they should go. Run straight? Turn to the side? The morak are coming right up behind them—

One lopes past Norra in a lumbering gallop, swiping at her with its long neck—the thing is twice her height and she just barely darts out of its way even as others come up behind her. Ahead, though she can't see it, the far side of the hill awaits. What then? Run down it, trying not to fall? Duck and pray the charging morak go over the edge?

The bounty hunter runs next to her, and when one morak comes behind her, Jas jabs at it with the barrel of her slugthrower—and the beast roves drunkenly toward Norra. It clips her and she staggers—

Her legs go out from under her—

There's Temmin, grabbing her by the belt to keep her from falling. It's just enough to help her get her legs back under her. Norra is about to thank her son—

She doesn't get the chance.

A sound hits them, a sonic hum. Suddenly, the morak are squawking and turning sharply away, the herd splitting in twain as if by an invisible wedge. Norra thinks, *Thank the stars for whatever is doing that.*

But then something lands in the grass in front of them—the thing rolls a few times like a flung rock. It beeps three times in succession. Then:

An implosive sound—*foomp* The air lights up around them, a hard pulse of bright light. It concusses the air, too, hitting her like a thunderclap. Norra is suddenly blind and deaf, her ears ringing, her vision washed away in a tide of searing white. She fumbles for the blaster at her side—she whips it out, and it's suddenly rocked out of her hand, clattering away.

A shape emerges in front of her as the white light begins to recede: a person-shape. Norra thinks: *Aram has us. We thought we were watching him, but he was watching us.*

She leans forward, starts to stand.

"Don't move," comes a voice. Quiet, but urgent.

Norra asks as her eyes adjust, "Who is that? Who's there?"

The figure steps forward. She spies two blasters held aloft, one in each hand, and one pointed right at her. "Name's Han Solo. Captain of the *Millennium Falcon*. Who the hell are *you*?"